THE
ASSASSIN

OTHER TITLES BY MARK DAWSON

HONG KONG STORIES VOL. 1

White Devil

Nine Dragons

Dragon Head

STANDALONE NOVELS

The Art of Falling Apart

Subpoena Colada

MARK **DAWSON**

THE
ASSASSIN

AN ISABELLA ROSE THRILLER

Published by Thomas & Mercer, Seattle

www.apub.com

Amazon, the Amazon logo, and Thomas & Mercer are trademarks of Amazon.com, Inc., or its affiliates.

ISBN-13: 9781503905498
ISBN-10: 1503905497

Cover design by @blacksheep-uk.com

Printed in the United States of America

Chapter One

Mexico

It was midday, and there was not a scrap of cloud in the sky. The desert stretched out, all the way to the mountains. The sun sat high overhead, pummelling the arid landscape until woozy waves of heat radiated up from the ground. There was not a breath of wind, either, and no prospect of any change for the rest of the afternoon. Isabella Rose reached into the car for the bottle of water that she had brought with her. She had already finished half of it, and what was left was tepid. It was wet, though, and it helped slake her thirst and wash away some of the dust that stuck to the top of her mouth and clogged her throat.

The car was an old Ford Torino GT that they had purchased from a dealer in El Paso before they crossed the border. Isabella slid into the cabin. The faded black seat had been cooking all morning and it was almost too hot to sit in. She opened the glovebox and took out the old iPod that had been left there by the previous owner. The device hooked up to the car's stereo and was loaded with playlists of songs from the eighties; Isabella ran her finger around the click wheel until she found the one marked 'Remixes' and pressed play. Queen's 'Another One Bites the Dust' started up. The bass line shook the speakers; she drummed her fingers in response. Isabella's mother, Beatrix, had played a lot of eighties music during the year they spent together. Isabella hadn't yet been born when the songs were released, but she found that she remembered many of them from Marrakech, and the familiarity was reassuring. Remembering her mother was especially reassuring when she was nervous, and she was nervous now.

Isabella wound down the window so that she could still hear the music outside and got out of the car. She had parked the Torino next to a small single-storey warehouse that had once accommodated the business of Jamie Flores, as noted by the painted sign on the wall. She clambered onto the hood of the car and boosted herself up to the roof of the building. She had left her things up there: she saw the pack with her pistol and ammunition, and the binoculars that she had rested next to it. She sat down, took the binoculars and raised them to her eyes. She scouted the environment, running through the same patient routine she had followed every ten minutes throughout the course of the morning. The road she was watching joined Ciudad Juárez to the northwest with El Porvenir to the southeast. Isabella's position was to the south of the road. The building she was atop had been abandoned, the windows smashed and the doors forced so that the insides could be scavenged. She had selected it when she'd scouted the area last weekend; the landscape around here was flat, and the raised vantage point offered excellent visibility in all directions. More to the point, it allowed a clear line of sight for half a mile, to the road that led away from the main highway and headed north, toward Tornillo and the new bridge that forded the Rio Grande and offered access to the Texas border. She would have plenty of notice when the vehicle that she was expecting finally appeared.

The rubber eyepieces were hot as she pressed them to her skin and watched the road. There was no traffic; the crossing was not busy, with the majority of the cars and trucks that passed between Chihuahua and

Texas using the three crossing points between Juárez and El Paso, to the northwest. This new crossing had only been open for two years, and it appeared to be less popular than had been expected. Cars and trucks went by every now and again, their passage presaged by clouds of dust that were visible long before the vehicles came into view. Isabella saw such a cloud now, and waited patiently until she could make out the details of the vehicle. It was a car, headed towards her. She watched as it turned right onto the highway and accelerated away in the direction of El Porvenir.

Queen ended, and 'Shout' by Tears for Fears started.

The town of Guadalupe was a short distance to the south. Isabella had driven through it, and had researched it online back at the house. It had been busy once, like the others in the Juárez valley that followed the Rio Grande. The whole valley had prospered as the cotton industry thrived. But now the town was largely abandoned, populated by stubborn older residents who were unwilling to leave their homes, and poorer ones who were unable to. Dozens of houses and businesses had been painted in colourful shades of pink, blue, green, orange and fuchsia. The local mayor had ordered that the buildings be painted as a tribute to the owners who had been executed or driven away by La Frontera, the cartel that ran this side of the border. It was the last civic order the mayor had given; his headless body had been found by the side of the road a week later.

Guadalupe was a major base of operations for La Frontera now. The truck that Isabella was waiting to meet would end its journey there. The vehicle belonged to them.

Isabella saw another cloud of dust on the horizon to the north. Another vehicle was approaching. She grabbed the binoculars and put them to her eyes. It was a truck. She stood so that she so she could get a better view of it.

La Frontera had been using delivery trucks to transport their drugs over the border into the United States, those same vans loading up with the hundreds of thousands of dollars from the sales of previous shipments and bringing the money back down south. They crossed the border at Tornillo, taking advantage of a crooked official who waved them through with minimal checking. The money ended up in Guadalupe, where the process began again.

Isabella put the binoculars in her pack, dropped it over the side of the building and slithered down after it. She got into the Torino, tossed the bag onto the passenger seat and switched off the ignition, silencing the music. She opened the pack and took out her pistol. It was a Walther PPS M2 Centerfire, with the slim and ergonomic profile that meant it fit comfortably in her hand. She had been practising with it for the last four months. She had spent enough hours sending rounds down the range that the smooth trigger-pull felt completely natural to her.

She got out of the car, shoved the pistol into the back of her cutoff jean shorts and covered it with the bottom of her T-shirt. Isabella was wearing cowboy boots that reached up to her calves. The jeans had been cut midway down her thighs, revealing plenty of her long legs. She wore an old Iron Maiden shirt, the band's logo stretched tight across her chest.

She walked away from the Torino and headed towards the approaching truck. She went out into the road, putting herself in its way, and waved her arm for it to stop.

Chapter Two

Isabella knew that there was a chance the truck would swerve and go around her. There was a plan for that, but she hoped it would be unnecessary. The vehicle drew closer, near enough for her to see the two men in the cab. The sun shone onto the glass, sparking back at her, but she could tell that they were talking.

The truck slowed down.

She waited in the road as it came to a stop. She put her hand to her face to shield her eyes from the reflection of the sun in the windshield, smiling shyly up at the cabin. Her heart was racing. She concentrated on the reassuring shape of the Walther against the small of her back.

The passenger door opened and a man stepped down. He was large, wearing a green shirt that was a little too small for his belly. His hair was cut close to his head and he wore thick stubble on his face. His nose was bulbous, his lips thin and cruel and his ears a little too small for his head.

'What's the problem, *chica?*'

The man addressed her in Spanish. Isabella spoke it fluently after the year she had spent here in Mexico.

'My car,' she said. 'It broke down.'

'You were driving it?'

'Yes,' she said.

'How old are you?'

'Sixteen. Old enough to drive.' Isabella smiled at him.

'What you doing out here?'

'Going to El Porvenir to see my friend. I've been stuck here for an hour. No one else would stop.'

'You wanna ride?'

'It just needs a push. It's happened before.'

The man shook his head. 'Too busy for that. We're already late.'

The driver's door opened and a second man got out. 'What's the problem?'

'Car broke down.'

'There's a repair shop in Guadalupe,' the driver called over.

'I haven't got a signal,' Isabella said.

'It's a couple of miles,' the first man said. 'You can be there in half an hour if you walk. Or you can come with us.'

The man reached over and rested his fingers on Isabella's shoulder. She felt a shudder of revulsion. She was losing control of the conversation.

Isabella tried to remember what they had planned, but her mind was a blank. She had been so certain of the order of things, but now that she was here, in the middle of the road with events unrolling around her, she had forgotten it.

'I'm sorry,' she said. 'It's okay. I'll . . . I'll wait for someone else.'

'Come on, *chica*. Don't be shy. We stopped for you now. You don't want us to waste our time, do you?' He ran his hand across her shoulder and traced his index finger up her neck. He hooked his finger under her chin and raised her face so that he could look down into her eyes. 'You're pretty, baby.'

The sun glared in her eyes. She stepped away from him.

'Don't be ungrateful,' the man said.

He reached for her again, his hand clasping her face and then sliding up and around until his fingers were bunched in the long blonde hair that fell down her back.

Isabella felt a flash of anger, and the control that she had worked so hard to master evaporated in an instant. He anchored his fingers around the back of her head and yanked her towards him; she drew back her right knee and drove it, hard, into his groin. He had pulled her close enough that there was only a narrow gap between them, but there was still enough space for her to strike him powerfully. He bent down, grunting in pain and surprise, but he did not let go of her hair. His left hand fell instinctively to cover his crotch, and as he doubled over, he dragged down on her head with his right. Isabella reached for his collar with her left hand and yanked down as she brought her left knee straight up. She struck him flush in the face, hard enough to feel the bite of his teeth against her patella. His grip on her hair loosened; she shook him off, shoving him with both hands so that he toppled down and landed on his backside.

Isabella reached around for the Walther, but just as she yanked it from her waistband, she noticed the driver coming around the front of the truck.

He had a stubby shotgun. It was levelled right at her.

The driver saw Isabella's pistol and pressed the stock of the shotgun harder into his shoulder. 'Hands!' he called.

The man on the floor raised himself onto hands and knees. Isabella glanced down at him; blood was dripping from his face. She felt the weight of the pistol in her fist.

'Put your hands up now,' the driver yelled, 'or I shoot!'

The gun was a Serbu Super Shorty with a three-round magazine. She had used it before: it fired full-power 12-gauge loads, and from this short distance it would blow her to bits. Isabella raised her hands, her Walther glinting in the sun.

The man on the ground got to his feet. Blood was running freely from his nose. His eyes were full of anger as he reached out towards her.

'Give,' he said, nodding at her Walther.

She had no choice. She kept her left hand raised and lowered her right so he could take the weapon. He looked at it, checking that it was loaded, his dextrous fingers betraying their experience.

'Nice piece,' he said. 'How'd you get it?'

'I bought—'

The man struck Isabella across the face with the back of his free hand. She wasn't expecting the blow, and the stinging impact caught her by surprise. She stumbled and fell, scraping her hands and knees against the grit that dusted the hot asphalt. The man kicked her in the ribs, the blow lifting her and flipping her onto her side.

He loomed over her. 'You're gonna pay for what you did, *chica*. You know who we work for?'

She looked up, shielding her head with her arms in case the man was tempted to kick her again. The sun was behind him, casting him in silhouette. He had her Walther in his hand, aiming it down at her.

'I'm sorry,' she said. 'I didn't mean to—'

He wiped his hand across his nose and looked down at the blood in disgust. 'What the fuck? You gonna try and roll us? You're just a little girl.'

'No,' she protested. 'I just wanted a ride. You frightened me.'

'Oh, we gonna give you a ride,' he said, turning to look over at the driver, both of them sharing an ugly laugh.

Isabella was looking at the man as it happened; he was standing over her, outlined by the sun, her Walther held out in front of him, his finger on the trigger. One side of his head exploded, a splatter of bone and blood and brains. His nearly decapitated body collapsed like a puppet with severed strings and sprawled on the road in front of her.

The boom came next, rolling in across the desert. The driver had seen what had happened to his friend, and he heard the boom, too. He realised what was afoot and, panicked, started to run down the road.

He didn't get far.

A gush of blood splashed out of his chest as a second round passed through his body from back to front.

The boom of the rifle followed once more, echoing over the open ground.

Isabella got to her feet. She touched her cheekbone and winced; it was sore. She pressed and probed until she was satisfied that the bone was not broken and then turned to the two dead bodies on the road. The passenger was nearest to her, a halo of blood slowly spreading out around the pulpy remains of his head. The driver had managed a few steps, but now he lay spreadeagled on the road.

Isabella clenched her fists in frustration.

Fuck it.

She had failed. Blown it. This had been her opportunity to demonstrate that she was ready. She had been training for this all year, trying to get better, and the first time she had tried to put that training into action she had frozen. The first time she found herself in harm's way and she had messed it up.

Fuck.

She looked down the road and saw a single figure in the distance. The heat-haze rose up, muddying her vision, but she could make out the long slender shape of the rifle. A woman was carrying it propped up on her shoulder, and she was coming this way.

Isabella took a moment to clear her head and then got to work. They needed to clean up. She crouched down next to the nearly headless man, grabbed him underneath the arms and started to drag him towards the back of the truck.

Chapter Three

Maia rested the rifle on her shoulder as she made her way down the road.

She had been watching the scene all morning. She had found a spot that was half a mile away, but the 4.5-14x50mm scope attached to her rifle was excellent, and it magnified everything so well that she had even been able to see the expression on the face of the man who was facing Isabella. Maia's shooting position was on the far bank of a dry creek that separated the highway from an abandoned facility that would once have been used to train horses. The raised lip on her side of the creek was higher than the opposite bank and, shielded by a collection of pathetic-looking bushes, she was able to sight the road while remaining hidden from view.

Isabella hadn't realised that she was there. The exercise would have been worthless if she knew she had backup, and it was with that in mind that Maia had secretly followed the Torino on her beaten-up Triumph when Isabella set out earlier. She'd waited for Isabella to pull over opposite the junction that led to the border crossing and then retraced her steps back to the settlement to the north that they had passed.

There she had seen a dirt track that ran south, and so she'd skirted around Isabella's position, left her bike outside Barreales and continued on foot. Maia had unpacked her rifle from the camo-coloured backpack she'd been carrying it in, unfolded the stock, extended the bipod and found a comfortable position to set the rifle in, on a convenient rock.

Isabella's preparation had been good: the spot for the ambush that she had chosen was excellent and she had been diligent in watching the road. Maia had seen the truck approaching and watched as Isabella flagged it down. She'd waited with a twist of tension in her gut as Isabella spoke to the man who got out of the truck.

She had willed the girl to grasp the advantage that surprise would deliver to her, hoping that she would put her training into effect. The plan required her to take both men out, but to do that she needed to find a moment where their attention was elsewhere. They couldn't have anticipated the danger they were in. How could they? Isabella was sixteen years old and they were cartel killers. What reason did they have to be afraid? All Isabella needed was a moment when the man turned his back to her; it would be the green light for her to strike. The driver, trapped in the cab, would be easy after that.

Maia had watched as the passenger grabbed Isabella's head. Her finger tightening on the rifle's trigger, reluctant to fire too soon and deprive Isabella of the chance to prove herself. And Isabella *had* fought back. She had shown guts. She had put the man down and reached for her pistol.

She would have had the opportunity to use it, too, if not for the driver and his shotgun.

Maia drew nearer. Isabella was crouching down; she grabbed one of the bodies by the arms and started to drag it to the rear of the truck. Maia put her hand into her pocket and felt the two shell casings that she had collected. They were still warm to the touch.

She had watched the scene play out and decided she couldn't wait any longer. The rifle was an Accuracy International AXMC chambered in .338 Lapua that she had purchased in Denver and then smuggled into Mexico. It was a bolt-action rifle used by military snipers around the world, and the .338 Lapua cartridge was the calibre with which Maia had the most experience. The passenger was a static target; Maia had zeroed the rifle at three hundred yards last week, putting three rounds into a six-inch square. Maia aimed slightly below her intended point of impact, took three deep breaths, exhaling for the third time and using the pause before she inhaled again as her money spot. She squeezed the trigger until the shot broke and then followed through, continuing the squeeze to the rear before releasing the trigger slowly to the front. The gun had a lot of recoil, maybe more than she'd noticed from the .338 in the past, and she allowed it to come straight back to her. She quickly worked the bolt – up, back, forward, then down – chambering the next round. The scope fell right back on the target, the confirmation that her fundamentals had been perfect.

She had watched the hit and immediately sighted the second target. The wind had picked up a little, with the vegetation two-thirds of the way to the target – the critical distance – swaying lightly from left to right. At the close distance she was shooting from, Maia knew that the wind would have little effect on the bullet's trajectory, but she adjusted her aim a touch and fired again. The cartridge sent a 300-grain bullet towards the man at 2,650 feet per second. At two hundred yards, the bullet hit with a devastating 3,800 pounds of energy – enough even to penetrate body armour, had the man been wearing any.

Maia was fifty feet away now. Isabella had moved the first man and was coming back for the second. Maia could see her expression: she looked angry.

'What are you doing here?' she asked bitterly as Maia reached her.

'I didn't want to leave you on your own. This wasn't easy.'

'I had it under control,' she said, but she was unable to look at Maia as she said it.

Isabella was angry, and Maia stumbled over what to say next. She found empathy difficult; the year that she had spent with the girl had helped her with that, but it still did not come naturally to her. Her career with Daedalus had made some things brutally plain to her, and one thing she had learned was that there was success and there was failure, and nothing in between. Maia had rarely failed, but the times when she was not able to meet her objectives – the first time that she had met Isabella and Michael Pope came to mind – had been rewarded with a curt debrief that made it clear that bad results would not be tolerated. She supposed she had taken those lessons to heart. She did not see the sense in sugar-coating a poor performance, and this was, by any definition, poor. Isabella would have been killed were it not for Maia. Isabella *had* failed. But Maia tried to hold her tongue. Words could sting. Perhaps encouragement was the better option.

'Fuck,' Isabella breathed.

'It's fine,' Maia said. 'It was the first time.'

'It's *not* fine,' Isabella said. 'This was supposed to be on me.'

'What happened?'

Isabella exhaled. 'I messed up.'

Maia checked the road in both directions. There was no traffic to be seen. She took the man's right leg, Isabella took the left, and they dragged him to the back of the truck.

'How? What went wrong?'

'He was a dirty pig,' Isabella said. 'I was going to shoot him, but then this one came out with his shotgun.' She toed the driver with the end of her boot.

'You were taking too long,' Maia said.

'I just blanked out.'

Maia could see that Isabella was upset and reminded herself that she should say something to encourage her. 'You got them to stop,' she said. 'That was good. They got out of the truck. They bought your story.'

'I think so,' Isabella said. 'But what should I have done? What would you have done?'

'You should have shot him as soon as he came out of the truck. The second man was still inside – you could have shot him through the windshield. It would have taken three or four seconds. There would have been nothing that either of them could have done.'

The cargo door at the rear of the truck was locked. Maia frisked the passenger and then the driver until she found the key. She unlocked the door and pushed it up, the partitions clattering as they ascended on rusted runners.

'I'm sorry,' Isabella said.

'There's no need to apologise. We'll try again. And, next time, you'll be better.'

The interior of the truck had shelves on both walls. There were parcels stacked on the shelves, each bearing labels with addresses and barcodes. Isabella hopped inside and pulled the passenger's body up over the lip of the loading area as Maia pushed. Isabella dragged him deeper into the cargo space and then came back to help with the driver.

'Had you been there long?' she asked.

'All morning.' Maia was about to criticise Isabella for not noticing that she had been followed, or for missing her as she found her shooting position, but again she held her tongue.

'Those were two good shots,' Isabella said.

'It was well within range,' Maia said. 'There was only a little wind.'

'Do you think I could've made them?'

'You've made more difficult shots.'

'But shooting someone like that . . . it's different.'

Maia didn't answer. That had not been something she'd ever struggled with. Her training had begun early, when she was still a small child. She had been given a thorough indoctrination that suppressed the notion that her targets were anything other than just that: targets. They were necessary waypoints on the way to the completion of her orders. Nothing more, nothing less. She never humanised them. She didn't know whether she was even capable of doing that.

Empathy and compassion? They were things she struggled with. She had been training Isabella, but she had wondered whether she might learn from the girl, too. She didn't know how much progress had made. Pulling the trigger on the cartel men had still been reflex, easy as shelling peas. She had done it automatically, without compun tion, and she knew that she would react the same way if she had to d it again.

'Keep watch,' she said as she hopped up into the back of the truck.

She had a knife in her backpack, and she used it to slice open the nearest box. Their day's work served two purposes: to advance Isabella's training, and to provide more of the funds they would need when the training was complete. She went along the shelves, slicing open box after box after box until she found the one that she wanted. She pulled it down, dumped it on the floor and sliced it all the way open.

There was money inside: lots and lots of money.

She took her rucksack off her shoulders and sent Isabella to get her bag from the Torino. They withdrew the big stacks of bills and transferred them into their bags.

'What now?' Isabella said.

'I'll take the truck, put my bike in the back and then drive it out into the desert. You take the car – I'll ride back. I've got to go and see Hector first, then I'll meet you at the house.'

Chapter Four

I sabella went back to the Torino. She cranked the key, and the car's 428 Cobra Jet motor, still reliable after all these years, grumbled into life. The car had the Cruise-O-Matic automatic transmission; she put it into drive and rolled the car over the uneven surface until she was on the road. She paused there for a moment, taking the iPod and skipping tracks until she reached AC/DC's 'Back in Black'. She glanced in the mirror and saw the truck pull away towards the south. She touched the gas pedal and rolled away in the opposite direction, feeding in more power until the car picked up speed. She ignored her usual caution and pushed down on the pedal even more, racing through San Augustín at sixty towards the outskirts of Juárez. She wound down the window and let the hot air rush into the cabin, drying the sweat that had gathered on her face.

She couldn't stop herself from revisiting what had happened; gritting her teeth at the frustration of it, she tried to fight back her disappointment. She had hoped that today would be the day they could move on to what they had been planning ever since she recovered from her broken leg. She had been working so hard, and for so long. It was what the training was for: to prepare her for the challenges that would come. They had been hiding south of the border since Maia smuggled them both across, and Isabella didn't want to hide any longer. There were things that they needed to do, and she was done with being patient.

Hiding, too, was demoralising, but she knew they had no choice in that. The conspiracy they had run from was large and powerful, and Isabella realised that the men who had so nearly killed them on the mountain wouldn't rest until she was dead and Maia had been recaptured.

And so they'd hidden. They had a small place in Juárez where they could pay the landlord in cash and where no questions would be asked of them. They lived entirely off the grid, with no bank account and the bare minimum of official documentation, all under their false names. They tried not to use cell phones, and when they did they relied on burners that they replaced on a regular basis.

Isabella raced by the streets that marked the beginning of the city limits and dabbed at the brakes to reduce her speed. The city was large and sprawling, a malignancy appended to its twin across the border, stubbornly growing despite the violence that had afflicted it for so long. Isabella looked out at an estate of new houses, which remained unsold despite the beseeching billboard ads on the highway. In the distance she saw the flickering lights of the city proper. It was so different from Marrakech. It was plain and brutal, baked by the sun and wracked by the violence that had once made it the most dangerous place on the planet. It lacked the romance of her adopted city in Morocco: the sounds and smells of the main square, the friendliness of the locals, the mystery of the souk and the dark alleys that cut through buildings that were hundreds of years old. She missed her *riad*, too, and wondered what had happened to it now that she had been away for so long. She doubted she would ever be able to return.

She thought about Maia's reaction as they'd cleared away the mess on the road. She had been brusque; there was no overt disappointment, no chastisement for the errors that Isabella had made, yet neither had there been any real encouragement or an acknowledgement that she was making progress. There rarely was. Isabella had come to understand Maia over the time they had spent together; rapport was something that was completely alien to her and she rarely showed anything that might approach warmth or affection. It wasn't that she was incapable of emotion – there had been moments when they had shared longer conversations, and, during those times, Isabella had come to detect what she thought might be the beginning of a closeness between them. Not a maternal relationship – Maia was only ten years older than she was, after all – but perhaps the beginning of something sisterly. Maia rarely laughed, but when she did it was with a hesitancy that was almost charming, and it was usually followed by a quizzical expression that suggested she was seeking confirmation that her laughter had been appropriate.

Isabella turned off the highway and slowed to negotiate the nest of streets that would eventually lead her to Calle Álamo and their little home. The Walther was on the seat next to her; she took it, reached over to the glovebox and hid it inside, next to the iPod and the detritus that had gathered in there over time.

She was agitated.

She needed to train.

Chapter Five

V ivian Bloom paused at the entrance to the building. The chrome nameplate next to the door at street level announced it as 'The Spire'. It was a glass-and-steel skyscraper that was unremarkable in Midtown Manhattan; just another minaret amid dozens of others that accommodated legal and accountancy firms, destinations for the thousands of anonymous drones that Bloom had watched emerging from the subway stations as his driver negotiated the choked streets.

Bloom went into the lobby. The project owned the entire building, although it would have been impossible for even the most thorough of forensic investigators to unravel the network of offshore companies and trusts established to bury the identity of the owners and the source of the funds that had been made available to purchase it. The ostensible holding company had been made to look as typical as possible: forty-eight of the fifty floors were rented out to legitimate businesses that would have had no clue as to the transactions that were discussed at the very top of the building.

The elevator chimed as it reached the top floor, and the doors parted. Bloom stepped out. There was a simple reception desk, with the name of a PR firm on the wall behind it. The firm was real, running real accounts for real businesses, but the office was all for show. The work of the firm was conducted elsewhere. This floor, and the floor below it, were used in order to advance the aims of the operation and the representatives who were responsible for it.

The receptionist smiled. 'They're in the conference room, Mr Bloom,' she said.

There were three men waiting for him inside.

'Good morning, Vivian.'

Theodore Carington was a career politician who had been driving his hawkish agenda since the administration of the first President Bush. He had served as Secretary of Defense for the younger Bush, and his influence had been crucial in persuading that administration to pursue the Iraqi regime following 9/11. Carington had maintained his influence and had become one of the senior players in the project. Bloom thought him a grubby and venal man, lacking the ideological purity that was Bloom's own motivation for being here. Carington was deep in the pocket of the military-industrial complex that had owned him for the entirety of his career.

'Teddy,' Bloom said. He turned to acknowledge the other two. 'Gentlemen.'

Jamie King was a part of that complex. He was sat next to Carington, tanned and with the appearance of almost obscenely good health. King was the chairman of Manage Risk, a vast private military contractor with interests all around the world, and his share price depended upon the world being a dangerous place. Bloom had an even lower opinion of him than he had of Carington, and their relationship – never close – had soured following the botched exchange at Clingmans Dome that had seen them lose the asset and fail to eliminate the problems represented by Michael Pope and Isabella Rose.

Professor Nikita Ivanosky was sitting opposite King. He was tall and slender, with a shaven head and a pair of spectacles that were a little too youthful for him. The man was in his late sixties and had defected from Russia when he realised that he wanted money rather than the gratitude of the state for the work he was doing, and that the most money could be found in the United States. Bloom thought that mercenary and found the scientist to be cold and aloof. Ivanosky evidently thought Bloom an annoying distraction and habitually directed his conversation to Carington and King – largely due to the fact, Bloom knew, that they were his paymasters and their continued patronage kept him in the gilded lifestyle to which he had become accustomed.

'Thank you for coming, Vivian,' Carington said.

Bloom waved the thanks away. 'There's the main meeting to attend,' he said. 'It's no inconvenience to get here a little earlier.'

Carington smiled. 'I just wanted to recap. It's been a year since we lost the asset. We haven't discussed it for several months. I thought it would be helpful if we sat down and assessed where we are.'

'I agree,' Bloom said. 'There's something I want to bring up, too.'

King ignored that. 'I can tell you where we are,' he said with his usual mixture of bombast and umbrage. 'We're exactly where we were a year ago. Nothing's changed. Not a fucking thing. We don't know where the asset is, *or* Pope, *or* his family, *or* the girl. We don't know shit.'

'Well, yes,' Carington said. Was he a little uncomfortable? That made Bloom anxious. 'Quite. That's why it might be that the time is right to discuss it now. Perhaps we can close the book.' He turned to Ivanosky. 'Professor – let's start with the asset. We've had no information since we lost contact with her. I'd like your opinion – what's the most likely reason?'

Ivanosky shuffled in his chair. 'It's very hard to say.'

'Speculate.'

Ivanosky fiddled with his spectacles. 'Maia would have needed a regular supply of citalopram to maintain stability. The change to the genome made them more naturally aggressive. The elevated levels of norepinephrine and dopamine do what we want them to do, but we've never been able to apply a natural check. They get weekly shots to keep them within safe tolerances. When we want to amp them up a little, we reduce the dose. When we need them to behave in such a way that they can more easily blend into society, we up the dose. We've become very good at using the drug – it's like an on-off switch. She would have to find a regular supply or . . .' Ivanosky paused.

'Or?' Carington prodded.

'Well, let's put it like this. Five years ago, we didn't have the control we have today. One of Maia's siblings was on a deep cover mission in Israel.'

'I remember,' King said. 'He dropped off the radar for a week. He went off his meds.'

Ivanosky nodded. 'We found him again after an unfortunate incident at a restaurant in Tel Aviv.'

'Unfortunate?' Bloom asked.

'He didn't like the way that his steak had been prepared. Killed the waiter who'd had the misfortune of bringing it to him, three other members of staff and two of his fellow diners. The Israeli police shot him. Fortunately for us, his cover held up. They didn't dig too deeply before we recovered his body and hushed it up. They put it down to a psychotic episode.'

Because the alternative would have been too fantastic to consider, Bloom thought. He'd had concerning thoughts at regular intervals during the last few years. Every new piece of information about the assets shifted what he thought was possible just a little bit more; on their own, the incremental changes were unremarkable – a *little* faster, a *little* stronger, a *little* more aggressive – until those increments were combined and the accumulated effect became startling, and frightening.

The thought of Maia, out in the world and completely unchecked, was appalling enough. The thought of her unshackled from the medication that kept her sane made it even worse.

'Could she have found a supply?' Carington asked.

Ivanosky removed his glasses and wiped them with a handkerchief he took from his pocket. 'Of course. We have caches of drugs for the assets within easy distance of most cities in North America, and plenty of other sites around the world. But we've had all of them under remote surveillance, and we haven't seen anything.'

'She's expecting that,' King said. 'She'd stay away.'

'Very likely. And citalopram is a generic medicine – you can get it as Cipramil. She could get it herself. It would be difficult, but it's possible. However, Cipramil is diluted compared to the pure doses that we administer. The amount that she would need to stay level is very significant indeed. She would have to be very inventive, and we haven't seen anything that makes us think that she's found a way to do that.'

'So?'

Ivanosky slid the spectacles back onto his head. 'So we think it is most likely that she's been un-medicated, or largely un-medicated. And that means we have to consider the chance that she's dead. We've seen suicidal behaviour in un-medicated subjects before. That's possible. It's also possible that she's been killed by someone else, although that would have been messy and we've been looking for incidents that we could attribute to her. Again, so far we've found nothing.'

'Fine,' King said. 'So we assume she's dead. Maybe we can put a line through it.'

'I think we maintain a level of caution until we know for sure. But if you're asking me to make an educated guess, I'd say that's the most likely outcome.'

Carington nodded, ready to move on. 'What about Pope and the girl? Vivian? Do you have anything on them at all?'

Bloom had put a team on Pope and the girl as soon as it was confirmed that they'd escaped the mountain. The team had pulled everything in the files they held on both of them. Pope's file was voluminous: throughout his adult life he had worked for the government, in the military and then for Group Fifteen. The vetting process for his transfer to the Group had been incredibly thorough, as was always the case. There were references in the file to friends and family who had been run down and checked, all without any indication that Pope had been in contact. They had scoured his online presence, but had found nothing there, either.

The girl's file was slender in comparison; most of their intelligence related to her deceased mother, but there had been references to properties in Marrakech that the girl was connected to, and to a man who ran a Krav Maga school there who had apparently been her instructor. They went back and checked the foster parents who had been responsible for her after Pope's predecessor as Control kidnapped her, but her file suggested that those relationships had not been warm and, in any event, it was moot: she had not been back to any of them.

Bloom had recently tried a different approach with Pope and had enjoyed a little success. But he was damned if he was about to mention that today.

He shook his head. 'Nothing,' he said. 'They got off the mountain and we lost them.'

King snorted derisively.

Bloom turned to him. 'Something you want to add, Jamie?'

'All of this could have been avoided,' King said. 'This whole goddamn mess. Pope and the girl made Syria more difficult. They interfered with the operation in Shanghai. We lost the asset after Washington because of them. If you'd handled it properly we wouldn't be having this conversation.'

'That's a very convenient assignment of the blame,' Bloom said. 'I should add, in case it's forgotten, that security for the exchange was a Manage Risk responsibility. If your men had done their jobs, neither Pope nor the girl would have been able to get off the mountain, and we would still have the asset.'

King was about to react to the barb, but Carington raised his hand and King held his tongue. 'You're saying they all dropped off the grid, Vivian? Pope, his wife and his children? All of them?'

'Captain Pope is a very capable agent. If he wants to stay out of the way, he'll certainly be equipped to do it. And you mention his family. They might be our main advantage in all of this. He's not going to want to do anything that puts them at risk. As long as he believes that we're not looking too hard for him, I think it's more likely that he keeps what he knows to himself.'

'But we *are* looking hard for him, aren't we, Vivian?' King said with unhidden sarcasm.

'Yes, Jamie. We are. Diligently and discreetly.'

'And the girl?' Carington asked.

Bloom shook his head. 'Again – we haven't found anything. But the last we saw of her was when the asset took her after the exchange. She was fifteen years old then. She's sixteen now. A teenage girl wouldn't be equipped to stay off the radar without help.'

'She's a child,' King said. 'And if we're operating under the assumption that the asset would have had some sort of psychotic reaction without her meds, then maybe she's dead.'

King looked over at Ivanosky.

'I think it's likely,' the professor said. 'Probably very likely. We've not been able to understand why Maia would have taken her. The assets don't form emotional attachments and I can't see what she would get from having the girl around. The girl would impede her. If Maia was minded to go underground, then she'd divest herself of anything and everyone that would make that more difficult. The girl would be the first thing to go.'

'All right,' Carington said. 'Unless anyone disagrees, and until we have evidence that suggests otherwise, I think we keep looking but we assume that Maia and the girl are both dead. Yes?'

Ivanosky nodded his agreement.

After a moment, King nodded, too. 'And Pope?'

'I think that's different. We keep looking for him. He's out there, him and his family. I'm not comfortable trusting that he'll keep his mouth shut. He knows what happened. He could cause a serious problem.'

'Are we done?' King asked, half rising from his chair.

'No,' Bloom said. 'Not yet.'

'Vivian said he had something he wanted to bring up,' Carington said.

King lowered himself back down to his chair with an impatient sigh.

Bloom laid his hands on the table. 'It strikes me that we're all here and there's something that needs to be discussed. We've been dancing around it for too long.'

'Vivian—' Carington began.

'No, Teddy,' Bloom said, speaking over him. 'I've been patient. We need to talk about Prometheus. I want to address it.'

Bloom had noticed the look that King shared with Carington, and knew that whatever he was about to say had been the subject of a pre-meeting to which he had not been invited.

'This is about sharing the technology?' Carington said.

'It is.'

'Then I'm afraid we can't agree to do that.'

'You can't or you won't?'

'Honestly?' Carington said. 'Both.'

King took over. 'There's no point pussyfooting around this,' he said. 'Are you crazy, Vivian?' He punctuated the question with an incredulous shake of his head. 'Prometheus was funded with American money.' He gestured to Ivanosky. 'We paid for him to come over, we built Daedalus to give him the tools he needed. He works for us. Anything he produces belongs to us. Why would you—'

'That wasn't what we agreed,' Bloom interrupted. 'We've been involved in this right from the start. You've had scientific support. There's British money tied up in it. And do I need to remind you who found your missing scientist in Venezuela?'

'That was a long time ago,' Carington said. 'Before my time.'

'But not before mine,' Bloom said. 'I was there. The CIA asked us when Koralev went AWOL. I helped to plan that operation. We found him.'

'You're out of your mind,' King spoke over him.

'Jamie's right,' Carington said. 'It's impossible. How could we share it? Be reasonable, Vivian. The research is a state secret – a multibillion-dollar state secret. You must be able to see that?'

'No,' Bloom said. 'I'm afraid I can't. We had an understanding that this was a shared project, and now you are reneging on that.' He found the ire that he knew they would expect from him; it was a show for their benefit. He had anticipated that there would eventually be a stonewall, and he had been working assiduously in expectation of it for the better part of two years. It would be better, though, if they did not suspect that.

Carington tried to pacify him. 'You're being unrealistic,' he said gently.

Bloom threw up his hands theatrically. 'I don't need to listen to any more of this,' he said.

'Don't be so dramatic,' King said.

Bloom stood and made his way around the table to the door.

'*Vivian*,' Carington said. 'Come on.'

'I'll see you at the main meeting.'

Bloom made his way outside. He felt calm. He had always known that they would stab him in the back, and now that they had, he could concentrate his energy on the alternative courses of action he had prepared. He had made himself indispensable in a dangerous world for decades. One did not manage that sort of longevity without contingencies.

And Bloom had several.

Chapter Six

Mexico

The house was in San Gerónimo, a reasonably upscale neighbourhood for a place like Juárez. Maia turned onto Calle Pedro Rosales de Leon and then turned again onto Del Mar Sur. It was a quiet, tree-lined street, with decent cars parked outside the properties. There was much more money in this neighbourhood than the streets around the place she shared with Isabella. The houses were set back a short distance from the road, many of them shielding their yards behind neatly whitewashed iron railings.

Maia rode the bike for a short distance until she reached 162, which was identified as such by the number painted on the blue trash can that had been left on the sidewalk to be collected by the city council. The property was on a single level, as were most of the others on the street, making up for what it lacked in storeys by dint of extending back a good distance. Hector had painted it a lurid green, insisting that the colour gave it character amid neighbouring houses that were resolutely monochrome. Maia thought it looked ridiculous. She flinched at the idea that there was anything to gain by standing out; her training had underlined the importance of the opposite, accentuating the benefits of being just another face in the crowd.

It was evident that the members of the cartel did not share that opinion. They drove expensive cars, wore ostentatious jewellery and declared their affiliation with gang tattoos. Maia knew why: they had nothing to fear from the authorities. They either owned the police or had terrified them into inaction. The men in the cartel were average and of mediocre intelligence; they had been given vast amounts of money and had no reason to be concerned about letting their neighbours speculate about how they had accumulated it.

She parked the bike on the side of the street and looked up and down the sidewalk. It was a little after three in the afternoon and there was no one around. The locals would be at work or sleeping through the hottest part of the day. That suited Maia well. There was a buzzer on the wall next to the gate. She pressed the button and waited until the lock was disengaged. She went inside the yard and walked to the front door.

Hector opened it. He was short and skinny, with a thin face and dark brown hair that was retreating at the temples despite the fact he was only just out of his thirties. He was entirely unremarkable and would have been able to pass as a provincial accountant save for evidence of meth addiction, and the tattoos that covered most of his skin. He was shirtless, and Maia saw the familiar piece on his chest that depicted the face of his mother beneath a cursive banner that read 'LA FRONTERA' and then, above it, an angel. He had a large piece on his back that featured the Devil and the Grim Reaper, and the skull design that was the cartel's calling card was etched on the side of his throat.

He stood there, just looking at her.

'Hello, baby,' Maia said in her perfect Spanish.

'Elizabeth,' he said.

'Can I come in?'

He stepped aside. Maia went through, immediately reacquainting herself with the property: a long corridor with doors that led to the living room, the kitchen, the bathroom and the three bedrooms. She paused for a moment to listen, but couldn't hear anything save the sound of the TV in the living room.

The door closed behind her, and she turned to face Hector. 'Is everything okay?'

He stared at her, a frown furrowing his brow. It was an unfortunate expression for him; glowering made him look even more stupid than normal. He didn't answer, his lip curling in an expression of diffidence as he went by her into the living room.

Maia could guess the problem, but there was nothing to be gained in bringing it up herself. He would have to tell her. She had cultivated the impression that she was something of a hopeless airhead, and revealing any sort of perspicacity would risk compromising herself.

She followed Hector into the living room. He rummaged around on the couch until he found the remote control and silenced the TV with a peremptory stab of a button. He glared at her, but still he didn't speak.

'What is it, baby?' Maia said, undoing the top two buttons of her shirt as she sat down. 'Something on your mind?'

Hector exhaled unhappily. 'You know what I was saying about the trucks?'

'Sure,' she said.

The glowering hostility and suspicion was gone, and in their place was angst. She saw his Adam's apple bobbing up and down in his throat.

'Did you tell anyone?' he asked her.

'No,' she said, shaking her head guilelessly. 'Who would I tell?'

'I don't know,' he said. 'Maybe you were at a bar?'

'No,' she said. 'Why would I want to go to a bar? You know I don't do that now. I don't want to meet anyone now I got you.'

The compliment stalled him, but didn't satisfy him. 'So maybe you said something to someone at work.'

Hector thought that Maia worked in one of the *maquiladoras* at the edge of the city.

'Who would I tell? It's a bunch of old women. You think I'd tell them? I don't even like any of them. And anyway, you told me not to, so I didn't.'

He sat down next to her and breathed out again. She knew what she might have to do to get him to relax, and the thought of it repulsed her, as it always did.

'Ah, fuck it,' he said.

'What's the matter? Tell me.'

'You know I told you about the one that was coming over the border at Tornillo? It was coming today, but it never showed. The men who were driving it have disappeared, too. No sign of them. They left El Paso, crossed the border like they were supposed to do at the time they were supposed to do it, but now it's like they never even existed. Them, the truck and the money?' He made a gesture with his fingers, closing and then opening them as he blew out his cheeks. 'Poof – gone. It's all gone, like magic. The bosses don't know what happened and they're freaking out about it.'

'Well,' she said, shuffling around on the couch so that she could face him. 'I swear I didn't tell anyone.'

Lying was easy for her. She had no moral compass, no conscience that could be pricked by the telling of mistruths. Her training had made her a consummate actor, compelling and credible, and she knew that she wouldn't give herself away. Not that the impression of veracity would matter to this particular audience; Hector was so dumb that she didn't need anything more than a straight face to fool him – and, more to the point, she had already decided that their relationship was going to be coming to a close tonight.

But she needed to ask him a question first. She needed to know what he had done, and whether that made her and Isabella vulnerable.

'Did you tell anyone else that you told me?' she asked.

'No,' he said.

'I just want to know if I should be worried. If you did say something, and they're already worried, maybe they get worried about me – about whether I could have said something to someone else. Baby? Do I need to be worried?'

He tried to wave away her concern. 'I didn't tell them,' he said. 'They'd kill us both if they thought I'd told you. That shit's totally confidential.'

'Then don't mention anything like that again. I don't know why you told me, anyway.'

'Because you asked,' he protested. 'You said you wanted to know.'

'You told me because you wanted to impress me,' she said. 'But you don't have to. I love you, baby. Nothing's gonna change that.'

She reached across and ran her fingertips down his face, her skin scratching against the bristles on his cheek. He relaxed, sitting back and closing his eyes.

'I got a bottle of tequila in the kitchen,' he said. 'You wanna go get it? I could do with a drink.'

Maia stood and went to the kitchen. There was a bottle of Patrón Silver standing on the countertop. Maia took out four shot glasses from the cabinet and rested them next to the bottle. Hector had rather superciliously made it his mission to educate Maia in the niceties of tequila. He said that Americans had no idea how to drink it properly, explaining that Mexicans didn't drink tequila with lime, preferring a shot of sangrita to accompany it. He had demonstrated how to make sangrita, and Maia quickly followed his instructions now. She took two plump oranges from the fruit bowl and squeezed out the juice, adding fresh lime juice, grenadine and a teaspoon of ancho chile powder. She cut two slices of jalapeño and dropped them into two of the shot glasses, and then filled both with the mixture.

There was one more ingredient to add. She reached into her pocket and took out a small vial. She listened for a moment to make sure that

Hector was still in the living room and, satisfied that he was, removed the top from the vial. It contained ketamine in its liquid form. She had purchased it from the same street dealer in La Mariscal who supplied the drugs she needed to keep her level. She tipped the clear liquid into one of the glasses of sangrita. It was impossible to detect.

She put the four glasses and the tequila on a tray and took them into the living room.

'Here,' she said, handing Hector the doctored sangrita as she opened the bottle of tequila and poured out three fingers into the two empty glasses. She handed one to Hector and raised the other in salute.

Hector ignored her gesture, grunted what might have passed for a thank you, took the tequila, knocked it back in one swift hit and then followed it with the sangrita. Maia sipped hers, enjoying the acidity of the sangrita against the tequila, the spiciness of the chilli acting as a bridge between the alcohol and the fruit.

Maia had laced the drink with a heavy dose and guessed that it would take thirty minutes before it rendered him helpless. She didn't need him to be unconscious to do what she needed to do, but this was a residential neighbourhood and she preferred to go about her business with discretion. She put the glass to her lips again and sipped, watching Hector as he poured out another measure of tequila and downed it once more.

Chapter Seven

Isabella undressed and looked at her reflection in the mirror. She still had the blowback from the driver of the truck on her neck, and as she touched her hair she found that it was matted with dried blood. She showered to wash it all away, then dried herself and pulled on her running pants and a T-shirt. She went through into the tiny room that served as both kitchen and living room. She boiled three eggs, shelled them and then spread them out between two pieces of toast. She ate, drank a pint of water and then filled a plastic bottle. She found her backpack and opened it on the table. She had a map, a GPS tracker, a Glock 21 and three boxes of .45 ACP ammunition.

She dropped the full bottle of water in the rucksack, closed the sack and put it on her shoulders, then slipped on her running shoes. She went outside, grabbed the iPod from the car and pushed the earbuds into her ears. It was burning hot, but she didn't let that put her off. She scrolled until she found her running playlist and hit play. 'Everything Counts' by Depeche Mode started up. She set off.

She headed west, out towards the boundary of the city. She fell into her usual stride, a comfortable pace that chewed up the distance and usually meant she could cover ten kilometres in around forty minutes. She followed the six-lane highway that cut a diagonal from the northwest to the southeast through the city. She went by stores and businesses, through a long one-mile stretch that was just empty scrub on either side, and reached the junction with Boulevard Municipio Libre. She took the turn, continuing due west until she reached the cemetery at Memorial Park. She left the road and picked up the trail in the park, starting the first of three clockwise loops.

She knew that Juárez was dangerous, but that lent an edge to things. It kept her sharp and alert. She and Maia wouldn't stay here forever, and, when they moved, the residual sense of threat that she felt here as she passed men on street corners and in parked cars would be replaced by a more immediate danger. For now, she had the gun in her pack. She almost welcomed an incident, hard-staring the men as they watched her go by. She wanted them to come on to her. The debacle in the desert had knocked her confidence, and she was hungry to prove herself.

'Under Pressure' started, and she picked up her pace.

This edge of the city had been blighted by the abandoned factory that sat atop the hill to the northwest. It had been owned by a Californian businessman who packed up when the economy tanked. A local reporter estimated that ten thousand tonnes of toxic sludge, including lead and sulphuric acid, had simply been left in open pits. Whenever it rained, the sludge would start to creep down the hill, leaching poison into local drinking water and poisoning the cattle that grazed nearby.

She completed the third loop. She felt good. She had measured the distance when she first plotted the route and knew that she had covered six miles so far. She was breathing easily and her legs were still strong. She stopped, took the bottle from her pack and glugged down half of it in thirsty gulps. She checked her watch: she had been running for forty-five minutes, and at a decent pace. She replaced the bottle, put the bag back onto her back and turned to make her way back again.

She picked up her pace for the return leg, checking with her watch and speeding up until she was running six-minute miles. She concentrated on her body, assessing everything; fatigue encouraged flaws in her running form, and she corrected them as she became aware of them. She found herself slouching and straightened her back, intent on holding her stance all the way to the end. She looked down at her watch and picked up her pace again.

She was drenched with sweat as she turned onto Calle Álamo. Maia had just arrived outside the house. Isabella slowed and pressed stop on her watch, waiting as Maia wheeled the bike off the street.

'Well?' Maia said.

Isabella held up her watch. The stopwatch had ended on seventy-four minutes.

'Good,' Maia said. 'But you can go faster. Tomorrow, seventy-three.'

Isabella allowed herself a rueful smile; Maia was still stinting in her praise. She shrugged off her pack and took out the water. 'How did it go?'

'It's done,' Maia said.

Isabella didn't need to ask what that meant. It didn't bother her. She had seen a lot of death in the last year, and she knew a man like Hector had, in all likelihood, doled out more than his fair share. His fate was predestined; just karma coming back around.

'Do we have anything to worry about?'

'No,' Maia said. 'He didn't tell anyone. We're fine.'

She made her way to the front door and unlocked it.

Isabella replaced the iPod in the glovebox and followed. She was hungry and tired.

Chapter Eight

Isabella showered for the second time that day, changed into comfortable clothes and looked in the cupboard for inspiration for their meal. There was nothing there. She had forgotten that she had used up all of their fresh food for the quesadillas she had made last night.

Maia had taken the Glock from Isabella's pack and was field-stripping it on their small table.

'What are you doing?'

'It's dirty,' Maia said. 'You need to keep it clean. If you have to use it and it doesn't fire, you'll get yourself killed.'

Isabella was used to the criticism by now; she knew that Maia meant nothing by it and that, in her own strange way, it was an expression of affection. She filled a glass from the faucet and drank it, and then pulled on her shoes.

'I've got to go to the store,' she said. 'We're out of food.'

Maia's attention was consumed by the pistol, breaking it down into its constituent parts and cleaning them all with a fastidiousness that was close to obsession.

'Maia?' Isabella said.

Maia looked up. 'Yes?'

'I've got to go to the shop – do you need anything?'

Maia shook her head and turned her attention back to the pieces of the Glock.

Isabella collected her purse and left the house. Bip Bip was just at the end of the street. Isabella went inside the store and started to think about what they needed. Money wasn't really a problem for them, as Maia had been rolling the local dealers for their stashes for the past few months, but she also siphoned off a decent amount to pay for the drugs that she needed, and then more for what she described as 'preparation'. Isabella liked to shepherd what was left. She spent frugally. They didn't have jobs and she was aware that extravagance would generate attention that they could not afford.

Isabella took a basket and started to fill it.

Chapter Nine

Maia looked down into the sink and watched the last of her blood as it circled the plughole and disappeared. She had felt weak when she had returned, but she didn't want Isabella to see it. There was no sense in worrying the girl until Maia was able to diagnose what was wrong with her, even though she already had a very good idea. She had been suffering from a litany of symptoms: fever, aches in her bones, lethargy and shortness of breath and bruising that came too often and too easily to be dismissed, especially when she had been so difficult to bruise until now. She looked at her shoulder in the mirror: it was a perfect case in point. The recoil from the rifle had left a deep bruise, a purple-and-red print in the shape of the buttstock. That would never have happened before.

The symptoms, taken individually, could be dismissed. Taken as a whole, though, and it looked as if something far more serious was happening inside her body. The bleeding had started a week ago. She'd bled from her gums and started to suffer nosebleeds that were difficult to staunch. Her nose had bled at dinner two nights ago. Isabella had fetched a dishcloth for her to use; Maia had seen the girl's concern, and explained it away by telling her that it was a childhood affliction that had started to reoccur.

But Maia had never suffered from nosebleeds.

It was more than that.

She rinsed out the basin, turned off the faucet and flushed away the bloody tissue that she had dropped into the toilet. She needed to see someone, but there was no one that she could turn to. Reputable doctors would have online records that could be searched. They would want to take blood; her sample would return unusual results that would lead to further investigation. It would lead to questions, suspicion and, eventually, discovery. And, in any event, she knew that the doctors in Juárez would be hopelessly ill-equipped to deal with her case. There were only a handful of doctors in the world who had the experience to diagnose and treat her, and they all worked in a secure CIA facility in Skopje to which she would never be able to return.

Ivanosky might be able to help her. But no, she couldn't go to him. Couldn't do that. She was on her own.

She was pulling her T-shirt over her head when she heard the door open.

Isabella.

She made sure that the sink was clean and that there was no other evidence that would reveal that she had been bleeding.

She went back into the living room.

A man she had never seen before was standing on the other side of the table. He was tall and broad, with a wide face and dark hair that he wore long, down beyond his collar. His face was distinguished by prominent cheekbones that seemed to accentuate the sallowness of his cheeks. His skin was marked by a scattering of old acne scars and he had a well-trimmed goatee beard and thick eyebrows. He was wearing a white shirt that was open at the throat, with chest hair and the dark ink of a tattoo visible in the gap.

He was carrying a large handgun. He raised it, levelling it at her.

'Good evening,' he said. 'You are Elizabeth?'

Maia stayed where she was, without speaking, and conducted as fast an assessment of her situation as she could. The man looked comfortable with the Beretta that he was holding, and he was certainly too close to miss hitting her, were he to fire. She could hear movement in her bedroom. There was at least one other person in the house. Her suspicions were confirmed a moment later when a second man came into the living room. He was armed, too, with a Beretta in his right hand. His face was covered in a collection of ugly tattoos.

The first man looked at the second. 'Well?' he said.

'There is no one else here,' the man with the tattooed face replied in guttural Spanish.

Maia glanced down at the broken-down Glock on the table; the first man noticed, and smiled.

His English was awkward. 'We come at bad time?'

'You could say that.'

'My name is Felipe,' he said. 'I expect that you have heard of me?'

'Hector mentioned you.'

She knew exactly who he was: Felipe Valdez. Hector had spoken about him as they lay in his filthy bed. Valdez was an enforcer for La Frontera, a *sicario* who was sent out to eliminate those who stood in the way of the cartel's business. He had been given the nickname of Las Muletas, or 'The Crutches', on account of the number of victims he had left with a bullet to the back of the knee. Those men and women had been fortunate, despite being crippled, for Hector told of dozens of others who had been executed, many of them in particularly gruesome ways. Valdez was particularly fond of *el guiso*, which involved boiling a person alive, or setting them alight with kerosene in a large metal barrel.

He picked up the Glock's slide and receiver and held them out for her to see. 'Why would woman who works in a *maquila* have a weapon like this? It is expensive, no?'

'This is a dangerous city,' Maia said. 'I like to be careful.'

Valdez handed the pieces of the Glock to the tattooed man. Maia glanced around the room for an alternative weapon. There was a block of cheap knives on the counter, but Valdez was blocking her way to them.

'What do you want?' she asked him.

'You mentioned Hector,' Valdez said. 'You were seeing him, no?'

'Yes.'

'Why?'

She didn't answer.

'It is strange,' he said. 'I explain why. You are American. You come here, to Juárez, to this shithole, because you say you are married to a Mexican businessman. But then you are not married anymore and yet you stay. You could go back to your comfortable life in America, but you do not. And then you have a relationship with a man like Hector. A cockroach. Why? You like danger? You like dangerous men?'

'I like Hector,' she said.

'When was the last time you see him?'

'This afternoon.'

He pursed his lips and nodded, as if considering the information. 'Hector – he has a loose tongue, no?' Valdez paused, smiled and shook his head. 'I say *has*, but I mean *had*. Hector don't talk about our business no more. He don't talk about nothing.'

'I don't understand.'

'Yes you do,' Valdez said. 'Hector is dead. You killed him.'

'What?' she said, feigning shock. 'What do you mean? I saw him this afternoon.'

'We have friends in house next to his house. We know Hector is unreliable. We know he is seeing strange American woman who does not go back to America, who says she works in a *maquila*, but we can't find out which *maquila*, who says she was married to a Mexican, who we can't find, and who chooses to fuck a man like Hector. And so, Elizabeth, we know you left his house today. And we go inside and find him, dead. His body – it is still warm. And all of this happen the same day one of our trucks goes missing after it crosses the border. And this truck, Elizabeth, it is carrying money. A lot of money. My boss – he want to know what happened to it. I said I find out, and I will. That is why I am here. You are going to tell me who you are working for. You will tell me what happened to the truck.'

'I don't know what you're talking about,' she protested. 'I swear it.'

'I expect you to say that. You will change your mind, I think, once we begin. But where is other girl? The young one – your sister, yes? I would like to see her, too.'

'She's not here.'

'I see that. But where is she? It would be easier if you told me.'

Maia felt an unfamiliar feeling: panic. 'She's out,' she said. 'I don't know where she is.'

Valdez was about to speak when he was interrupted by a third man coming inside. He was bald, and when he spoke, Maia saw that his front teeth had been fitted with gold caps.

'The girl has gone out,' the man said in Spanish. 'Luís saw her. She has gone to the store. They say they will collect her when she comes out. You want to take her to the warehouse?'

Valdez nodded. 'Take her straight there.' He turned back to Maia. 'You understand Spanish?'

'Yes.'

'So you understand what we just say? You don't need to tell us where she is. We know. She is brave, to go out on her own on streets like this. In Juárez. Very brave. It is a dangerous city. Girls go missing here all the time. Anything could happen.'

'If you hurt her—'

'What?' the man said, speaking over her. 'What are you going to do, *chica*? You are both going to come to a place we have. Somewhere we can talk where no one bothers us. And then you are going to tell me what I want to know.'

Maia took a step back and tensed, enjoying the release of adrenaline and the prospect of doing what came naturally to her.

'You are going to tell me what Hector say to you,' Valdez went on, 'and you are going to tell me who you told, because I know one thing for sure: you and your kid sister did not take out one of our trucks all by yourselves.'

Maia stared him out. 'No,' she said, 'that's exactly what we did.'

Valdez turned to one of the other men. 'You hear that? She say she took the truck herself.'

They laughed, but when Valdez turned back to look at her across the table, his eyes flashed with ire.

'You come with us now. We talk about what happened.'

'I don't want to go with you,' she said.

'I'm not asking, *chica*. You come. Now.'

She stared at him. 'Make me.'

Chapter Ten

Isabella came out of Bip Bip. She noticed a white panel van outside. Isabella wouldn't normally have paid it any heed, but it was parked in an unusual fashion: positioned at an angle across the parking lot, blocking four cars and another van from leaving. Its rear end was pointing towards the entrance to the store and there was a man waiting there, leaning against the side.

It made her nervous, and so she lowered the groceries to the ground and pretended to put her earbuds in her ears. The pause provided her with an excuse to watch the van and the man for a moment. He was smoking a cigarette; he glanced at her, his eyes flicking away again with a lazy disregard. She doubted that he had even noticed her. His insouciance was reassuring. Isabella picked up the bags of groceries and started out across the lot.

She was ten paces from the entrance when she heard the rear doors of the van open; she turned, trying to maintain her composure, and saw a man jumping down. It wasn't the man that she had seen smoking; he was approaching her from behind. She felt a jolt of panic, but before she could do anything, she felt strong hands on her shoulders. The man grabbed her, his arms wrapping around her chest so he could haul her off her feet and muscle her towards the open van. She struggled, raking her foot down the man's shin and then, as he was distracted, butting the back of her head into his face. He cursed and loosened his grip enough for Isabella to work her right arm free.

The man who had jumped down from the back of the van rushed forward. He drew back his fist and tried to punch her; Isabella jerked her head aside at the last moment and his knuckles scraped across the side of her temple. She kicked out at him, but he was able to block her. He punched again, and this time he was more accurate. The blow clipped her on the side of the chin. Her knees went weak and she experienced a momentary flash of darkness.

Her awareness returned a second later; she was being dragged towards the back of the van. She struggled again, but the blow to her head had sapped her strength, and the man behind her had taken the chance to enfold her in a tighter grip.

She glimpsed the van, trying to remember as much as she could in the event that it was important later. It was a Ford Econoline, an older model, with two darkened windows in the rear doors and Mexican plates with the notation 'Tamaulipas' beneath the registration. The interior of the van was dark, but Isabella could see that there was a third man inside and that a mattress had been spread out across the floor.

She was lifted up and pushed into the van. She tried to slither down again, but the two men were up close behind her and they shoved her deeper inside. One of them put his hands on her hips as he forced her ahead. He was too close for her to lash out at with a kick, and he was strong. The man inside grabbed her and hauled her the rest of the way. Isabella felt another shove as she was forced deeper into the cargo space. She landed on her back on the mattress.

The van went dark as something was pulled over her head. A hessian sack; she could feel the coarse fibres against her face. Someone pressed down on her shoulders. She grunted with pain as her wrists were brought closer together. Her hands were forced into plastic bracelets and then she heard a zip sound as a cable tie was tightened. Someone sat on her legs and pinned them down.

The doors slammed shut. She heard the sound of a hand slapping against the partition that separated the cargo space from the cabin and then, in answer, the engine rumbled to life and the van jerked and rolled as it pulled away.

Chapter Eleven

ake you?' Valdez said incredulously.

There were three of them: Valdez, the bald guy with the gold teeth who had taken the phone call about Isabella and the man with the tattooed face. At least two of them were armed; Valdez had his Beretta and the man with the tattooed face had one, too. She assumed that the bald man was carrying.

'You hear that? She wants me to make her!'

Maia stayed where she was.

Valdez stepped forward. 'Are you out of your mind, *chica?*'

He came around behind her. Maia felt the muzzle of his gun between her shoulder blades.

'Fucking *move*,' he said.

The gun told her exactly where he was. The muzzle was a light pressure, gentle enough that she guessed that he was an arm's length away.

Maia walked towards the door. Valdez's colleagues left the room before she could reach it.

She stopped.

She felt the gun between her shoulders again.

Valdez jabbed her. 'I said move!'

Maia dropped down to her haunches, driving the point of her elbow into Valdez's gut as she brought her right leg out and around in a fast semicircle, her calf crashing into his ankles and sweeping his legs out from under him. She continued spinning until she was facing him, then leaned forward and drove her right fist into his face.

Valdez tried to aim the Beretta. Maia grabbed him by the wrist, forcing his hand down and pinning it to the floor. He fumbled with his left hand, finding the lamp on the table and crashing it against the side of her head. The porcelain smashed against her temple and her vision dimmed for a split second. She kicked out, monkey-flipping up, with her left hand still gripping Valdez's wrist. The momentum wrenched the gun out of his grasp and it skidded away, resting out of reach beneath the couch.

Valdez reached down and yanked a knife out of a sheath that he wore around his ankle. He got up and lunged at her with the blade; she blocked his attack and then hopped back to avoid the backhand and forehand swipes that followed. Valdez moved forward and stepped straight into her high kick, which landed on the side of his jaw and sent him stumbling across the kitchen into the gap between the wall and the freezer.

The door behind Maia opened; she glanced back and saw the bald man and the man with the tattooed face had come back inside the room.

She sensed movement and whirled back to face Valdez. He was staggering towards her. She opened the door of the freezer compartment into his face.

He slid to the ground.

Maia spun.

The man with the tattooed face rushed her. He threw a punch; Maia tried to block it, but wasn't able to sweep her arm up and around in time. His fist crunched into her cheek, snapping her head to the right.

She fell back, reached across to grab a skillet from the kitchen counter and lashed out, crashing the flat side into his face and then crouching to deal a backhanded swipe at his right arm so that he dropped his Beretta.

The bald man with the gold caps on his teeth grabbed a kitchen knife and raised it above his head. He stabbed down at Maia in a clumsy motion. She parried the knife with the pan, struck him in the knees with it and then whipped it up so that the edge crashed into his face.

She felt the burn of the endorphins in her blood. Her muscles tingled and her senses were alight.

The man with the tattooed face was on his knees. He reached for the Beretta that he had dropped. Maia swivelled and put him down again with a forehand swing to the head.

Meanwhile the bald man had staggered back to his feet. He let go with a big right-handed hook that caught Maia on the side of her head. She ignored the tingle of dizziness, swung around and crashed the pan into his face. He spat out his gold teeth as he, too, went down.

Maia sensed motion again and turned just as Valdez collected the Beretta and aimed it at her. She swung the pan to knock the weapon out of his hand and then kicked him in the sternum, the force of the impact sending him back against the refrigerator. He bounced off it and stumbled back in her direction. Maia grabbed his jacket with both hands and pivoted, transferring her weight quickly and easily and with enough force to fling the man through the air. Valdez landed in the centre of the cheap glass coffee table that had come with the house, the surface shattering into a million pieces as his body jackknifed over the metal frame.

The Beretta was on the floor. She picked it up.

Valdez was on his hands and knees, his palms bleeding as he crawled slowly across the broken glass that sparkled on the floor. Maia traversed the room and rested the muzzle against the top of his head. He turned, looking up, the muzzle now pressing against his ear. He didn't speak, and Maia didn't encourage him to try.

She pulled the trigger.

He fell flat, his arms splayed out, the glass beneath his body gleaming as if he had come to rest on a bed of diamonds.

She turned and went to the man with the tattooed face. She shot him, point-blank.

The bald man scrabbled away from her. She reached him and pressed the muzzle between his eyes.

'Where is the warehouse?' she said.

The man gulped, blood pouring from the stumps where his gold teeth had been.

She pressed harder, tilting his head back with the gun. 'Where is it?'

'Guadalupe.'

'Where in Guadalupe?'

'You cross the river and turn right. There is a track. Half a mile.'

She pulled the trigger. The man collapsed and lay still.

Maia took a moment to catch her breath. She felt the bloodlust, the craving that she could only suppress with her weekly injections, felt it swelling until it pushed and strained against her defences. She inhaled and exhaled, once and then a second time and then a third, until the greed receded and her hands stopped shaking. She caught her reflection in the window: her face was bloodied, a mixture of her own blood from where she had been hit and blowback from the kill-shots she had dealt. Her T-shirt was red and tacky, too; more blowback.

The fracas had lasted less than a minute, but they were seconds that Maia was loathe to let pass. Isabella was outside and the cartel were going after her, too.

Maia knew that she should at least stop to clean the blood from her face and change her shirt, but she didn't have time.

She shoved the pistol in the waistband of her jeans, grabbed the knife that the man with the gold caps had dropped on the floor, snatched the keys for the Torino from the counter and left the house at a flat run.

Chapter Twelve

I sabella couldn't see a thing, but tried to assess her situation. There were three men in there with her: the two who had pulled her off the street and the man who had stayed inside the van. Add the driver: that made four. She hadn't recognised the men who grabbed her, and she had been unable to make out the details of the third man before they put the sack over her head. The cable tie that secured her hands had been pulled as tight as possible, and she could feel her fingers numbing as the blood flow was restricted. One of the men was on her legs and she had no leverage. There was no point in struggling.

They drove.

She tried to gauge the passage of time, but it was difficult to judge in the darkness of the hood. Thirty minutes, she thought, the sound of the city quietening down to a dim hush as they continued on their way. The three men spoke in Spanish. She listened to their conversations, quickly determining that the man who had been inside was the most senior of the group. There was talk of the local cartel, and she noted the occasional mention of names – del Rio, Valdez – that recalled reports she had read in the newspapers. Valdez and del Rio were senior figures in the La Frontera cartel – wanted for multiple homicides. Then they spoke of a recent murder and, although her Spanish wasn't perfect,

Isabella was left with the firm impression that they had been involved. She concluded that the men were *sicarios*, hitmen who disappeared the men and women who stood in the way of the cartel's business.

The noise outside the van lessened even more. Isabella concentrated, searching for any clue as to where they might have taken her, but could hear nothing of use. They rolled off the asphalt and onto a rougher surface, the van's old suspension creaking as they bumped along. Eventually, after another few minutes, the van came to a rest.

She heard a *thunk* as the door was unlocked and then a groan as it opened. She felt cool air on her bare arms and heard the sound of feet crunching on loose stones as the three men got out of the back of the van. Another door opened – the driver's, she guessed – and she heard muffled conversation. She sat up and then shuffled towards the door, sliding off the mattress until she was able to hook her heels over the lip of the cargo space.

'Where you going?' one of the men said in accented English.

He grabbed the front of her shirt and dragged her out of the van.

The other men laughed. She counted the different voices: there were definitely four of them.

The hood was yanked away and she blinked against the light. Her eyes adjusted quickly; it was dusk, and the light was dim.

They were in some sort of industrial area. There was a building ahead of them; it looked like it was a warehouse. She glanced left and right and saw that there were other warehouses all around her. The van had stopped on a forecourt. There were a handful of other parked cars, but there was no sign of anyone who might be able to help her.

She was on her own.

The four men were arranged around her. She quickly took them in, and chose one – to her left, at nine o'clock – as the most dangerous. He wasn't the biggest, but he wore prison tattoos down both arms and looked lean and powerful. She guessed that the man to his left, at her twelve, was two hundred and fifty pounds, although most of that was fat.

The third man was skinny and angular, although his expression was cruel and promised unpleasantness. The final man, at her six, was shorter and squat, with a thicket of hair that sprouted out of his open shirt.

Isabella got to her feet. 'Let me go,' she said to the man with the tattoos.

He laughed at her.

'Who are you?' she asked.

'My name is Francisco.'

'Undo my hands.'

'No.'

'You scared of me? I'm sixteen. What am I going to do?'

The man made a joke about how he preferred his women to have a little fight in them, and the laughter continued; it afforded Isabella another moment to prepare.

She stared at him. 'Are you frightened, *hijo de la gran puta?*'

Son of a whore. The insult stopped Francisco short, and now the other men, instead of laughing with him, looked over at him and started to laugh *at* him.

His eyes flashed with fury. 'You want to say that again?'

'What? *Hijo de la gran puta?*'

Francisco spat at her feet. 'Find Claudio,' he said to one of the other men, waving his hand towards the warehouse. He turned to the skinny man. 'Stay with the van.'

Two of the men approached her and grabbed her roughly by the arms.

Isabella caught sight of another man approaching from around the corner of the warehouse. She wondered, for a moment, whether his arrival might provide a distraction that she could take advantage of, but her hopes were quickly dashed. The man had a bunch of keys in his hand, and he tossed them over to Francisco.

'It's all yours,' he said.

Francisco acknowledged the man and went to unlock the door.

The men dragged Isabella across the forecourt.

Chapter Thirteen

The warehouse was dark, lit only by the dying light from outside. It was a medium-sized space, filled with a collection of different items: there was a delivery truck very much like the one that they had hijacked on the road south of the border; behind that was a long table upon which she saw several large sets of scales, as well as cardboard boxes and three automatic rifles; behind the truck and the table, lined up against the wall, was a tall stack of plastic-wrapped bricks. Each brick was a dirty, off-white colour; Isabella recognised them as the product that was the stock-in-trade of La Frontera – cocaine that had been imported from Colombia and was due to be moved north to feed the American market.

The men tossed Isabella down onto the rough concrete floor. She lay there for a moment, her wrists still held together in front of her body by the cable tie. She heard footsteps behind her, then the clunk of a heavy switch being pulled; the space was filled with a harsh artificial glare from fluorescent lights suspended high overhead.

She heard footsteps approaching and then felt hands grabbing at her shirt. She was yanked up and dragged across the space to the wall, next to the pile of narcotic bricks. She didn't try to walk; the toes of her shoes scraped on the floor, drawing ripples through puddles of brackish water that had formed from rain that must have fallen into the warehouse through a hole in the roof. The man turned her around and dumped her so that her back was against the wall.

She blinked into the light. It was the man with the prison tattoos who had introduced himself as Francisco.

'What's your name?' he asked her.

'Isabella.'

He nodded. 'You're gonna stay here a while. My friends, they're bringing your sister. Then we gonna ask you both some questions.'

Isabella drew her knees up to her chest and looked away from him. It seemed defensive, as if she might be hoping to shelter behind her legs, but that wasn't why she did it. It gave her the chance to place her feet flat on the floor.

Francisco noticed, but missed the danger that her intentions presented. He reached a hand out to stroke her cheek. 'Relax, *chica*,' he said. 'We're not so bad. You and your sister answer the questions, maybe we take you back home again.'

Isabella pressed down with her feet. The soles of her sneakers gripped against the rough concrete. 'I don't even know who you are,' she said.

He spread his arms to take in the room: the drugs, the weapons on the table, the other accoutrements. 'We are La Frontera,' he said, as if that were enough. 'You wait here. When your sister arrives, then we talk again.'

He ran his fingers down her cheek, then rose to a standing position and started to walk away.

Isabella took her chance. She locked her feet against the floor and pushed down hard, pressing with her thighs. She slid up the wall, her back scraping against the cold concrete, until she was upright. The fat man and the shorter man with the open shirt were looking their way, but rather than call out a warning, they grinned and pointed, as if what

Isabella was doing was nothing more than a childish prank and not something to be taken seriously.

Francisco noticed the men's gestures and stopped. He began to turn back, but he was too slow. Isabella rushed him, jumping at the last to reach over his head so her bound wrists slid down his face, her forearms settling on his shoulders. She wrapped her legs around his waist, locked her ankles over his groin and then pulled back. The tie caught around Francisco's throat; the plastic tie was long enough that Isabella could bring her fists around to the side of his neck, and she yanked back as hard as she could. He gasped and spluttered as his airway was compressed, reaching up with his hands and trying to slide his fingers between the plastic tie and his larynx. He wasn't able to; Isabella had cinched in the hold as tightly as she could, and she had the advantage of leverage.

Francisco stumbled back towards the wall. Isabella braced herself for the impact; she crashed against the concrete, but held on, pulling back hard again. Francisco bounced her against the wall a second time, but Isabella kept her position. She gritted her teeth and yanked once more, eliciting a strangled choke as the man fought for breath that would not come.

The spectacle might have been amusing at first, but now, with Francisco's distress obvious, the other two men took it more seriously. The fat man lumbered over, and the man with the open shirt went to the door and called for help.

Francisco slumped to his knees. Isabella released her legs so that she could stand; she placed her knee in Francisco's back and pulled back again. His hands fumbled at his throat, impotent and pathetic.

The fat man drew near. He had a knife in his fist, and he raised it to the height of his head and then stabbed down with it. Isabella's range of motion was curtailed, but she was able to hop to the side. The point of the blade scraped down the outside of her right arm, drawing a furrow that started at the tip of her shoulder and ended above her elbow.

The stab unbalanced the fat man and he stumbled ahead, the knife continuing down and burying itself up to the hilt in Francisco's side, just beneath his armpit. Francisco didn't scream; the sound he made was little more than a choked-out moan.

The fat man fell to his knees. Isabella hopped in his direction, transferred her weight from left to right and drove the flat of her foot into his sternum. He fell back. Isabella's hands were still around Francisco's throat and she couldn't follow up; she let go, reaching forward so that she could bring her bound wrists up over his face. The knife was still buried in Francisco's side; she grabbed it with both hands, yanked it out and then spun around just as the fat man swung a punch at her.

She ducked underneath it, his knuckles brushing against the top of her head, and then rotated her wrists so that the blade was perpendicular to the floor and plunged it, two-handed, into the man's gut.

He slumped to his knees, his mouth wide open with the shock of what had just been done to him.

The man with the open shirt took a moment to react, as if what he had just seen had rooted him to the spot.

She sprinted forward, running as quickly as she could, heading right for him.

He pulled a pistol and tried to aim it, but Isabella was on him too quickly. She ducked and the bullet passed wide and overhead. It landed in the stacked packages of cocaine with a deadened thud, the impact expelling a fine cloud of powder that bloomed like a firework and then drifted down to the floor.

Isabella lowered her shoulder and buried it in the man's chest. He must have outweighed her by a hundred pounds, but the collision staggered him. She grabbed his right hand in both of hers and twisted the gun down. The man's index finger was still in the guard and the sudden motion bent it back; Isabella yanked hard and was rewarded by the sound of the finger breaking. Her wrists were still restrained, but she had enough play in the cable tie to do what she needed to do. She twisted the gun until it came free.

The man howled at the pain from his broken finger and staggered away from her.

Isabella took aim and fired twice.

The gun boomed, the noise echoing in the wide space, the recoil jerking the muzzle up both times. The first shot missed to the right, punching through the partially raised metal door, but the second found its mark. The man fell down onto his backside, his hands clasping his gut.

Isabella looked for the two men behind her. Francisco had made it back onto his feet and had staggered over to the table. As she brought the gun around and aimed, he lowered an automatic rifle and sprayed half a dozen rounds at her. He was dazed and the bullets were little more than spray and pray, all of them passing harmlessly overhead. Isabella dropped to one knee, sighted and fired. Francisco's head snapped back as the round struck him in the face. His arms windmilled hopelessly as he lost his balance and fell backwards, bouncing off the floor, his leg spasming twice before he lay still.

She went over to where he had fallen. She aimed down and fired into his body, then stalked the fat man. He was sitting against the wall, his hands resting helplessly around the hilt of the knife that still pierced him through the gut. He looked up at Isabella, the contemptuousness that had characterised his face now replaced by dread.

'Please,' he begged in English. 'I have a wife. I have kids. Two—'

Isabella shot him, the gun jerking up, a fine spray of blood washing over her.

The man slumped, and Isabella took a moment to gather her breath. She looked down at her arm; her shirt had been sliced open, and the furrow that had been carved across her flesh was now running freely with blood. She hadn't even noticed the pain before, but now that she could see the injury, it throbbed enough to make her wince. It was a flesh wound, perhaps half a centimetre deep, not enough to damage the muscle beneath. She flexed the arm to check; there was no impediment to her range of movement. She would have to dress it.

She examined all three men: they were all dead. But she knew she was far from safe. There were at least two others outside, and they must have heard the sound of gunfire. She bit her lip against the pain in her arm as she raised the pistol, holding it out in front.

She made her way to the door.

Chapter Fourteen

Isabella pressed herself to the wall and listened. She couldn't hear anything. She slid down the wall until she was on her haunches and then risked a quick glance around the doorway.

She saw the van. The driver was inside, but as Isabella drew closer, gun raised, she realised that he was slumped forward and unmoving. The window on his side of the cabin had been shattered and a spray of blood had splashed across the partition behind his seat.

Isabella saw another two bodies. She recognised the first: it was the man who had tossed the key to the warehouse to Francisco. He was sprawled out across the forecourt, a leaking entry wound in the side of his head. There was a second body around the corner of the building; Isabella could see a pair of legs sticking out.

She spun around, aware of someone standing behind her.

'Relax.'

It was Maia.

'Jesus,' Isabella breathed.

Maia had taken a beating. Her face was bloodied, with contusions across her cheekbones and on her temple. There was dried blood in her scalp, and her T-shirt had been speckled with it.

'Are you all right?' Maia asked her.

'Yes,' Isabella said. 'You?'

'Fine.'

'But you're covered in blood.'

'Most of it isn't mine,' Maia said. She pointed at Isabella's shoulder. 'You've been cut.'

'Hurts a bit.'

Isabella turned so that Maia could look at it more closely.

'We'll need to close it up,' she said. 'What happened?'

'One of them had a knife.'

Maia ducked beneath the warehouse door and looked inside. She paused there for a moment and then ducked back outside again.

'You did that?'

Isabella nodded.

Maia didn't speak. Instead, she looked over at Isabella with an inscrutable expression on her face.

'What about you?' Isabella asked. 'What happened?'

'They knew about Hector,' Maia said. 'They saw me this afternoon. I wasn't careful enough.'

'And they came to the house?'

'Yes.'

Isabella did not need to ask what had happened to them. She had seen what Maia was capable of on more than one occasion. The men who had accosted her would have had no idea of how dangerous she was, and by the time they had corrected the errors of their ignorance, it would already have been much, much too late.

Maia took a knife that Isabella hadn't seen before and indicated that Isabella should raise her hands. She sliced the cable tie in two.

'They took you at the store?' Maia asked.

'When I came out.'

She gestured towards the open door. 'You didn't need me.'

Isabella felt a throb of pain from the cut on her arm. She winced.

Maia led the way to the Torino. 'It's time to leave,' she said.

'Do you think . . .'

Isabella didn't finish the sentence. She had been going to ask if Maia thought she was ready, but she found herself tripping over the words. It was, she realised, because the answer mattered to her. She was afraid that Maia would say that she was not, and that, perhaps, she would never be ready.

Maia answered anyway. 'Yes,' she said. 'You're ready.'

Isabella paused. She found that, even after everything, she was nervous. 'What now?' she said.

'We've got work to do.'

Chapter Fifteen

New York

Bloom's hands were damp, and his finger left a smear of perspiration on the button for the top floor. It had been an anxious time. He had engineered the confrontation with Carington and King, but that didn't make the consequences of it any less daunting. It had been the green light to put his own plan into effect and, once it was in motion, it would soon have too much momentum to stop.

The stakes were high, and he had to persuade them of two things: that he was still engaged with the project, despite their snub, and that his anger was authentic. He couldn't afford for them to doubt him. The burden was on him, and there was no one with whom it could be shared. It was a lonely responsibility. The things that they had spoken about were wrapped up in a secrecy so absolute that there were just a handful of people that Bloom could discuss them with.

It was the secrecy that was the cause of his anxiety. Bloom was a spook, and had been for more than half a century. A reflex towards the suppression of information was habitual. Necessary. The confidences from his earlier career as a Cold War spy could bring down governments; the secrets that he had been made party to over the course of the past decade were far more pernicious.

The collusion that had birthed Prometheus was itself wrapped up within an even larger conspiracy. The main project – the scheme that had persuaded Bloom to delay his retirement for as long as was necessary to put it into effect – had consumed him for the last five years. The assets that had been produced by Prometheus were key to advancing the aims of the project, but they were subsidiary to it. That Daedalus had been tampering with germline DNA would cause a cataclysmic shock were it ever to be made public. But that astonishment would be nothing compared to the horror that would follow if the deceit that underpinned everything that the project had done and continued to do came to light.

Bloom leaned back against the side of the elevator as it ascended. Yes, he thought – it was lonely work. The scale of it, and the consequences that would follow if it was revealed, meant that Bloom could tell almost no one what he was doing. There was a kind of perverse relief in meetings like this morning's, when details could be discussed. The secrecy consumed everything, including – and perhaps especially – the relationship between the attendees of today's meeting and their governments. Bloom would not report his attendance to *his* government; the knowledge that he was here, and the knowledge of his involvement in the operation, was restricted to a vanishingly small cohort of intelligence apparatchiks and mandarins in Whitehall and Vauxhall Cross. They shared his world view, and although the threats that they faced had forced them to take measures that were abhorrent, they all knew those measures were essential.

Bloom and the others who were involved in the project had been responsible for the deaths of hundreds of thousands of civilians in the last two years.

They had fomented the war in Syria.

They were responsible for the atrocities they had antiseptically coined the 'precipitating events' . . .

The attack on Westminster.

The shooting down of British Airways Flight 117.

The bombing of Dulles Airport.

Bloom thought back to the earliest meetings, held as the strands of the scheme were knitted together. The conspiracy's sheer outlandishness was their cover. The merest suggestion that those events were anything other than terrorist outrages would be rejected out of hand as impossible, and anyone who claimed otherwise would be derided as a nut. The preposterousness of the scheme had provided them with their cover, and they had operated beneath that cover long enough to engineer the conflict that they all wanted.

Some wanted war for venal reasons. Bloom's motives were pure: the conflict was necessary to put an end to the slow, inexorable spread of militant Islamism.

The elevator reached the top floor. The doors slid back and Bloom disembarked. He made his way into the conference room and sat down.

The room was full. Bloom counted twenty delegates, and none of them were talking to one another. The CIA represented the host country, and they were joined by representatives from the Canadian Security Intelligence Service, the Australian Secret Intelligence Service, the French Directorate-General for External Security, the German Militärischer Abschirmdienst and a carefully curated selection of others from Western countries that shared the same opinions and were inspired by the same motivations. There was always an underlying sense of duplicity at these gatherings, the sure knowledge that not everyone was made privy to every single piece of information. There was deep cooperation here, but that didn't mean that there was parity between all parties. That was to be expected, Bloom knew, given that most of the men and women involved in the operation had backgrounds that had them concerned with state secrets. They were so steeped in lies and paranoia that open and honest sharing would always be impossible.

Carington tapped both hands against the edge of the table. 'You all know why we're here – the national conventions are soon and it's looking bad for us. We need to review where we're at and how it might affect us. Nora?'

The woman to Bloom's left was Nora Scott. Bloom had commissioned additional background research into her after she had been brought onto the committee a year ago. She was a career spook and had been the CIA station chief in Pakistan for five years. Her husband had been assassinated after an al-Qaeda cell detonated a bomb they had hidden underneath his car. Her motives for being involved with the project were, at least, purer than those of Carington – and, especially, Jamie King. Bloom had chosen to be involved for rational and practical reasons, and while he had a natural aversion to emotional motivation, at least revenge was predictable.

'Teddy is right,' she said. 'We have a problem. The Republican side of the equation is fine – we're confident that Hawken will win, and we know that we've got enough to control him. The issue is Gary Morrow. He's going to win the Democratic nomination at a stroll and he's making a virtue out of the fact that he's not an internationalist. More than that – you've seen the debates – he's campaigning on a platform of isolationism. Putting America first, to borrow his phrase – he's the second coming of Charles Lindbergh. He's not interested in continuing the wars of the previous administration. And we have to face facts – a lot of people agree with him. There's just no appetite for war, not after the past year.'

'Not even after Washington?' said the Canadian representative.

'It's a twenty-four-hour cycle, and Washington was last year. Old news. And the public has seen too many dead children and too many soldiers coming back in body bags. It's Vietnam all over again.'

'What polling do you have?' said one of the representatives from French intelligence.

'We commissioned our own,' Scott said. 'Assuming he wins the nomination, and he will, we're looking at near-certainty that he takes Pennsylvania, Florida, Ohio, Wisconsin, Iowa and Michigan. And if he turns those blue, he'll win the election easily.'

Carington turned to Bloom. 'And it's similar in Europe – Vivian?'

'It is,' Bloom said. 'The French want out. The Germans never wanted in, and they've pulled their planes back.' The representatives from France and Germany did not demur. 'It's difficult for us, too. The opposition in Parliament is stridently anti-war. They're trying to force a vote of no confidence in the government, and most of the people I speak to think that's very likely to happen. The government will lose the vote, there will be an election and the new government won't share our view. Most people see globalism as the problem, not the solution to the problem. They want less of it. They want to close the borders.'

'Globalism is a problem everywhere,' Jamie King said.

Bad for business, Bloom thought, although he managed to restrain himself from rattling King's cage.

Carington exhaled. 'We were hoping that we wouldn't need another event to nudge opinion back in our favour, but perhaps that was optimistic. Our purpose is too important to allow it to be derailed when we're so close to success. We can't allow Morrow to win the nomination. We have a number of options open to us to prevent that from happening. I think, unless anyone else disagrees, we should look into developing one of them.'

Bloom looked around the room. There were no objections.

'Very good,' Carington said. 'Shall we begin?'

Chapter Sixteen

Mexico

Maia drove, stopping for the first time at the side of a quiet road where they wouldn't be disturbed. It was seven in the evening. The sun had slipped down behind the jagged mountains on the horizon. Isabella watched as a goods train rumbled through the desert, silhouetted against the ochre, passing in and out of the shadows that reached out across the sand.

Maia went around to the back of the Torino and retrieved the first aid kit that they kept in the trunk. She had put it there in readiness for their hits on the cartel trucks, but they had never needed to use it until now. Isabella took off her shirt so Maia could examine her wound. It was still bleeding, but the flow was sluggish as the blood started to thicken and clot. Maia emptied a bottle of water over Isabella's arm, irrigating the wound. She took out a bottle of antiseptic lotion, soaked a swab and cleaned the injury. Isabella gritted her teeth at the stinging pain. Maia threaded a needle with a suture and took Isabella's hand.

'This will hurt,' she said.

Isabella turned her head to look away as Maia prepared to stitch up the wound. The pain was sharp and intense, but Maia was dextrous and in just a minute she had finished the stitches. She took out a sterile dressing and covered the wound.

'You're done,' she said.

Isabella's shirt was soaked with blood, but she had nothing else to wear. She put it on and flexed her arm, feeling the stitches pulling against her skin.

'Okay?' Maia asked.

'Let's go,' Isabella said.

Maia drove them back to Juárez. They skirted the city and then took Highway 45 to the south. There were around 200 miles between Juárez and Chihuahua. It was a straight north–south run and, once they had left the city behind them, the traffic was sparse. They had to get away from Juárez. What they planned next would attract attention from the police, and the cartel owned the police all along the border.

It was half past eight when they stopped again at a gas station on the outskirts of the hamlet of Samalayuca. Maia had tried to wipe away as much of the blood from her face as she could, but there was still plenty matting her hair and staining her clothes. The right side of her face was badly bruised, with a lattice of tiny cuts that had crusted over. They decided that it would be better for her to stay in the car, and so Isabella got out and filled up the tank with gasoline. When she was done, she went into the store and grabbed two big bottles of water and two packets of taquitos. She went to the counter and, despite her better judgement, pointed to the hot dogs that were turning under heating lights inside a glass case. She held up two fingers and waited for the attendant to prepare two of the dogs. She paid for the gas and food, laying down one of the fifties that they had taken from the cartel.

'*Baño?*' she asked once the attendant had handed her the change.

The man grunted, offered a truculent '*si*' and pointed out of the dusty window to a separate building on the other side of the forecourt.

Isabella went back to the car.

'It's over there,' she said.

Maia got out of the car. Isabella opened one of the bottles and took a long slug of water as she watched Maia cross the forecourt to the toilet block. The heat was stifling. She poured a little of the water over her head, scrubbing it into her scalp and letting it run down her neck to her back and chest. She felt uncomfortable. It wasn't just the heat, although she would have preferred not to have had to make the journey until it was a little cooler.

More than that, it was the knowledge that they had taken the first step on the path that they had been planning for all year.

It had seemed theoretical until now: abstract possibilities that had been possible to dismiss; prospects that they could discuss, but something that would never really come to pass. Sometimes, Isabella had even been able to persuade herself that they could stay where they were. Juárez was unpleasant and their house was a hovel compared to the *riad* in Marrakech that she knew she would never be able to return to, but, despite the circumstances, the two of them had been there a year and had carved out something resembling a life. Isabella had never been settled anywhere for long enough before now to have grown comfortable.

She didn't remember her early childhood, but the years that followed her abduction from her mother had been spent in a series of foster homes, a peripatetic existence where happiness and stability had always been mirages, apt to disappear without the slightest of warnings.

Then Beatrix had found her, and the year that they had spent together had been the best time of her life, but even that had been threatened by the knowledge that her mother would not be able to rest until the men and women who had betrayed her had been punished. And then, near the end, came the news of her cancer and the realisation of the absolute impossibility of them staying together.

Isabella had enjoyed Marrakech, but she had been restless, and vulnerable to the offer that Michael Pope had put to her. Since then, everything had been fluid and confusing: the explosion in London, her kidnapping and imprisonment in Syria, her time on the run with Pope and then the events in Shanghai and Washington.

Perhaps it could have been different?

But those thoughts never lasted long. Reality was impossible to ignore. Isabella and Maia were marking time until Isabella was ready. Maia was preparing her for what would come next. The training was rigorous, and pushed her to boundaries that she didn't know she had. Her mother had taught her the fundamentals and Pope had refined them, but her time in Juárez had been of an intensity that was altogether different from both of those experiences. Isabella knew that she was ready – physically *and* mentally – and she knew, too, that once Maia reached that conclusion then they would abandon their sanctuary and put themselves in harm's way once more.

And now they were.

Maia was single-minded and relentless. She wanted revenge for what had happened to Doctor Litivenko. Pope had been convinced that Maia had been in Washington to kill the doctor, but Isabella now knew that was far from the truth. Maia had been there to *protect* Litivenko, and her failure to do so, and the fate that had met the woman who had filled a maternal role in her miserable life, had fostered in her a determination to find justice.

There was something else, too. There had been weekends when Maia had disappeared, leaving on a Friday and returning late on Sunday. Maia never spoke about what she had been doing, and refused to answer when Isabella pressed her. All she would say was that she was making 'preparations', but she would not tell Isabella what, exactly, those preparations entailed. Isabella couldn't guess what it meant, but she had decided there was no point in pushing any harder. She had no one else and so, for better or worse, she had to trust Maia. The woman had saved her life and was training her. There was nothing else for it: Isabella was grateful for what Maia had done, and she wanted to help her.

Isabella took another mouthful of water as Maia returned. Her shirt was damp from where she had attempted – with only partial success – to remove the bloodstains. Her hair was wet, the blood rinsed out, and her skin was clean. The bruise on the side of her face looked more pronounced now that it was the only thing to look at.

'Ready?' she said.

Isabella nodded and slid into the hot cabin.

Maia started the engine. The old car had a fan, but all it did was recirculate the hot air. They both shut their doors and wound down their windows and Maia pulled away.

Isabella opened the glovebox and took out the iPod. She pressed the buds into her ears and pushed play. 'Golden Brown' by The Stranglers began.

'We've got three hours to Chihuahua,' Maia said. 'Get some sleep. I don't know when you'll get the chance after we get there.'

Chapter Seventeen

Isabella didn't think she would be able to sleep, but the heat inside the cabin and the steady rumble of the tyres on the asphalt had a soporific effect that quickly lulled her to sleep. It was a fitful slumber marked with dreams of her mother.

She awoke to find Maia gently shaking her by the shoulder.

She opened her eyes and blinked. 'What time is it?'

'Quarter to midnight,' Maia said.

They were parked in a lot that served a couple of businesses on the side of the highway. This part of the road was undergoing improvement work and had been reduced to one lane by double lines of orange-and-white cones. It looked as if a new pedestrian bridge had just been built; the concrete was pristine white, unmarked by the cartel graffiti that was so conspicuous in Juárez. The dark was deep, and the lights of the few cars that passed them glowed brightly.

Isabella turned her attention to her immediate surroundings. The lot was little more than a dusty square of unfinished ground and, aside from their Torino, the only cars that were parked there were pickup trucks and vans. The businesses were all marked by signs that had been fixed to the facades of their buildings: Ferreteria Rosales was a general store, while Estetica Diamante looked, rather incongruously given the location, to be a beauty salon. There was a series of dilapidated huts and shacks to the north, with a yard of scrap cars behind them.

'There?' Isabella said, pointing at the general store. It was open, advertised by the garish neon sign in the window that flashed '24/7' off and on.

Maia nodded. 'It's as good as anywhere.'

Isabella took a deep breath.

'Okay?'

Isabella nodded her head.

'You know what you're doing?'

'Yes. I haven't forgotten.'

'Do exactly as we said. When you come out again, start walking south. Make it look like you're hitchhiking. You won't get far.'

Maia reached down onto the floor of the car, collected a Beretta and gave it to her.

'Where's the Glock?' Isabella said.

'I was stripping it when they came in. I didn't have time to put it back together. The driver of the van had this. It'll be fine.'

Isabella examined the weapon. It was an APX: high-strength alloy steel with dovetail sights, chambered in 9mm. She checked that it was ready to fire; it was. She hiked up her top and pushed it into the top of her cut-off shorts.

'Be careful,' Maia said.

'I will.'

'You remember where you need to take them?'

Isabella nodded. 'North of Rancho de Peña. I can find it.'

'I'll be there. And when they bring you?'

'I know,' Isabella said. 'I know what to do.'

Isabella got out of the Torino and shut the door.

Maia reached across to wind down the window. 'Good luck,' she said.

Isabella stepped back and watched as Maia put the car into drive and rolled away, continuing south towards the outskirts of Chihuahua. She waited until she couldn't see the car any longer and then, fighting down the feeling that she was alone and about to start a process that she knew was terribly dangerous and entirely unpredictable, she crossed the forecourt to the buildings beyond.

Chapter Eighteen

A bell rang as Isabella opened the door and stepped into the store. She looked around: it was a long, thin room, with a line of wooden shelves arranged down the middle. There were two chiller cabinets with beer and soft drinks, baskets that contained bags of potato chips and the shelves displayed rows of canned goods, toiletries and kitchen products. The room was lit by overhead panels, one of them flickering and buzzing with a loose connection, and ventilated by spinning fans that were fixed to the ceiling. The counter was at the front of the store, by the door. Behind it was the clerk, an old man with leathery brown skin, wisps of white hair that were stuck to his scalp with sweat, and dirty yellow teeth.

Isabella went to the first cabinet, opened it and took a bottle of Snapple. She felt a knot of trepidation in her gut and, as she closed the door, she saw that her fingers were trembling.

She knew why: this was it.

No going back if she did what they had planned.

She took a deep breath, opened the Snapple and took a sip.

'Hey,' the man behind the counter said. 'You pay first, *then* you drink.'

His Spanish was a lazy drawl, but she understood it. She put the cap back on the bottle and tightened it, grabbed a packet of tortilla chips and went to the front of the store. The counter was in front of a rack of shelves with cigarettes and spirits. The till was an old-fashioned model that showed the prices as they were rung up. She looked up above the shelves and saw a cheap CCTV camera pointing down at her; on the counter, a monitor showed the black-and-white feed.

The man glared at her with unconcealed hostility. 'You hear me?' he said. 'You don't drink until you've paid for it.'

Last chance.

Isabella clenched and unclenched her fists. She took another deep breath, put the bottle and the chips on the counter and then reached around for the Beretta. She took it out and aimed it at the man.

She nodded at the till. 'Open it,' she said.

The man froze, staring at the gun, at Isabella and then back down at the gun again.

'*Now*,' she said, jabbing the gun towards him.

The man didn't argue. He opened the till and stood back from it. Isabella glanced inside; there was a meagre amount in the tray, but that wasn't really the point. She stepped around the counter, indicating that the man should back into the corner. She reached down for the money, resting her fingertips on the tray for a moment to make sure that she left her prints. She took the notes and stuffed them into her pockets and then backed away, glancing up at the camera long enough to ensure that the police would have a good view of her face. She pointed the gun at the ceiling and fired a single shot. The cartridge ejected; Isabella saw it hit the floor and roll away. She would leave that here, too. She would leave as much evidence as possible.

'No police,' she said, wagging the index finger of her left hand from side to side to emphasise her point.

Isabella kept the gun trained on the man as she backed away, bumping the door with her backside and stepping out into the warm night once more. She shoved the pistol back into her shorts and crossed the forecourt again, making her way beneath the pedestrian bridge and setting off to the south.

Chapter Nineteen

Maia had been right: Isabella didn't get far.

She heard the sirens before she had been walking for even ten minutes. The highway ran into Ejido Ocampo, a small village on the northern approach to Chihuahua that was little more than a collection of low-slung shacks. She was opposite a business advertised as 'Super y Carniceria', a refrigerated truck parked outside so it could be loaded up again for tomorrow's rounds. Isabella stopped on the wide dirt run-off that separated the business from the highway and turned around to watch as the red-and-blue flashing lights accelerated towards her through the darkness.

There were two cars, each of them carrying two cops – three men and a woman. They got out, all of them with guns drawn and aimed.

'*Manos!*' the nearest cop said.

Isabella raised her hands.

'*Ponte en el suelo,*' he yelled, pointing at the ground.

Isabella dropped to her knees, her hands still raised. The cop approached, his gun aimed at her head. He told her to lie flat with her hands behind her back. Isabella did as he instructed, taking a breath and trying to ignore her fear.

She could feel control slipping away.

A small push.

The officer reached her, put his knee in the small of her back and leaned his weight into it. He was heavy and she winced. The man grabbed her right wrist and cuffed it, reaching for her left and cuffing that, too.

A little momentum.

The man moved aside so that the female officer could frisk her. Isabella had made no attempt to hide the Beretta. It was in her waistband, the butt pressing into her back. The woman pulled it free and continued her pat-down.

Things gathering pace.

Once the woman was satisfied, she stepped back so that the first officer could haul Isabella to her feet.

'*Cuál es tu nombre?*' he asked her.

'What?'

'What is your name?'

'Isabella Rose,' she said, realising as she did so that it was the first time that she had given her real name for almost a year.

'English?' the man said, the word a little awkward in his mouth.

'Yes.'

The officer gestured to one of the other men. This one evidently spoke better English. 'You are under arrest on suspicion of armed robbery,' he said, still stumbling a little with the unfamiliar words. 'You have the right to remain silent. Anything you say can and will be used against you in a court of law . . .'

He continued with the rote warning, but Isabella tuned him out. It didn't matter. It was too late for her to change her mind now. They had started something from which there could be no turning back. They couldn't stop it. They could only be ready, for better or worse.

The officer finished his warning. 'Do you want to say anything?' he said.

She shook her head.

The rear door to one of the cars was opened and Isabella was pushed inside. Her hands were still secured behind her back, and she adjusted her position so that she was sitting side on, in an attempt to maintain the flow of blood. The compartment was separated from the front of the car by a mesh cage. The officers conversed at the side of the road for a moment. They looked back at her and laughed; a shared joke, perhaps, at the sixteen-year-old girl who had robbed a grocery store, shot up the ceiling and had then been so stupid to think that she could just walk into the city without being picked up.

The officer who had read her rights to her got into the driver's seat and his female colleague got in next to him.

'Where are we going?' Isabella asked.

'Chihuahua,' the man replied. 'We get you processed.'

'I want to call my embassy.'

'Later,' he said.

'But I can call them?'

'This is not America,' the man said. 'You get a phone call when we say you do.'

The woman spoke into the radio, reporting that they had arrested a suspect and that they were bringing her back to the station.

Isabella settled back, her shoulder resting against the warm upholstery. She closed her eyes and tried to picture what would happen next. Maia would be busy, but it was Isabella who had the more difficult task to perform. She had never been very good at lying. Maia had tried to show her how to be persuasive, but Isabella knew that it was something that required her to make a considerable improvement. She had no choice now. She would have to do her best.

She would make herself into the bait and hope that they would bite.

Chapter Twenty

They drove her into the centre of Chihuahua.

It was twenty past midnight when they reached the police station. There was a sign in front of it that read 'Comandancia de Policía Zona Sur'. It was next to the firehouse, and there was a mixture of police cars and fire trucks gathered outside the modern-looking white buildings. Three pickup trucks painted in blue and white and with 'POLICIA' stencilled across them had been arranged as a makeshift chicane to make it impossible for a car to approach the entry gates at speed. This was still cartel country, and Isabella had read the stories on the Internet of how the police had been attacked.

The officer drove carefully between the parked cars and paused at a yellow-and-black painted gate until their identity had been established. The gate opened and the man in the guardhouse to the left raised a hand in greeting as they rolled through and into the wide, open space beyond. The facility was demarked by a wire-mesh fence, with five or six acres of scrubby ground abutting the L-shaped complex of buildings. The driver swung the car to the left and then sharply to the right, parking in a yard with a collection of other police cruisers. He got out of the car, opened Isabella's door and helped her out.

Isabella was taken into the building, where they made their way into a reception area. There was a counter and, behind it, a bored-looking female officer who was tapping her fingers across a keyboard. She looked up as Isabella approached.

'This is her?' she asked the officer. 'From the grocery store?'

The man said that it was.

The woman turned her gaze on Isabella. 'What is your name?' she asked.

'Isabella Rose.'

'And you are English.'

'Yes.'

'What are you doing in Mexico?'

'I've been travelling.'

'Really?'

'Yes.'

The woman noted down the details on a form with carbon paper beneath it. 'You understand why you have been arrested?'

'Yes,' Isabella said.

'You robbed a store, no?'

Isabella nodded.

'You admit it?'

'Yes,' she said.

'And you were found in possession of an unlicensed weapon.'

'Yes,' she said.

If her confessions surprised the officer, she didn't show it. The woman tapped on the keyboard until she was satisfied with whatever it was that she had composed and then looked up again.

'A detective will speak to you tomorrow,' she said. 'You will stay here tonight. Understand?'

Isabella said that she did.

'First you must be processed. Fingerprints, photographs. Yes?'

'Yes.'

The woman gave a nod, and the male officer took Isabella by the shoulder and led her away from the desk. He led her into an adjacent room where a technician was waiting. She was lined up against a chart on the wall that gave an indication of height and given a board upon which was displayed her name and a series of numbers that contained the date and, Isabella guessed, the number that she had been assigned for the purposes of the Mexican penal system. She was photographed face on and then in profile. The technician checked the photographs on a monitor and, satisfied, moved to a waist-high table that held an ink blotter and two pieces of paper that had been divided into grids. Isabella was brought across. The fingers of her right hand were inked and then pressed down onto the first piece of paper. The process was repeated for her left hand.

The technician examined the prints and, presumably satisfied, grunted something to the officer. Isabella was led outside, to a door that opened onto a long flight of bare concrete steps. There was another door at the foot of the stairs, with an intercom next to it and a security camera fixed to the wall above. Isabella descended, the officer at her back. The man thumbed the buzzer, looked up at the camera and waited for the door to be unlocked. Isabella heard the *thunk* as the bolt was withdrawn and stood back as the officer pulled the door towards them. He put his hand between her shoulders and pushed her into the gloomy room beyond.

The smell was the first thing that Isabella noticed. The room was full of the stench of human excrement. It was dark, with just a little dim light; there was enough for Isabella to make out a large cage at the other end of the room. She could see a handful of women in the cage and, even though it was dark, could feel their eyes on her. The walls looked to have been painted a deep crimson colour; Isabella wondered if that choice had been made in an attempt to hide the blood and shit that would otherwise have been starkly visible.

A second officer appeared from the shadows and unlocked the cage door. The man behind her nudged her in the back again.

'I want to make a telephone call,' Isabella protested.

'Please – inside.'

Isabella did as she was told.

'Hands through the cage.'

There was a slot in the bars. Isabella put her hands through the slot and waited as the officer unlocked and removed the cuffs.

He turned and started for the door.

'Wait,' Isabella said. 'I want to speak to my embassy.'

'Maybe tomorrow,' the policeman said. 'Not tonight. Tonight, you stay here. We see about it tomorrow.'

Isabella stepped away from the bars. There was no point in protesting. The telephone call was important, but Maia had explained that it wasn't essential. The fact that her details had been entered into the Mexican judicial system – her prints and her photograph, together with her real name – would sound an alarm that would, in turn, alert those men and women who were looking for her. It would tell them that she had surfaced and where they could find her. She would call the embassy, but it wasn't a prerequisite for the baiting of the trap. Isabella thought of that as she lowered herself to the bench and rubbed the spots on her wrists where the cuffs had abraded the skin.

Chapter Twenty-One

T here were a dozen other women in the cell with her. Most of them, Isabella guessed, had been arrested for prostitution or drug offences, and all of them looked at her with surly hostility as she took her place on the bench. They must have heard her speak to the officer, for it wasn't long before she heard coarse imprecations that included the suggestion that she was a little gringo bitch. None of the other women sat next to her, and she knew there was a good chance she would have to put on a show to persuade the others that it wasn't worth their time to try to take advantage of her.

She was right.

Less than an hour had passed before one of the other women sauntered over to her. She was big, with pendulous breasts, arms and legs that quivered with fat and a head that was almost too big for her shoulders. Her eyes were small and mean and her skin was covered in tattoos.

The woman positioned herself in front of Isabella, close enough for her to smell the sweat on the woman's body. She didn't say anything; instead, she reached down and rested her hand on Isabella's cheek and then ran her fingertips down her skin to her shoulder.

Isabella didn't speak, either. She reached up with both hands, grabbed the woman's pudgy wrist and then stood and ducked around her, quickly yanking her arm so that it was behind her back. She pushed the arm all the way up so the woman's hand was between her shoulder blades, let go with her left hand and used that to crash the woman's head against the bars of the cell. She held her there, pulling the woman's hand all the way back until there was pressure on her wrist and shoulder.

'No,' she said, not bothering to add anything else.

She held the grip, pushing up to increase the torque on the woman's joints.

'*Por favor*,' the woman gasped.

'*Entender?*' Isabella hissed.

'*Si*,' the woman said. '*Si, si. Lo siento.*'

Isabella gave one final upward yank and then released her grip. The woman staggered away from the bars, massaging her wrist. She glared at Isabella, but when she saw that Isabella was staring right back at her with an implacable expression, she retreated to the other side of the cage.

The other women had watched the display. Isabella turned her gaze onto all of them, daring them to step up; none of them did.

Isabella took her seat on the bench once more. She didn't expect to get any sleep tonight, but neither did she think she would be bothered again. She turned around so that she was sideways on the bench, brought her knees up to her chest and leaned back against the bars.

She closed her eyes and tried to relax.

Chapter Twenty-Two

There were no windows in the basement, and it was difficult to judge the passage of time without a clock or a watch. The noise from the floor above gradually grew more obvious and, eventually, the door to the basement opened. A woman in a cheap suit came in, spoke to the guard at the table and then followed the officer to the cell door. The guard collected a pair of handcuffs from a hook on the wall and then pointed at Isabella.

'You,' the woman said. 'Here.'

Isabella got up and went to the door. The guard told her to put her hands through the slot, and she did. The bracelets were fixed around her wrists and pressed together until the locks clicked. The guard opened the door and beckoned that Isabella should come out.

The woman in the suit grabbed her by the elbow and led her towards the exit. Isabella climbed the stairs back to the first floor of the building and was led into an interrogation room. There was a table, two chairs and a digital recorder on the table. A paper sack had been left on one of the chairs.

'Sit,' the woman said, indicating the empty chair.

Isabella sat down and waited as the woman unfastened one of the cuffs and attached it to a metal hoop that had been fitted to the wall.

She glanced around the room as the woman ensured that the cuff was secure. The paint was peeling off the walls, graffitied messages had been scored into the bricks and the surface of the table, there were brown stains on the floor and mildew was growing in the corners.

The woman went around to the other side of the table and sat down. 'Would you prefer to speak in English?'

'Please,' Isabella said.

'I'm Detective del Castillo,' she said. 'My first name is Salma. You can call me that if you like. My English is okay?'

'It's fine.'

'I used to live in El Paso,' she said. 'I remember most of it. Now, then – you're Isabella?'

'Yes.'

'Isabella Rose. And you're sixteen years old, Isabella – that is correct?'

'Yes.'

'Where are your parents?'

'I don't have any.'

'No?'

'They died a long time ago.'

'But you should have an adult here with you. What we are going to talk about is very serious. Do you have anyone I could call?'

'No. It's just me.'

'Then a lawyer?'

'You don't need to baby me. I'm fine.'

The detective looked at her quizzically. 'You need a lawyer.'

Isabella held her eye. 'I'm fine.'

'You don't have money?'

'Not much.'

'We can get a public defender if you can't afford one yourself.'

'No,' Isabella repeated. 'No lawyer. I don't need one.'

'Are you hungry?' Del Castillo didn't wait for Isabella to answer; it was as if Isabella's seeming indifference had caught her off guard. 'We will talk now, and then I will make sure you have some breakfast. The food is not special here, but it will fill your belly. A burrito, perhaps. You like burritos?'

'Sure,' Isabella said, very aware that the detective was intent on winning her trust by playing the maternal card. Isabella didn't care. She wouldn't be here long enough that a relationship would be important, and she preferred to abbreviate this conversation by confounding the detective's expectations.

'You have been living in Mexico, Isabella?'

'Travelling.'

Del Castillo smiled patiently. 'Really? Where?'

'I was in San Miguel de Allende for the winter.'

'Did you like it there?'

'It was nice.'

'Where were you headed next?'

'America.'

'But you did something very stupid.'

Isabella shrugged.

Finally, Del Castillo frowned with irritation. 'You know that you are in a lot of trouble? Yes?'

'Yes.'

'So less of the attitude – okay?'

Isabella gave a half-shrug and leaned back against the chair.

Del Castillo took an evidence bag out of the paper sack and put it on the table. The Beretta was inside the bag. The detective took a second bag from the sack and laid that next to the gun. It contained the small amount of money that Isabella had taken from the store.

'Let me tell you what we have, Isabella. We have security camera footage of you in the store. We have an identification from the man you robbed – we showed him the photograph they took last night and he said that it was you. The officers who arrested you found this gun and this money on your person. We found a spent 9mm round in the store. We'll test it – I bet it matches this gun. This isn't going to be a difficult case to prove, Isabella. You are going to be found guilty of armed robbery and being in possession of an unlicensed firearm and you are going to be sent to prison. But you are so young. Sixteen is no age, especially not for someone in a Mexican jail. I would like to help you. But, before I can do that, I need you to help me. I need to understand why you did it. Perhaps I can say something to the judge. If there is a reason why you did what you did, then . . .' She let the sentence drift away.

'I did it,' Isabella said. 'I was stupid, but I did it.'

'Why?'

'I needed the money.' She shrugged. 'I'd run out, and I needed more. What else do you want me to say?'

'What's wrong with you? You *want* to go to prison?'

Isabella ignored the question and asked one of her own. 'What happens next?'

Del Castillo shook her head, as if what she was hearing made no sense to her. 'Do you understand, Isabella? You will go to jail. Not for a week or a month. Not even for a few months. For years. Six or seven years, perhaps. You will not be sixteen when you come out, and you will be a different person. You should think about that. It is a serious thing.'

Isabella held up her hands. 'I don't see the point. I did it – you said you can prove it, so what's the point in arguing? I confess. Now what?'

Del Castillo stared at her, rubbed a hand against her cheek and then exhaled through her nose. The warmth in her voice was gone when she spoke again. 'Fine. We've shown that an offence has been committed, so your case will go to the Ministerio Público. The *agente* will look into whether there is enough for the case to be prosecuted. He will find more than enough. You'll be turned over to a judge and then there will be a hearing within forty-eight hours. The judge decides whether to let you go or prosecute you. In this case, I think he will prosecute. You will be imprisoned until your trial. There is no bail. And you are guilty unless you can prove you are innocent. Do you understand?'

Isabella nodded. 'When do I see the judge? Now?'

'No,' said del Castillo. 'Not now. I am uncomfortable with this. I don't think you realise how serious this could be for you. You need to speak to someone else before we think about what to do next.' She stood. 'You said you wanted a phone call. I think that is wise. I can do better, perhaps. I will speak to your embassy. They will send someone to talk to you. Maybe they can talk some sense into you.'

'Thank you,' Isabella said. 'Can you tell them I need to speak to Vivian Bloom?'

'Who's that?'

'Just tell them they need to tell him that I'm here.'

'Vivian Bloom,' the detective repeated. 'He works at the embassy?'

'No,' Isabella said. 'He works in London. Ask them to pass him a message.'

'What do you want me to say?'

'They should tell him I'm here. Give my name. And he needs to know that I want to talk about Prometheus. And Maia.'

'Who's Maia?'

'They'll know. They need to tell Bloom that I know where she is.'

Chapter Twenty-Three

London

Bloom had taken the red-eye from New York. He had managed to sleep as they passed over the Atlantic, but he was stiff and only half awake as he made his way through the lobby of the dull and anonymous building off Whitehall. The meeting of the Intelligence Steering Committee had been scheduled on short notice, and Bloom was keen to get started. The building had not been decorated for years, in common with most of the other governmental properties in the neighbourhood. The Committee prized discretion in its work, and these backwater buildings offered more of that than the glitzier, showier offices that could be found on Whitehall itself.

The Committee was responsible for the oversight of The Firm, the classified organisation that carried out the most clandestine work of MI5 and MI6, the two state security agencies. It was an inter-ministerial body comprising senior Cabinet members and civil service mandarins. The invitations for this particular meeting were even more limited than usual. The business on the agenda was too sensitive even for the restricted security clearances necessary for membership of the Committee; a smaller, more elite gathering had been called.

Bloom took the lift to the third floor and went through into the conference room. It was panelled in warped oak and lit by an ornate chandelier that might have been impressive once, but was now dusty and unreliable, its bulbs buzzing and some of them flickering on and off. Two people were waiting at the table: Sir Benjamin Stone, the chief of the Secret Intelligence Service, and Eliza Cheetham, the director-general of MI5. Stone was in his early sixties, bearing a little too much weight, and with lank hair that always looked as if it would benefit from a wash. Cheetham, on the other hand, was elegantly dressed and had a handsome cast to her face that recalled great beauty when she was younger. Her smile was taut as she took her seat. Stone, too, looked anxious.

'Well, Vivian?' Stone said. 'How was the trip?'

'They're moving on the plan to get rid of Morrow. They're keeping it domestic – we won't be involved.'

'That's a relief,' he said. 'We've more than played our part.'

'Quite,' Bloom agreed.

'When?'

'There's a rally in Sioux City next week.'

'It'll be decisive?'

'Carington seemed to think so.'

'Well, we can leave them to sort out their own mess,' Cheetham said, motioning with her hands as if pushing the problem away.

'I'll prepare a detailed briefing when I know more. We won't want to be caught short.'

'Certainly not,' Cheetham agreed.

'The PM will need to be carefully handled. All the usual bromides: special relationship, shoulder-to-shoulder against terror . . . It should all be reflexive by now.'

'It'll be handled,' Stone said. 'We'll be ready to prepare him as soon as they've done it. Did they say how?'

'They're sending two of their assets. That brings me to what I want to talk to you both about.'

'Prometheus?'

Bloom nodded.

'You spoke to them?' Cheetham asked.

'Yes. And it's exactly as we expected. They're going to try and fuck us.'

Bloom's propensity for vulgar language – potentially disorientating thanks to his background and age – was well known to Stone and Cheetham, and neither of them reacted to it.

'Can't say I'm surprised,' Stone said.

'What happened?' Cheetham asked.

'I reminded them that we have been promised access to the programme and they said it was impossible. They won't change their position. It's worth billions to them.'

'But we knew that,' she said.

'We did. But we had to ask – it would have been easier than the alternative.'

'There is one?' Cheetham asked.

Bloom reached across the table for a china cup and filled it with coffee from the dispenser that had been left for them. He handed it to Cheetham, poured another for Stone and then a final one for himself.

'Vivian?' Stone pressed.

'I suggest we un-fuck ourselves,' Bloom said. 'Have you heard of the Gen 75 Committee?'

'Nuclear research,' Stone offered.

'Correct,' Bloom said. 'This is going back a few years, of course. Everyone knows we were involved in the Manhattan Project. The Americans, the Canadians, us. But the Americans refused to give us anything on the bombs they dropped on Hiroshima and Nagasaki. They passed a fucking statute *forbidding* it. We spent a year trying to get Truman to cooperate, but Truman said no. They wanted to keep it for themselves. So Attlee put together a committee to look into getting our own version of the bomb. The Gen 75 Committee, also known as the Atom Bomb Committee. They set up a site at Aldermaston and eight years later we had Blue Danube – our very own bomb.'

'And you see an equivalence here?'

'Oh, most certainly. But this is worse. No one else is anywhere near to the level the Americans have reached. We're certainly not. I've seen what they've done. I've been to the Daedalus facility they're running in Skopje. I've seen the monsters they've built at first-hand. We could set up our own programme tomorrow, but it would be decades before we could get to the level they're at now. It wouldn't take eight years – I doubt we could do it in eighty. And, by then, where they're at now will look primitive in comparison. We can't let them build up that kind of head start.'

'So what do we do? Ask nicely if they'd consider changing their mind?'

'No,' Bloom said. 'That'll never happen. We need to take the initiative.'

'How?' Stone said. 'We go after Ivanosky? Was he there?'

'Yes,' Bloom said. 'I had a team of headhunters on him from the moment he landed at JFK to the moment he left.'

'So we make a run at him?'

Bloom shook his head. 'He's too valuable. The Americans have him heavily guarded. If we could have snatched him in New York, we would have – but we couldn't. And he's back in Skopje now. Getting to him there is impossible.'

Cheetham smiled thinly, her patience wearing thin. 'But you have an alternative?'

He smiled. 'Of course. I knew that they'd react this way. I told you they would. So I engaged a freelancer two years ago to get us the information we need to catch up.'

'You haven't mentioned it before.'

'I have contingencies for my contingencies. It wasn't relevant until now. You remember Litivenko and her husband?'

'The defectors?'

Bloom nodded. 'I thought they would be able to get us what we need. I had the freelancer intercede on our behalf. We were close – very close. Captain Pope went to bring them in, but there were complications, as you know.'

'A bullet in the head,' Stone said gruffly. 'You could call that a complication.'

Bloom opened his briefcase and took out a tablet. He put it on the table, navigated to the file he wanted, and tapped it to play.

'*British embassy,*' said a female voice through the tablet's speaker. '*How can I direct your call?*'

'*My name is Salma del Castillo,*' said a second voice, this one also female. '*I am a police detective in Chihuahua. I have arrested a British national for armed robbery. She is young. She needs someone from the embassy to help her.*'

'*What is her name?*'

'*Isabella Rose.*'

Bloom watched Cheetham and Stone. Their faces recorded their surprise.

'*And you're where?*'

'*She's at Comandancia de Policía Zona Sur – Chihuahua, southern command.*'

'*Thank you. I'll pass that along and we'll get someone there to see her. Likely be a day or two.*'

'*That's fine. There's one other thing. Something she said to me.*'

'*Yes?*'

'*She wants to speak to Vivian Bloom.*'

'*Who?*'

'*My prisoner has a message for him. Her name is Isabella Rose. She tells me she wants to speak to Señor Bloom. She says she has information*' *about Prometheus. And she says that she can tell him about Maia – where she is.'*

Stone shook his head. 'Well, I'll be damned.'

'It's legitimate?' Cheetham said.

'We're checking. But early indications are good. A sixteen-year-old girl with a British passport was arrested yesterday evening just north of Chihuahua. She was questioned and gave her name as Isabella Rose. And she knows my name and the name of the asset – I don't know how else any of that would be possible.'

'And we thought she was dead.'

'It would appear she's more resourceful than we gave her credit for.'

'What now?'

Bloom stroked his chin. 'We're going to go and get her. I'd like to know what she can tell us about the asset. You heard what she said: she can tell us where she *is*. Present tense.'

'Could be where the body is,' Stone suggested.

'Could be. But wouldn't you like to find out? I can't tell you how much satisfaction I'd get if we could find Maia before the Americans.'

'Who are you going to send? Headhunters?'

'I've sent an old Group Fifteen team to Mexico for backup,' Bloom said. 'But we can do better than that. I have someone in mind. Someone Isabella will trust.'

'Who?'

'Control,' Bloom said. 'I know where Pope is. And I'm going to persuade him to help us.'

Chapter Twenty-Four

Ho Chi Minh City

Michael Pope parked the car and turned to look at the villa. The property was in District 2, Thao Dien. It was in the French Colonial style, a common sight in this part of the city. There was a wrought-iron gate in front of a pleasant courtyard that was large enough to park the two mopeds that Pope's wife and daughters used to get around the city. There was an indoor swimming pool and a set of outdoor steps that swept up to the living accommodation on the second floor. There were a further two floors that offered four bedrooms and two bathrooms and a space for sunbathing on the roof. It was a pleasant house, and Pope had been happy when they had found it and secured the agreement to lease it for a year. It was two thousand dollars a month, which had stretched their budget even before Pope moved out. It was almost crippling now, but he refused to countenance that they should default and find somewhere else. He had taken the cheapest place for himself that he could find so that they could continue to afford it. His wife, Rachel, argued that it made no difference, that their changed circumstances had an effect on their finances and that they would have to face facts. Pretending otherwise was foolish, wishful thinking, she had said, but Pope refused to hear it. He had arranged more hours at the club and started to look for a second job. He didn't care how hard he had to work; he wasn't about to have his girls move out of the house. Having somewhere nice to live was the only thing that made their lives bearable.

He looked through the bars of the gate to the windows on the second floor. The drapes were drawn and the French doors were open. He saw movement in the room inside and, almost unaware that he was holding his breath, he waited until his younger daughter, Clementine, came out onto the balcony. She was wearing cut-off jeans and a T-shirt that Pope remembered buying for her in the airport gift shop as they arrived in the city a year ago. He clenched the wheel tightly, his throat thick with emotion. Clem was joined on the balcony by her older sister, Flora. Pope watched as they spoke.

He wanted to go to them, to clasp them both in an embrace and never let them go. But that couldn't happen. He would have to wait. Rachel had made it clear that he wasn't welcome at the house, and he didn't want another argument.

He had a bottle of Táo Mèo rice liquor on the seat next to him. He grabbed it, twisted out the cork and put it to his lips. The liquor was made from sticky red rice fermented with yeast, and it tasted strongly of rose apple. He had been drinking from the bottle all afternoon, and he had started to feel the buzz.

He watched until they both went back inside and, wiping the back of his hand across his damp eyes, he took another long gulp of the wine and then dropped the bottle onto the seat again. He put the car into drive and rolled away from the kerb.

Chapter Twenty-Five

Pope parked the car in a lot on the edge of Pham Ngu Lao and walked. District 1 of the city comprised narrow lanes and back alleys that ran off the main thoroughfares of De Tham, Bui Vien and Do Quang Doa streets. The whole area was famous as a hub for backpackers who were making a stop in the capital. A vibrant street-drinking scene had developed, with a number of ad hoc bars setting up every night. Pope bought a pint of *bia hoi* draught beer from a roadside vendor and found a vacant plastic stool in the middle of the street. He looked around. The street was a crazy riot of colour and noise. There were low-key restaurants, and cheap nightclubs where prostitutes of both sexes would gather to take advantage of the drunken foreigners. There were tour companies and kiosks offering excursions to nearby landmarks, together with hostels and guesthouses and 'mini-hotels' that rose six or seven storeys, but almost always came without an elevator. The space between the buildings was festooned with wires and cables, and the walls were fitted with countless signs advertising the businesses that were accommodated inside: ABC Laundry; Spa & Nail Violet; Tiger Beer; Circle Cellphones. The clientele sitting on the stools around Pope were young, for the most part, a mixture of nationalities who came for the cheap beer, the chance to score dope and the atmosphere. There were locals, too, men and women who were drawn in by the budget prices and the closeness to the city's main attractions.

He checked his watch. It was a little before eight thirty; he had a few minutes before he was due to start his shift. He put the plastic cup to his lips and drank down the pint in three hungry gulps. He tossed the empty cup into the trash, grabbed his bag and set off again.

The club was called VIP Karaoke. It was nestled between two other similar bars, all of them seemingly competing for trade by dint of the garishness of the neon that drenched their exteriors. Pope had been working there for four weeks. A man called Pham was the manager. He was supercilious and unpleasant, but Pope had needed a job and Pham had been prepared to offer him one despite the lack of satisfactory references. Pope was English, which meant that he could communicate with the vast majority of the traveller clientele, and he had the look of a man who it would obviously not be wise to annoy. The money was meagre and it was often paid late, but Pope could work as many hours as he wanted. He had also taken to supplementing his earnings with bottles of Johnny Walker that he filched from the store cupboard and knocked back in the toilets.

The bars all had awnings that extended out onto the street, with tables and stools fighting for space on the sidewalk. Pope nodded hello to the girl who worked the ticket booth as he went down to the basement and the tiny space that served as the staff restroom. He put on the VIP Karaoke-branded shirt and checked that his knuckledusters were safely in the pocket of his trousers. The bar encouraged young backpackers to drink to excess – and, as a result, trouble was a frequent occurrence. A big fight five weeks earlier had seen a stool thrown through the club's windows, and the ensuing brawl had put Pope's predecessor in hospital; the fracas had provided a vacancy that Pope had been able to fill, but he wasn't about to go to work without an equaliser in the event of similar trouble.

It was a terrible place. They played Europop through cheap speakers that were not equipped to deal with the volume from the amplifier, with the result that the sound was distorted. Strip clubs were outlawed in Vietnam, but industrious entrepreneurs got around the restrictions by setting up *karaoke om* bars. Where *xe om* meant a motorbike where the passenger hugged the rider, *karaoke om* meant a club where the guests were allowed to hug the girls. And, of course, 'hug' was interpreted liberally; provided that money changed hands between the owner of the bar and the customer, it was permitted for the guest to do much more than simply hug the women. Those bars that had under-the-counter arrangements with corrupt local officials allowed the women to remove their clothes and dance on the tables as tourists massacred songs from the karaoke machine's extensive catalogue.

Pope went into the bathroom and filled the sink with cold water. He cupped his hands and filled them, then dunked his head. The water was cool on his hot skin, and he splashed more onto his face in an attempt to clear away the fug of the alcohol that he had consumed.

There was a dusty and cracked mirror above the basin and Pope looked up into it. He had aged over the past twelve months. His hair was greying at the temples and lines had formed across his weather-beaten face. He stared at his reflection. There was a coldness in his eyes that he didn't recognise. He reached up with his fingers, pressing hard against his forehead and cheeks and then kneading his eyes. His head buzzed from the alcohol. He knew that he should stop drinking, but also that he wouldn't be able to. He could ignore the sadness and the guilt when he was drunk; it was the only solace he had left.

He drained the sink, dried his face with a fistful of toilet paper from the cubicle and went up to the door to start his shift.

Chapter Twenty-Six

Pope's shift finished at two in the morning. The bar kept going for another couple of hours, but Pham's brother worked the last shift so that the tight bastard could save a few dong. A group of drunken backpackers had been the worst of it. Nothing else had happened that Pope couldn't fix with a stern glance, and so he collected his pay and made his way in the vague direction of his car.

He knew that he had been drinking too much. It had started months earlier, before the trouble at home. The atmosphere in the house had been tense. He knew that he was being cowardly, and that it would be better to address it in the hope that they might be able to find a solution. But wasn't that wishful thinking? How could they find a solution? How could Pope find a way out of a situation of his own devising, one that had forced him to uproot his family from their happy, settled lives and transport them halfway around the world because he was certain of what would have happened to them if they had stayed? The lives of his wife and daughters had already been threatened once. They had been abducted. He had managed to get them back, but now, he knew, he had only saved them from one crisis before dumping them into another.

And it had been too much for the family to bear. The fights with his wife had grown more and more unpleasant until they'd fought to a standstill. She'd told him that their marriage was over, that he had wrecked everything and that she wanted him to leave. Pope couldn't argue with her. He had agreed. She was right: he *had* ruined everything. He told her that he would fix things, but he had been saying the same thing every day for months and nothing was different. He didn't know how to fix things. They couldn't just go home. They had to hide. All they could look forward to was to move from one place to another when things got too hot. They couldn't put down roots, not even in a place like this. They would be found eventually, and, if that happened, Pope wouldn't be able to guarantee their safety.

He had argued that he needed to be with them in order to protect them, but she had brought up his drinking and used that against him. He was never there anyway; what difference would it make if he moved out?

Pope reached into his pocket and took out his wallet. It was full of the evidence of his fake life, the legend that he had adopted in order to disappear. He was George Watson, an English teacher who had come to Vietnam in order to find work. His wife was Yvette and his daughters were Chloe and Kylie. He had a picture of his girls in one half of the opened wallet, and he rubbed his finger across the plastic that guarded it. He knew that he needed to address the situation, but he had no idea how to do that.

Guilt. He could feel it, stirring in his gut again, whispering in his ear, telling him he was to blame.

He found his car and slid inside. He started the engine and set off.

Chapter Twenty-Seven

P ope had taken an apartment on Nguyen Van Huong Street. It had a single bedroom, a living room and a tiny kitchen. It was all that he could afford while still paying the rent on the house.

He opened the door and went inside. The apartment was on the sixteenth floor of the block, and offered a wide view of the city. It had been clean and tidy before Pope moved in, but a month later it was a mess. He only owned a small collection of cheap clothes, and these were strewn across the bed and the floor. The place was too small for a washing machine, and so he had to do his laundry in a communal place at the foot of the building. The kitchen sink was stacked with dirty plates and takeout boxes, and empty cans of Saigon Special were scattered around the overflowing trash can. Pope was an army man, and most of his life had been governed by the discipline that had been drummed into him as a new recruit. Those habits were a tie to the certainties of his old life, but now, just as his relationship with his wife had frayed, those ties were fraying. Pope knew that he should fall back on his old routine, but he had slipped too far away from it now for him to care.

He went to the kitchen, opened the cupboard and took down a bottle of rice wine that still had a little left in it. He poured the alcohol into a glass, put it to his lips and drank it down in one gulp. It was sharp, and he winced as it burned the back of his throat. There was enough left in the bottle for another swig; he dispensed with the glass, putting the bottle to his lips and drinking until it was empty.

He stared down at the bottle and, irrationally furious that it was spent, he flung it against the wall. It smashed, loudly, the fragments clattering down against the tiled floor. He stumbled out of the kitchen and into the tiny bedroom. He yanked out the bottom drawer of the closet and upended it. Dirty clothes fell to the floor, along with a heavier item that landed with a dull thud and glinted in the light. He reached down and picked it up. It was a M10 RB, the revolver that the American army had used during the Vietnam War. Pope had bought it from a black-market dealer in Ben Thanh Market, paying two hundred dollars for it and a box of ammunition. He opened the gun, ejected five of the rounds, spun the chamber and closed it up again.

He shut his eyes, put the heavy barrel in his mouth and pushed the muzzle against his palate. He didn't give himself time to think; he put his finger through the guard and pulled the trigger.

Click.

He tried again.

Click.

He tried a third time.

Click.

He was overcome by fury. He took the gun out of his mouth, catching the foresight against his gum as he did so and drawing blood. The coppery taste of it filled his mouth and brought him back to himself; he stared down at the gun and, his fingers trembling, released his grip on it and let it fall to the floor.

He felt dizzy, and then he felt sick. He put his hands out to balance himself on the edge of the upended drawer.

He fell down on the unmade bed, his face resting against the mattress with its brown stains and odd odours, and closed his eyes.

He was asleep within moments.

Chapter Twenty-Eight

Pope woke at midday. His head was splitting with a brutal hangover, and as he rolled off the bed to go to the bathroom, he saw the revolver on the floor and remembered what he had tried to do. He took the gun, removed the round and collected the five others he had ejected from the chamber. He put the ammunition back into the box and took it into the kitchen. He was tempted to take it and the revolver to the river and toss them out as far as he could. But that would be foolish. He knew there was a chance he would need a weapon in the future – it was why he had purchased this one in the first place – and he did not feel comfortable with the notion that he might have to face the assassins they would send after him unarmed. They were different – they were *monsters* – and he needed something to level the playing field.

He decided on a different course of action: he put the ammunition in the kitchen cupboard, on the top shelf behind the dirty crockery and the boxes of noodles. He returned to the bedroom and put the revolver in his bag, stuffing clothes atop it and shoving it all back into the drawer. It would be easy enough to find and load the weapon if he needed it, but it would take long enough that he would not be able to act on drunken impulse. He would have to *mean* it.

He stood under the feeble shower for ten minutes, scrubbing the water into his face and scalp, and brushed his teeth until the tang of the alcohol was gone. He dressed in the cleanest clothes he had and then went into the kitchen to fix something to eat. He saw the shattered remains of the bottle that he had smashed against the wall and, with a fresh burst of shame at what he had so nearly done, he found a dustpan and brush and cleaned up. He didn't stop, using his abashment as motivation and tidying the apartment. He put the dirty clothes into a bag and the clean ones into the wardrobe. He binned the packaging from the cheap and unhealthy food that he had been living on and then scrubbed the work surfaces and the sink until they were spotless. He filled a bucket with soapy water, got down on his hands and knees and washed the floor. He took the bucket into the bathroom and did the same in there, too. Finally, he made his bed. He worked quickly, reprising the routine that had been drilled into him when he was a recruit, the same process he had started his days with for nearly thirty years until he had allowed himself to slip. He started at the foot of the bed, tucking the end of the sheet between the mattress and the box springs. He went to the head of the bed and pulled the other end of the sheet so it was taut, made neat hospital corners at the top and bottom and then smoothed out the wrinkles. He spread out the top sheet and the blanket and tucked the sides in.

He stepped back. The apartment was tidier.

Pope realised that he was hungry. He opened the refrigerator; it was empty.

He put on his shoes, grabbed his money and his phone from the counter and made for the door.

Chapter Twenty-Nine

P ope waited for the number 43 bus at the end of the road. He took a seat at the back and watched out of the window as the driver started off to the southwest. They left Thao Dien, crossed the Song Sai Gon River and made their way to Dong Khoi.

Ho Chi Minh City was one of the busiest, most chaotic places that Pope could remember visiting. It was why he had chosen it when they were looking for somewhere to hide. The streets around the central district were busy with traffic, with delivery vans and taxis fighting for space with hordes of scooters and tuk-tuks. Locals and tourists jostled and bumped outside the stores and restaurants. Pope got off the bus in Da Kao and picked a patient path through them to the restaurant that he often visited for breakfast. The Café de la Poste was on Cong Xa Paris, offering an excellent vantage point to observe the throngs of people who gathered around the cathedral and the post office.

There was a kiosk on the sidewalk where tourists could get day-old copies of foreign newspapers; Pope bought a copy of the *New York Herald Tribune* and took it to the restaurant, sitting at an outside table. He ordered scrambled eggs and bacon together with an orange juice, and opened the newspaper. He flipped through the first few pages. The focus was, as ever, on the continuing Syrian conflict.

Pope had devoured the news obsessively ever since they had arrived in the city. The first few months of their exile had coincided with the start of the war. People back home had been whipped into a frenzy by the Westminster attack, and then, not long afterwards, by the shooting-down of British Airways Flight 117. Years of misadventure in Afghanistan and Iraq had meant that the prevailing mood was one of isolationism, but those two atrocities inverted things with the ease of simply flipping a switch. The security services produced supposedly irrefutable evidence that proved both attacks had originated within the caliphate that had been established across Syria and Iraq.

Pope knew the fallacy of that argument. He knew that the reality was very different to the version that had been prepared and served up. He knew he had helped to manufacture the case for war, too. And he knew that public opinion was being manipulated so that the war could be prosecuted. The same manipulation had been effected in America with the bombing at Dulles Airport, an operation that had been met with the same success in changing the national agenda. Pope and Isabella had been in the airport that day, and had been caught up in the explosion.

Pope knew that there was another purpose hidden within the grander objective. The conspiracy had used the bombing to murder Aleksandra Litivenko, the scientist they were delivering to Congress. She had been going to testify that she had been working on Prometheus, the beyond-top-secret project responsible for Maia and the other agents who implemented the conspiracy's agenda.

War had come quickly, and it had been relentless. The USA, the UK and a coalition of willing partners had proceeded with the usual shock and awe campaign that began with an aerial bombardment and then continued with troops crossing the border from Turkey and head-ing south. There had been protests in the United Nations. China had pushed for an immediate cessation in hostilities, but had been ignored. Russia and Iran increased their backing for the beleaguered regime, launching their own offensive, which sent mechanised divisions north from Damascus and secured a wide swathe of territory from the capital to Aleppo.

But then, almost as quickly, the mood had changed again. The news was full of pictures of the schools and hospitals that had been flattened by coalition bombs. Innocent civilians, already punished by years of living under ISIS rule, were now made to suffer once more. The risk of an accidental escalation between the United States and Russia became more acute when a MiG-29 was shot down by a Sea Sparrow surface-to-air missile fired by a US Navy frigate twenty miles off the coast of Latakia. Governments around the world struggled to adapt. At home, the British government had lost a motion of no confidence and had been forced to call a general election. The opposition's new leader – Anthony Johnson, a telegenic former human rights lawyer – said that the electorate was presented with a binary choice: an incumbent party offering more war, and his quickly ascending left-wing faction promising that Britain would withdraw from the coalition and press for an immediate armistice.

The mood for peace proved to be contagious; one by one, all of the coalition partners pushed for a diplomatic solution. The upcoming American presidential election offered the same choice as its British equivalent: a continuation of the conflict under the Republican candidate, Scott Hawken, or the cessation of violence and the withdrawal of troops under the Democrats and Gary Morrow.

The waning influence of the hawks in Washington and London had been a solace to Pope. If men like Johnson and Morrow could finally get their hands upon the levers of power, then perhaps they could put an end to the fighting. And Morrow had gone further, threatening to dismantle the CIA, close Guantanamo, pardon the whistle-blowers who had exposed American corruption and rein in the drone programme that he said had sown hatred for his country across the Middle East. Pope had read the reports and could barely credit that a mainstream politician could hold those views and still stand a realistic chance of electoral success, but polls were polls and the evidence was difficult to refute.

That the same change to public opinion was taking place within the UK, too, was a source of dark amusement to Pope. He thought of old spooks like Vivian Bloom – the puppetmasters who still held the strings and made the politicians dance to their tunes – and found a little satisfaction at the dismay and alarm that he knew they must be experiencing. Bloom lived in the ugly margin of chaos created by conflict. He might claim philosophical justifications for his position, but Pope was too jaded to buy those; the existence of Bloom, and the men and women like Bloom, depended on strife. Without it, they would be rendered obsolete. They needed the cycle of war as much as they needed air, and so they encouraged it as much as they could.

The newspapers were full of hope: the world was changing, they said, and the old order was being steadily eroded. The more optimistic leader-writers proclaimed that it was being replaced by something new and better. Pope doubted that was true – the regime would not go quietly into the night – but, even if it was true, it did not give Pope satisfaction. The climate would have to change much more than it had before it would be safe to think about going home. Pope knew too much, and the men who had reason to be frightened of him had long memories and much to lose.

Chapter Thirty

Pope finished his breakfast and ambled towards the cathedral. The grand building with its twin spires reached out from the western edge of the lawned square that offered at least a semblance of tranquillity amid the chaos of the city. He wanted to sit for a while to think.

He walked around a tourist bus parked next to the building and climbed the steps that led through the large archway and into the coolness of the vast space inside. There were TV screens set into the ornate stone pillars – Pope guessed they were to show the lyrics to the hymns – and free-standing rotary fans circulated the air. The pews stretched all the way to the far side of the building, and the floor was paved with a geometric pattern that was dizzying if you looked at it for too long.

He walked along the transept and sat on a pew next to the aisle, then closed his eyes and tried to tune out the noise in his head.

'Hello, Pope.'

He started at the sound of his name and turned around. The man who had spoken had taken a seat in the pew directly behind him. He was dishevelled, wearing an old jacket that was patched at the elbows and a pair of dirty jeans.

Pope felt the clutch of shock and then fear. He glanced up and down the aisle. There were twenty or thirty tourists enjoying the respite from the heat outside, and members of the cathedral staff were going about their business.

'Get away from me,' he hissed.

The man was wearing a ball cap with frayed edges around the peak and the logo of the old American software company Atari on the front. Pope and Isabella had called him that, and the name had stuck. The man's face was cast into shadow by the cap, but Pope could see that he was grizzled with day-old stubble, and his teeth, when he smiled, were crooked. He was wearing a pair of dark glasses that obscured his eyes.

'Five minutes,' he said. 'I just want to talk to you.'

'I'm not interested.'

'You will be. Please. Five minutes, that's all. I've been looking for you for a year, Control. You've hidden well.'

'Obviously not well enough.'

'I came here just so I could speak to you. I flew in last night. No one else knows I'm here. And I don't intend to reveal where you are. I just want to talk. That's it.'

Pope and Isabella didn't know his real name; he had never told them, and they had never pressed. He had helped them negotiate the aftermath of their misadventure in Syria, and had helped Pope to find his family. That didn't mean that Pope trusted him. On the contrary: Atari had been very open that he was following his own agenda, one on which he had not been willing to elaborate beyond that he wanted to expose Daedalus and the programme that was responsible for Maia and the other monsters who had been sent after Pope and Isabella. Pope had come to the firm conclusion that Atari had offered his help as a means to an end, and that he cared very little for him or Isabella.

And yet, here he was. A reminder of what Pope had been involved in, and the price he was paying for that involvement.

'Please,' Atari said. 'Five minutes. If you're not interested in what I have to say, I'll leave.'

The man took off his glasses. His eyes were dark, lively with intelligence and active with wary agitation.

Pope considered his options. He could leave, but he remembered how determined Atari was from their previous encounters. He wouldn't stop until he had delivered whatever message it was that he had come here to deliver. If he had found Pope, then he certainly knew where his family lived. It would be easier and more discreet to hear him out.

Pope tried to justify his decision on the grounds that Atari might have information that would be important to his family's security, although he knew that was just him trying to fool himself. There was no point in pretending otherwise; he was curious.

'Five minutes. No more.'

Chapter Thirty-One

How did you find me?'

Atari adjusted the brim of his cap. 'Your daughter has been sending messages to a friend in London. She used a café in Tan Dinh. The first message triggered the alarm, and we hijacked the webcams on all of the terminals for when she came back the next day. Once we had a location for her, it wasn't difficult to find you.'

Pope wasn't angry. He had told Clem and Flora that they were not to contact anyone from their old lives, but he could not condemn them for their loneliness. It, along with everything else, was his fault.

'Consider it a free tip in the event that you decide you're not interested in what I have to say.'

'I'm not going to be interested.'

'But you'll hear me out?'

'What's the point?'

'If I can find you, they can find you, too.'

'"They"?'

'You know who I mean.'

'But they haven't found us yet.'

'They're not as good as me,' Atari said smugly. 'And they don't have the same imperative that I do. I need your help. They don't. But they will find you. You know that as well as I do. You know much too much to be left unattended. They're coming.'

Atari paused as an elderly couple walked by them. Then he spoke again. 'It took me a year, but I found you. It's not possible to stay off-grid forever. Twenty years ago? Maybe. You go and live in a kibbutz or an ashram – perhaps. But not today. They *will* find you, Control, and when they do they'll dispatch one of their agents to finish the work they started. And it'll be on their terms. You saw what their monsters can do. You won't have a chance, even if you have the luxury of knowing when and where they'll come for you. But you don't have that luxury. You won't see them coming.'

That was true: Pope *had* seen what they could do. Maia, a woman barely half his weight, had thrown him around like a rag doll. He'd seen her leap ten feet in the air to grab the skid of the helicopter that was rescuing his family from the ambush on the mountain. Litivenko had explained the aims of the project that had birthed them. Daedalus had been tasked with producing metabolically dominant soldiers, and evidently they had succeeded. Pope had no intention of seeing what else they could do.

'We'll move again,' Pope said. 'We'll keep moving.'

'And they'll keep looking and, eventually, they'll find you. I'm not saying this to try to frighten you. It's just a statement of fact. If it were me, I'd be looking to make the first move.'

'It isn't you, though, is it? I'm sorry. I'm through with all that. I lost my kids once. That's not going to happen again.' Pope looked at his watch. Atari had two minutes left, but he wasn't minded to allow him them. He stood. 'I'm sorry,' he said. 'I can't help you.'

'What about Isabella Rose?'

Pope stopped. 'What about her?'

'You're not curious about what happened?'

'She's dead.'

'No,' Atari said calmly. 'She isn't.'

119

'She fell from a helicopter. Twenty feet. I saw her fall.'

Atari shook his head. 'We've been looking for her, too. She was harder to find than you. We got her in the end. Would you like to see?'

Atari didn't wait for him to answer. He reached into his satchel, took out a tablet, woke it up and handed it to Pope. He saw a photograph of a teenage girl.

'This was taken yesterday. I'm not sure I would have recognised her. She looks different, doesn't she?'

Pope sat. He didn't turn away from the tablet. The girl in the photograph was Isabella, although there was something different about her beyond just the changes that another year had brought. She had been photographed against a plain backdrop and she was staring into the lens of the camera with an expression that mixed the vulnerability of youth with an edge that he couldn't remember from before. There was fresh steel in her eyes. She had been fifteen the last time he saw her, and a year had passed since then; she was sixteen now, but she looked so much older than that.

'Where is she?'

'That's where it gets even more interesting,' Atari said. 'Swipe right, please.'

Pope did as Atari suggested and saw a second picture. Isabella was photographed against the same backdrop, but this time she was in profile. On her shoulder Pope could see the tattoo of the rose he remembered. The rose that she had inked there as a testament to the man she had killed in her mother's memory.

'These are police mugshots?'

'Yes,' Atari said. 'She's been arrested in Chihuahua.'

'She's in Mexico?'

Atari nodded.

'Arrested for what?'

'Armed robbery.'

Pope shook his head. '*What?*'

'There's a store to the south of the city. She put a gun in the owner's face and robbed the till. They picked her up outside with a 9mm pistol.'

'I don't believe it.'

'Really? I remember her as a fairly extraordinary young woman, with an unfortunate history. And a year has passed. We have no idea where she's been or what she's been doing.'

'And?'

'Swipe right again, please.'

Pope did as he was told. The next page was a transcript of a police interview.

'Do you speak Spanish?'

'Not very well,' he said.

'I'll give you the summary. Isabella was interviewed the morning after she was arrested. What you've got there is her confession.' He found a passage and translated it. '*I did it – you said you can prove it, so what's the point in arguing? I confess. Now what?*'

Pope was assailed by a strong sense of responsibility. Isabella had died on the mountain. He had seen her fall before he had been forced to run. He had seen her fall twenty feet and hit the ground and lie still. He had been unable to stay on the mountain; his wife and girls were aboard the helicopter and the muscle that had turned up with Bloom had known that he was on the slopes. He had been badly outnumbered.

'How did she get off the mountain?' he asked.

'We have no idea.'

'What about Maia?'

'You delivered her to them, captain. We have to assume that they have her back.'

Pope had been unable to forget the woman. The coldness, the lack of emotion; the moving through life like an automaton. He flicked back to the encounter in his apartment in Montepulciano, and the way she had beaten him as if he were nothing more than an insolent schoolboy rather than a grizzled soldier most certainly *not* used to having his rear end handed to him like that.

'The detective in charge of Isabella's case made a very unusual telephone call yesterday. Here – we intercepted it.'

Atari took the tablet, navigated to another app and tapped the screen.

'*British embassy,*' said a female voice through the tablet's speaker. '*How can I direct your call?*'

'*My name is Salma del Castillo,*' said a second voice. '*I am a police detective in Chihuahua. I have arrested a British national for armed robbery. She is young. She needs someone from the embassy to help her.*'

'*What is her name?*'

'*Isabella Rose.*'

The conversation continued. The detective said that the British national was being held at the southern command of the Chihuahua police. The woman from the embassy said that someone would be sent to attend to her but, before the call ended, the detective added one more thing.

'*She wants to speak to Vivian Bloom.*'

'*Who?*'

'*My prisoner has a message for him. Her name is Isabella Rose. She tells me she wants to speak to Señor Bloom. She says she has information about Prometheus. And she says that she can tell him about Maia – where she is.*'

'*I see. Did she tell you what that means?*'

'*No. That's all she said.*'

The call came to an end.

'What's she talking about?' Pope said. 'Why does Isabella want to speak to Bloom?'

Atari took the tablet. 'You know as much as I do, Control.'

Pope felt blindsided. Isabella was always at the back of his mind. He thought about her every day. He was responsible for her, too. If it wasn't for his credulousness in prosecuting Bloom's agenda, and Pope's callousness in recruiting a teenage girl to work for him, Isabella would still have been in her *riad* in Marrakech. She would have had the chance to rebuild her fractured life. But Pope had deprived her of that chance. And now, staring out of the screen, were the consequences that had been handed down to her.

Atari put the tablet away. 'You know the organisation that I belong to wants to expose what Daedalus has been doing. We want them shut down. Litivenko's testimony was our best chance of doing that. We thought the chance was gone. But maybe not. Isabella has been off the grid for a year. She's sixteen and we haven't seen even the merest glimpse of her. We can only conclude that she has had help. She mentioned Maia. If they've been together, it's imperative that I speak to her. If I could find Maia . . .' He paused. 'But I can't just go and do that. Isabella is in police custody. We need to break her out. And that's something particularly well suited to your set of skills.'

'You want me to bust her out of jail?'

'Yes.'

Pope exhaled. 'I can't.'

'Can't or won't?'

Pope shook his head.

'I thought that you were close?'

'We are,' he said. 'I mean, we were. It's not that I wouldn't, it's just . . .' He paused, closing his eyes as if that might help to protect him from the fresh surge of guilt. 'It's my family – I can't risk leaving them again.'

'But you're not living with them.'

Atari dropped in that information with a casual flourish that filled Pope with anger. He must have realised it was a bad tactic, as he back-tracked quickly.

'I know this must have been difficult for you. Bringing them here, uprooting them – I can only imagine how hard that is. But this is a way back for you – for all of you. How long are you going to stay here and hope they won't find you? They will, Pope. They will find you and they'll come for you. Put them on the back foot. Take the fight to them.'

'That's naïve.'

'Not as naïve as doing nothing. If we can find Maia and show the world what she represents, everything changes. Daedalus is finished. Prometheus is finished. Anyone associated with the project will go to jail. And you don't need to do much to make that happen. Just help us get to Isabella.'

'And my family? While I'm away?'

'I'll make sure they're safe. You'll have my word.'

'You can't promise that,' Pope said. 'I know what Bloom and the others have been doing. The war – I helped make all of that possible. With that *and* Prometheus . . . the stakes are too high. You can't protect them, so don't pretend that you can.'

'But I—'

Pope cut him off. 'And I can't trust you. I don't. I *won't*.'

Atari did not give up. 'You *know* what they've done,' he said. 'They've killed hundreds of thousands of people in Syria. Men, women and children. And you know the role you played in that. You helped them build the pretext. You feel guilty – fine, I get that – but here's a chance to put things right.'

'Fuck you,' Pope said.

'So what about Isabella? You're just going to leave her?'

'Fuck you. I have nothing else to say.'

Pope stood. Atari stood, too.

'Think about it,' Atari said. 'I'll be here again tonight. Think about what you'd need from me before you'd be ready to say yes. If I can do it, I will.'

Pope didn't reply. He stepped out into the aisle and set off for the exit. He glanced back when he reached the top of the stairs. Atari was still there. He was watching him. Pope turned back and descended the stairs, exchanging the cool of the old building for the damp, sticky broil of another hot Vietnamese afternoon.

He did not look back again. He had no intention of returning.

Chapter Thirty-Two

Pope drove to the house. He parked outside and gazed through the bars of the gate. The windows were closed and there was no sign of activity either inside the building or in the garden. He looked at his watch. It was a little after three. Rachel often went to the store after lunch, and sometimes took the girls to Le Van Tam Park. Pope had enjoyed going there with them. It was usually busy with men and women enjoying Vietnamese dancing, and others taking informal fencing lessons or just relaxing away from the traffic that clogged the streets.

He put his hands on the wheel and then rested his forehead against them. He was confused.

He closed his eyes and thought about his meeting with Atari. He had not wanted to be found. It was the last thing they needed. It was, he knew, another repudiation of something that he was supposed to be good at. Tradecraft. He had dragged his family halfway across the world because they needed to disappear, but he had not even been able to arrange that.

He looked into the footwell and saw the glint of a bottle that had rolled down from the seat. He reached down and collected it. It was rice wine, and it was half-full. He held it by the neck and was about to open the top when he caught himself. He shook his head at the bottle, and what it signified. How had he allowed this? He had watched what happened to agents who were in Group Fifteen for too long. John Milton had fallen into alcoholism and it had nearly killed him. There had been others, just the same, their lives disintegrating, only able to silence their consciences by drinking themselves into a stupor. He was disgusted that he had permitted himself to become such a pathetic cliché.

He dropped the bottle back into the footwell and started the engine. He gave the house one final glance, put the car into drive and set off.

It was seven thirty when Pope made his way back to the cathedral. He left his car in a long-stay garage, paying for a month up front, and then walked the rest of the way. The square outside the building was still busy, a bustle of tourists taking selfies in the fading light and taking tables at the restaurants and cafés thereabouts. Pope sat down at a table and ordered a coffee, nursing it as he watched the entrance to the cathedral. Atari arrived after ten minutes. Pope saw him on the other side of the square, still wearing the same battered old cap. He walked with a lazy slouch, crossing the road and making his way up the steps and into the building. Pope drank the rest of the coffee, laid a note on the table to cover the bill and followed.

Pope paused at the entrance, looking into the interior of the cathedral. Atari had taken the same seat as this afternoon. He was sitting alone, hands folded in his lap, staring straight ahead. Pope waited a little longer, watching for any signs that might suggest he had not come alone. Nothing stood out.

Pope made his way down the aisle and stood next to him.

Atari looked up. 'Hello, captain,' he said. 'I didn't know whether I would see you again.'

'I haven't decided what I'm doing yet.'

'So why are you here?'

'I have some questions.'

Atari spread his hands to encourage Pope to ask them.

'Tell me about Isabella.'

'What do you want to know?'

'Everything. Start with where she's been.'

'We don't know for sure. I've been looking ever since she went missing, but yesterday was the first time I've been able to find her. And I'm good at finding people, Control.'

'She's very resourceful,' Pope said.

'She certainly is,' Atari agreed.

'What else?'

'We've got more of the interview with the police.'

'And?'

'She didn't say very much. She told them that she was in San Miguel de Allende for the winter. It's popular with ex-pats, it makes sense – I'm checking it out. She said she was heading north, to the States, and that she needed money. That's why she robbed the store.'

'What happens to her next?'

'They'll put her in front of a judge. We don't know when, but not long. In the next day or two. She'll be handed over to the prosecutor and a judge will decide whether or not to go ahead.'

'Can she get bail?'

'Not in Mexico. She'll stay in prison while she waits for her trial. That's why we need to move quickly. The police station where they have her now is going to be difficult to get her out of, but we stand a better chance there than if they move her to a jail.'

'That would be something for me to work out,' Pope said.

Atari glanced over at him. 'Does that mean you'll help?'

He thought of Isabella, locked up and alone, and knew that he wouldn't be able to say no.

'Maybe,' he hedged. 'You said you'd help.'

'What do you need?'

'New papers.'

Atari reached into his jacket pocket and took out a British passport. He handed it to Pope, who looked at the document. It was the real deal, with the red cover and the symbol that signified it was equipped with a biometric chip. Pope opened the passport and flipped through to the page that bore the bearer's details. He saw his own picture, the same as the picture in his legitimate passport, but with a new name next to it. He was to be Charles Mackintosh.

'I took the liberty of assuming that you'd say yes,' Atari said with just a hint of apology. 'What else?'

Pope slid the passport into his pocket. 'Transport to get me there and a car at the other end.'

'There's a red-eye to Tokyo that leaves at midnight. Tokyo to Dallas and then Dallas to Chihuahua. We've reserved a seat for you. It's a twenty-four-hour trip. You'll be on the ground the day after tomorrow.'

Pope laced his fingers and pushed down, popping his knuckles. He had already made up his mind to help Isabella, but he still found Atari's assumptions a little annoying. Was he so easy to read?

'Anything else?' Atari asked him.

'A gun,' Pope said. 'I'll need a gun.'

Chapter Thirty-Three

Skopje

Ivanosky had a villa on the slopes of Mount Vodno. It had a pool, a well-stocked wine cellar and a terrace that overlooked the city. Ivanosky had seen similar places on the market for over a million euros. The property was provided by Daedalus, a luxury that was quite plainly intended to make up for the inconvenience of having to live in Macedonia. The professor lived alone, and as he put on his raincoat and grabbed his umbrella from the stand next to the door, he found himself wondering again whether he should get a dog. He had been considering it for some time and had always found an excuse to put it off. Perhaps now was the time. His work with Daedalus had been unsatisfactory for too long now, and he thought that he might enjoy a little distraction when he returned home, and perhaps a reason to stop himself from practically living at the lab. There were spectacular walks within five minutes of his front door and having a dog would do him good. He resolved to look into it when he got back that evening.

His driver was waiting for him at the end of the drive.

'Good morning, sir,' he said.

The man spoke with an American accent. He had been seconded to Daedalus by Manage Risk. His ostensible purpose – other than driving Ivanosky back and forth between the laboratory and his villa – was to protect him from the threat of abduction, something that they had taken very seriously in the aftermath of the breakthroughs they made twenty years ago. Ivanosky and the research for which he was responsible were worth billions of dollars. It did not require a great leap of faith to see how attractive he would be to a rogue government: the Iranians, the North Koreans, the Chinese – even the Russians, from whom he had fled all those years ago.

Protection was the given reason that he was guarded, but Ivanosky knew the man had been posted to keep an eye on him, too. Aleksandra Litivenko's attempted defection had rattled Jamie King, and security had been increased after the threat she had posed had been neutralised. Ivanosky was old and tired, and did not have the energy or the wherewithal to consider running like she had. He didn't want to, either. He was dedicated to his work, and that dedication had not swayed even in light of the developments that he was still keeping from King and the others.

'Where to, professor?' the man said as he pulled away.

As if he had a choice.

'The lab,' he said.

Chapter Thirty-Four

Ivanosky changed into his lab coat and sat down at his desk to check the results of the tests that had been completed overnight. Moros was still sick. All of his relevant biomarkers were elevated, with his sialic acid and lactate dehydrogenase particularly high. They had been treating him with massive doses of cytarabine and daunorubicin, but the drugs were having no discernible effect. They had idarubicin and fludarabine left to try, but Ivanosky had always seen those as a last resort. He didn't hold out much hope that they would be successful. He was running out of options.

He collected his tablet and checked his emails as he made his way to the elevator. He saw another intemperate missive from Jamie King and swiped it away to be dealt with later. King was impatient and difficult and had made it increasingly plain that he viewed Daedalus and the research they had been doing here as his own personal property. In some ways, Ivanosky thought, King regarded *him* as a chattel, too. Ivanosky found it frustrating. They had needed to disguise the funding for the project and Manage Risk had been chosen for that purpose. Billions of dollars had been diverted from classified black budgets, with some of it made to look like legitimate payments for the services that the company provided to the government. Ownership of the research was complicated, and King was being typically presumptuous. Ivanosky tried to ignore it – his focus was on his work – but it was becoming increasingly difficult to do that.

The elevator descended to level four and slid to a gentle stop. '*Warning,*' said the recorded voice. '*Authorised personnel only. Biological hazards present.*'

Ivanosky waited for the airlock to open and then stepped outside. The corridor led to the left and the right, the light overhead reflecting back from the flawlessly white plastic panels. Ivanosky walked to his left until he reached a door that was stencilled with the legend 'Infirmary 2'. He leaned forward so he could position his forehead against the moulded headrest, and waited for the scanner to read and cross-check his iris. The door unlocked with a gentle hiss of compressed air and then slid back.

Ivanosky went inside.

They had four infirmaries, and all of them had been refitted to attend to the crisis that had developed over the course of the past twelve months. Ignoring previous losses, they'd had six active assets from the M cohort. Of those, Maia was missing and presumed dead. Morpheus was dead, killed by Maia during the botched operation that had been intended to exchange her for Michael Pope's family. There were four others – Macaria, Moros, Mercury and Mithras – and, within the space of a year, all of them except for Macaria had developed the exact same type of cancer that had blighted the cohorts that had gone before them.

Mercury and Mithras had only just been diagnosed, and the clinical staff had been able to stabilise them enough that it was possible for them to remain in the field.

Moros's cancer was further advanced. He was lying in the infirmary's single bed, hooked up to a battery of diagnostic equipment that displayed his physiological data on an LCD panel that hung down from the wall. He had cannulas in both arms, and the IV lines fitted into each of them dripped the cytotoxins that Ivanosky was using to try to keep the cancer at bay.

'Good morning, Moros,' he said as he downloaded the data from last night.

'Good morning, professor.'

'How are you feeling?'

'Much the same. Weak.'

'Have you eaten?'

'I have no appetite.'

The sick assets were suffering from acute myeloid leukaemia. Ivanosky had traced the disease back to myeloproliferative neoplasm, a condition that affected the bone marrow. The marrow normally made blood stem cells that became mature blood cells over time. A blood stem cell would become a myeloid stem cell or a lymphoid stem cell. Eventually, a lymphoid stem cell became a white blood cell. Ivanosky had observed the myeloid stem cells as they became immature white blood cells called myeloblasts. These myeloblasts did not become healthy white blood cells, and built up in the blood and bone marrow so there was less room for healthy cells and platelets. Ivanosky had noticed it first in Moros when he complained of anaemia and easy bleeding. The leukaemia cells had spread outside of the blood to other parts of the body. The rogue cells had also formed a solid granulocytic sarcoma; they had removed the tumour only to find that three more grew in its place. They removed those, too, but the cancer was still there. Still mutating. Still growing.

Giancarlo Esposito came into the room, and Ivanosky went over to join him. The doctor was a world-renowned oncologist who had, until recently, been the director of the Yale Cancer Center and physician-in-chief at Smilow Cancer Hospital at Yale New Haven in Connecticut. A seven-figure package had persuaded him to join Daedalus, and now that he had joined and was privy to the astonishing research that Ivanosky had pioneered, that and the money – together with implied threats to his family's future well-being – had secured his silence and his dedication.

Ivanosky raised his eyebrows questioningly; Esposito shook his head.

'Well?'

'It's spread. Central nervous system, skin, gums.'

'The chemo?'

'You saw the data. It's not having any effect.'

'Not slowing it down at all?'

'Not appreciably. He's reporting much more serious fatigue, he's bruising more easily than he was last week and there are petechiae on his chest, back and down both legs.'

'How long does he have?'

'I've never seen leukaemia move so quickly. It's hard to be sure, but I wouldn't bet on much longer than two or three months.'

Ivanosky nodded. He had seen it before. Every cohort that he had worked on had succumbed to it eventually. Almost all of the previous subjects had died within the first few years of life; a handful had survived into a second decade, but none of them had survived beyond twenty. The M cohort were twenty-six, and Ivanosky had allowed himself the luxury of thinking that they would be spared. He had been unable to replicate his success with them, and all subsequent cohorts had been unstable. That the Ms had prospered was his saving grace; if they were all to die, as he knew now that they all would, he had little doubt that Daedalus would be shuttered. His life's work, and his reputation, would be worthless.

'Excuse me? Professor?'

It was the intercom. Ivanosky looked up at the window of the observation suite. Felicia Quayle, one of his assistant doctors, was standing there with her hand raised to attract his attention. He went to the intercom and held down the button to speak.

'What is it?'

'Jamie King wants to speak to you, doctor. He says it's urgent.'

Chapter Thirty-Five

I vanosky took the call in an empty office next to the infirmary. He switched on the monitor and joined the encrypted channel. Jamie King's face filled the screen.

'Jamie,' Ivanosky said, hoping that there would be no new questions about the cancer.

'The girl's been found,' King said abruptly.

'What girl?'

'Isabella Rose.'

Ivanosky needed a moment to process that. 'What? Where?'

'Mexico. Near Chihuahua.'

'I don't understand. She was *found*?'

'She was arrested,' King said. 'She held up a store. I don't know exactly what happened – we're still interpreting the intercepts. But we have a message from the Mexican police to the British Embassy saying that she wants to speak to Vivian Bloom about Maia. She says she knows where she is.'

Ivanosky couldn't hide his excitement. 'She's alive? She said that?'

'She said she knows where she is. We can ask her what that means when we bring her in. That's why I'm calling you. We need to go and get her before Bloom. Where's the nearest asset?'

Ivanosky put the palms of his hands on either side of his head and pressed, trying to impose a little order on the riot of thoughts in his mind. 'We've got Macaria and Mercury in Sioux City,' he said. 'They're setting up for Morrow.'

'We need both of them there?'

'I'm not involved in operational planning,' Ivanosky protested. 'That's you.'

'So we'll manage with one. Choose one to go to Mexico and pick her up.'

Ivanosky assessed his options. The operation in Sioux City was likely to be the most demanding, and Macaria was the healthier of the two.

'We'll send Mercury,' Ivanosky said.

'Fine. Contact him. We'll arrange for a chopper to pick him up from the Air National Guard base in Sioux Falls and fly him to Chihuahua. We can get him on the ground in eight hours. Tell him he'll have a full debrief in the air.'

Ivanosky was about to respond when he saw that the screen had gone black; King had ended the call.

He pushed his chair away from the desk and stared at the black screen. He didn't know how he felt: anticipation, relief, excitement and something else that he couldn't quite place.

He realised what it was: it was foreboding. Maia had chosen to leave the programme. She had shot and killed her own brother as she made her escape. Ivanosky knew that her motivation must have been connected to the death of Litivenko, but the assets were not supposed to act on emotional impulse. What she had done was so far beyond the scope of the standard behaviour he had observed for so many years that he hadn't known where to start when he tried to decode it. Perhaps now, if he could bring her to the laboratory and speak to her, he might be able to understand.

He called the ops room. 'Send a flare to Mercury,' he said. 'Category One. I need to speak to him now.'

Chapter Thirty-Six

Mexico

Pope's flight touched down in Chihuahua at 8.58 a.m. local time. He had been travelling for over a day. He passed through the terminal and took the transfer bus to the long-term parking lot. A rental car had been left there, the Hertz tag still hanging from the stem of the rear-view mirror. He went around to the back of the car and, looking to ensure that no one was watching him, he ducked down and felt underneath the fender. His fingers brushed up against the key, secured there by a strip of tape. He tugged the tape away, peeled the key from the adhesive and opened the trunk.

There was a bag inside. He unzipped it: there was a pistol, together with a shoulder rig and a box of ammunition. The gun was a Sig Sauer P224. Pope examined it quickly, hidden by the open lid of the trunk: it looked reasonably new, fired just a few times and with the serial number filed off. He put the gun back into the bag and unzipped the pouch at the front. He found a new cell phone with a hands-free kit, together with an envelope that contained four SIMs. There was also a wallet, complete with a collection of credit cards in the name of Charles Mackintosh and a wad of Mexican pesos. Finally, there was a pair of high-power binoculars. Pope took the cell phone and one of the SIMs, replaced everything else in the bag, dropped the lid of the trunk and got into the car.

He put the SIM into the phone and switched it on. A single number had been programmed into the memory. Pope tapped it.

'Good morning, captain,' Atari said when the call connected.

'Just like old times,' Pope observed. 'I wish I could say that it was a pleasure.'

'How was your flight?'

'Long. But I'm here now.'

'And you've got everything you need?'

'I think so.'

'Good. There's been a development. You're going to need to get on the move.'

Pope switched on the engine. 'Go on,' he said.

'Isabella is being taken to the courthouse for the first hearing of her case.'

'When?'

'The hearing is at eleven. We don't know when they'll move her, but it'll take fifteen minutes to drive to the court from the precinct house.'

Pope looked at his watch. 'I'm on my way,' he said.

He ended the call, tossed the phone onto the seat and set off, taking his place in a line of traffic waiting to negotiate the automatic gates. Pope was at the barrier when he realised that he had left the money in the trunk. He was about to stop and get out when he saw a ticket in the central cupholder. He took it, fed it into the slot and shook his head in reluctant admiration as the gate jerked up to let him through. Atari was ridiculously thorough. He could be irritating, but that was a trait Pope knew would come in useful before this trip was over.

Outside, waves of heat radiated up from the baked asphalt. The city of Chihuahua was to the west, a collection of low buildings encircled by the ragged peaks of the Sierra Madre. Pope thought of the pistol in the trunk and started to give a little more consideration to how he was going to accomplish what he had come here to do.

Chapter Thirty-Seven

I sabella woke up with a sore back, and she needed to stretch out the kinks. She worked through the exercises that she had put together to keep herself limber. She started with her feet and worked up her body, ending with five hundred crunches and then a hundred pull-ups using the bars of the cell. It was stuffy in the basement, and she was quickly damp with perspiration.

They had kept her in the cell for three days, with short breaks for exercise in the yard behind the station. She had been visited by someone from the embassy in Mexico City yesterday, and the woman and del Castillo had made sure she could be kept out of federal prison until her first hearing. Del Castillo had said that she could only keep her here until then; it was likely she would be transferred after the hearing.

Isabella hoped it wouldn't come to that.

The other women watched her exercise. Most of the prisoners from the previous night had been removed from the cell as the police station came to life; Isabella guessed that they would be processed, and either charged or released depending on the strength of the cases against them. Six newcomers had arrived in their places, and now they were lounging on the bench around the perimeter of the cage. From the belligerent stares they shone at her as she exercised, Isabella wearily accepted that she was going to have to give another demonstration to buy herself a further day's peace. Two of the women appeared to know each other, and they conspired together, punctuating their conversation with inimical glances in Isabella's direction.

Isabella had decided not to wait and was about to get up and go over to them when the door to the basement opened and del Castillo came inside. The two women settled down as the detective spoke with the guard, who then came across to the cage.

'Isabella,' the detective said, pointing at Isabella. 'Here.'

Isabella got up and went to the bars. 'What's happening?' she asked.

'You're being taken to court,' del Castillo said.

'Why?'

'Your hearing. You are going to be charged.'

The detective shackled Isabella's wrists through the slot in the bars and then indicated that she should step back so the door could be opened. Isabella did as she was told, making her way out into the basement and then up the stairs to the first floor. She waited for the detective to open the door at the top and went into the reception space that she had been brought to when she arrived at the station. They continued on to the exit at the rear of the building and went outside into the yard. It was hot, with the sun already blazing down onto the compound.

'What time is it?' Isabella asked.

'Ten fifteen. Your hearing is at eleven.'

There was a Mercedes Sprinter in the yard with its rear doors open. It had been fitted out as prisoner transport: a closed compartment had been fashioned in the rear of the vehicle, and Isabella could see a row of bench seats down each side. There were two uniformed police officers – one male and the other female – waiting outside the van.

The detective removed her hand from Isabella's shoulder. She was about to say something, but stopped. She looked frazzled. She was probably busy in a precinct like this, and time spent on a prisoner who was blasé about her prospects was time that could be better spent elsewhere, even if that prisoner was young and apparently heedless of the gravity of the situation that she faced.

The uniformed policeman took Isabella by the arm and led her to the van. Isabella got into the back and sat down. Her cuffs were attached to a bracket that had been fitted to the bench; she sat with a leg either side of it. The compartment was separated from the front of the van by a thick mesh screen. Isabella was able to look through the screen and then out through the windshield; she saw the other cars and vehicles in the compound and, beyond the fence, the peaks of the mountain range in the distance.

Three other female prisoners were brought outside and put into the back of the van. They were all hard-faced and none of them looked at her.

'Isabella,' del Castillo said.

Isabella looked back.

The detective held up a hand. 'Good luck.'

The female officer shut the rear door and got into the driver's seat. Her male colleague joined her alongside. The engine started and the driver reversed the van, turning the wheel and rolling towards the gate.

Isabella felt a tremble of adrenaline.

Chapter Thirty-Eight

There was a strip mall on the north side of Highway 16. The road was busy here, with three lanes running northeast and three running southwest. Pope had parked his car in the forecourt of Pollo Feliz, a takeout restaurant offering cheap boxes of chicken pieces and fries. There was also a pharmacy, a hair salon and a branch of the Oxxo grocery chain. The positioning of the mall was convenient; Pope had reversed his rental car into a parking space so that he could look out through the windshield across the traffic to the entrance that led into the police compound.

Pope had been here for an hour. Atari had sent a series of documents that he had been able to read on the long flight: a summary of the interview that Isabella had given after her arrest; confirmation that the police were recommending that she be charged for armed robbery; the corresponding change on her arrest record; and notification that she was to be handed over to the prosecutor for the first hearing of her case. Atari said that Isabella would not be released on bail, and that it was most likely that she would be taken to a local prison after the hearing. Pope knew that the best chance of retrieving her would be before that happened. Atari had been given firm intelligence that she would be moved, and there was no guarantee he would be able to provide any other intel once she had been passed into longer-term custody. There would be little chance of breaking her out of a jail, either.

The odds of success were best now. He didn't want to wait.

Pope had found a map of Chihuahua in the glovebox and had plotted out the most likely route along which Isabella would be taken. The courthouse in Chihuahua was located on Avenue Benito Juárez, near to the Catedral Metropolitana. They would travel on Federal Highway 16 from the police station, turn onto Avenue 20 de Noviembre and then take Calle 11. Google suggested that the four and a half kilometres would be covered in seven minutes, although it also suggested that the traffic was often heavy.

He had bought a box of chicken pieces from the restaurant. The box was on the seat next to him and he reached inside, snagged a wing and took a bite. It was the first thing he had eaten since he had taken off. He had skipped the bland meals that the airlines had provided on his flights between Vietnam, Japan and Mexico, and had spent most of the time drinking miniatures of whiskey. When the attendants had stopped serving him, he had slept. He had woken somewhere over the Pacific with an unpleasant hangover that was rendered even worse by the dryness of the ventilated air. The chicken was stringy and coated in grease, but he was hungry and he didn't have time to be fussy.

He thought he saw something across the road. He tossed the unfinished chicken bone back into the box, collected the binoculars and put them to his eyes. A van was passing through the gate that led to the police compound. Pope held the glasses steady and watched as it rolled down the slope and waited to turn left onto the highway. It was a black Mercedes Sprinter, with a grille on the hood that could be moved up to cover the windshield and tinted windows on either side. 'POLICIA LOCAL' was written along the side.

Pope put the glasses on the seat next to the takeout box, started the engine and rolled the car to the edge of the lot. The lights changed and the van pulled out, crossing the eastbound traffic and joining the line of cars, trucks and pickups that were headed west. Pope gave it a short head start before he nosed out onto the road, muscling into a narrow space and ignoring the angry gesticulation from the driver whom he had forced to brake.

The Sprinter was fifteen cars ahead, in the middle lane, waiting for the lights to change. Pope was comfortable with that. He didn't want to get too close, yet he didn't want to drop too far behind, either. He knew where it was going. He would stay back for most of the way to ensure that he was correct about its route, and then, when he was sure, he would get ahead so he could be at the courthouse before it arrived. There was no reason to think that Isabella would be accorded any special attention. She was just a girl, and their lack of concern was flagged by the fact that she was in a normal van rather than one of the armoured trucks that the police around here often used; those were more akin to military troop transports and would have presented a whole host of problems for him. This van was less of a concern. Pope was confident that he would be able to get to her.

The lights changed to green and the line of cars slowly moved forward.

Pope followed.

Chapter Thirty-Nine

Isabella shuffled across the seat, trying to arrange herself so that the metal bench was a little less uncomfortable. She looked up and glanced through the front window. They had been travelling for ten minutes. The driver and the guard were relaxed, listening to a local radio station that played Spanish pop between interminable ads for local businesses. The other prisoners were quiet, either staring down at the floor or watching out of the window as they drew closer to the courthouse. Isabella guessed that, for most of them, this would not be a new experience. None of them looked nervous; instead, they displayed a boredom and cynicism that marked them out as habitual criminals.

The van slowed as the traffic congealed around a junction. There was an empty billboard to their left and a Pemex gas station to their right. There was a side road that led up a hill immediately after the gas station; halfway up that road, Isabella saw a delivery truck with two passengers inside the cab. The driver had parked twenty feet up the hill; there was no traffic requiring him to do that, and it didn't look as if he were making a delivery. The angle allowed the occupants of the van a clear view of the main road. As the police truck edged a little closer, Isabella saw that the driver had his hands on the wheel. The smoke from the exhaust indicated that the engine was running, too.

Rather than the usual brown of the delivery company's uniform, the men were dressed in black.

And they were wearing ski masks over their heads.

Isabella checked the driver of their van. She was talking to the officer in the passenger seat, tapping her fingers on the steering wheel as the latest Rihanna song played on the radio. She was distracted. Hadn't seen a thing.

Isabella braced herself, planting her feet a little farther apart, pressing her shoulders back against the wall and reaching down to grab onto the restraining bracket with both hands.

Maia had spoken about this.

She had known that it would happen.

Their enemies had found her after a year of frustration, and now they couldn't resist taking the bait.

The traffic moved ahead. The police van reached the gas station and the delivery truck rumbled into life. It sped down the hill, passed the bar on the corner and rushed directly at them.

The police driver didn't see the danger until it was much too late.

The truck crashed into the right-hand side of the van. Isabella gripped the edge of the bench tight as they were swung around madly by the impact, bouncing into a car in the stationary line of eastbound traffic and spinning through two full revolutions before the van overbalanced and tipped over onto its side.

Isabella's side of the van lurched up into the air and she was thrown off the bench.

Chapter Forty

Pope followed the van as it approached the junction with Avenue 20 de Noviembre and went straight on. It was taking a more indirect route, perhaps to avoid traffic. The lights flicked to orange as Pope approached them and, rather than stop, he put his foot down and raced across the intersection. The driver of the car merging from the right sounded his horn and Pope winced at his appalling tradecraft. He knew that anyone with an ounce of awareness in the van would make him immediately, but he was prepared to gamble that the two cops he had seen in the front were little more than glorified taxi drivers, and that they wouldn't be paying attention to their surroundings. The van moved on as if nothing had happened; Pope crossed his fingers and hoped that he had got away with his rookie move.

He was wearing the phone's hands-free kit, and he dialled the single number on the SIM's memory.

'Isabella is moving,' Pope reported. 'I'm behind them.'

'Maia?' Atari asked.

'No sign of her, or anyone else.'

'When are you going to do it?'

'Outside the courthouse. Either before they go in or when they come out.'

'Be careful, captain. You're on—'

Atari continued to speak, but Pope didn't hear him. The police van was approaching the next junction. There was a gas station to the right, with a side road that climbed a steep hill heading north. Pope saw the delivery truck facing down the slope. He watched it start down towards the busy junction, picking up speed and aiming at the prison van with an accuracy and an intention that made it very clear that what was about to happen was not an unfortunate accident.

The impact was sudden and vicious, and the crunch of the rending metal was easily audible above the usual sounds of the busy road. The prison van was knocked off course; it skidded across the road, crashing into the stationary line of eastbound traffic, spun around twice and then toppled over onto its side.

The truck was brought to a controlled stop. It rolled forward for a few extra yards until it blocked the way for any traffic that might have tried to go around the accident and continue west.

'Captain?'

Pope ignored Atari and got out of the car. He glanced up at the hill beyond the gas station as a man in a ski mask walked down the slope to the highway. The man was wearing all black and had come out of another van that was parked on the hill; this one was a dirty white colour and it was pointed up the slope. He was holding a machine pistol in one hand and a pair of long-handled bolt cutters in the other. The man passed a bar on the corner and kept going, walking calmly, moving behind the crashed truck and out of Pope's line of vision.

There were nine cars between Pope and the crash, arranged three abreast in three rows. Pope walked between the eastbound and westbound traffic and pulled his pistol from its holster.

The driver of a Ford that had only narrowly missed being sideswiped by the truck got out of his car and went up to the driver's window. Pope was four cars away, but he could hear the noise as the man thumped his fist against the window. There were two men inside the truck, both of them wearing masks; the driver opened his door and stepped down to the street. Pope's view was obscured by the angry driver, but he heard the crack of a gunshot and saw the man topple backwards.

A woman in the car next to Pope screamed. Pope paused. The driver from the van was carrying a pistol. Pope gripped his Sig in both hands, aimed for the body and fired. Both rounds found their mark, striking the man in the torso. He stumbled back against the side of the truck and slid down until he was resting on his backside. The woman screamed again.

The passenger was still inside the truck. Pope sighted him through the open driver's side door and fired three rounds. One missed, slamming into the dash and detonating the airbag, and the second passed through the cabin and out the other side. The third round caught the passenger in the thigh. Pope was rewarded with a scream of pain.

Pope kept the gun levelled and moved ahead. He was about to fire again when he saw a flash of motion in his peripheral vision. He turned just in time to see another man come out from the rear of the dirty white van up the hill. He was wearing black clothes and boots, and his face, too, was covered by a black mask. The man was holding a long gun in both hands, and as Pope came to a stop and looked for cover, the man shouldered it and aimed in his direction.

Automatic gunfire rang out, a rattle that preceded the thudding of 9mm rounds as they crashed into the bodywork of the line of cars. Pope dropped down to his haunches between them, shielded by an Acura to his right. The woman screamed again. The fusillade continued, with a round passing through the Acura and blowing out the windshield. Glass was tossed out of the frame and onto Pope as he lowered himself to the ground, the asphalt hot against his cheek as he pressed himself flat and looked underneath the Acura and across the road. The shooter was still there, his weapon aimed in Pope's direction, the muzzle flashing out an irregular starburst of fire.

'Pope,' Atari's voice said in his ear.

Pope ejected the half-spent magazine and slapped in a fresh one.

'Pope – what's happening?'

'The van's been hit.'

'By who?'

The occupants of the cars on the highway panicked. They got out of their vehicles and started to run. The driver of the car ahead of Pope put his Citroen into gear and tried to move out of the way. The car crashed against the one in front of it, reversed, and crashed into the car behind. Pope got up and inched forward, bumping against the men and women who were fleeing to either side of him. He stayed low, in the cover of the cars, jostling a man out of the way as he tried to reach a place from which he might be able to return fire.

'Who is it, Pope?'

He reached the gap between the Acura and the Citroen and stood, aiming his Sig over the hood of the car in front. He managed to get a shot off, but there was no time to aim and the round went nowhere near its target, cracking into the wall of the nearest building with a puff of plaster. The shooter drew a bead on him and fired again. Pope ducked as the volley passed overhead, blowing concrete chunks out of the wall of the garage all the way on the other side of the road.

The Citroen jerked forward and back as its driver tried again and again to get clear, but then its windshield detonated, and blood splashed across what was left of it as the driver was hit. The car slammed into the one ahead of it once more, the engine revving helplessly, the man's foot still pressed down on the gas.

'Pope!'

'I don't know,' Pope said. 'Are you tracking me?'

'You're at the junction of Highway 16 and Nicolás Bravo.'

'I could do with some of your magic right now.'

Pope used the Citroen as cover, poking his head over the hood as steam jetted out of the punctured radiator. The man in black was still there. He was changing his magazine. Pope rested his arm across the hood, held the Sig in both hands and squeezed off three rounds. He was a hundred and fifty feet away, too close for anything other than a miracle to find its mark, and his luck was out. But the shots went close, and the man scurried back into the shelter of the scruffy van.

Pope thought about what Atari had been able to do in Shanghai. He had bought them precious moments with a series of improbable distractions, and Pope badly needed something similar now.

The shooter was still out of sight. Pope took the opportunity and advanced, making his way from cover to cover until he was behind the truck.

'Come on,' he hissed into the in-line microphone of the hands-free. 'I'm outgunned.'

'I'm working on it.'

Pope pressed himself against the hot metal of the truck and wiped the sweat from his eyes. He was breathing hard and his palms were wet.

He gripped the pistol and readied himself to make a move.

Chapter Forty-One

Isabella looked around. The women in the back of the van were in various states of distress: the two who had been on the same side as her had been thrown across the gap and had crashed against the opposing bench and wall. Neither of them were moving, draped limply with their arms held out behind them, the cuffs still attached to the restraints. The women on the other side of the truck had fared better; they were still on their bench, although they had been flung around. The glass in the windows on their side of the van had broken, with jagged shards pushing inside between the bars. Isabella looked ahead, to the cab. The passenger was still in his seat, held in place by his belt. The driver, on the left of the cabin, had her shoulder through the broken window; her arm was pressed against the ground and she was struggling to undo her seat belt.

The van was still facing in the right direction. Isabella looked through the shattered windshield and saw a single figure walking purposefully towards them. Steam was billowing out of the van's radiator and it obscured her view. She could see enough to guess that the figure was male. She could see that he was dressed in black with a mask on his face and that he was carrying a machine pistol. He was holding a pair of bolt cutters in his left hand, with the pistol held out straight in his right.

The driver managed to undo her belt and reached down for the sidearm that was holstered on her belt.

The man in black aimed the machine pistol and fired a quick burst into the cab. The driver was hit first, her body juddering as the rounds passed through her body, then sliced through the upholstery of her seat and pinged against the metal chassis behind her. The passenger had taken the brunt of the crash and might already have been dead, but the second volley that studded his body right down the centre line made sure of that.

The man passed the front of the truck and made his way around to the rear. Isabella heard a crunch as the bolt cutters snapped through metal, saw the handle turn and then blinked into a sudden blast of light as one of the rear doors fell open. She saw the man's legs first and then the rest of him as he opened the other door. He stepped into the overturned cabin, his boots crunching against the shattered glass, and made his way to Isabella, letting the pistol hang on a strap that he wore over his shoulder. He reached down with his hand to take Isabella's chin and raised her face so that he could look at her. Isabella held his gaze. She could only see his eyes through the slits in the mask, but they were the same pale blue as Maia's.

Isabella heard the sound of three gunshots, and then an answering clatter of automatic fire. She wondered if the police were here, and whether they would be able to upset what had been planned. She hoped not.

The man ignored the firefight. He moved quickly and efficiently, positioning the jaws of the cutters around the chain that connected Isabella's cuffs to the bracket and closing the handles. The chain snapped but Isabella's wrists were still restrained, and the man reached down for the cuffs and grabbed them, dragging her out of the van. The other prisoners watched fearfully, unable to retreat any farther than the play of their chains would allow. But the man gave them no attention, looping his right arm around Isabella's waist and lifting her easily off her feet.

She saw a flash of movement from behind the delivery truck: a man ducked out of cover, a pistol in his hand.

The man was ten feet away.

Isabella recognised him at once.

Pope.

He raised his pistol and aimed it.

The man tightened his grip on Isabella, holding her between his body and Pope. Isabella looked into the barrel of the gun and then up at Pope's face. He looked back at her and their eyes locked; he held the gun steady, but his face twisted with frustration. She knew why: she was in the way and he dared not shoot.

'Put her down,' Pope called out.

Isabella's captor backed away.

Pope's jaw bulged as he grit his teeth. 'Last chance. Put her down.'

He was bluffing. Isabella could see it, and the man behind her must have been able to see it, too. Pope had no shot, not unless he was prepared to take the chance that he might hit her.

Isabella held Pope's gaze and gently shook her head.

He stared at her. Did he understand what she meant?

Her captor retreated.

There was no time for Pope to speak. He dove around the corner of the truck at the same moment as she heard the rattle of automatic gunfire from somewhere behind her, up on the hill. A line of jagged holes was ripped in the flank of the UPS truck.

Her abductor hurried now, carrying Isabella up the hill to a dirty white van she had not noticed before.

She didn't struggle. She had no interest in trying to escape. This was what she wanted. It was what they had planned. The man went around to the back of the van, opened the door and pushed her inside. He clambered inside, slammed the door shut and then slapped his hand against the partition that separated them from the cabin.

The engine growled and the van jerked forward.

Chapter Forty-Two

The glass in the van's rear windows was tinted, but Isabella was able to see out as they hurried away from the wrecked van. They picked up Avenue 20 de Noviembre and raced to the north, hurrying past the Cerro Coronel mountain that dominated this part of the city. They reached the main highway and turned to the east, settling into the fast lane and maintaining a steady speed.

The man who had taken her from the truck brought his hand up to his face to remove the mask. Isabella had never seen him before, and yet he was immediately recognisable. He had blond hair and blue eyes and the shape of his face was not quite symmetrical enough to be attractive, yet indistinct enough that he would be unmemorable.

One of Maia's brothers.

The man reached into his pocket and took out a cell phone. He dialled a number and put the phone to his ear.

'We have her,' he said, speaking in a voice without an accent. There was no inflection at all, his enunciation as flat as his face was without expression.

There was a reply, but Isabella was unable to make anything out save the buzzing of the voice.

'We're on our way now,' the blond man said. 'We'll be there in two hours. I don't foresee any reason for concern. She's compliant.'

He ended the call.

'What's happening?' Isabella asked him.

He stared at her, but didn't respond.

'Where are we going?'

'We want to talk to you,' he said. 'If you do as you're told, you'll be fine.'

The man stared at her, his blue eyes dull and expressionless.

'Who are you?'

'You can call me Ambrose,' he said.

Isabella looked away. She wanted him to think that she was frightened. It wasn't difficult to do that, because she *was* frightened. Things were going the way that they had planned, but that reassurance was not enough to dull the ache that she felt in the pit of her stomach.

They reached the edge of the city and kept driving, heading into an open landscape of scrub and brush, with the mountains forming a jagged horizon in the far distance. There were small farmsteads on either side of the road, and regular elevated billboards carried vast advertisements for businesses in the city behind them. It didn't take much longer before they started to pass signs for the 'Aeropuerto Internacional', and five minutes later, as the driver turned to the left, the terminal buildings came into view in the rear windows.

The driver followed a service road that led to a medium-sized building. They passed through a gate in a wire-mesh fence and, as they stopped, Isabella saw an airstrip behind the building. There was a helicopter on the strip, its blades already spinning. Isabella didn't recognise it, but as Ambrose opened the door and pulled her outside, she could see that it bore the insignia of Manage Risk, the global military conglomerate she knew was involved with Daedalus and the plot into which she and Pope had been sucked.

Ambrose held her by the arm and led her towards the helicopter. His grip was firm, and Isabella knew that she would not be able to break free even if she wanted to. He ducked his head as they entered the downdraught of the chopper, and Isabella closed her eyes and mouth to protect herself from the fragments of grit and debris that had been disturbed by the wash. They still stung her cheeks and forehead and the skin of her arms, but she ignored the discomfort and allowed Ambrose to boost her up into the cabin. He indicated that she should take one of the empty seats and reached across her to secure her safety harness. He sat next to her, fastened his own harness and then stared forward impassively.

The driver of the van jogged up to the helicopter, signalled to Ambrose and received a thumbs-up in return. The man slid the door across and closed it. The pilot opened the throttle and fed power to the engines. The noise grew louder and louder until it was deafening. There was a pair of headphones on a hook next to the seat and Isabella reached her cuffed hands over and awkwardly put them on.

The helicopter lifted off the ground and started ahead, the nose dipping gently as the pilot gathered speed and began a slow climb. They cleared the fence at the side of the facility and turned to the right. Isabella looked down at the dirty van and the terminal buildings spread out below them, and at the medium-sized jets that jockeyed at the gates, watching as one of them lumbered down the runway and launched itself into the air.

Isabella took a breath and tried to settle her nerves. She knew that it was just over three hundred miles from here to the border. The helicopter would likely travel at a hundred and fifty miles an hour. She had two hours to prepare herself for the performance that she would have to put on once they arrived. She had been practising it for weeks, going over it again and again when she went out for her runs, but that had been easy. There were no consequences if her rehearsals were substandard. It didn't matter if things went wrong or if she stumbled over her lines.

Now she would be performing for real, and the ramifications she would face if they didn't believe her would be severe indeed.

Chapter Forty-Three

The police arrived two minutes after the dirty van drove away. Pope's hire car was trapped in the snarl of traffic and there was no prospect of him being able to use it if he wanted to get away and avoid attention. There were plenty of witnesses on the highway who would have seen him shoot the two men in the truck and then engage the man with the automatic rifle. He had no interest in being questioned by the authorities, and so he crossed the highway and walked briskly along Calle Nicolás Bravo to the southwest. Another road joined from the left and Pope took it. There was a building site to his right, with unfinished brick walls and a stack of sewage pipes ready to be lowered into a trench. There was a small white Chevrolet van parked next to the pipes; Pope put a rock through the van's side window, opened the door from the inside, hot-wired the engine and drove away, headed south.

He had disconnected the call to Atari, but now he dialled the number again.

'What happened?' Atari said.

'They've got her.'

'Who?'

'Our friends. They drove a truck into the police van and busted her out. There were at least four of them, all wearing masks. I shot two of them, but they still got her. Nothing else I could do.'

Atari cursed. 'Which way did they go?'

'You don't have coverage?'

'It's Mexico, Pope. It's practically the third world.'

'Northeast. Towards the airport.'

'I'll see what I can find,' Atari said. 'Where are you now?'

Pope glanced out of the window. The road ended in a junction with Avenue 20 de Noviembre. Pope indicated right and joined the larger road.

'I'm getting out of the area,' he said. 'It's going to get a little warm.'

'Stay in the city,' Atari said. 'I need someone on the ground. I'll try to find out where they've taken her.'

Two police cars rushed by in the opposite direction, their lights flashing and their sirens wailing.

'Call me if you find anything,' Pope said.

He ended the call and slipped the phone back into his pocket. He felt a sudden blast of frustration and slapped the wheel with both hands. He could have taken a shot, but he couldn't have been sure that he would miss Isabella. He had done the right thing, but that didn't mean he felt any better about it.

He had let her down again.

He gripped the wheel and accelerated. He would find her. He had abandoned her once before, and he wouldn't do that again. It was his fault she was caught up in this mess.

He was going to make things right.

Chapter Forty-Four

New Mexico

I t was difficult to keep track of their route from the cabin of the helicopter. The pilot took them up to altitude and then prepared the helicopter for a smooth and easy cruise. Isabella was able to look out of the window and could see that they were headed due north. It looked as if they were following the route of the 45D, the highway they had taken on their way out of Juárez. She thought that she recognised some of the towns they passed over, and she was sure she could identify the swathe of green that made up the protected national park at Médanos de Samalayuca. They took a sharp turn to port and passed around Juárez itself, the sprawl of the city running up against the natural border of the river and then the conjoined twin of El Paso beyond it. Finally, they turned to the east and started to descend.

Their destination was obvious now: it was a very large military complex, as big as a town. She saw rows and rows of buildings, a network of roads and a mixture of military and civilian vehicles. The base had been built on a wide plain in the shadow of a large mountain range, the foothills rising to jagged peaks on the horizon.

They were descending to a landing strip. She saw a big cargo plane at the end of the apron and counted five helicopters, one of which lifted into the air and passed them as they continued their descent. The pilot touched them down gently and went through the procedure of checking the systems before he shut them off.

Ambrose undid his harness and reached across to undo Isabella's, taking the headphones from her head and replacing them on their mount. A man in olive fatigues jogged out across the apron towards them, holding on to his cap as he stepped into the rotor wash. He opened the door and stood aside as Ambrose disembarked. Isabella noticed the same Manage Risk insignia on his lapel as she had seen on the fuselage of the helicopter, and as she got down to join Ambrose, she saw it two more times: once on the side of the jeep that had brought the man out to meet them, and once again on a tall sign at the edge of the landing strip.

'We're ready for you, sir,' the soldier said to Ambrose, leading the way back across the strip to the jeep.

Isabella got into the back of the vehicle and Ambrose sat alongside her.

'Where is this?' she asked him.

'Fort Bliss.'

Isabella was surprised to have received an answer and pressed her luck. 'Why am I here?'

'No more questions.'

The soldier put the jeep into gear and they set off, leaving the airstrip through a manned gate and driving deeper into the facility. They drove for five minutes before the driver turned off and followed a narrower road that led to a series of low-slung buildings that were encircled by a tall fence. Isabella saw the Manage Risk insignia once more as a gate was pushed back and the driver brought them inside the compound. Then he stopped, got out of the jeep and went around to let Ambrose and Isabella disembark.

'This way, sir,' the soldier said, leading them into the nearest building.

Isabella watched for anything that might distinguish it, but saw nothing. It was a single storey, with blacked-out windows and an array of communications equipment on its roof. She looked beyond it, scouting the compound: there were armed soldiers on the gate, and outside the fence she saw two patrols cross on their circuits – two teams of two men, each team with a dog. Traffic passed on the road that they had used to get here; above, an arrowhead formation of three Apaches clattered noisily by.

The soldier led the way inside. There was a woman at a desk in the room beyond; the man conferred with her, signed a form on a clipboard and indicated to Ambrose that they should follow him. Isabella was prodded in the back and continued inside, turning down a corridor that led to a wider space that was faced on all sides by doors. They were sturdy doors, made of metal, and they each had a peephole that could only be opened from outside. There was a guard in the reception space; the soldier took a tablet from the man and tapped in a series of details, handed it back and stood aside. The guard pressed a button and one of the doors buzzed as it was unlocked. The door opened and the soldier went across to pull it back all the way.

Ambrose nudged Isabella once more. The idea of confinement here – of being locked up in the middle of a military facility totally at the whim of the company that had tormented her mother and then chased her and Pope around the world – was disturbing, but she knew she had no choice. She was here now, the plan was afoot and there could be no backing away from it.

She kept reminding herself: this was what they had planned for.

It was what they wanted to happen.

And Maia would be there when she needed her.

Isabella stepped through the door. It was a cell. There was a bed, a toilet behind a low wall and a metal chair. There was nothing else.

Isabella went over to a single, barred window in the opposite wall and looked out. She thought of Maia and wondered where she was. She had no way of knowing. Their plan called for Maia to make the final preparations, but now Isabella found that she was assailed by a wave of doubt. What if Maia changed her mind? What if she decided to disappear? Because, at the end of it all, what did she owe Isabella? Nothing, not really. Certainly nothing that would compel her to put her own life or liberty at risk by following through with a plan that Isabella was worried, now, was the height of foolishness. Surely Maia would realise the folly of it and leave. They would never see each other again.

She closed her eyes and found a central point of calm.

No.

That wouldn't happen.

They were both invested in following events through to their conclusion.

Maia wanted Ivanosky for the murder of Aleksandra Litivenko in Washington.

They both wanted to unpick the conspiracy that they had facilitated.

The only way that they could get what they wanted was for Isabella to find her strength and follow this path to its end.

She stepped away from the window and lay down on the bed. It was early in the afternoon, but she was tired. She knew that she would need all of her strength for the days ahead. She closed her eyes again and listened to the clatter of another helicopter as it passed overhead. It was just fading into the steady hum of the base's natural noise when Isabella drifted away to sleep.

Chapter Forty-Five

I sabella woke up after a fitful and unsatisfactory rest, and when she went to the window, she saw that the sun had almost set. The day's last glow was fast descending beneath the mountains on the horizon, painting the sky with a palette of reds and purples and oranges. The base was as busy as it had been when she had last looked, with vehicles rumbling along the road beyond the periphery of the wire-mesh fence.

She turned at the sound of the door being unlocked. It opened and two people came inside: a man and a woman. The man came in first. He was older, wearing a pair of wire-framed glasses that sparkled against his wrinkled, leathery skin. The woman was short, with long black hair that she wore tied back and a pair of glasses that lent her face a stern and severe aspect. The man closed the door and stayed by it. The woman came all the way inside.

'Hello, Isabella,' she said, smiling. It looked wrong on her face, as if she had only been able to manage it with effort.

'Who are you?'

'I'm Doctor Quayle. I work for Daedalus Genetics. Do you know what that is?'

'Yes,' Isabella said.

'Did Maia talk to you about it?' Quayle mentioned Maia's name easily and naturally, without ascribing any special value to it.

'Yes,' Isabella replied. She looked over at the man by the door. 'Who are you?'

'Doctor Ivanosky,' he said.

Maia had described Ivanosky, and had said that he, more than anyone, wouldn't be able to resist the bait. Isabella felt a shiver of anticipation. It was working. Now she had to sell it.

'He's a colleague,' Quayle explained. She went over to the bed and sat. She patted the mattress next to her. 'Come and sit down,' she said.

Isabella stayed where she was. 'I know why I'm here,' she said.

'You do?'

'You want to know where I've been for the last year,' she said.

Quayle smiled again, baring a mouthful of small white teeth. She reminded Isabella of a piranha. 'You're right, Isabella. We do.'

'Shall we make this quick? What you *really* want is to know about Maia.'

Quayle chuckled. 'We do.'

'So Bloom got my message then?'

'We're not here for Mr Bloom,' she said. 'We've been working with Maia. And, yes, you're right. We'd like to know what's happened to her, very much.'

'I want to propose an exchange,' Isabella said. 'I tell you everything you want to know about the last year, and everything I know about Maia . . .'

'And what do you want?'

'You take me to Morocco with new papers and enough money for me to get on with my life. You get what you want, and you'll never hear from me again.'

'Morocco?'

'I used to live there,' she said. 'And they don't have an extradition treaty with the United States or Mexico.'

'You've been thinking about this a lot.'

'I was locked up in a Mexican jail for three days,' Isabella said. 'I've had a lot of time to think.' She looked at Quayle. 'Well?'

'It's an interesting offer. Maybe. But you'll need to cooperate. You need to answer all of my questions. Everything. Do you understand?'

'I do. But I'm not going to say anything until you agree to give me what I want.'

Quayle shook her head. 'It's not going to work like that, Isabella. You have to demonstrate your good faith. You need us more than we need you.'

'Really?'

'Have you seen the inside of a Mexican prison? A real one – not the police cell they kept you in? They'll give you ten years for what you did. You won't come out until you're in the middle of your twenties, and that's if you come out at all. We *will* help, Isabella, but you have to give us good value. And you have to give it to us first.'

'Then we have a stalemate. I'm not saying anything until I know I'm going to get what I want.'

Quayle looked over at Ivanosky; Isabella saw him give a slight incline of his head.

'Okay,' Quayle said. 'We'll take you to Morocco.'

Isabella had known that it would be easy enough to extract the concession from them, and that the concession would be worthless. She knew, of course, that they could not be trusted. She didn't know how they would assess her, but her hope was that they wouldn't credit a six-teen-year-old with the wisdom to see through a false promise. But when all was said and done, whatever they offered her was an irrelevance. She wasn't going to Morocco. She just needed them to take the bait.

'Fine,' she said. 'What do you want to know?'

'You're ready to talk now?' the woman asked.

'Yes.'

Quayle gave a nod. 'Good. Let's go back to Clingmans Dome. You were with Captain Pope?'

Isabella nodded. She noticed Ivanosky pay closer attention.

'I was,' she said.

'He had arranged to swap Maia for his family. There was an incident—'

'You mean you betrayed him,' Isabella corrected.

Ivanosky stood a little straighter. 'What happened to him?'

'I'm sorry,' Isabella said. 'Who did you say you were?'

'Answer the question,' he snapped.

'I don't know,' Isabella said.

That would have been the honest answer until the events of this morning; the last that she had seen of him before today was when they parted ways on the road that led to the parking lot at the top of the mountain. She knew that he had taken position in the trees that clung to the flanks of the mountain, and she knew that he had provided covering fire during the exfiltration, but that was all she could say. She had wondered about what had happened to him and his family many times in the year that had passed, but Maia had made it very clear that he was probably dead – and, in any event, there was no way for her to know. Pope would have had no choice but to disappear, just like she and Maia had. Even if they had been able to find him, to communicate would have been dangerous.

'You must have an idea,' the woman pressed.

'I don't. I was going to get out on the helicopter with his family and he was going to leave on foot. But then one of your agents pulled me off the helicopter. I don't know whether Pope is alive or dead. Him or his family. I don't know what happened to any of them.'

'So tell us what happened to you. Were you hurt?'

'I broke my leg.'

'And then?'

'Maia took me.'

'Where did you go?'

'West. She found a place in the middle of nowhere. She said it was a house that she had used before. I think it was in Tennessee. It was quiet. The place was empty. There was no one for miles.'

'How long did you stay there?'

'Long enough for her to set my leg.'

'She did it herself?'

Isabella nodded.

'That's nonsensical,' Ivanosky said. 'Why would she do that? You were nothing to her. You would only have slowed her down.'

'I don't know,' Isabella said. 'You'd have to ask her.'

Ivanosky snorted derisively.

Quayle continued. 'And then?'

'We stayed there for two days. She said that she wanted to keep moving. I think she was worried that you would be able to find her.'

'Where next?'

'Mexico. She had false papers. We crossed at El Paso and found somewhere to stay in Juárez.'

'You were in Juárez? For how long?'

'Most of the year.'

'And then?'

'We headed south.'

'Why?'

'We were going to head to Venezuela. She said she knew someone who could help me get home.'

'Just you and Maia?' Ivanosky said. 'Happy families?'

Isabella shrugged. 'You asked me. It's the truth.'

'What about the practicalities?' Quayle said. 'What did you do for money?'

'We robbed the cartel. Maia had a contact. Someone she met in Juárez – a man. He told her when and where they brought their money over the border. We waited for them. We ambushed a truck when it arrived and took the money.'

She could be reasonably candid, but she needed to be creative with the timings so she didn't undermine what would come next.

Ivanosky remained unconvinced. 'And you stayed with her all this time? You didn't try to get away?'

'Why would I do that? She was helping me. She fixed my leg. She helped me get away, and then she showed me how to stay hidden. I didn't want you to find me and she didn't want to be found, either. She kept me safe.'

'What – you were *friends*?'

'I suppose so.'

'Don't be so ridiculous,' he spluttered.

Quayle persevered, evidently trying to deflect Ivanosky's irascibility. 'Why would she stay with you? It's very out of character. She must have said something.'

'I don't know,' Isabella replied. 'Maybe she was lonely.'

Ivanosky snorted again. 'They don't *get* lonely. They don't have feelings.'

'Then I don't know what else to say.'

He came farther into the room, passing through a shaft of grey light that placed faint shadows in the crevices around his eyes and mouth. 'You said she *was* helping you. You used the past tense. What happened?'

Isabella's throat felt dry; this was it. 'We got to Chihuahua. Maia had a place for us to stay. This old RV, in the middle of the desert. We went into Chihuahua to get supplies and the cartel found us. They followed us and forced us off the road. They would have killed us both, but Maia fought them off. There were three of them. She killed all of them, but they shot her. I got her into the car and drove us away. We went back to the RV. I knew we couldn't continue – she was badly hurt.' She rested her fingers against her stomach. 'The bullet went in here. I tried, but I couldn't stop it bleeding.'

Quayle looked across the room at Ivanosky. 'What are you saying? She's dead?'

171

Isabella nodded.

Quayle glanced over at Ivanosky again, this time with a frown. 'And then?' she said.

'I didn't know what to do. The car was shot up, and it wouldn't start. I didn't know where the money was – I didn't have anything, so I robbed a store. I was going to use the cash to buy a plane ticket to Morocco.' Isabella shrugged helplessly. 'But I got caught. They were going to send me to prison. I didn't have anything else that I could do.'

'So you told the police you wanted to speak to your embassy.'

'Yes.'

'About Maia?'

'Because I knew that someone would notice. I couldn't think of any other way to get help. Like I said – out of options.'

Ivanosky shook his head. 'I don't believe you,' he said. 'I don't believe any of it.'

'What more do you want me to say?'

'I want you to tell us the truth, you little bitch, not a pack of lies because you think it's what we want to hear. We're not naïve. Do you really think we'll forget all the trouble you caused and just send you off to start your life again?' He shook his head. 'No. That's not how this is going to go at all.'

'You said you'd let me go.' Isabella turned to Quayle. 'I've told you what I know. It's the truth.'

The woman shrugged. 'I'm afraid I agree with Doctor Ivanosky. It's all very unlikely.'

It was time. The bait had been dangled long enough. Isabella swallowed on a dry throat and prepared to play the card she knew they would never be able to resist.

'What about if I took you to her?'

'What?' Ivanosky said.

'You know where she is?' Quayle said, betraying her enthusiasm.

'I buried her. I can take you there.'

Chapter Forty-Six

Isabella struggled for sleep again, eventually lulled by the sound of the military equipment that rumbled beyond the window of her cell. She woke before dawn to the noise of movement outside the door, then slid off the bed and rinsed her face to banish the last remnants of sleep. She was drying herself as the door opened. The two from yesterday – Quayle and Ivanosky – were there. Ivanosky came inside, leaving Quayle in the antechamber.

'Miss Rose,' the old man said, 'I'm sorry about yesterday. I lost my temper. I shouldn't have done that.'

Isabella didn't answer.

Ivanosky sat down on the side of the bed. 'Did Maia speak to you about me?'

'Yes.'

'What did she say?'

'That you worked with her.'

He nodded. 'I worked with her for many years. I was very fond of her.'

He put his hands down and slowly levered himself upright. 'You offered to take us to her body. You know where she is?'

'I buried her. I know exactly where she is.'

'And she was shot?'

Isabella nodded. Ivanosky looked as if he was still considering everything that Isabella had told them. It was clear that he was senior, and that he would be the one that would make the decision. Maia had predicted that he would weigh his curiosity against a natural distrustfulness, and Isabella found herself digging her nails into the palms of her hands as she waited, hoping that his curiosity would win out.

'All right,' Ivanosky said. 'We will fly to Mexico.'

'When?'

'Now. Where did you bury her? Chihuahua, yes?'

'South of there.'

'Please, Isabella, one thing: don't try to mislead me. I can be your friend, and you need a friend very badly now. If you take advantage of my friendship, I won't be inclined to help you. There are people here who would be very happy to take you back to the Mexican police. There are other people here who think that would be too generous after the trouble that you and Mr Pope caused. But it doesn't matter what they think. I make the decision. I can help you, but only if I think that I can trust you. Can I do that? Can I trust you?'

She looked into his eyes and held his gaze. 'Why would I lie?' she said. 'I don't have anyone else who can help me. I just want to go home.'

Chapter Forty-Seven

They came back for Isabella thirty minutes later. She heard the sound of footsteps in the lobby outside her room, followed by voices and then the key in the lock. She slid off her bed and stood as the door opened. There were two people outside: Quayle, and a man wearing black fatigues and heavy black boots. This man – Isabella could tell that he was military – came inside first.

'Hands,' he said.

She didn't protest, raising her hands and holding them together as the soldier took a pair of cuffs and attached them to her wrists.

'Good morning, Miss Rose,' Quayle said.

'Where is Doctor Ivanosky?'

'We'll meet him on the apron.'

She was solicitous, but her words were underpinned by an eagerness that was impossible to miss. Maia had been right: they were all desperate for news about what had happened to their lost asset, and that desperation had overridden any caution that might have meant they were more circumspect in how they reacted to the story and to Isabella's offer. Maia had explained Ivanosky's character, that he was arrogant and overbearing, and she had predicted that he would refuse to delegate this particular task to someone else. So far, her assessment of him and how he would react had been unerringly accurate.

'Are you ready?'

'Yes,' Isabella replied. 'The sooner I get out of here, the better.'

'If you take us to Maia, everything will be taken care of.'

Quayle's lies were as obvious as her enthusiasm. Isabella knew there was no way they would just let her walk. There was no way they would return her to the Mexicans, either. She knew too much. They would check out her intelligence and, once they had satisfied themselves that she had nothing left to offer, she would be disappeared. A shot to the back of the head in the desert, or a fall from the helicopter as it returned north. Whatever happened, she knew that she would be taking a one-way trip.

The guard led the way out of the building to a blacked-out SUV bearing the Manage Risk insignia. A driver was waiting inside the vehicle, the engine running. Quayle got in first, sliding all the way across the seat so that Isabella could follow. The guard came next, pressing up against Isabella so she was squeezed between them. Quayle told the driver to drive. They left the compound through the gate and set off back towards the airfield.

Quayle turned so that she could look at Isabella. 'We're going to take a helicopter,' she said. 'Where are we going? I know you said south of Chihuahua. But where?'

'Follow Route 16 to just before the junction with Route 24. There's a place just after there – Rancho de Peña.'

'It's near there?'

'Yes.'

'What kind of place?'

'It's an old junkyard. There's a hut. She said she'd been there before.'

'And that's where you buried her?'

'Yes,' Isabella said. 'There's a camp just outside it.'

Quayle said something to the driver; he, in turn, spoke into a radio that he had clipped to his jacket. He looked like a soldier, too. Isabella wondered if that was to be the full complement today – two soldiers and two scientists – or whether they would be joined by more.

The SUV passed through the gate onto the landing strip and Isabella saw that it was going to be more. There were two helicopters waiting for them. She recognised them as Bell UH-1Y Venoms. Super Hueys. Utility helicopters that could perform a number of functions, they were typically used by the United States Marine Corps.

A group of four soldiers had gathered on the apron near to the aircraft, checking their weapons and other equipment. The SUV pulled up beside them and the soldier next to Isabella stepped out. He reached back inside the vehicle and helped Isabella to disembark. The four men watched her emerge, one of them turning to his colleague and saying something that provoked a chuckle. Isabella could guess what he had said: *All this security for one sixteen-year-old girl.* But it wasn't for her, of course. Maia was something else, and Ivanosky knew it. He was being careful, just as he should.

A second car pulled up and Ivanosky stepped out. He walked across to them.

'Are you ready, Isabella?'

'Yes.'

The soldier looked over at the doctor, received a sharp nod that he should proceed and, with his hand on Isabella's shoulder, he impelled her towards one of the Hueys.

'This had better not be a wild goose chase,' he muttered into her ear as they approached the bird. 'I fucking hate Mexico.'

Isabella didn't reply. She let the soldier lead her to the open door and clambered inside. He indicated that she should take the seat on the far side of the cabin and she did, sitting down as he buckled the safety harness around her. Quayle got in next, sitting opposite Isabella.

Ivanosky followed, and then the soldier closed the door and sat down diagonally opposite Isabella.

The pilot started the engines, the rotors slowly beginning to turn. Isabella looked out of the window next to her and saw the four soldiers gathering their equipment and making their way to the second chopper, which was also going through its start-up routine.

The soldier pointed to the headphones next to each seat and indicated that they should put them on. Ivanosky put on his own pair and then helped Isabella with hers. There was a microphone on an arm attached to the side of one of the headphones, and he moved it around so it was in front of her mouth.

'Can you hear me, Isabella?' he said.

'Yes.'

'We'll need to keep these on so we can hear each other. The pilot can hear you, too. You'll need to tell him where to go when we get there. Do you understand?'

'Yes.'

'Two hundred and thirty miles to destination,' the pilot reported, his voice clear over the growing whine of the engines. 'Flight time will be ninety minutes. We'll be there for zero-eight-hundred hours.'

'Let's get started,' Ivanosky said.

The pilot slowly increased the thrust until the Super Huey lifted up into the air. They started forward, cleared the fence and then tracked around until they were facing south. Isabella saw the second helicopter gain altitude as it settled into close formation behind them. She turned away from the window, leaning back in the seat and concentrating on her breathing. Her heart was racing. Ninety minutes. It wasn't long. She assessed the odds. There were five armed soldiers, two pilots and two co-pilots and two scientists.

Maia had anticipated a heavy presence, and she had been right.

Isabella hoped that she was ready.

Chapter Forty-Eight

Mexico

The day's new sun painted the clouds on the horizon in yellows and oranges as they passed over the southern outskirts of Chihuahua. The pilot picked up the route of Highway 16, swooping across the landscape as they traced its path to the south. They passed a large body of water on the right of the road that Isabella remembered from the scouting that she and Maia had undertaken together, and then they flew over the small hamlets that gathered around the highway.

They continued for another five minutes until Isabella saw a turn-off that she recognised. There was a white wall and a white gate that only partially blocked the way ahead. The track was unpaved and continued west towards a series of steep hills.

'There,' she said, pointing.

Ivanosky looked out through the same window. 'That track?'

'Yes,' she said. 'Follow it.'

'Follow the track,' Ivanosky said to the pilot over the intercom, and after a quick word of acknowledgement, the man nudged his stick to bring the chopper around. He reduced their altitude, too, until they were just a hundred feet above the ground.

The track wound left and right, carving a lazy path through the foothills as the land started to ascend towards the higher ground. Isabella realised that she was clenching her fists and, anxious not to betray her nerves, she opened them and laid her hands in her lap. The cuffs restricted her movement significantly; she had hoped that they might have removed them by now, but it seemed as if she was going to have to improvise as best she could.

'How much farther?' Ivanosky said.

Isabella waited a moment to answer until she saw the shack. She pointed. 'There,' she said.

She looked down as they flew over the settlement. There was a collection of buildings to the south of the track, shielded by stands of trees that had grown up on either side of a desiccated riverbed. They had first found this place in the winter, when a fast-flowing stream ran along the bed, water pouring down from the mountain to irrigate the land. The buildings were gathered around a meadow that had been over-grown when Isabella was last here; it was different now, and the lack of moisture and the battering from the sun had flattened the weeds, with patches of scrub showing from the air. The compound was demarked by a fence made of old tyres that had been arranged between wooden posts. There were three old wooden shacks and a big RV that had been driven here at some point in the past and left to die.

The pilot slowed the Huey and took up position just to the south of the camp. The branches of the trees bowed down in the rotor wash, and eddies of dust were thrown up from the ground.

'There?' Ivanosky said, pointing out of the window.

'Yes,' she said. 'That's where we stayed.'

'Which one?'

She pointed to the abandoned RV. 'In there.'

'And where is her body?'

'I buried her behind the shack on the far side.'

The soldier opposite Isabella spoke over the radio. 'Asset is reported to be buried on the western edge of the compound,' he said.

The second chopper edged forward, pulling slightly away from their Huey so that the men inside it were afforded a better view.

'There's a cairn,' one of the men radioed back.

'Is that it?' Ivanosky asked her. 'You put stones on top?'

'Yes,' Isabella said. 'I didn't want the coyotes to get to her.'

'Nighthawk,' the soldier radioed. 'You see anything?'

'Negative,' came the reply.

'Try infrared.'

'I already have. No heat sources. No nothing. The area's clear.'

'Put down and check it out. We'll maintain position.'

'Affirmative.'

The second Huey landed, almost disappearing in the storm of dust that the rotors disturbed. Isabella saw the side doors open and the four men inside disembark. They proceeded in pairs, relaying orders and information across the troop net. The two pairs split up: one went to the RV and the other towards the collection of shacks.

Isabella held her breath. She dared not look too excited, yet it was difficult to hide the trembling of her fingers.

The two men reached the first shack.

Chapter Forty-Nine

T he two soldiers took up position on either side of the door of the shack and, working on hand signals, one man kicked the door open so that the other man could go in. He led the way with his rifle raised while the first man stayed in the doorway.

She glanced across the compound to the RV. The vehicle had been allowed to fall into a state of terminal disrepair. The wheels had been removed long ago, and the chassis was now suspended on four piles of bricks. The windows were all intact, but they had been obscured by vines and creepers that had crawled over the front of the vehicle, as if trying to wrap themselves around it so they could drag it down into the earth. The bodywork was bent and buckled and the panel that protected the engine was hanging by a single screw.

The attention of the three others in the chopper cabin was fixed on the scene on the ground below them. No one was paying attention to Isabella. She moved her cuffed hands back so she could rest her thumbs against the button that would release the straps of her safety harness.

The second pair had reached the RV. They adopted a similar position as the first team, with a man on either side of the door that was set into the side of the vehicle. One of the soldiers reached up for the handle as his partner prepared to breach the vehicle.

The man yanked down on the handle . . .

. . . and the RV exploded in a huge, fiery detonation.

Both soldiers were tossed away from the vehicle; Isabella saw them as indistinct blurs that preceded the flames that shot out. The pressure wave rolled out in all directions, and the Huey was caught up in it and buffeted to the side. Isabella heard the pilot's curse through the intercom as he wrestled with the stick to maintain control.

Isabella pressed down on the release mechanism. She shrugged her shoulders out of the harness and threw herself across the cabin at the soldier. The man was gawping at the blast and reaching for the pressel that would open a radio channel to the men on the ground. He didn't see Isabella until it was too late. She crashed into him, the sudden impact pushing him back into his seat. He was still fixed in his harness, and the lack of mobility and his surprise almost made up for the fact that Isabella's hands were restrained. She put her hands together, palm against palm, straightened her fingers and drove them into the man's throat. She struck him in the trachea, her fingers firing into the cartilage and collapsing it. Beatrix had taught her the defensive move at the start of her training, suggesting that she use it after deflecting a punch, in the moment when her attacker's attention was diverted from the threat that a counter-strike might pose. The larynx was a pack of cartilage, cords and muscles that were bound to each other, elastic enough to recover its original form in the event of a strike. But until that happened, it led to a difficulty in breathing and was extremely debilitating.

The soldier was finding that out now. He instinctively reached up to cover his head from a follow-up strike, leaving his weapon unguarded.

Isabella grabbed the butt of the pistol, yanked it out of the holster, held it against the man's head and pulled the trigger.

Ivanosky was covered in blood and brain matter.

A second detonation roared up from the ground. Isabella caught the flash of it in the corner of her eye. It was the shack. Bits of debris were blown high into the air, fragments of wood and stone ringing against the fuselage of their chopper.

Quayle struggled with her harness. Isabella lost her balance as the Huey slid to the side, swept there by the pressure wave from the second blast. She fell against the fuselage, shrugged her shoulders to force herself back into an upright position and aimed the weapon for a second time. Quayle released the harness at the moment that Isabella fired. The round tattooed her in the shoulder and she bounced back down in her seat.

Ivanosky tried to grab Isabella. She saw him coming, her attention exclusively on him now that the more significant threats had been neutralised. She felt his hands around her waist, but he was old and weak, and she was easily able to twist and break his hold. She pistol-whipped him in the side of the face, the blow landing with enough force to bounce his head against the window. He lolled in the seat, stunned, and Isabella turned around to face the cockpit. The co-pilot was struggling with a weapon that he wore in a holster on his belt; Isabella drew a bead on him and squeezed off a single round. His head detonated in a shower of blood and brain matter. The windshield was punctured by a neat incision surrounded by a spiderweb of cracks. The man jack-knifed forward and then back again, held in place by the harness that he hadn't had time to disengage.

Isabella took aim at the pilot.

'Take us down,' she said.

The pilot worked the collective and the Huey descended, touching down at the eastern edge of the compound.

Through the window, Isabella watched the chaos consuming what had, until just a few moments earlier, been a deserted and quiet space. The RV and the shack had disappeared. Maia had taken position three hundred yards to the north, in a spot that Isabella had found. She was hiding inside a small cavity in a face of rock that would shield her from all but the most thorough of aerial searches – and with excellent sight lines into the camp, it was more than sufficient to watch the soldiers approaching the booby-trapped RV and shack.

Maia and Isabella had assembled the two bombs from propane tanks and electrical detonators, running the detcord along a narrow trench they had dug from the clearing to the hiding spot. The tanks themselves were hidden beneath an inch of loose earth below the RV and the shack. Maia had triggered them at the moment when she was sure the blasts would do as much damage as possible.

Now she was finishing up. Her hiding place also offered an excellent shooting position. One of the soldiers from the shack was still alive. Maia took him out, taking aim with the AXMC and firing a round into his back. He fell, dropping his rifle and bouncing down to the ground, his hands fluttering to the precise opening that had just been made in his sternum.

The pilot of the Huey struggled to get his bird back into the air. The engines roared and the scrub was flattened as the rotors picked up speed, but the aircraft was too big to be nimble. Then the angle of the chopper altered, and Isabella could see Maia. She was laying prone with her cheek pressed up against the rifle. She took a moment to aim and then began unloading the rest of the magazine in a steady fusillade that detonated the windshield and peppered the two men behind it. The Huey had only managed to rise six feet into the air; now, with the pilot slumped forward against the stick, the nose pointed down and the vehicle slammed back onto the hard earth. The fuselage struck at an angle and crumpled like paper. The chopper tipped over, the blades snapping like dry twigs as they slapped at the ground. The engine roared, suddenly impotent, before the fuel tank was pierced by shrapnel and the helicopter exploded.

Ivanosky groaned as he came around; he opened his eyes and gasped, 'What . . . I . . .'

Isabella pushed the muzzle of the gun against his forehead. 'Be quiet,' she said. 'Do as you're told. There's someone who wants to meet you. Open the door.'

He reached over, pulled down on the handle and muscled the door back.

'Out,' Isabella said.

He unclipped his harness and shuffled across the cabin. Warm morning air blew inside, freighted with the smell of burning kerosene and the odour of escaped gas. Ivanosky tripped on the sill of the door, falling through it and landing flat on his face.

Isabella slid across the seat just as Maia reached them.

Ivanosky rubbed his eyes.

Maia had left the rifle and was armed with a Glock that they had stashed in the RV. Her face was slathered with camo paint, green and black stripes that hid her face in blocks of dull colour.

'Hello, doctor.'

Chapter Fifty

They put Ivanosky in the trunk of the Torino and drove north, following Highway 45 all the way back to Juárez and then turning to the west. Cacti and outcrops of rock flashed by on either side, and Isabella saw the occasional blur of motion from animals that slunk low and waited for them to pass. A coyote trotted out ahead of them, quickly disappearing as it crossed over the road and hurried away.

It was a six-hour drive, and it was mid-afternoon when they finally saw the first signs for Los Tríos. Maia continued on for a mile until they reached an abandoned gas station on their left. Isabella noticed a forecourt with six decrepit pumps, a collection of broken-down pickup trucks in a yard at the back, and signs that advertised diesel at prices that hadn't been seen for many years. Pieces of trash had blown into the scrub that had been allowed to grow alongside the white-painted wall that enclosed the yard. There was a single-storey building with boards over the windows and half-hearted graffiti on the walls. Atop a pole next to the pumps was a sign that read 'Mohawk', and the name of the station was repeated on the fascia of the abandoned building. The mountains rose up from the horizon; rocky peaks that scraped against the grey clouds that had swept across the landscape.

'Is this it?' Isabella asked.

'Yes,' Maia said.

Isabella had never been here before. She wondered if this was where Maia had been coming on those weekends where she disappeared. Isabella looked at their surroundings. There was nothing else within sight. If Maia had wanted isolation, this was it.

There was a gap in the wall that led through to the yard. Access was prevented by coils of barbed wire that were strung out between wooden fence posts planted in the dirt. Maia got out of the car, uprooted the posts and moved the fence aside. She drove through and parked around the back, the car hidden from the road by the building.

Isabella saw that Maia was bleeding from the nose when she returned to the car.

'What?' Maia said, noticing Isabella's expression.

'Your nose.'

Maia dabbed her fingers to her nostrils, held them up and saw the bloodied fingertips. She exhaled impatiently, reached into her pocket and took out a handkerchief. Isabella hadn't noticed it before, but she saw, as Maia held it to her nose, that it was stained with dried blood.

'It's nothing,' Maia said.

'Are you—'

'It's nothing,' she said curtly. 'Just a nosebleed. You need to focus, Isabella. We need to get him inside.'

They went around to the trunk and opened the lid. Ivanosky was curled up inside the compartment. He was old, and the long drive must have been uncomfortable for him. Maia reached down and helped him to sit.

The old man looked up. 'You're bleeding.'

'It's nothing,' Maia repeated impatiently.

'Let me look at it.'

Maia ignored his request. 'Listen carefully,' she said. 'We're a long way from anyone who would be able to help you. I would rather you cooperated willingly. I don't want to hurt you.'

Isabella thought that she could detect a little deference in the way Maia spoke to Ivanosky. Maia had explained the role that the doctor had played in her life; he was the scientist responsible for the Prometheus programme, in charge of the development of the research that had ultimately led to Maia and her siblings. He was, in many ways, the nearest thing that she had to a father. The ties of fealty would be difficult to unknot.

'What am I doing here?' he said. 'What do you want?'

Maia didn't answer. Instead, she reached down and helped Ivanosky slide his legs over the lip of the compartment. She allowed him to put an arm over her shoulders and then assisted him in getting out and down to the ground. Maia indicated that Ivanosky should make his way to the door at the back of the property. He shuffled forward on stiff legs. The door was secured by a padlock that was evidently brand new. As Isabella waited for Maia to unlock it, she saw that the door had been strengthened. The cross braces were made from fresh wood, and it looked as if the deadbolt and lockset plates had been replaced.

Maia opened the door. It was dark inside, and Ivanosky paused on the threshold.

'What is this?' he said.

'This is where we're going to be staying,' Maia said.

'Why? For what?'

'We need your help, doctor.'

Chapter Fifty-One

Maia took a flashlight from a shelf next to the door, switched it on and led the way through the building. They stepped over discarded tyres, stacks of piled-up wood and ash that marked out long-dead fires. There were two more doors inside, both secured by padlocks; Maia removed the padlock on the nearest door and opened it.

Isabella followed her inside, passing through a darkened room that looked as if it might once have been a store. There was a lantern on the floor. Maia reached down to light it, and then hung it from a nail that had been driven into the wall. The light slowly gathered, casting out the shadows until they could see that the room had been furnished sparsely, with three bedrolls on the floor, a table, a sink and a stove. There were twenty-four plastic bottles of water against the wall, still in their shrink-wrapped covering, together with cans of food.

Maia's bleeding had stopped, and she put the handkerchief back in her pocket. Isabella wanted to talk to her about it, but she could see that Maia would quickly shut the conversation down, and so she said nothing.

'We'll rest here,' Maia said.

'What are we doing?' Ivanosky said.

'I told you,' she replied. 'You're going to help us, doctor.'

'How? Are you unwell?'

Isabella thought that he looked at Maia with sudden concern; Maia spoke before he could ask anything else.

'We will discuss it later.' She pointed at the bedroll nearest the wall. 'Please,' she said.

Ivanosky didn't protest. Maia took him to the bathroom and then brought him back, indicating that he should sit down on the bedroll. She took out a pair of handcuffs from a bag on the table, and attached one of the bracelets to the old man's ankle and the other to a waste pipe that led away from the old, stained sink.

'This isn't necessary, Maia,' Ivanosky said, jangling the cuff. 'I'm old, and look where we are – I wouldn't get a hundred yards.'

'I don't want to worry that you might be foolish enough to try.'

Ivanosky sighed and settled back against the thin bedroll. 'I didn't think I would ever see you again,' he said. 'None of us did. We all thought you were dead.'

Maia ignored him, busying herself with a can of soup. She removed the lid, poured it into a small saucepan and rested it atop the small gas stove.

'What happened? Where have you been?'

'Here,' she said. 'Mexico.'

'For the whole year?'

Isabella looked over at Maia through the golden light as Maia stirred the soup. Her face was as blank and inscrutable as ever. She didn't answer the question.

'Have you self-medicated?' Ivanosky asked her.

'Yes,' she said.

'Citalopram?'

'Yes. You don't need to worry – I'm level.'

'Where did you get it from?'

'That doesn't matter.'

'But you've had no episodes?'

'No,' she said. She poured the soup into three cups and took one over to him. 'No more questions, please. You need to eat and then rest. You will be busy for the rest of the day.'

Maia brought the second cup to Isabella. It was tomato soup, sweet and warming. Isabella drank it down.

Maia took out a knife, sheared through the plastic wrapping that held the bottles of water together and gave one each to Isabella and the professor. Isabella cranked off the cap and drank. She was thirsty, her throat dry and clogged with dust from the desert road. Ivanosky did the same, resting the bottle on the floor next to his bedroll.

'I'll be outside,' Maia said. 'There's a generator for power. I need to get it started. You should rest.'

'What are we here for, Maia?'

'We have work to do.' She turned to Isabella. 'Stay with him.'

Isabella nodded, and watched as Maia left the room.

Ivanosky finished the rest of the soup and put the mug down on the bare floor. 'How much of what you told me is true?' he asked.

'She told you to rest,' Isabella said.

Ivanosky ignored her. 'It's remarkable, what she's done. To stay out of sight for a year with no recourse to her usual regimen. I wouldn't have said it was possible. Tell me – has she been well?'

'What do you mean?'

'Her nose was bleeding. Has that happened a lot?'

'No.'

'Has she complained of fatigue?'

'No.'

'Has she been bruising more easily?'

'No. What is this? Why would you say that? She's fine.'

Ivanosky looked as if he might answer, but then changed his mind. 'Forget it,' he replied.

'No more talking,' she said more firmly, although it appeared that he had already decided he would be silent and rest.

Isabella realised that she had no real idea what they were going to do next. Maia had explained that she wanted Ivanosky for his involvement in Litivenko's murder. She needed to question him, and then exact a measure of her revenge. Isabella had accepted that, but now that they had him and they were here, she found the lack of clarity unsettling. He was going to *help* them? What did that mean?

She started to wonder if Maia had told her everything.

Chapter Fifty-Two

Fifty minutes passed before the lightbulbs that hung down from the ceiling started flickering on and off, eventually glowing brighter until they gave out enough light to banish the shadows that had been cast by the lantern. Isabella could hear the sound of an engine from outside; Maia had started the generator.

Isabella heard the remaining padlock being unlocked and then the second door as it was opened on squeaking hinges. Footsteps approached, and Maia came back inside, knelt down next to Ivanosky and checked that the handcuff was still fastened, then took Isabella gently by the arm and moved her to the door.

'I need to speak to you,' she said.

Maia led the way into a second room. Isabella looked around. It had been set up as a laboratory. There were four distinct workstations, and an array of equipment was laid out around them. Isabella didn't recognise much of it, but she could see a centrifuge that looked like an oversized rice cooker, as well as microscopes, scanners, refrigerators, a piece of machinery with a row of nozzles that looked as if they could inject liquids into several test tubes at once, analytical equipment, two laptop computers and a row of rugged metal flasks, which she thought might be used to store frozen samples. There were boxes of medical consumables, too: test tubes; disposable gloves; plastic coveralls that were still in their packaging.

'What is this?' Isabella said.

'I haven't been honest with you,' Maia said.

'What?'

'Ivanosky isn't just here because of Aleksandra.' Her voice was as flat and dispassionate as ever, but Isabella could see that she was trying very hard to deliver something with sensitivity, as if she feared Isabella might react badly. 'It's part of it, but it's not the most important reason.'

'So what is he here for?'

'For you.'

Isabella looked away from her, and turned to the equipment that looked so incongruous in the dusty, dilapidated wreck of a room. She took a step back from it. 'What?'

'You know that I'm . . .' Maia paused, looking for the right word. 'You know that I'm *different*, Isabella? Yes?'

'Of course.'

Maia looked straight at her. 'Have you ever thought that you might be different, too?'

Isabella smiled nervously. 'Come *on*. Stop joking.'

'I'm not,' Maia said, and Isabella realised: Maia didn't joke. She'd never heard a joke from her once in the year that they had spent together.

'Then you're crazy,' she said, unable to stop her jittery laugh.

Maia kept her eyes on her. 'You remember when you fell from the helicopter? You broke your leg. Do you remember that?'

'Of course I remember.'

'I took you to the hospital in Murfreesboro. They fixed your leg. They took a flap of skin from your back and attached it to your leg, where the bone came through. They took a lot of skin. The doctor who treated you showed me how quickly you'd healed. They'd done the operation only six hours earlier when he showed me, but it was already healing. He said he would have expected that amount of healing to take two or three days.'

'This is stupid,' Isabella said, taking another backward step.

'He showed me your leg, too. The flap had already attached. He said he'd never seen anything like it – but *I* had seen it before. I'd seen it with me – I heal quickly. The same as my brothers and sisters. Much faster than normal.'

'You're crazy,' Isabella repeated.

Maia reached out and took Isabella's wrist in a firm grip. 'I'm not,' she said. She reached out her other hand, her fingers hovering over Isabella's right shoulder where the *sicario*'s knife had sliced down the outside of her arm. 'Can I look?'

Isabella glanced down. The dressing that Maia had fixed over the long wound was visible beneath the sleeve of her T-shirt. She had been so distracted that she hadn't asked for it to be changed since she had been arrested.

Maia pulled up the sleeve of her T-shirt until it was over her shoulder, and then carefully peeled away the dressing. The gauze was stained by dried blood and the pus that had drained from the wound, and she tossed it into an empty plastic barrel that had been used to gather the discarded packaging from the equipment in the room. Isabella raised her arm so she could look down at where the knife had sliced through the skin. The ugly track of the cut had faded away, the skin knotted back around it. Some of the stitches that Maia had put in had come out, stuck to the dressing, and the others were in the process of being expelled. New skin had formed inside the wound, pulling the edges of the cut closer and drawing them together.

'That only happened five days ago,' Maia said.

'So?'

'Look at it. That looks like it's been healing for a month.'

'I . . .' Isabella started to respond, and then stopped.

'I'm the same,' Maia said. 'Exactly the same.'

Isabella lowered her head and kneaded her temples between her fists. 'This is nuts.'

'So why not let Ivanosky take a little of your blood and test it?'

'Because it'd be a waste of time. Because it won't show anything.'

'So there's no harm in trying.'

Chapter Fifty-Three

Maia released the handcuff from Ivanosky's ankle and brought him through into the makeshift laboratory.

His mouth fell open. 'What is this?' he said, looking around the room.

'I want you to run some tests.'

'On you?' he asked. His face clouded.

'Not just me,' she corrected. 'On both of us.'

Ivanosky turned his attention on Isabella. 'What? Why?'

'I want you to run a DNA comparison – hers against mine.'

The old man's forehead creased. 'That doesn't make sense, Maia. Why would I do that?'

Maia gestured to the equipment. 'Do you have what you need?'

Ivanosky walked along the countertops, examining the machines that had been put out there. 'You've been thorough,' Ivanosky said.

'I can remember,' she said.

'From Skopje?'

She didn't answer. 'Do you have everything?'

Ivanosky looked at her with a bemused expression on his face. 'I'm sorry,' he said. 'I still don't understand. You brought me here for that? To test her?'

'Will you do it or won't you?'

Ivanosky frowned, but then shook his head and shrugged. 'Fine,' he said, waving his hand as if to sum up the ridiculousness of the situation in which he had found himself. 'Fine.'

'What do you need?'

'Blood from both of you.'

Maia put her hand on Isabella's shoulder. 'Is that okay?' she asked. Isabella nodded that it was.

'I'm going to need syringes and a tourniquet,' Ivanosky said.

Maia went over to a cardboard box on a shelf and took out two disposable syringes, a pack of alcohol wipes and a latex tourniquet with a button clasp. She handed the items to the doctor. 'Be careful,' she cautioned him.

Ivanosky ignored the warning and turned to Isabella. 'Give me your arm,' he said.

She did as he asked.

He swabbed her arm with an alcohol wipe, fitted the tourniquet and tightened it. Isabella didn't know how to feel; the whole situation was bewildering. Ivanosky ran his finger down the inside of her arm and, once he found a vein that he liked, he slid the needle inside and drew enough blood to fill the barrel. Isabella winced at the scratch of the needle and then the ache. Ivanosky withdrew the needle, unscrewed the barrel from the syringe and labelled it.

'How long will it take?' Maia asked.

He gestured helplessly at the equipment. The Pyrex containers on metal racks and other clinical-looking equipment looked more like a lab for cooking crystal meth than somewhere that was ready for scientific analysis. 'A day,' he said. 'Should have it tomorrow.'

Maia didn't react to the estimate, save for a nod of her head. She rolled up her sleeve and offered her arm to the professor. 'Do it.'

Chapter Fifty-Four

There was little to do to make the time pass any faster. Maia insisted that Ivanosky stay inside during the rest of the day so as to avoid being seen from the road. She relented when it was dark, removing his cuffs and taking him outside to the back of the building. She followed close at hand, ensuring that the old man would not think to try anything that might put them in jeopardy before she could stop it. He realised that there was nothing that he could do, and was content to sit with his back to the wall of the building, watching the shooting stars race across the heavens and listening to the howls of the coyotes.

'How does the test work?' Isabella asked.

Ivanosky looked to Maia as if for permission to answer; she gave a shallow nod of her head. 'It's like a paternity test,' he said. 'I isolate the DNA in the samples from the cells and make millions of copies. You use an enzyme to copy a particular stretch of DNA over and over again; the more DNA I have, the easier it is to read and compare your genetic codes. I split the DNA molecules at particular locations to separate them, then I take the code at those points to create two distinct DNA fingerprints. And then I compare them. It's very basic.' He glanced over at Maia. 'I'm not sure you needed to go to the effort of bringing me out here to do that. You can get this done on the Internet.'

'Not what we need,' Maia said.

Isabella had prepared a flask of coffee. She poured it out into three paper cups.

Ivanosky took one. Isabella saw that his hands were trembling. 'What are you going to do with me when this is done?'

Maia didn't answer.

'Are you going to kill me?'

She still didn't answer.

'You don't have to say,' he said.

He paused, and for a moment no one spoke. Isabella looked at him, at his apparent resignation, and didn't trust him for a second. She had noticed the way his eyes darted around, as if searching for a flaw, something that he might be able to exploit so he could get away from them. Only there was no flaw – Maia had been thorough, and, at the end of the day, he was an old man who was outnumbered and outmatched.

Ivanosky broke the silence. 'There's another reason, too, isn't there?'

'For what?'

'For why you're doing this.'

Maia looked away.

'You're dying, aren't you?'

Maia didn't answer.

'What?' Isabella said. 'What does he mean?'

'Maia?' Ivanosky said. 'You should tell her.'

'Yes,' Maia said. 'He's right. I'm sick.'

Isabella's mind scrambled. 'How? The bleeding? You said that was just a nosebleed.'

'It's not just that,' Maia said quietly. She looked to Ivanosky. 'The others?'

'You're the fourth,' he said. 'Morpheus was first. We only found out when we did the autopsy after you shot him – I suppose we should thank you for that. Moros was next. It started with fatigue, then weight loss, then bleeding and petechiae. He's in the infirmary now. He won't leave. Mithras has it, although it's not advanced yet. Macaria is clear, but we know that won't last long. And then there's you.'

'You're sick with what?' Isabella said.

'Cancer,' Ivanosky said when Maia didn't reply. 'We thought we'd managed to avoid the cancers with Maia and the others, but we were wrong. We've never been able to maintain genetic stability. The science . . .' He exhaled wearily. 'The science is difficult.'

'I want you to test my blood for it,' Maia said. 'I want to be sure.'

Ivanosky nodded.

Isabella felt as if the ground was shifting beneath her for the second time that day. She blinked her eyes. 'You didn't tell me,' she said, bewildered.

'I didn't want to . . .' Isabella thought Maia was going to add 'upset you', but instead she said, 'I don't know for sure.'

Isabella turned to Ivanosky. 'What kind of cancer?'

'A kind of leukaemia. Acute myeloid leukaemia. It's a cancer of the white blood cells. It's very rare. The process of making blood cells in the marrow gets out of control and too many abnormal cells are made. The abnormal cells fill up the marrow, so the body can't make enough normal cells. Some leukaemia cells get into the bloodstream. They don't work properly. You end up with increased risk of infection, and anaemia and bruising, because fewer healthy red blood cells and platelets are being made.'

'Can you cure it?'

He sipped his coffee and then spoke again. 'Normally? Yes – normally, it's curable. Patients go into remission with chemo. But we haven't been able to cure it in the assets. I've seen it before. Many times. We've never been able to stop it with them. And we've spent a lot of time and money trying to. It's beyond me, I'm afraid.'

They heard the rush of a rare car as it approached and then sped on, its lights visible in the dark as it hurried away from them.

'Of course,' Ivanosky said, 'I can't tell the people who paid for the work to be done. The industrialists. The intelligence community.'

'They don't know yet?' Maia asked.

'No. I haven't told them. But if we lose you and the others . . .' He let the sentence drift away. 'What would be the point of me then? My work doesn't come with a pension and a gold watch. I can't leave, even if they don't want to do the work any longer. I already know much too much. They can't have me taking my work to the Russians or the Chinese. So, I suppose the question about what you're going to do with me is pointless. Maybe it's best this way. Just make it quick.'

If Maia was upset about the direction of the conversation, and the unhappy prognosis that had just been outlined for her, she did not show it. Isabella realised that she must have known for a while, and that she had already processed and accepted it.

Maia got up, took her cup with her and sipped from it. 'What about Macaria and Mercury? Are they still operational?'

'They were,' he said. He gestured to Isabella. 'Mercury was responsible for getting her out of Mexico. He reported that he was feeling sick as soon as he landed. He collapsed ten minutes after I arrived. I sent him back to Skopje.'

'And Macaria?'

'Healthy for now. They've just sent her back into the field.'

'For what?' Maia asked.

He smiled, but it was a smile without humour and there was no light in his eyes. 'She's going to go out with a bang. Gary Morrow has a rally in Sioux City. Macaria is going to assassinate him before he can stop the war my benefactors want so much. They'll make it look like it was the Syrians or the Russians – anything to make a ceasefire impossible. Morrow wants the war to stop, but they'll make him into a martyr for it to continue. That's always been their aim. A never-ending cycle of violence. There's a lot of money to be made in misery.'

'Don't pretend like you regret it,' Isabella said.

'I'm not pretending,' he said. 'It was always about the science for me. It always has been. But this kind of science' – he gestured to Maia as if she were a piece of equipment – 'is expensive. It's so expensive that there are very few ways that you can get the money you need. It was the same when I started, in Russia. I had to make some difficult choices there, just as I have had to make them here. I can live with myself. The rewards are worth it.'

He was quiet, and they listened to the sounds of the desert for a moment.

Maia broke the silence. 'Who killed Aleksandra? Was it Moros?'

'They used stooges, just like they did in London.'

'But Moros was in Washington. I saw him.'

'He was involved.'

'Who else?'

'Macaria,' he said.

'Were they both at the airport?'

Ivanosky nodded. 'As fail-safes. It turns out they weren't needed. Why? What difference does it make now?'

'Because I'm going to kill them both,' Maia said.

'What good will that do? They'll die anyway. The cancer will take them before you can.'

'No,' she said. 'It won't.'

Chapter Fifty-Five

Isabella was woken by the sound of raised voices from the laboratory next door. She crawled off her bedroll and got to her feet. She heard Ivanosky speaking. 'Is this a joke?'

'No,' said Maia.

'You brought me all the way out here to trick me?'

'It's not a trick.'

Isabella crossed the room. Light was leaking through the boards that covered the windows, and when she checked the time on her phone, she saw that it was seven. She made her way into the makeshift laboratory. Ivanosky was standing in front of an open laptop. Maia was next to him.

Ivanosky glared at Isabella, then jabbed his finger at the screen. 'You manipulated the samples?'

'No. How could I? You took the blood.'

Ivanosky threw up his hands and whirled away. Isabella walked over to the computer and looked at the screen. It showed a graph. She stooped down so she could examine it more carefully. The Y-axis bore the legend 'CHROMOSOME'; it was divided into segments labelled '1' to '22', with a further two rows notated as 'X' and 'Y'. Each segment contained a multicoloured bar that extended to the right of the screen, with each bearing a mark that was referred to as 'telomere/centromere'. Isabella had never seen anything like it before, and it made no sense at all.

'What is it?' she asked. She pointed at the screen. 'What does it show?'

'You switched the bloods,' Ivanosky repeated, gesturing angrily to Maia. 'You must've done.'

'No,' Maia said again. 'I didn't.'

'Then you're going to have to tell me why her profile is *exactly* the same as yours.'

Isabella paused and looked up at him. 'What does that mean?' She turned to Maia. 'What does he mean?'

Ivanosky waved his hand at the screen. 'You have forty-eight chromosomes.'

'And?'

He snapped back at her, 'You should only have forty-six.'

Isabella shook her head. 'I don't understand . . . I don't . . .' She lost the thread of the sentence before she could finish it.

Maia came over and guided her to the room's only chair. 'Sit down.'

Ivanosky went to the laptop and scrolled down. 'I have forty-six chromosomes arranged in twenty-three pairs. The last pair are the sex chromosomes – they differ between men and women. But that's it. Always the same.' He was talking rapidly, as if he would be able to answer his own questions amid the welter of words. 'But my life's work has been to amend that pattern.' He flicked his fingers in Maia's direction. 'That's what we did with Maia. A twenty-fourth pair so we could add new genetic modules or remove them when they become obsolete. They all have it, all the same. All just like this.'

He stalked along the line of machines and then, as he turned back to face her again, he stopped.

'How old are you?' he asked her.

'Sixteen.'

Ivanosky paused for a moment, as if making a calculation. He nodded. 'It's possible. It fits.'

Isabella felt dazed. 'What does?'

'*Jesus*,' he breathed.

Maia regarded him sternly. 'Professor?'

He took off his spectacles and rested them on the keyboard. 'I used to work with a man,' he said. 'Igor Koralev. He was a geneticist. Russian. We both emigrated to the United States from Russia. He worked with me at Daedalus. Igor was brilliant. A genius, really. One of the most impressive men that I ever knew. It would have taken *years* longer to get to where we are without the work that he did. Perhaps we would not have got there at all.'

'I don't remember him,' Maia said.

He kneaded his eyes. 'You wouldn't – you were very young. A little girl. And then . . .' He paused. He put his spectacles back on and spoke more harshly than before. 'Igor was greedy as well as brilliant. We were well paid, but he always wanted more. He disappeared. Just fell off the face of the earth one day. The CIA couldn't find him. It was the British who picked him up in the end. He'd run to Venezuela.'

Isabella looked from the doctor to Maia as if she might be able to find something in their faces to confirm the riotous direction of her thoughts, but she could not.

'Igor didn't just disappear, though,' Ivanosky continued. 'He stole from us. We'd been working on improving the genetic alterations that we pioneered with the M cohort. There were two cohorts after that one. The Ns and the Os. Both unsuccessful. There were five children in each, and they all died. Cancers. Leukaemia, just like . . .' He waved a hand in Maia's direction, and the words petered out. 'None made it past their first birthdays. We tried and tried, but we couldn't replicate our success – we've never been able to. But Igor kept experimenting. We didn't know until later. His P cohort produced a single viable embryo. He implanted it and brought it to term. It was a girl. Igor called her

Phoenix. And when he went, he took her away with him. She was six months old.'

Isabella dipped her head, spread her fingers and pressed them against her brow. 'When was this?'

'Nearly sixteen years ago. '

She felt sick.

'The British sent two agents to bring him back,' he went on. 'The CIA interfered and Igor was killed.'

'And the baby?' Isabella said.

Ivanosky shrugged. 'Never found.'

Isabella said, quietly, 'Who were the agents?'

'I have no idea. They never told us.'

'My mother . . .' Isabella's head pounded, the words crowded out by the onset of a sudden, crushing throb of pain.

Maia reached for her. 'What?'

She tried to stand, but found the effort disorientating. She reached down for the counter and used it to brace herself.

'Sit down,' Maia urged.

Ivanosky suddenly looked avid. 'What about your mother?'

'She worked for the government. She . . .'

Isabella's heart beat faster and faster and her head pulsed. The sentence trailed off, but the thought remained, burning bright: Beatrix had told her, in the time that they had spent together before she died, that she had once been sent on a mission to Venezuela.

Isabella stumbled away from the chair, knocked against Maia and pushed her away, and ran to the door.

Chapter Fifty-Six

Isabella shoved the door open and went outside. The sun had crested the mountains, and dry heat washed over her. She lurched away from the building, her thoughts a commotion of confusing and conflicting information. None of it made sense, but then none of what had happened to her over the past year made sense, either.

She thought of the broken leg that had healed in weeks.

She yanked down her shirt and looked at the cut on her shoulder, almost invisible now.

She tried to turn her thoughts away, but she could not. There was a voice in her head, whispering doubt and uncertainty, and she couldn't shut it down. The voice started to tug on the knots that bound her history together. The fibres started to part and fray. How much of what her mother had told her was true? If she had lied about the most fundamental thing – that she was her mother – how could Isabella trust a single word that she had said?

She stumbled and fell, dropping to her knees in the hot sand.

The voice whispered now, and she couldn't stop it.

Your mother was not your mother.

You're not normal.

You're like Maia.

Different.

Altered.

You've been tampered with.

Another vicious wave of dizziness crashed over her and she had to put her hand down to stop herself from collapsing onto her face. Her fingers slid into the sand and she tried to focus on that, feeling the grit between her fingers, anchoring herself to it, anything to tether her to something tangible, something real, something that she could trust.

How much of what she had been told was a lie? She had always been able to remember her father's face, his gentle kindness and patience, from before he had been murdered and taken from her. But if Lucas Rose wasn't her father, then what did that mean? Who was?

What about the years she had spent in foster homes as the agency who had abducted her from Beatrix kept her for the leverage that she provided? She had tried to wipe out that whole decade, to treat those years as lost, but what if that time was more truthful than the time she had spent with Beatrix after she found her again?

What if those memories were more reliable than the three years before Isabella was abducted?

Or more dependable than the year in Marrakech after Beatrix found her and before she was killed while settling the scores of her betrayal.

What if . . .

What if . . .

She felt weak and sick.

'Isabella!'

She closed her eyes, trying to find a point of steadiness amid the maelstrom that threatened to yank her from all of her certainties and send her tumbling into a void of ambiguity and doubt.

She heard footsteps coming towards her.

'Leave me alone,' she mumbled, not sure if anyone could hear her.

She put her head in her hands, forming fists and then sliding them down until she was able to grind her knuckles into her eyes. She pressed hard, as if she might find an answer in the explosions of light that deto-nated against her retinas.

'Isabella.'

'Leave me alone.'

She took her hands away, opened her eyes and blinked into the sudden, ferocious daylight. She felt a hand on her shoulder. Maia was crouching next to her.

'It's all right,' she said. 'I understand. Let me help you.'

'*Leave me alone!*'

She tried to run, but Maia was too quick. Her hand raced out, crossed the distance between them and fastened around Isabella's wrist. She tried to shake it loose, but Maia was too strong for her.

'Please, Isabella. I can help you.'

Isabella heard the sound of an engine and they both looked up.

The Torino swung around in the yard and crashed through the fence.

Maia let go of Isabella's arm, turned from her and ran.

The car skidded across the loose dirt at the side of the road, gravel and sand spraying out as the wheels struggled for purchase.

Maia planted her hands on the white-painted wall and vaulted eas-ily over, landing on the other side and sprinting hard.

The car, and then Maia, disappeared behind the building. Isabella got to her feet and watched. The car raced back into view, picking up speed as it headed east, towards Juárez. Maia followed, but she couldn't keep up. She slowed to a jog and then stopped, her hands on her knees as she bent low to catch her breath. The car kept going, clouds of dust marking its escape until it passed out of sight.

Maia collapsed to her knees.

'Maia!'

Isabella ran, her feet sinking into the sand. She cleared the wall, made it to the firmer surface of the road and sprinted. When she reached her, Maia was gasping for breath. Blood ran from her nose, dripping down to the dirt where it gathered in a sticky brown puddle.

Maia tried to stand, but didn't have the strength. She toppled backwards, landing on her backside in the dust.

'Don't move,' Isabella said. 'Just take it easy. I'll go and get you some water.'

'We can't wait,' Maia said. 'The professor . . . he'll bring them after us. We have to leave.'

'Look at you,' Isabella protested. 'You can't even stand.'

'Help me up.'

Isabella looped her arm around Maia and pulled. She managed to stand, and with her arm around Isabella's shoulders she was able to walk back to the gas station.

'I'm sorry,' Isabella said. 'This is my fault.'

'No, it isn't.'

'If I hadn't—'

'It's not your fault,' Maia insisted weakly.

'What do we do? He's got the car.'

'We have to find another. There's a town that way.' Maia pointed to the north.

'How far?'

'Five miles.'

'You'll never be able to walk that far.'

'I will,' she said. 'We'll get water from inside and then we have to go. They'll be coming for us.'

Chapter Fifty-Seven

Ivanosky drove as fast as he dared. The handling on the old Torino was challenging, and it bounced and juddered over the uneven surface of the road as he raced east.

He had to try to keep his attention on the road, but it was difficult. His head was spinning with what he had discovered in the desert. Isabella Rose was Phoenix? He could hardly credit the possibility. They had lost the child fifteen years ago. He remembered more of what the CIA team had reported when they returned to Langley. A search team had found the place that Koralev was using to hide out, but they had been ambushed and the four agents had been killed. A second team had found them: three had been shot to death and the fourth had had his throat slit. The team also found a bedroom that had been made into a nursery, with a crib and other evidence that suggested a baby had been there. There was no sign of the child. Whoever had taken out the first team had taken the baby, too.

They had assumed the hit was the work of a rival government. The Russians and then the Chinese had been the chief suspects, but they had never been able to confirm exactly what had happened.

Until now.

The British had located Kolarev. Could they have found his house? Had they been responsible for the murder of the first team and the abduction of the child?

There were too many questions; Ivanosky didn't know where to start. And what about the girl? She was sixteen and there was no obvious sign of the cancers that had blighted the N and O cohorts, and latterly afflicted the Ms. And, he realised, there had been no mention of the girl regulating the out-of-control norepinephrine and dopamine that made Maia and her siblings so dangerous. Had she found another way to keep herself in check without citalopram? Perhaps she didn't even need to.

The possibilities spun away in countless directions. Ivanosky found that he was excited; he barely gave a moment's thought to Maia's cancer. It seemed less important now. The girl's existence – the confirmation that she was Phoenix – gave him new faith that his work could be salvaged.

His career might not end in the ignominy that he had feared.

He just needed to secure her and take her back to the laboratory.

Ivanosky raced by a series of low-slung buildings until he saw a phone booth next to a blue-painted building that announced itself as a Catholic chapel. It was little more than a shanty, with 'Jesús D'Nazareth' painted along the wall and a temporary sign calling the faithful to worship flapping listlessly in the breeze.

Ivanosky hit the brakes, dust pouring out of the wheel arches. He turned the car around, pulling up outside the booth. He got out into the sticky morning heat, took the phone off the hook and called the unlisted number that was reserved for emergencies only. The operator who answered the call was as professional as he would have expected; he gave her the fake name that would be traced back to him, said that he wanted a taxi and, when she asked, gave her the location that he read on a faded sticker stuck to the board that was fixed to the wall above the telephone.

'We'll be there as soon as we can, sir,' she said.

'What does that mean?'

'No more than an hour.'

'Faster than that,' he snapped. 'I need it now.'

'We don't have any drivers in your vicinity.'

'I need to come in *now*.'

'Stay where you are, sir. A driver is on the way.'

Ivanosky slammed the receiver back into its cradle and stalked back to the car. 'Driver' meant 'helicopter', and it would come from Fort Bliss. It was close. But an hour was too long. He slid inside the car and moved it off the road, reversing it onto a dirt track between the chapel and the ochre-painted building to its left. The track offered access to a small number of houses that had been built to the south of the main Juárez road. He rolled slowly along the track until he saw an empty yard between two shacks. He turned into the space and parked.

He took a moment to breathe. He had no idea whether Maia had another means of transport, but if she did, he knew that she would come after him. She would have killed him once she was finished with him. She had been trained to ensure that operations were never compromised, and she would have needed to ensure that he could not raise the alarm. That was even more pertinent now.

Yes, he thought. Maia would have to try to find him, and the prospect of a second meeting, out here in the middle of nowhere, was not an appealing one. The thought chilled him.

He got out of the car and went to the edge of the yard. The main road into the city was quiet. He was well hidden, and he allowed himself to feel reassured. Even if she did give chase, there was no way she would be able to find him here.

He looked at his watch. It was still early. He would stay here, out of sight, and wait to be exfiltrated.

Chapter Fifty-Eight

Ivanosky heard the sound of a car fifteen minutes later. He left the security of the yard and walked to the front of the chapel. He put his head around the corner; there was a car parked next to the phone booth. The engine was running and the driver's door was open. He couldn't see the driver, though, and that made him feel a little anxious. He turned, ready to go back to the Torino, but before he could take another step, he was intercepted by a man who slid out from the gate that opened into the chapel's rear yard. The man had a gun in his right hand.

'Walk over to the car, please.'

Ivanosky froze, but the man reached out and shoved him firmly on the shoulder. He stumbled ahead, kicking up dust as the man pushed him again towards the car. Two more men appeared from either side of the junction. All three men had the look of soldiers: they had on jeans and desert boots, dark glasses covered their eyes and they wore their hair close to the scalp. He felt the first man's gun in his back as he reached the Torino. The man opened the door and pushed him down and ahead so he had no choice but to get inside.

The man slid into the back next to Ivanosky, pushing the gun into his ribs. One of the others opened the door on the other side of the car and lowered himself inside, the two men sandwiching Ivanosky between them.

The third man got in the front and started the engine.

'What is this?' Ivanosky said. 'Who are you?'

'Nice and quiet, please, sir,' the man with the gun said.

The man spoke with an accent.

A British accent.

'Who are you?' Ivanosky repeated.

He felt a sharp prick of pain in his leg, and as he turned and looked down, he saw the man on his other side had just stabbed him in the thigh with a syringe.

'What the . . .' he started to say, but a swell of torpor rolled over him and he could barely move his lips. His muscles felt as heavy as lead, his eyelids drooped and then closed and he exhaled in peaceful drowsiness as sleep caught him up and overtook him.

Chapter Fifty-Nine

Sioux City

The woman thanked the cabin crew as she disembarked the American Eagle jet and crossed the airbridge to the terminal building at Sioux Gateway Airport. She had flown from Quebec City to Montreal, then from Montreal to Chicago, where she had stayed overnight. She had caught a third flight this morning to bring her to Iowa.

Her name, at least according to the credit card that had been used to purchase the flights, was Katie LeFebvre. Katie was a businesswoman from Montreal who was travelling to Iowa to meet a local manufacturer of highway construction machinery. The company she worked for was interested in a potential order, and Katie was here to negotiate the contract.

But Katie LeFebvre wasn't her real name. It was one of a series of fake legends that she adopted as needed when she wanted to pass across borders without drawing undue attention to herself. The woman had fair skin and blonde hair, and bland features that were not quite symmetrical enough to be considered attractive and yet not unattractive enough that they would stand out. She had varied her appearance in line with the picture on her fake passport: a long honey-blonde wig with pronounced highlights, gold stud earrings and a pair of glasses that made her look older. She wore a business suit: not too expensive to stand out, and yet of sufficient quality to match the budget of a successful middle manager who cared about how she looked.

She walked through the terminal. She had no checked baggage to collect, with just a carry-on case that she wheeled behind her. She passed through the arrivals lounge, through the sliding doors that led to the taxi stand and, since no one else was waiting, made her way to the car at the front of the line. The driver was leaning against the hood of his car smoking a cigarette, which he dropped and ground underfoot as the woman approached. She asked him for a ride to the Holiday Inn Express on Southern Hills Drive. The driver put the case in the trunk and the woman slid onto the rear seat.

'Where'd you come from?' the man asked as they pulled away from the kerb.

'Montreal,' she said.

'Long trip?'

'Too long.'

'What you here for?'

'Business,' she said.

'Not for the rally tomorrow?'

'No.'

'They're expecting three or four thousand,' he suggested, as if he hadn't heard her answer. 'They were just saying on the radio. Gonna be busy. He's getting more and more popular. You ask me, he's gonna win the election.'

The woman caught him looking at her in the rear-view mirror and gave an incline of her head to acknowledge him. Then she took out her phone and made herself busy with it to cut any further conversation short. She wanted to be friendly, but had no interest in pointless small talk. She had work to do, after all, and she needed to put herself in the right frame of mind.

Her codename within the Prometheus programme was Macaria. She had been travelling for two days before she had departed the Aéroport International Jean-Lesage de Québec. Her journey had originated in Macedonia, and it had taken her to Canada where she had adopted the Katie LeFebvre legend before continuing on to Sioux City.

She would abandon Katie soon enough, though. She had things to do, and she needed to be someone else in order to do them.

Chapter Sixty

Mexico

They waited in line to cross the bridge into Texas. The Rio Grande was ahead of them, the six-lane bridge accommodating both vehicles and pedestrians. They had hiked north from Los Tríos to Puerto Palomas, where they had found a beaten-up Chevrolet outside a house on the edge of town. They had taken it, driving back south and then following Highway 2 to Juárez and then to Guadalupe. The Tornillo crossing was familiar to them, since that was where the cartel truck had come south before they hijacked it.

Maia was driving. She edged them forward, a little closer to the booths where the immigration officials would check their passports. Isabella had put their documents on the dash; they were excellent fakes, and Maia had expressed no concern that they would be stopped.

That wasn't enough to prevent a little flutter of nerves in Isabella's stomach as they edged ahead again, however.

'What will she do?' she said to distract herself.

'Who?'

'Macaria – how will she do it?'

'I don't know.'

'Another bomb?'

'Maybe.'

'But there'll be a lot of people there. What about them?'

'She won't care.'

'But we do. We'll stop her, won't we?'

'If we can,' Maia said.

'If we can? That's got to be the first thing we do – right?'

'No. The priority is finding her.'

'But we have to tell the police.'

'If we do that, they'll abort and we'll lose her.'

'So we find another way.'

'No. They're onto us now. It won't be as easy as it was before. We won't be able to surprise them.'

Isabella gritted her teeth. 'We can't take the risk,' she said.

Maia turned to face her. 'You'll do as I say, or I'll leave you here. Do you understand?'

There was a harshness in her voice to which Isabella was unaccustomed. But she knew better than to push against her. She believed that Maia meant what she said.

'Okay,' she conceded. 'We'll do it your way.'

Maia turned back and, seeing that a new booth had opened, she pulled out of the lane and crossed over to it. She wound down the window, took the passports and handed them over.

Isabella watched. She wasn't prepared to take the same chances that Maia was apparently prepared to take. She wanted to help her – she wanted her to find Macaria – but Isabella wasn't prepared to gamble with the lives of the people who would be at the event. She started to think about how she might help Maia find her sister while also preventing another loss of life.

'Thank you,' Maia said as she took the passports back from the immigration official.

'Welcome to America,' he replied.

Chapter Sixty-One

Sioux City

Macaria returned to her hotel at nine in the evening. The meeting with the manufacturer had gone well, and after being taken out to Ida Grove to see the equipment in action, she had returned to the company's offices and closed the terms of the deal.

Now, though, Macaria was ready to attend to the real business she was here to transact. She went through into the bathroom, removed the wig and glasses and undressed. She took a quick shower and then went into the bedroom. She felt something warm and wet on her top lip, and as she looked in the mirror, she saw that a single pearl of blood had rolled out of her right nostril. She looked at it quizzically; she didn't suffer from nosebleeds. She took a square of toilet paper and mopped up the blood, then balled it up and flushed it away. No sense in worrying. It was nothing.

She put on a pair of jeans and a black turtleneck, took her credit card, her phone, two hundred dollars in cash and the hotel keycard and left the room. There was a way out at the end of the corridor and so, rather than go back through the lobby again, she opened the door, stepped outside and closed it behind her. She found herself at the side of the building. She crossed an overgrown verge that had not been tended to for some time, took out her phone and opened the app for Uber. She requested a car, noting that it would take five minutes to reach her, and made her way to the pickup point on Southern Hills Drive.

———

Macaria told the driver to drop her off outside the Mount Olive Baptist Church. She set off to the east, towards Floyd Boulevard, but then changed back to the west when his car was out of sight. She turned left onto Virginia Street and walked a block to number 1111. It was a small property, with windows on the first floor and a gable end on the second. The house had a narrow access road on its right-hand side and Macaria walked along it. There was a side door that was locked when she tried the handle and, beyond that, a garage at the rear of the house. She looked up and saw an open window on the second floor and, after checking that she wasn't being observed, she leapt up and grabbed the lip of the garage roof and hauled herself up. The roof had been covered with aggregate to weigh down the felt, and Macaria trod carefully to avoid making too much noise. The window was a sash, with the bottom portion slightly open. She reached it and pushed it up enough for her to be able to slide inside.

The house was quiet. It was owned by a twenty-nine-year-old woman called Madison Wagner. Macaria had studied the file that had been prepared for her by the surveillance team, and she knew that Wagner was unmarried and childless. As far as the surveillance team could ascertain, there was no one who would report her missing for a day or two. Nevertheless, Macaria had been trained to be thorough, and she went downstairs and cleared each room, one by one. She saw nothing that gave her pause to doubt the report: it looked like the home of a single woman of modest means.

An ironing board had been left out in the kitchen, and next to it there was a neat pile of clothes. Macaria went through each item until she found what she was looking for: a tunic and a pair of black trousers. Both were made from a polyester and cotton mix, and both bore the logo of the Sioux City Convention Center. Macaria separated them from the pile and put them on the ironing board.

In the kitchen was a small table with a dirty plate bearing evidence of the dinner that Madison must have eaten. There was a small collection of personal effects on the table, and Macaria sorted through them and removed a set of car keys and a keycard that was marked with the same logo as the clothes. She put the keycard and the car keys on top of the clothes, took a knife from the wooden block and then climbed back upstairs.

There were two bedrooms. The first was empty, but as she stepped carefully into the second, she could hear the sound of light snoring.

She stepped all the way into the room.

There was enough light from the streetlamps outside leaking through the gap in the curtain for Macaria to be able to see that there was a woman in the bed.

She held the knife a little tighter as she made her way to the side of the bed, and gently sat down on the mattress.

Chapter Sixty-Two

Mexico

Two and a half days had passed since Pope watched Isabella be pulled from the wreckage of the police van. He had taken a room at the Hotel Don Ruben on the southern edge of Chihuahua. It was cheap and out of the way, and he had stayed in his room for the most part. He had reported in to Atari every day and had worked his way through the minibar while he waited for information as to what had happened to Isabella and where she might be.

It was 10.40 at night when his phone finally buzzed on the table. He had been watching Mexican soccer on ESPN, and he switched off the set as he got up to retrieve the phone.

'About time,' he said.

'I've got something for you,' Atari replied without acknowledging Pope's impatience.

'Go on.'

'We've been able to intercept Manage Risk comms. It's a little clearer what happened now – both what you saw and what came next. You were right – it was them. They just got there before we did. We think one of their assets was involved.'

Pope thought of the man who had taken Isabella out of the overturned van. He thought of his eyes through the slit in the ski mask: pale, cold, impassive – the exact same as Maia. 'Tell me something I didn't know,' he said.

'They flew her out of Chihuahua to a facility at Fort Bliss. They kept her there overnight, and then flew her back into Mexico early yesterday morning. We've got chatter between two Hueys and ATC as they went across the border.'

'Where to?'

'Rancho de Peña – a few miles to the south of where you are now. And they flew straight into an ambush. They weren't taking chances – they went down there with two fire teams. Maia destroyed both helicopters and killed everyone they sent. Maia and Isabella set them up. Check your phone – I'm sending you something.'

The phone buzzed with a file download invitation. Pope opened it and saw a satellite picture. He saw the sinuous curves of a track that cut through a desert landscape, with a settlement to the north and scrub to the south. Nestled within one of the road's curves was a smaller settlement, dotted with the unmistakeable signs of debris. Pope zoomed in and saw the wrecks of two helicopters, marked by the distinctive shape of the rotors and, as he zoomed in again, what he thought might have been bodies.

'When was this taken?' he asked.

'Eight thirty this morning.'

'You said it was Maia – how do you know that?'

'Who else could have done that?'

'Isabella used herself as bait,' Pope said.

'And they took it. She must have persuaded them to take her down there. Maybe she told them she had something on Maia they couldn't ignore. Who knows – it doesn't really matter. Whatever she said, however she persuaded them to go there, they went for it. And it gets more interesting, too. Nikita Ivanosky was on board one of those helicopters.

He flew into El Paso the day before yesterday, and we've had intercepts to say that he's missing. I think the reason Maia laid the trap was to get to him.'

'Where is he now?'

'That I don't know,' Atari said. 'There's no sign of him. He wasn't one of the dead men the police took to the morgue.'

'So Maia has him?'

'That seems the most likely.'

'But why would she do something like that?'

'We know she's gone rogue. I think this is all about revenge.'

'For what?'

'There's something I haven't told you. Aleksandra Litivenko was responsible for her within Daedalus. The data that Litivenko was going to give us was related to her – her physiology, a DNA workup, report debriefs . . . Litivenko was the closest thing that Maia had to family and then they killed her.'

'Fine,' Pope said. 'Let's assume I can buy that she's capable of being motivated by something other than what they tell her to do. That doesn't explain why Isabella is still with her. Why would she be doing this? Helping Maia? It doesn't make sense. Why would she do that?'

'I could hazard a guess: they've been together for a year. It wouldn't be the first time a hostage has been unable to leave their captor. Maybe she's frightened. You know what Maia and the others are like – you've seen them first-hand.'

'I don't know,' Pope said. 'That's a reach.'

'I said it was a guess,' Atari said. 'But I don't have anything else for you on that, other than that I know where she is.'

Pope pressed the phone to his ear. 'What? Where?'

'I'm sending another picture.'

The phone buzzed in his hand again. Pope opened the file and saw an image of two women passing beneath a security camera. He recognised Isabella immediately. Maia was with her, a hand resting on the girl's shoulder.

'That was taken at a gas station outside Deming in New Mexico three hours ago. They got over the border somewhere and now they're on the move. They were heading northeast when we lost them.'

'Where are they going?'

'I think they're going to Sioux City.'

'Why?'

'Because there's a Gary Morrow rally there tomorrow.'

'What does that—'

Atari interrupted him. 'Look again.'

The phone buzzed for the third time. Pope opened the files and scrolled through two photographs. The first was a grab from a security camera, and it showed a woman wearing the mustard-coloured uniform of a McDonald's server. Her face was tipped up towards the camera, but it was partially obscured by the bill of her branded cap.

'I don't know who that is.'

'The first picture was taken at Dulles last year, the same day as the bombing.'

Pope looked at the second photograph. It, too, had been taken from a security feed. It was of a woman wearing a business suit, wheeling a carry-on suitcase as she passed through what Pope took to be an airport lounge.

'The second one?' he said.

'That was taken at Sioux Gateway Airport this morning. She's in disguise both times, but the best disguise can't beat a biometric scan. It's the same woman. We think that's one of the assets. Her name is Macaria. It's obvious why she's there. Morrow will put an end to the war if he's elected. All of their actions ever since you've been involved have been to foment conflict. The Dulles bomb brought the Americans into the war. Morrow is threatening to bring them out of it again. I think that woman has been sent to assassinate him.'

'And Maia?'

'Let's say this whole thing was so that she could get hold of Ivanosky. Let's say she took him somewhere so she could interrogate him before she killed him. I think he told her that whoever that woman in the pictures is, she was responsible for Litivenko's murder. She was there when the bomb went off. I think Maia has gone there to kill her.'

'Jesus.'

'Isabella is in very serious danger, captain.'

Pope felt sick. 'So I need to get there.'

'I have a ticket waiting for you at Chihuahua Airport. There's an American Eagle flight connecting in Dallas at six tomorrow morning.'

'Tomorrow? That's too long. I need to leave now.'

'You won't be there in time if you drive. If you get the flight you'll be in Sioux City in plenty of time. The ticket will be waiting for you at the airport.'

Pope tried to work out what Atari was thinking. It was difficult: the man had always been inscrutable.

'What do you really want? You're not doing any of this because you care about Isabella.'

'You know why – I'm doing this because I want to change things. I want the same thing I've always wanted – I want you to help me to expose them.'

'So go public. You don't need me to do that.'

'I will, but I need more evidence. We need to show the world what Daedalus is doing. The best way to do that is to present them with something that can't be ignored. We want one of the assets, alive and in one piece. If we can get Maia or Macaria, we can bring everything down around their ears. That's what we want you to do.'

'And Isabella?'

'You go and get her and I'll make sure you both get out. Safe and sound.'

Pope knew that he couldn't say no. He was already entangled in Atari's scheme, and besides, he couldn't leave Isabella again. He had abandoned her once. His selfishness should have cost her her life; that she was still alive was a miracle. He had failed her mother and ignored the promise he had made to keep her safe. But he would make up for it. He would do everything he could to make up for the damage that he had done to her life.

'I'll go,' he said. 'But one more thing – the last time I went up against Maia, she kicked my arse. She's not going to cooperate when I tell her to come with me. You got any smart ideas that'll even the odds?'

'I do,' Atari said. 'There will be equipment waiting for you when you get there. Everything you need.'

Chapter Sixty-Three

Sioux City

Macaria arrived at the convention centre at five in the morning. It was only a mile from the house on Virginia Street and so, rather than take Madison Wagner's car, she had decided to walk. She picked up the sports bag that had been delivered to the house an hour earlier and set off, walking the quiet streets to the south and arriving at her destination fifteen minutes later. She made her way to a private lot at the rear of the building next to a rusting dumpster. The road was quiet, between Jackson Street and Jones Street, and she was not observed as she walked to a plain red door next to a stained metal bin that was, judging by the sign that was affixed to it, used to store spent cooking oil. She put the sports bag down, took the keycard that she had found at Wagner's house and slid it through the reader. The lock buzzed. Macaria opened the door, picked up the sports bag and went inside.

It was dark. She found the light, switched it on and allowed the door to close behind her. There was a rack on the wall that held timesheets, and a machine next to it that was used to stamp them in and out. She paused for a long moment and listened to the sounds of the building: it was quiet, save for the tired creaking of the pipes.

Macaria shouldered the bag and opened a door that led deeper into the building. She saw a corridor beyond, with walls in need of paint and black bags of trash stacked up haphazardly outside another door that she guessed must lead to a refuse area. She paused for a second to listen, heard nothing, and set off to find the store cupboard that Wagner had described before Macaria had opened her throat.

She found it a short walk away. She swiped the keycard to unlock the door and went inside. The walls were lined with shelves on three sides, and there were two large janitor's carts parked up against the far wall. Macaria took one of them, turned it around so she could get to the doors of the cart's small storage cupboard, put the sports bag on the floor next to it and set to work.

Chapter Sixty-Four

They arrived in Sioux City at eight in the morning the day after they had left Mexico. They had been on the road for twenty-four hours. Isabella had insisted that they share the driving and Maia had not demurred. Isabella thought that Maia looked tired, and she had drifted off into a fitful sleep almost as soon as Isabella had taken the wheel for the first time outside Puerta de Luna.

They had travelled northeast through New Mexico, Texas, Oklahoma, Kansas and Nebraska. At six in the evening the previous day, Maia had been sleeping again when Isabella had decided they should find a room to rest and, while she drove, had booked them a room at the Holiday Inn in Liberal. Isabella nudged Maia awake and told her that they were going to stop. Maia had checked their progress to ensure they had the time; satisfied that they did, they had checked in and both slept for four hours.

There was another nine hours between Liberal and Sioux City, and they had taken half of the drive each. Maia was at the wheel when the city came into view for the first time, at just before eight in the morning. Isabella had called ahead and booked a room for them at the Hilton Garden Inn. Maia took Interstate 29 to the north, as it met and then followed the Missouri River.

Isabella gazed out of the window as they headed into the heart of the city. It seemed small and spread out, far removed from the tightness of Juárez – or, before that, the crazy hustle of Washington or the cities that she and Pope had passed through on their way there. She thought back to the time she had spent in Syria, to the cityscapes that had been flattened by years of war and the men and women who slouched as if the spirit had been sucked out of them. She felt as if she were approaching a conclusion, a period that would punctuate the end of the ordeals of the past twelve months. That it might happen here, in a quiet Iowan city, seemed almost anticlimactic.

'Isabella?' Maia said.

She had been gazing vacantly out at the waterfront. She settled herself in her seat. 'I'm okay,' she said.

They passed billboards that were emblazoned with pictures of Gary Morrow. His campaign logo was ubiquitous: in the rear windows of cars waiting at junctions; on signs that had been planted at the side of the road; and on banners in the windows of the properties they passed as they continued north. They passed signs for the Sioux City Convention Center, too.

'We'll rest until midday and then we'll go to the rally,' Maia said.

Isabella nodded.

Maia tried to speak again, but she was interrupted by a hacking cough that wouldn't stop. She signalled that she was going to pull over and turned off the road. She opened the door and stepped out, the coughing seemingly getting worse. By the time Isabella had joined her at the side of the road, Maia had spat out a mouthful of blood onto the asphalt. She was unsteady on her feet and did not resist as Isabella reached her arm around Maia's waist and guided her to the kerb. She helped her to sit and went back to the car for the bottle of water they had picked up when they refuelled the car. Maia filled her mouth, swilled the water around and then spat it out. She took another mouthful and drank it down.

'It's getting worse,' Isabella said.

Maia tried to speak, but the coughing returned. She held up her hand as she waited for the spasm to pass and then shook her head. 'I'm fine,' she said weakly. 'Just a cough.'

Isabella was going to tell her that she was wrong, but she could see that Maia wouldn't agree with her and that the effort of an argument would take more out of her. She decided to hold her tongue, and instead she helped Maia to her feet and took her around to the passenger seat. She went back to the other side of the car, stepping over the blood on the road as she slid inside. She couldn't help thinking about whether their plan was foolish, and whether they would be wiser to turn around and drive away again.

Maia wouldn't agree to that, either, she knew. She was consumed by her desire to finish what Litivenko had started. It might have been the only thing that was keeping her upright. Isabella knew that she wouldn't turn away – and she knew, with certainty, that unless she stayed to help her, Maia would have no chance of success.

Maia had risked her life for Isabella. And as much as Isabella was trying to put it to the back of her mind, there was a connection between them now that could not be ignored. Isabella had so many questions, and she had no one else to ask.

Isabella had no choice. She couldn't abandon Maia now.

Chapter Sixty-Five

Isabella opened her eyes to find that Maia was already awake.

'How are you?' Maia asked.

Isabella had retired as soon as they had reached the hotel room earlier that morning, and she realised that she had fallen asleep while Maia was still up and awake. Maia's bed looked as if it was undisturbed.

'How long was I asleep?'

'Two hours,' Maia said.

'Did you rest at all?'

'No,' Maia replied. 'I went out for these.'

Isabella sat up. Maia's skin had recovered some of its colour, and she looked far less weak than she had appeared earlier. Her unsteadiness was gone. She had an AT&T bag and took out two boxed cell phones.

She tossed one over to Isabella. 'We'll use these, and dump them when we're done.'

'How are you feeling?' Isabella asked her.

'Better,' she said.

'But—'

'I'm fine, Isabella,' Maia said – and then, qualifying, added, 'I'll *be* fine. Really.'

Isabella looked for her clothes. She knew what Maia was saying wasn't true, but there was no point in arguing. Maia wouldn't listen to her.

'Here,' Maia said, handing Isabella a sandwich wrapped in cellophane. 'You need to eat.'

Isabella unwrapped the sandwich and took a bite. It was limp and uninspiring, but she was hungry and she knew that she would need to be at her best for what might happen at the rally.

Maia gave her a bottle of Coke. 'Do you have any questions?' she asked her.

'About?'

'What we are going to do today.'

'No,' Isabella said. They had discussed the plan during their long drive. It was familiar. 'I know what we're doing.'

'I just want to be clear. You don't take any action yourself. You're there to watch. Do you understand?'

Isabella cranked the lid of the Coke and took a long drink. 'Yes,' she said. 'I understand.'

Maia stared at her. 'Say it.'

'I'm there to watch.'

Maia nodded. 'And if you see something?'

'I'll tell you.' Isabella felt a flash of annoyance. 'You don't trust me?'

'I do,' Maia said. 'Ivanosky will have told them that we know. They might call it off. Or, if they don't, they'll be more careful. This isn't the Mexicans. Macaria is like me. She's dangerous.'

'And like me, too?'

Maia looked as if she were about to reply, but then paused and looked down. When she gazed up again, it was as if she had changed her mind about what she was going to say. 'I find it difficult to put myself in your shoes,' she said. 'I wish I could, but I can't. I've never been able to do that. Empathy . . .' She paused again. 'I'm not good at it. But I want to help you, Isabella. I *will* help you. But we have to do this first. If Macaria is here, I have to find her.'

'What about what we talked about? When do we tell the police? We have to tell them.'

Maia's face flickered with annoyance. 'We will,' she replied. 'I told you we would. But if we do it too soon, Macaria will abort. You have to trust me.'

Isabella decided that there was no point in pursuing the conversation any further. They had already talked it out. She went into the bathroom and turned the faucet in the shower. The water began to fall; a reassuring hiss as it splashed against the tray. She went to the basin and looked into the mirror fixed above it. Who was she? She had stared at her reflection for hours in the darkened windshield as they had crossed the country and not even recognised herself. Everything she had thought she knew about herself had been undermined. She couldn't trust her memories. Her mother had lied to her. Her heritage was a mystery. Who was she? *What* was she?

She could only judge herself by what she did, by the standards to which she held herself. Maia was too good a liar for Isabella to work out whether she was being truthful or just telling her what she wanted to hear. Isabella knew that Maia was consumed by the prospect of revenging Litivenko. It had driven her for a year, and now she was close to achieving it. Close enough to ignore the likelihood that Ivanosky might have tipped off Macaria and her support team that they were coming. Close enough, too, to ignore the risk to the hundreds, and likely thousands, of Iowans who would be there. Isabella thought of them. Some would be on their way now, readying themselves, perhaps excited by the prospect of what they were planning for the day.

She had already made her decision, and now she acknowledged it to herself: she wouldn't gamble with their lives. She would allow Maia's plan to go as far as she dared, but she would go no further than that.

She looked back into the bedroom. She could see Maia in the reflection of the mirror inside the wardrobe door. Isabella did not know how Maia would react if she disobeyed her, but that uncertainty was not a good enough reason for her to change her mind. She thought of her mother: she had lived her life by a code, and Isabella was going to do the same. If there were to be consequences for that, she would deal with them when the time came.

Chapter Sixty-Six

The Sioux City Convention Centre was a curious looking building in the centre of town, in a large block between 4th and 5th Streets. It was ugly, with two arched entrances that accommodated a series of double doors that led in from the street. American flags flew from reproduction street lamps that were trying, and failing, to evoke an earlier time. The building faced onto an untidy parking lot that was already busy with buses and cars bringing in the Iowans who had travelled to see the candidate in person.

Isabella and Maia were on 4th Street, waiting to be admitted. The street thronged with men, women and children. Isabella guessed that there must have been two thousand people in the multiple lines that snaked towards the doors. Isabella looked at the people nearest to them. They were wearing T-shirts and caps branded with message that had propelled Morrow to the verge of the presidency: *America First*. The mood was festive, and excitement trilled through the air. Isabella didn't share their excitement; she felt sick. No one had any idea of the risk they would be taking if they went inside the doors. How could they know?

Isabella watched for anyone she might recognise. She had seen two of Maia's brothers before: Blaine had been at the exchange at Clingmans Dome and Ambrose had taken her from Mexico. There were very clear resemblances between them, but Maia had undercut the suggestion that Isabella might be able to pick out Macaria, saying that she would almost certainly be in disguise.

Isabella looked at the building. There were armed police on the doors. Members of staff were conducting random bag searches on those waiting in line. Other officers walked up and down outside with sniffer dogs.

'It looks thorough,' Isabella said.

'It won't be enough to stop her,' Maia said quietly.

They waited their turn, slowly moving forward. There was a group of protestors on the other side of the street, penned in by a row of temporary railings that separated them from the crowd. They were chanting anti-Muslim slogans, and a call-and-response between one of the protestors and the others around him argued that the troops should not be called back, and that the war needed to be won. They had hung a banner across the railings: 'DEMAND VICTORY IN THE MIDDLE EAST'. Other banners mixed political and religious zeal, with several badges displaying the cross, with the message 'Thanks Be To God Which Grant Us This Victory'.

They reached the front of the line.

'Tickets, please,' asked the attendant.

Maia handed over the pages she had printed out at the hotel's business centre. She had applied for tickets on her phone while they drove north from Mexico, and they had been allotted without any kind of security check, or even confirmation of party affiliation. The attendant glanced at the printout, glanced at Maia and then Isabella, and waved them through.

The doors opened into a wide lobby area. Four scanners had been installed, and it was necessary to pass through them before entering the main body of the centre. Isabella had asked whether they would need to be armed, but Maia had warned her that the security would make it impossible; Isabella could see that she had been right. Isabella took out her phone and loose change and removed her belt, putting everything into a tray and sliding it towards the X-ray machine. She stepped through the arch; the machine was silent and the guard beckoned her on, indicating that she should quickly gather her things and go through.

Isabella fed her belt back through the loops of her trousers and watched as Maia went through the next scanner along; her machine was silent, too.

Isabella looked around. The lobby opened into the main auditorium, with corridors leading away on both sides to access restrooms and concessions. The crowd was milling in the lobby, some looking at the merchandise on sale at a large booth to the right, while others bought drinks from a bar to the left. It was loud, with an electric buzz of anticipation that strummed and throbbed as the crowd waited to go inside to listen to their hero speak.

Maia drew nearer. 'Ready?' she asked quietly.

'Yes.'

'Go into the hall and keep your eyes open. If you see anything—'

'I know. I'll tell you.'

'Leave the line open all the time.'

'I know. I will.'

Maia nodded, turned and made her way through the clutch of people in front of the merchandise stall and into the corridor beyond. Isabella looked around the room at the dozens of men and women slowly filtering through the doors into the auditorium. She took out her phone, plugged in her earbuds and pushed them into her ears. She allowed herself to be jostled towards the doors and, settling into the slow-moving line, she shuffled ahead.

Chapter Sixty-Seven

The crowd was gradually dispersing as the delegates made their way into the conference hall. Pope waited patiently as the line shuffled forward. The security was decent, with each person being required to show their tickets before passing through a body scanner.

Pope could see a clock on the wall inside the lobby: it showed ten minutes past twelve. He could see a reasonable police presence throughout the facility, with several men and women in sharp suits with earpieces that marked them out as secret service. Morrow was a high-value target, and no chances were being taken.

'Sir?'

Pope was next in line. He stepped forward, handing over the ticket that Atari had magicked up for him. The security guard checked it, gave a nod of satisfaction and then ushered him towards the scanner. Pope emptied his pockets and removed his belt, dropping the items and his empty rucksack into a tray and sliding the tray into the X-ray machine. He passed through the arch with the same feeling of unease that he felt whenever he had to negotiate the devices at airports. He was always irrationally paranoid that he had neglected to remove his weapon, or that he would have ammunition about his person that he had forgotten. The reason for his unease this morning was the opposite: he was unarmed, and that knowledge was disconcerting given what he was expecting to find when he got inside. He was going to have to rely on Atari's continued ingenuity to even the odds a little in the event that Maia was here and he could find her.

He passed through the scanner without setting it off, collected his personal belongings from the tray, looped his belt back through his trousers and slung the empty rucksack over his shoulder. It was twelve thirty now. The event was due to begin in half an hour. He would have to be quick.

He set off, passing through the crowd until he reached the corridor that Atari had described to him. He followed it until he found the men's room and went inside. The bathroom smelled of disinfectant and urine. There were four cubicles and a row of urinals, together with several sinks and two hand driers. He checked that the cubicles were empty – they were – and then waved his hand under both driers to set them off. He made his way to the furthest cubicle from the door, went inside, closed the door and slid the bolt through the lock. He lowered the toilet lid, stood on it carefully and reached up to push at one of the ceiling tiles. It was light, and he was easily able to dislodge it and then turn it around through forty-five degrees so that he could rest it on the open aperture. He reached up into the space and patted around with his fingers, trying to find anything that might have been left there.

There was nothing.

The first hand drier cut out, followed shortly afterwards by the second, and so Pope compensated by flushing the toilet with his foot and waiting for the hiss as the cistern refilled itself. He replaced the first ceiling panel and shuffled across so he could get to its neighbour. This one was easily dislodged, too, and Pope had to look away as a cloud of dust and fragments of dried paint fell down into his face. He reached through the gap and felt something cold and hard. He stood on tiptoes and, careful not to drop the item, he brought it down. It was a black moulded plastic case with a handle and two metal clasps. He rested it on the cistern as he replaced the ceiling tile, then lowered himself to sit on the lid and examined the case more closely. A legend on the front read 'Taser X26P'. He flipped the clasps and opened the case. It was fitted with a foam inset and, nestled within, was a taser. Atari had said that they wanted Maia in one piece, and that he would provide the equipment to help Pope to do that. He looked in the case once more and found a leather wallet that held a syringe, which was preloaded with a clear fluid.

He hid the taser and the syringe in his rucksack and put the empty case back in the ceiling space.

Then he took out his phone and called Atari's number.

'Got it,' he said.

'Good. Anything?'

'I'm looking. You?'

'Nothing yet. This is probably going to be on you.'

Pope ended the call, slid the phone back into his pocket and stepped out into the bathroom again. It was still empty. He put the rucksack over his shoulder and made his way back outside.

Chapter Sixty-Eight

Macaria pushed the janitor's cart along the corridor until she reached the series of booths that were set into the wall at the back of the auditorium and were reserved, usually, for camera crews and for sound and lighting technicians. She had visited the booths earlier, when the centre was still empty, and had chosen the one at the end of the line. It was empty, without the equipment that she had found in the neighbouring booths, and the dust on the small table near to the window that looked down onto the stage showed it had not been used for weeks. Macaria opened the door, pushed the trolley inside, closed the door behind her, wheeled the cart back up against it and used her foot to lock the castors so that it couldn't easily be moved. She would have a warning were anyone to attempt to come inside.

She made her way to the window. It was arranged in two panes, and the bottom one could be opened. Macaria undid the clasp and pushed the panel a little to open up a small gap.

The auditorium was beginning to fill as the crowd made its way inside. She checked her watch: twelve thirty.

Thirty minutes.

She went back to the cart. It was reasonably large, with two removable vinyl bags on either side that were used to hold trash, and a front storage area that was accessed through a pair of lockable polypropylene doors. She reached into the vinyl bag on the right of the trolley and took out the component parts that she had taken from the sports bag. She laid them out on the floor: upper and lower receiver assemblies, bolt assembly, bipod and sights. She opened the cart's storage and removed a box of ammunition and an optical scope.

The rifle had been delivered to the house, and Macaria had spent an hour ensuring that it was correctly zeroed. She had disassembled it carefully, and now she needed to put it back together again with the same care and precision. The scope was fitted to a mount that could be separated and re-joined without interrupting the adjustments necessary to keep the rifle zeroed.

Macaria moved the small table to the window and set up the rifle so the bipod was resting on it, the muzzle a good six inches inside the room and invisible from outside. This would not be a difficult shot. The distance between her shooting position and the stage was not significant, and there were no environmental factors to consider. She was standing behind the rifle, bent at the waist so she could push the butt end of the stock up tight against her shoulder. She looked through the sight, nudging the aim across the stage until the lectern was settled dead centre in the cross-hairs.

She rehearsed the routine that she would go through.

She took a breath, exhaled and then slid her finger through the guard. She breathed in and out.

In and out.

In and then out a final time, allowing herself an envelope of three seconds when she would be relaxed enough to take the shot.

She pulled away from the rifle, removed it from the table and placed it carefully on the floor.

She looked at her watch.

12.45.

Fifteen minutes to go.

Chapter Sixty-Nine

Isabella made her way inside the auditorium. She had studied the information on the centre's website and had noted that it could accommodate up to three thousand visitors. It was going to be at full capacity today. She looked up at the raised stage. A temporary backdrop had been put up at the back, decorated in patriotic red, white and blue, with 'Morrow' printed in large capital letters. There was a lectern, similarly decorated, with a microphone arranged atop it. She saw the transparent glass panels of two autocue machines, and behind them a row of temporary barriers fencing off the stage from the rest of the room. Men and women, some of them with children, had already filled the auditorium halfway to the back. They held campaign banners aloft, some of them raising their cell phones to take pictures of the empty stage and their fellow attendees. There was a festive, almost jubilant atmosphere. The campaign's momentum was almost tangible, and the prospect of success was infectious.

Isabella dialled Maia's number. 'I'm in,' she said into the hands-free mic. 'It's busy. Where are you?'

'Backstage.'

Isabella could hear the sound of footsteps.

'Have you seen anything?'

'Nothing,' Maia said. 'Stay inside. Pay attention. If you see anything, tell me. If you see anyone that worries you, tell me. Don't do anything yourself.'

'I know,' Isabella said testily. 'You told me already.'

'Leave the line open.'

Isabella walked ahead until she was at the back of the crowd and stopped. She studied the wings of the stage; she guessed the speakers would emerge from there and wait their turn. It was dark, though, and she couldn't see anything save a man in a suit speaking into a lapel mic.

She looked around. The men and women were dressed casually in jeans and T-shirts, many of them bearing the campaign logo or variations on the same theme. There was a buzz of excited conversation in the room, the thrill of anticipation that they were about to be so close to the man in whom they had invested so much hope. Isabella tried to ignore them, to tune out the noise and the pageantry so that she might be better attuned to the threat she knew could very well be a few feet away from her.

She looked at the time.

12.55.

Five minutes.

She couldn't wait any longer.

Couldn't take the chance.

She turned away so she wouldn't be overheard, put Maia on hold and dialled 911.

Chapter Seventy

Macaria waited and watched.

The governor of Iowa came on stage first and delivered an enthusiastic speech, extolling the virtue of the candidate and what he would do for the state – and, beyond that, the country as a whole. Macaria lifted the rifle from the floor, placed the bipod on the table and aimed the barrel out of the open window. She lowered herself to the sight and leaned forward until she had acquired the perfect position: no offset in her shoulders, lined up straight to allow for rapid shooting with minimal muzzle rise. Her feet were shoulder-width apart and her right foot was staggered six inches behind her left. The stance would absorb and reduce recoil; she could cede a little accuracy in favour of being able to put three or four shots into her target.

She watched through the scope as the governor ran through a tired call-and-response routine with the crowd, leading them in a choreographed protest against the 'elites' who were forcing young American men and women to fight in wars that had nothing to do with them. The crowd booed and cheered on demand, their placards and banners raised in a forest that provided a distracting foreground that Macaria could have done without. The moment passed, however, and the signs were lowered as the governor moved on to thank the volunteers who were canvassing for the candidate. There was a show of hands from those party loyalists who were giving their time to advance the cause, and then, almost without transition, the governor extended her arm to the right.

'Ladies and gentlemen, please give a rowdy Iowan welcome to the next President of the United States: Gary Morrow!'

'The Stars and Stripes Forever' played through the venue's PA system and the crowd raised their signs and waved them with wild enthusiasm. Macaria held her concentration, aiming the rifle off to the left. Morrow appeared from the wings, waiting at the edge of the stage for a moment and applauding the crowd. He was wearing a dark blue suit, a white shirt and a tie that was a shade lighter than his jacket. He set off across the stage, still clapping, and Macaria tracked him, holding him in the cross-hairs. The upraised signs flashed colourfully across the bottom of the sight and the music came to an end, the crescendo distorting through the cheap speakers. Morrow reached the microphone and adjusted it.

Macaria centred the rifle's pistol grip in the V at the junction of the thumb and index finger of her trigger hand. She held the gun high on the back of the grip and supported the forestock with her left.

Morrow pointed to the wings with his left hand. 'Thank you, Alexa,' he said. 'That's your governor right there, ladies and gentlemen! Isn't she doing a *terrific* job? Just terrific. Give her a round of applause.'

The crowd obliged, whooping and cheering.

Macaria stared into the sight, centring Morrow's head in the cross-hairs. She started to apply pressure on the trigger, gradually pulling it back.

'I am thrilled to be back in the great state of Iowa right here with the incredible men and women of Sioux City. We've had quite a week. On Saturday I was in Virginia with thousands of brave men and women of the United States military. Do we love the United States military?'

There were loud cheers.

'And now this morning I'm back in the centre of the American heartland to spend time with thousands of true American patriots. And, let me tell you, we are going—'

Macaria heard the change in the timbre of crowd's cheering before she saw what had prompted it. She kept her cheek pressed to the rifle but, before she could squeeze the trigger all the way to the rear, two dark-suited men hurried out and bundled Morrow away. She pulled up from the weapon so she could see what was happening: the two men, Secret Service agents judging by their dark suits and the earpieces pressed into their ears, manhandled the candidate off stage. He was gone in less than four seconds, and Macaria's chances of successfully prosecuting the operation went with him.

There was no time to question what had happened. She placed the rifle on the floor, crossed the booth and, taking a breath to compose herself, moved the cart aside, opened the door and stepped out.

Chapter Seventy-One

The crowd had gasped as the two Secret Service agents hurried onto the stage and bustled Morrow into the wings.

Isabella was halfway between the front and rear of the auditorium and found herself going against the flow of the crowd ahead of her as people turned and started to hurry towards the exits. Isabella turned with them and was bumped and nudged along with the tide.

She glanced up. There were lighting rigs suspended from the ceiling at various points, and three separate projection booths at the back of the room. A bright spotlight shone from the window on the immediate left, and she could see the glow of electrical equipment through the middle window. She was about to turn around when she saw something in the window to the right. It was a quick flash of movement and then something long and straight sliding back until she couldn't see it any longer.

'Maia!' she hissed, cupping her mouth and the in-line microphone. 'What's happened?'

'Morrow's just been taken off stage.'

'What?'

'They just came and grabbed him.'

There was no reply, save the sound of Maia's footsteps.

'I saw someone. The booth to my right.'

'Someone?'

'I don't know – it might have been a sniper.'

'Copy that.'

'What do we do?' Isabella asked.

'Abort,' Maia said. 'Go back to the hotel.'

'What about—'

'Abort,' Maia repeated. 'Get out now.'

Chapter Seventy-Two

Maia was in the guts of the building. The corridors were suddenly busy as staff hurried along them. She heard the squelch of static from a police radio and stepped aside as an officer trotted by her. She held her breath, but the officer was distracted and did not stop. She continued on and was approaching a crossroads in the corridor when a woman wearing a cleaner's uniform walked right across the junction. She was moving quickly, with a look of determination on her face. She was clearly in a hurry. She did not look into the corridor and had not, as far as Maia could tell, seen her.

But Maia saw her.

And she recognised her instantly.

Macaria.

She was in disguise, but Maia knew it was her. She was certain of it.

Macaria walked over the junction and disappeared from view. Maia picked up her pace, reached the crossroads and turned to follow the direction that her sister had taken. She was ahead of her, no more than twenty feet. The corridor curved around a corner.

Maia picked up her pace.

She found herself wondering, for a moment, whether she was doing the right thing.

Maia thought about Litivenko. Her siblings were still working for the people who were responsible for her murder. Macaria and Moros had been there when she was killed. They were involved. They were complicit, just as Maia had known they would be.

She would make them pay.

But Macaria would surely have a handgun or something else that she could use to defend herself, and Maia was unarmed.

Maia was fifteen feet away from her now and closing in. She looked beyond Macaria and saw the figure of a man coming around the curve in the corridor. Macaria stepped over to the side so that she and the man could pass each other by.

The man looked up, saw her and slowed.

Maia stopped. She recognised him.

It was Michael Pope.

His hand went to his jacket and pulled out a chunky object. It was a taser. He aimed it at Maia.

'Stop,' he said.

Macaria turned around, perhaps fearful that she had been the object of the man's instruction. She saw Maia and, for a moment, their eyes locked. And then she turned and hurried away.

'Hands up,' Pope said.

Maia raised her hands above her head.

'Don't,' she said.

Chapter Seventy-Three

T he crowd was marshalled through the lobby and out into the bright sunshine. Half a dozen police cruisers had drawn up outside the conference centre, and officers were haranguing the men and women to get away from the doors so that the scrum behind them could leave, too. Isabella was jostled as she passed through the doors. One of the officers found a bullhorn and used it to encourage the crowd to keep moving.

Isabella raised the in-line mic closer to her mouth. 'Maia?' she said. There was no response.

'Keep moving, folks,' the officer with the bullhorn called out. 'Move away from the doors.'

Isabella let the mic fall back down and glanced to the left and right. Some of the attendees were crossing 4th Street so they could head back to the buses that were parked in the large lot opposite the building. Others were going to their cars, and others still were gathering in little clutches to breathlessly talk about what they had just seen.

Isabella's attention had been drawn to the sound of a car's horn as a Buick narrowly avoided reversing into the side of a bus when she saw her: a woman dressed in what Isabella took to be a cleaner's uniform, waiting to cross the street. The woman was ten feet away. Isabella's eye was caught by the woman's blonde hair, but it was when she turned to look back at the conference centre that she mistook her for Maia. They shared the same features: the shape of the nose, just a little larger than usual; the same angled cheekbones; the same pale eyes. The woman turned away from her, negotiated the crowd on the sidewalk and set off to the west, passing beneath a Stars and Stripes flag that was fixed to one of the old-style lamp posts and heading towards the big Howard Johnson hotel.

It wasn't Maia, but the resemblance between her and the woman was so close that it could not be a coincidence. Isabella had never seen one of Maia's sisters, but she was sure that the woman was related to her.

It had to be Macaria.

'Excuse me,' she said, squeezing between two women who were speculating about whether what they had just witnessed was real or a false alarm. They parted just enough for Isabella to slide through. The crowd started to thin out as she moved away from the immediate vicinity of the centre, and she was able to pick up speed. Macaria was twenty feet away, walking quickly but not so fast as to draw attention to herself.

Isabella followed her.

Chapter Seventy-Four

H ands,' Pope repeated.

Maia raised her hands above her head.

Pope closed in on her, the taser aimed squarely at her chest.

'Please,' Maia said. 'That was my sister. I have to go after her.'

Pope looked at her. She looked different to how he remembered. There was something *lesser* about her. She looked unwell.

'Where's Isabella?' he said.

'Outside,' Maia replied. 'Why don't you speak to her?' She slowly lowered one of her hands, turned her head and pointed to her ear. Pope saw that she was wearing an earbud and that a wire ran down the side of her neck and into her jacket.

'Keep your hands up,' Pope said.

'Please, captain. I need to follow my sister.'

Pope brandished the taser. 'Stay where you are,' he said.

'Speak to Isabella. I'll put the phone on speaker. I'm going to reach into my pocket to get it now.'

She didn't wait for him to give permission. She brought down her right hand and started to reach into her jacket.

Pope couldn't take the chance that she might have a weapon.

He pulled the trigger. Two prongs ejected from the unit, streaking across the distance between them and landing on either side of Maia's sternum. The shock discharged, twelve hundred volts unloading down the filaments and pumping into her body. Maia grimaced, but she didn't go down. Pope triggered another blast; a buzzing and clicking sound was emitted by the unit as a further charge was sent along the filaments. Maia winced and, moving stiffly, took her hand from her pocket, grabbing the prongs and yanking them out.

She turned to face him. 'Get out of my way, captain,' she muttered.

Pope launched himself at her. He was much heavier than she was, and her muscles were still stiff from the taser. She was unable to get out of the way and their bodies collided, Pope lowering his shoulder at the last minute to strike a blow against the side of her head. She bounced away, staggering against the wall. Pope overbalanced and fell to his knees, turning back just in time to raise his right arm to deflect the kick that she launched at him. He caught her ankle and yanked her off her feet. Maia landed on her backside; Pope scrambled atop her, his left arm barred across her chest and all of his weight pressing down on her. She struggled, but she was unable to move him. She was weaker than Pope remembered; the effects of the tasering, perhaps, or maybe she really was unwell.

He reached his right hand into his pocket, took out the syringe that he had moved there and used his teeth to pull off the protective sheath.

She saw what he was doing. 'No,' she protested. 'Please! Don't.'

Maia looked up at him as he leaned down close enough to press the needle into her neck. She mouthed something, her voice little more than a gasp. Pope ignored it. He depressed the plunger and injected her with the anaesthetic.

The strength ebbed out of her body and her breathing became shallow.

Pope kept his left hand on her chest, pressing down, and then reached into her jacket with his right hand and found the pocket. There was no gun. She wasn't going for a weapon. All she had in there was the phone, just as she had said. Pope took it and looked at the display: there was an open call. He put it on speaker.

'Isabella?' he said.

There was a moment of silence before he was rewarded with the sound of a voice he immediately recognised.

'Who's this?'

'Pope.'

'Pope?'

'Yes,' he said. 'Where are you?'

'Where's Maia?'

'I've . . .' He paused, disorientated by the turn that events had taken.

'Where is Maia, Pope?'

'I'm with her. It's fine. You don't need to worry about her now.'

'What?'

'What's happening, Isabella? Where are you?'

'What do you mean I don't have to worry? Let me speak to her.'

'You can't. I drugged her.'

There was no reply, just the sound of Isabella's footsteps.

'I came to help you,' Pope said.

'No,' she said. 'Maia doesn't work for them anymore. She's not like you think she is. She wants to finish what Litivenko started – I'm helping her to do that.'

Pope closed his eyes. He suddenly felt stupid and afraid.

'Pope?'

He took a deep breath.

'Pope! Get Maia out of there.'

'Where are you?'

'I'm following Macaria. Heading west. Just crossing Jackson Street.'

'I'm coming,' he said.

He felt the touch of fingers on his wrist. He looked down: Maia had somehow found the strength to reach for him. Her eyes were pleading as she tried to speak, but her voice was too quiet for him to hear it.

He lowered his ear so she could speak into it.

'Help her,' she breathed. 'My sister . . . will kill her.'

Pope nodded and went to rise, but Maia held onto his wrist.

'Isabella,' she said, barely audible. 'She's . . . different.'

'How?'

'Special,' she said.

Her eyes closed; she could barely open them.

'What does that mean? "Special"? How is she special?'

'She's . . . like . . . me.'

She exhaled deeply, her fingers loosening and sliding off his wrist, and she lay still.

Chapter Seventy-Five

Macaria went by the big Howard Johnson hotel. She made her way beneath the bridge that connected the Wells Fargo bank with the office building on the opposite side of the street, skirted a grassy area with a fountain and other water features and turned right onto Nebraska, heading north.

Isabella followed, leaving plenty of distance between them. Her mother and then Maia had taught her how to tail someone without being seen, and she tried to remember everything that they had said. She knew Macaria would be skilled in counter-surveillance, and that it was unlikely she would be able to follow the woman on her own for very long. She would just have to do her best.

Macaria passed beneath another footbridge and made her way along the sidewalk next to the Sioux City Public Museum. She reached the junction with 5th Street. The Martin Luther King Jr Transportation Center was on the other side of the crossroads. It was a large five-storey block that included a parking garage and the Greyhound terminal. A long line of traffic moved sluggishly, and the woman was forced to wait for the lights to change before she could cross over.

The earbud in her ear buzzed. 'Isabella? Where are you?'

It was Pope. She could hear the sound of his breathing and the thud of his running feet.

'The corner of Nebraska and 5th. Where's Maia?'

'Don't do anything. Wait for me. I'm a minute away.'

'Where's Maia? Did you get her out?'

The lights changed and the traffic stopped.

Pope didn't answer.

Macaria stepped into the street and started to cross.

Isabella trotted after her.

Macaria was in the middle of the crossing when a SUV with blacked-out windows raced along 5th, shot across the junction and braked sharply, blocking her path. The doors along the side of the vehicle slid back and two men jumped down. They were both carrying bulky black-and-yellow tasers.

Isabella heard an engine behind her, and as she swung around she saw an identical vehicle skid to a halt. The doors to the second vehicle rolled back and two more men jumped down.

These men had tasers, too; they were equipped with laser targeting units, the red beams painting bright dots on her chest.

'Don't move!'

She turned to the sound of the voice. Macaria was backing up, retreating from the two men who were approaching her.

There was nowhere for her to go.

'Stay where you are.'

The order wasn't directed at Macaria. It was for Isabella. She turned and saw two men cautiously approaching her.

Macaria spun around and sprinted. The man on the left discharged his taser; the cartridge hissed as the compressed gas expanded, firing the charge electrodes at her. Both probes landed in Macaria's chest and Isabella heard the crackle of electricity as the current travelled down the wires. Macaria stopped short, falling to her knees. She reached up to the electrodes and ripped them out before getting back to her feet.

The man who had tased her was too close. Macaria launched herself at him. Isabella saw her block the man's clumsy attempt to club her with the taser, grabbing his wrist and then forcing his elbow in. Isabella heard him scream, and then the gunshot-loud crack as his arm snapped. Macaria took advantage of his disability to grab a pistol from a shoulder rig, pressing it into the man's chest and firing from point-blank range.

Isabella heard someone bellow her name.

She turned and saw Pope.

'Run!' Pope yelled at her.

Isabella felt two stings: one between her shoulder blades and the other at the small of her back. She heard the crackle and fizz of the discharging current and then felt her body stiffen like a board. She lost the ability to move her arms and legs and couldn't prevent herself from falling to her knees. The sensation was like the worst cramp that she could imagine and there was nothing she could do to make it stop. She realised that she had toppled over onto her back, and as she looked up at the square of sky between the sides of the buildings at the intersection, she saw a man she didn't recognise lean over her and press his hand against her neck. She felt a sharp scratch, and then a sensation of the purest cold passing up into her head and down towards her shoulder.

Her vision blurred.

She heard the rattle of automatic gunfire, although it sounded muffled, as if she were listening to it underwater.

Unconsciousness swept over her.

Chapter Seventy-Six

Pope barged a path through the crowds that were milling outside the conference centre. He walked briskly but, consumed by anxiety, he quickly broke into a run. He hopped down into the street to avoid the slow-moving pedestrians on the sidewalk and sprinted to the junction with Jones Street.

He heard Atari's voice in his earbud.

'Where are you, captain?'

Pope didn't know how to respond, and so he said nothing.

'Pope? Report. I'm tracking you outside of the building. Why have you left?'

He had to say something. 'It's too hot inside. They've evacuated the building.'

'Why? Was there an attack?'

'No. But they cleared the room.'

'Did you see Maia or the girl?'

'Negative,' he said. 'I'll call in later. Pope out.'

He reached down for his phone and ended the call before Atari could speak again.

Pope turned onto Nebraska just as a black SUV rushed past him. Its passage was marked by a barrage of angry horns as drivers watched in bewilderment. The SUV shot beneath the footbridge that spanned the street and then slammed on its brakes, slaloming left and right as it slid to a sudden stop in the middle of the intersection ahead. Pope saw a second black SUV parked on the other side of the junction; the two cars were parallel to one another, blocking the traffic.

Pope saw two pedestrians caught between the two vehicles. They were both female. The one furthest from him was wearing what looked to be a cleaner's uniform. She was the taller of the two, with blonde hair that ran down to her shoulders. The second woman had her back to him, but she was shorter and more slender.

Pope didn't need to see her face to recognise her.

It was Isabella.

She turned as the first SUV came to a halt. Two men got out of the vehicle. Both of them were carrying identical tasers to the one that Pope had used to subdue Maia. The same model that Atari had left for him. Pope reached for a weapon that wasn't there and swore. He would have to improvise.

He ran. There was a large office block between him and the intersection. The second floor protruded out over the sidewalk, supported by a row of concrete pillars. A man emerged from the building and wandered into Pope's path. Pope shouldered him aside, sending him sprawling to the ground, and ran on with imprecations ringing in his ears.

Another pair of men had emerged from the first SUV. They, too, carried the distinctive black-and-yellow tasers.

Isabella froze as one of the men behind her called her name.

They had both aimed their tasers at her. Pope could see red laser dots dancing across her torso.

The woman in the cleaner's uniform bolted. One of the tasers fired; Pope could hear the crackle and buzz. The woman was struck and fell to her knees, but yanked out the probes and stood. She launched herself at the man who had tased her, grabbed his arm and, with frightening ease, snapped it.

The man nearest to the injured man pulled an MP4 sub-machine gun and levelled it.

'Isabella!' Pope yelled.

Isabella turned to the sound of his voice.

'Run!'

She turned back at the same moment that one of the men behind her fired his taser.

She fell to her knees and the shooter went to her.

The other man, alerted by Pope's shout, whirled around to face him. He dropped the taser and pulled a handgun from a holster that he wore on his belt.

The man raised his arm. Pope dived to his right, throwing himself into the cover of one of the pillars. The gun barked twice, and Pope was showered with sharp fragments of concrete as a round crashed overhead.

He heard the rattle of small-arms fire, but this time it was not aimed at him. He risked a look around the pillar. The woman in the cleaner's uniform was on the ground, the man with the MP4 aiming down at her as he cautiously approached her.

The man who had tased Isabella hauled her out of sight behind the SUV, and the shooter who had fired at Pope covered their retreat. Pope glanced over at the other side of the intersection and saw that the other woman's body had been dragged into the first vehicle. He heard the rumble of the engines. The shooter got into the cabin and the driver buried the pedal, the car racing up the hill that led away to the north. It was followed by the second, with both vehicles running the red lights at the next intersection along.

Pope stepped out of cover and watched them until they crested the hill and disappeared.

Pope knew the two men who had taken Isabella. He was sure of it, and the details were coming back to him. Both men had been waiting for a transfer into Group Fifteen. The man who had tased Isabella was Firth, and he had come to them from the Special Boat Service. The second man was Parker, and he was SAS. Pope had been involved in their recruitment. The reports from Trafalgar Park, the Group's training facility in Wiltshire, had been excellent. Pope would have had no problem in approving their transfer, yet that was moot now that the Group had been disbanded and he had been forced into hiding.

So what were the two of them doing here?

And why had they taken Isabella?

Chapter Seventy-Seven

Maia opened her eyes. It took her a moment to realise where she was: in the back of an ambulance. The vehicle was moving; as it swung around corners, she felt the straps that secured her to the gurney. The straps were not so tight as to restrain her, but as she tried to raise her arms, she found that she could not. Her muscles were sluggish and torpid, and she remembered the injection that Michael Pope had administered. He had knocked her out. Whichever sedative he used had been powerful, and it was still in her system.

'Hello.'

She tilted her head so she could see who had spoken. It was a female medic, dressed in a white shirt with a blue cap on her head.

'How are you feeling?'

Maia tried to speak, but her throat was dry and her mouth felt as if it was stuffed with cotton wool.

'You want some water?'

Maia gave a slight nod. The paramedic got up and, supporting herself against the side of the vehicle, made her way to the front of the vehicle.

'What . . . happened?' Maia mumbled.

'They found you unconscious backstage at the centre. Couldn't wake you up, so they called us. What were you doing there? Trying to get outside?'

The woman moved back towards Maia again. She only managed a couple of steps when the driver slammed on the brakes. The paramedic was thrown backwards, crashing into a second gurney and then falling to the floor. The tyres squealed as Maia's gurney rattled against its stays, and she slid back and then forward, held in place by the straps around her body.

The ambulance came to a sudden stop.

Maia heard the sound of another vehicle's door opening and then the unmistakeable muffled bark of a suppressed pistol. Glass shattered and the ambulance's horn blared out.

The rear doors opened and natural light streamed inside.

The paramedic was on her knees; Maia heard the pistol exhale again, blood splashing the wall as the woman fell to the floor.

Her gurney was released from its stays and wheeled backwards out of the ambulance. Maia squinted in the bright sunshine that blazed down on her, trying to blink it away so she might see who was behind her. She could not; instead, she felt a sharp scratch against her neck and tumbled into the darkness once more.

Chapter Seventy-Eight

Time passed, but it hardly touched her. Isabella drifted in and out of consciousness, the grey veil lifting for a moment before it settled over everything again. She could only recall fragments.

She remembered waking to the steady drone of powerful engines, her ears popping with a change in air pressure. She remembered trying to move her limbs, only to find that she could not, and then a whispering of soft words, a scratch against the side of her neck, and darkness.

She remembered snatches of conversation, words that made no sense and a voice that she thought she recognised.

She remembered the rumble of a different kind of engine, a sensation of motion as she was driven around a corner; the feeling of tight bonds around her wrists and something else fastened around her waist, holding her down so she was unable to move.

She remembered more voices, different ones, their words buzzing with agitation and excitement, and then, as she prised open her eyes, she saw men and women looking down at her, their faces covered, only their eyes visible. She remembered bright lights that were shone into her own eyes, pain in the crook of her elbow as something sharp was pushed into her vein, the feel of the rough fabric that was looped around her wrists and ankles, the taste of blood in her mouth after she bit down on her tongue.

She remembered trying to get up, to free herself from whatever it was that held her in place, and then the return of the grey that faded into the darkness, and the sleep that consumed her.

Chapter Seventy-Nine

Birkenhead

Michael Pope stood on the deck of the *Stena Lagan* and watched as Birkenhead came into view. The crossing from Belfast had been scheduled to take eight hours, but delays in the loading of the ferry in Northern Ireland meant that they were running a couple of hours behind schedule. Pope didn't mind. He had been travelling slowly and deliberately, and, even as he approached his final destination, he wasn't in a rush.

He had taken advantage of the time to catch up on his sleep and to refuel himself with the complimentary food in the business lounge. It had been a long six days, and he was tired. He had travelled south through Mexico, crossing the border at Motozintla and making his way into Guatemala. He had flown from there to Panama City, transferring onto a connecting flight to Vienna. He had changed again in Austria, flying Lufthansa to Dublin. Then he had taken the train north to Belfast and booked a one-way crossing on the ferry because he knew that there would be minimal security, certainly in comparison to what he would have subjected himself to if he had landed at an airport on the mainland. The border between Ireland and Northern Ireland was easier to cross than had been the case twenty years ago, when he had been stationed in the province during The Troubles – and, once he was across, he was inside the United Kingdom. Entering the mainland by sea was an old spy's trick from years gone by, and it was the best way Pope could think of to avoid triggering an alert that he could not afford. There would be no immigration procedures to go through; he would not need to show his fake passport and his bag would not be inspected.

The ferry edged its way to the dock. The big bow doors were lowered and vehicles started to roll down. Pope went to the car deck and climbed aboard the bus that the ferry company used to embark and disembark foot passengers. The engine rumbled into life and the driver drove them slowly and carefully out of the belly of the boat, down the ramp and onto the dock.

The terminal was still a good distance from Liverpool. Pope bought a ticket for another bus to transfer him to the train station at Hamilton Square, and then bought a ticket to London, connecting in Chester.

The train was due to depart in an hour.

Chapter Eighty

Downton

Vivian Bloom's driver turned off the southbound A36 and followed Shute End Road towards Downton. The country house that appeared on the left was Trafalgar Park and it had once been a Group Fifteen property. It had been referred to then as 'The Creche', and they had used it to assess and train new recruits. The property was enormous.

They passed slowly along the narrow country lane until they reached the hundred-year-old brick wall that marked the periphery of the thirty acres of water meadows that surrounded the house. The wall was as old as the house it protected, although it had subsequently been augmented with the addition of motion sensors, floodlights and security cameras.

The driver turned off onto the neat drive that led to the house. He came to a stop before the wrought-iron gates, waiting for the car's registration to be scanned and compared to the list of plates that were authorised to enter. The gates opened and the vehicle moved ahead, passing through the brick pillars and onto the Lime Walk, a long drive lined with majestic lime trees that approached the side of the house.

Trafalgar Park had been vacant since the Group was disbanded, but Bloom had known that it would suit his present purposes very well. He had spoken to the scientists who had been leading the British response to Daedalus at nearby Porton Down and invited them to visit so they could lay out the specifications for the perfect research facility. The agents that had been retained from the defunct Group had been put in charge of securing the facility. Bloom had unlocked substantial funds from secret intelligence budgets that were kept far away from the prying eyes of parliamentary oversight committees.

The work to convert the house and grounds to its new use was still ongoing. The extent of the opportunity that had been presented to them in Sioux City had taken them somewhat by surprise, and they were rushing to keep up. The security, in particular, was still not in place. Bloom had instructed the agents to spec out their requirements without concern for the cost; the ability to defend the facility was paramount, and he would find the money. They had the existing surveillance, but the additional measures – and the soldiers who would be transferred to Trafalgar Park to bolster the existing platoon – were still pending. He would be restless until these measures were all in place.

Bloom did not like to think that the house was vulnerable, even a little, and resolved to speed up the process as much as he could.

'Here we are, sir,' his driver said, pulling up in the wide gravel space that was in front of the porch.

Chapter Eighty-One

Bloom went into the house. The first floor was busy: security contractors who had signed the Official Secrets Act were busy upgrading the internal systems, replacing the outmoded equipment that had been more than sufficient for the house's previous use, but was lacking when it came to the purpose it would now be put to.

Bloom ignored them. He went into the staircase hall and ascended. The second and third floors of the house were in the process of being adapted so they could accommodate the research that would soon be starting there. The work was not finished on the second floor; Bloom walked along the main corridor, glancing into the old bedrooms to find that they had all been stripped out, leaving large empty spaces into which a host of scientific machinery was being fitted. Bloom wouldn't normally have any idea what each expensive item was supposed to do, but since he had signed off on the precise specifications, he could hazard a guess at some of them: there was a workstation with a UVC disinfection lamp that was designed to clone and amplify RNA and DNA; there were thermal cyclers and microtube coolers designed to chill samples; there was a large centrifuge and bench-top freezing systems; and, on a white enamel desk, there was a computer powerful enough to run the modelling and analysis that he had been told would be necessary.

He reached the end of the corridor and ascended again. The top floor was finished. A wide landing linked the staircases at the east and west ends of the house, and four doors led off it. There had been a warren of rooms here, but the internal walls had been reconfigured to produce larger spaces, two of which had then been converted into infirmaries.

There were armed guards next to the staircases. They were there not so much to make sure that no one else entered the floor – that task was for the guards downstairs – but to prevent those on the floor from seeking to leave.

That included Nikita Ivanosky.

The professor was sitting at a desk that had been installed for him in the middle of the landing, beneath a well that admitted a shaft of greying light from above. The desk had been equipped with two computers, but the professor's attention was taken by a sheaf of papers that he was slowly reading through.

'Good afternoon, professor,' Bloom said.

The scientist looked up, peering at Bloom through his spectacles. 'Good afternoon,' he said, a little tersely.

Ivanosky had originally been unhappy with what had happened to him. That, Bloom thought, was fair enough. A hacker had intercepted the professor's panicked call back to Manage Risk after he had escaped from Maia, and had routed the information to Bloom. Manage Risk had two stand-by teams on hand in Mexico, and one of them was positioned in Juárez after the evidence suggested that was where Isabella had been hiding. It had been a race to get the team to Ivanosky's position before Manage Risk could send in their exfiltration team.

The snatch squad had collected him and driven west to Puerto Peñasco, where they made a rendezvous with an SBS team who had come ashore in the meantime. Ivanosky had been transferred aboard a fifty-foot sailing yacht that took him south through the Gulf of California to a second rendezvous with HMS *Atherstone*. The professor was then taken south to Guatemala, where he boarded a Gulfstream G280 that had more recently been used for the rendition of Islamist terrorists by the Secret Service and the CIA. He had landed at Biggin Hill three days after the operation to apprehend him had been launched. It had been a resounding success.

Maia and Isabella Rose were captured while Ivanosky was in transit. The professor's surliness had lifted when he was told of the news. Bloom knew why: Ivanosky wasn't interested in *who* he worked for, he only cared about the work itself. Bloom had sat in on Ivanosky's debriefing, and had learned of the cancers that were gradually claiming the M cohort. Ivanosky had explained that he hadn't told Jamie King yet. He said that he knew how King would react, and feared that the programme – and his life's work – would be dissolved. The stunning discovery that Isabella Rose shared the same genetic makeup as Maia, and that she was healthy, had reinvigorated the old man. The prospect that he would be able to work on the girl's DNA to try to discover the difference between her and the others had clearly been too tantalising for Ivanosky to care about who would ultimately benefit from his research.

The research was all he cared about. Perfecting his work was his main preoccupation.

Bloom would give him the chance to do that. In the meantime, he had ordered a sweep of Beatrix Rose's files for any suggestion that might lend credence to the professor's assertion that Isabella was Phoenix.

Bloom sat down in one of the empty chairs on the other side of Ivanosky's desk. 'How are they?' he asked.

Ivanosky took off his spectacles and rubbed his eyes. He stood. 'I'll show you,' he said.

Chapter Eighty-Two

Bloom followed Ivanosky to the infirmary. The soldier standing guard at the top of the stairs turned at their approach, and, perhaps recognising Bloom, turned away again and wrapped his fingers around the grip of the rifle that was attached to a strap he had around his torso.

Ivanosky went into the room and Bloom followed. It looked like a luxury hospital suite. The finishes were in soothing palettes, with natural wood flooring and panelling and plush rugs. A wide window looked out onto the expansive grounds, with a chalk stream wending its way between the trees. There was a single bed in the room. The mattress had an expensive bariatric pressure relief system that alternated pressure points to ensure that the possibility of sores was minimised. Maia was lying there, a single blue sheet covering her midriff and torso. Her arms and lower legs were bare save for the leather straps that had been fastened around her wrists and ankles, holding her to the bed. She was wearing a respirator over her face, electrodes had been attached to either side of her forehead and lines had been fitted to cannulas that were inserted into the arteries in the crooks of both arms.

'She looks sick.'

'She is. The cancer moves through them quickly. Her condition worsened during the flight.'

'You said it was leukaemia?'

'Acute myeloid leukaemia. It affects the bone marrow. Rogue blood cells form sarcomas – tumours. I won't know for sure until I can get her to an imager, but my guess is that she has several and they're getting bigger.'

'Can you do anything?'

The professor shook his head. 'We haven't been able to stop it in any of the others. You'd treat with chemotherapy and a bone marrow transplant normally, but neither had any effect. She's presenting with the exact same symptoms. The prognosis is the same. I doubt she has much more than a month left. Might be less.'

Bloom went over to the bed. Maia's hair looked thin, and as he looked more closely, he could see loose hairs on the pillow, and more than there should have been. Her skin was wan and there was a sheen of perspiration on her forehead, with drops of it slowly creeping down the rubberised seal that was pressed around her mouth. Her breath hissed in and out, accompanied by a chorus of soft bleeps from the monitors behind the bed.

'The others?'

'Moros might be dead already, and Maia killed Morpheus. Your thugs killed Macaria, of course.'

'You've read the report? She broke the arm of one of the men. They had no choice.'

Ivanosky waved away the protest. 'Mercury and Mithras are the only other ones left, and they're symptomatic, too.'

Bloom straightened up. 'The girl?'

'She's different,' the professor said.

'Show me.'

Ivanosky led the way back onto the landing and to the other infirmary.

Isabella Rose was lying in an identical bed. She, too, was restrained, although she wasn't wearing a respirator.

Bloom went over to the bed. He reached down and brushed aside a lock of hair that had fallen over her eye. The pictures that he had seen following her arrest in Mexico had made her look much older than her sixteen years; now, though, as vulnerable as she was, she looked younger.

'What do you know?' Bloom asked.

'She shares almost the same genetics as Maia and the others.'

'Almost?'

'Small differences. I'm going to need time to work out what they are.'

'And cancer?'

'Nothing. She's a healthy young girl.'

'And she doesn't need drugs?'

'Maia said that she had natural control of her norepinephrine and dopamine. She's never taken citalopram. I need to find out why that is.'

'When are you going to wake her?'

'This afternoon,' Ivanosky said. He looked at his watch. 'In an hour. Are you going to be here?'

'I have to go back to London,' Bloom said. 'I have someone I need to see. But I'll be back at the weekend. If you need anything, you'll have it. You just have to ask.'

Ivanosky nodded.

Bloom turned away. 'I'll expect your report in the morning,' he said over his shoulder as he set off.

Chapter Eighty-Three

London

Pope arrived at London Euston at 13.37. He took a taxi from the rank outside and told the driver to take him to Chalton Street in Euston. He watched through the windows as they made the short drive, to ensure that they were not being followed. The driver pulled up outside the Regent Theatre, then Pope asked him to wait and crossed the road to the building that housed the Safestore facility. There was a lot of student accommodation in the streets around here, and Pope guessed that the facility was most often used by foreign students to house their belongings outside of term time. The staff were lazy, there was no security of note and he had always been able to go in and out with the minimum of fuss.

He showed his fake passport at the desk. The clerk glanced at it without really looking and waved him through. He went into the main building and found the locker that he had first rented over five years ago. Everyone who rented a locker or room was required to supply their own padlock; Pope thumbed the combination, popped the clasp and opened the door. There was a single leather sports bag inside. He took it out, shrugged it over his shoulder, locked the locker again and made his way back to the taxi.

'Where to, mate?' the driver asked.

'Trafalgar Square,' Pope told him.

Pope went to the branch of Next on The Strand and bought a pair of jeans, a shirt, a padded jacket and a new pair of boots. He walked the short distance to Northumberland Avenue and took a room for three nights at the Citadines hotel. He rode the elevator to the third floor, found his room and went inside. He undressed and showered for twenty minutes, sloughing off the grime that had accumulated during his journey, and then wrapped himself in a towel and went into the bedroom. He took the leather bag that he had collected from Euston, opened it and spread the contents out on the bed. There was a Glock 9mm pistol, and a shoulder rig with two magazines in the inverted mag holders; there was a knife in a scabbard; a boxed pay-as-you-go phone with a selection of unused SIMs; a wallet containing a series of credit cards and membership cards in the name of Frank Euler; a roll of banknotes; and a selection of items that he could use to disguise his appearance.

Pope decided on what the intelligence community would deem a 'light' disguise. He took a false beard, a wig and a pair of dark-rimmed glasses and went through into the bathroom. He washed his face, dried it carefully and peeled away the adhesive backing from the fake beard, which was made from human hair and looked real. Pope glanced out of the window and saw the dark clouds overhead. That was good. The hair tended to frizz up on humid days, but that wouldn't be an issue in this cool, damp weather. He worked carefully, looking at his reflection in the mirror as he positioned the beard and pressed it down. A label inside the wig identified it as cappuccino; it was a dark brown colour, and it matched the beard. He took the wig and, securing it with double-sided tape and toupee glue, he settled it onto his head. It looked authentic, with soft movement and a neat tapering into the neck.

He put the glasses on, opened the wardrobe and regarded his new appearance in the full-length mirror fixed to the inside of the door. He was pleased: he would be unrecognisable to anyone working from a photograph of him, and difficult to identify even for anyone who was more familiar with him. What was more, the beard would make it difficult for him to be identified by facial recognition algorithms that relied on precise measurements of the jawline and cheekbones in order to determine a match. The disguise would also be easy to remove in a restroom stall in the event that he needed to effect a quick change.

He took out the clothes that he had just purchased and dressed. He checked his appearance once more and, satisfied, he fastened the shoulder rig around his torso. He took the Glock, popped out the magazine and checked that it was loaded. It was. He slapped it back into the magwell, racked the slide to put a round in the chamber and settled the weapon in the holster. He put the jacket on, zipping it up so the rig and the pistol were hidden. He took the phone, two of the SIMs and the wallet, and made his way outside.

He looked at his watch.

Time to get started.

Chapter Eighty-Four

Bloom's driver took him back to London. He turned off the road and into the underground garage that was beneath the building on the north bank of the Thames. It had been erected in the sixties, filling the space in a terrace that had been wrecked by a Luftwaffe bomb. The building was constructed from brick and concrete and was entirely without style or grace. The brass plaque outside the main entrance read 'Global Logistics'. The company had been the front for Group Fifteen, and the office that had putatively been its registered office had been, in fact, the headquarters for the agency.

The driver opened Bloom's door and accompanied him to the elevator. They stepped out of the car on the third floor and Bloom led the way through the dusty wood-panelled corridor to the conference room. He told his driver to wait outside the door. The man was armed; Bloom didn't expect trouble, but it paid to have him within easy reach if it did prove to be necessary. The man he was here to meet was urbane and had never shown any proclivity towards violence, but Bloom was a cautious man. His aversion to risk had always stood him in good stead; one did not remain in the business of intelligence for as long as he had without it.

He opened the door without knocking and went inside.

A man was sitting at the conference table.

'Hello, Bloom,' he said, straightening up and reaching across the table to offer his hand.

Bloom took it and they shook. He didn't know the man's name. He'd never bothered to ask, knowing that any name that was given would be fake. He was scruffy and unkempt, and he habitually wore a battered old cap with a logo that had been identified by a younger associate as belonging to an old American video game company. Bloom had been referring to him vaguely as 'the hacker', but the others had started calling him Atari and the sobriquet had stuck.

Atari had been working for Bloom for two years. Bloom had instigated a full background check on him when he had originally tendered the man's services. The analysts at GCHQ had spent weeks looking into him, but there had been nothing to find: no online identity, nothing that might identify him; no employment history, no pictures, no relationships.

Nothing.

Bloom had been ready to walk away until the man had suggested that he would be able to deliver the doctor who was responsible for the Daedalus asset codenamed Maia, together with the data that she and her husband were trying to sell.

Bloom had taken that to be providence; he had been looking for a way to get his hands on the research from the Prometheus programme ever since it had become clear to him that the Americans would shut him out, and he had – cautiously – agreed to engage the man.

Atari had suggested that Michael Pope would be the perfect emissary to bring the doctor and her husband in, but events had conspired against them. Jamie King had been forewarned of the doctor's duplicity and had sent two of the Daedalus assets to interrupt the Shanghai exchange. Atari had adapted his plan; he had located the fleeing Litivenko, and Pope had been sent to collect her. The plan should have been simple: Pope would give Litivenko's data to Atari, who would give it to Bloom; Litivenko would provide testimony to the congressional committee that had been established to investigate Daedalus. It would have been perfect. Atari had already secured a bought-and-paid-for senator to push a congressional hearing concerning the work that Daedalus was doing; Litivenko's testimony would have brought the project into the light and stalled its progress. Bloom would then give the data to his own geneticists and they would be able to use it to catch up with what Daedalus had already achieved.

But, once again, they had been thwarted.

The doctor had been murdered at Dulles before she could be delivered into protective custody.

The data had been lost.

Michael Pope and Isabella Rose had gone rogue.

It had looked bleak, but now, a year on, events had taken a more satisfactory turn.

'How are things? Atari asked.

'Very good,' Bloom replied.

'How is she?'

'Maia? She's sick.'

'And Isabella?'

'Under mild sedation.'

'But she isn't ill?'

'She appears to be in perfect health. They're still testing, of course, but the early signs are promising.'

'What are you going to do with her?'

'That's not really any of your concern now, is it? You've done what you agreed to do.'

'Ivanosky will start poking and prodding her.'

Bloom shrugged. 'As I said – not your concern.'

Atari laced his fingers on the tabletop. 'Don't you find it . . . immoral?'

'Come now,' Bloom said, the corner of his mouth turning up. 'You're not going to talk to me about morality, surely?'

'Fine,' Atari said. 'Not immoral. You don't find it wrong, then – what they've done to her? What they'll do now?'

'I try not to concern myself with rights and wrongs,' Bloom said. 'We have to find an edge, and Isabella is it.'

'And the edge is important enough to steal from your closest ally.'

Now Bloom chuckled. 'I *know* you're not that naïve. We should ask Captain Pope what he thinks about that, shouldn't we – or we could ask Isabella, perhaps? Today's allies are tomorrow's enemies. Alliances are fluid. The end result is the only thing that matters. We had to have that research. You brought up morality – we have a moral case. We contributed to it, even more than we originally believed. Her mother found Isabella when she went missing sixteen years ago. She brought Isabella here. She was already ours. They wanted to take her from us. You just helped bring her home.'

Atari held Bloom's eye and, for a moment, Bloom entertained the thought that he might really have developed a conscience. The moment did not last. Atari grinned, and tapped his left hand on the table two times. 'Yes,' he said with a smile. 'Relationships are transitory things. And, since you brought it up, we should end ours on a positive note. You still owe me rather a lot of money.'

'You'll be paid,' Bloom said, stifling his weary impatience. Atari was good – better than good, he had turned into something of a miracle worker – but he had a price. He didn't come cheap, and it was obvious that he had come here intent on collecting.

'When?' Atari said. 'You're already a week overdue.'

'You'll be paid this afternoon. Tell me how you'd like it done, and I'll make sure it happens.'

Atari reached into the pocket of his dirty jeans and took out a scrap of paper. He flattened it out and then slid it across the table. Bloom took it. Atari had written the details of a numbered bank account with Banque Privée BCP (Suisse).

'There, please,' Atari said.

'Of course,' Bloom said, folding the paper and sliding it into his waistcoat pocket. Atari's fee had been significant; Bloom had needed to be creative to find the money without attracting oversight.

'Is that it?' Atari said. 'Are we done?'

Bloom held up a finger. 'Not necessarily. What about Michael Pope? You said you'd find him.'

'That's been trickier than I expected,' Atari admitted. 'I lost him in Iowa. But I'll find him eventually.'

'There's a bonus if you do. Another million.'

Atari pursed his lips and rubbed his chin. 'Pope's a dangerous man,' he said. 'But I know where his family is. I think I can flush him out, but it won't be cheap. A million isn't going to cut it.'

'Fine,' Bloom said with a wave of his hand. 'If you can tell me where to find him, I'll pay you another three.'

Atari grinned at him. 'You really want him gone, don't you?'

'Just find him.'

Atari stood and put out his hand again. 'It was good to work with you. Good luck with the research. I'll take care of Captain Pope.'

Bloom found Atari insufferable, and was tempted to leave his hand hanging, but he took it. 'Goodbye,' he said.

'Goodbye, Bloom. I'll be in touch when I have something for you. Won't be long.'

Chapter Eighty-Five

Pope waited outside the old Group Fifteen building all afternoon and into the evening. The man who had taken a shot at him in Sioux City was an ex-soldier with connections to the Group. Pope had contacted a former colleague he still trusted while he'd waited for his connecting flight in Vienna, and had learned that the Group's old building had recently been allocated to another government agency. His contact had worked as an analyst for the Group, and she had found herself transferred to the new operation. There was little more to go on beyond that, save the information that the new agency was proceeding under the same security clearances as the Group had, and that Vivian Bloom had been seen inside on several occasions. Pope knew that it was a long shot, but he was down to long shots. He had nothing else to try.

He changed position regularly, always making sure that he had the entrance in view. He caught sight of his reflection in the glass panel of a bus shelter and was reassured by how different he looked: the fake beard changed his appearance entirely and the dark-framed glasses hid his eyes. He knew, too, that there was no way that Bloom – or the security that would have been assigned to him – could have expected that he was here, in London.

It was half seven when he saw Bloom coming down the steps that led out of the building. He was accompanied by two men. They had neatly trimmed hair and cautious, wary expressions on their faces. Pope recognised them both: Firth and Parker. He had seen them in Iowa, the two agents who had taken Isabella.

The three men descended the steps and turned right, heading north along Abingdon Street. They continued on, passing Parliament Square on the left and the Houses of Parliament on the right, and then followed Whitehall to the north. They turned right onto Whitehall Place and headed east.

Pope crossed Whitehall, jogging between a gap that was left between two buses, and then turned right, too.

Bloom had walked to the northern side of Whitehall Place. It started to drizzle, and the old man picked up his pace. Pope stayed on the other side of the street, allowing the procession to draw away a little. It was a narrow road set between identical buildings that had been crafted from slabs of Portland stone. Metal bollards separated the sidewalk from the street on both sides. Bloom passed a blue plaque that marked the site of the original Scotland Yard, crossed over Scotland Place and, opposite the statue of five men that memorialised the Royal Tank Regiment, he turned left, climbed the steps beneath a metal canopy and went into a hotel. Pope waited for the two bodyguards to go inside and crossed over. The hotel was the Corinthia, marked by a Union Jack and an Italian flag, which draped limply from poles on either side of the entrance.

Pope walked on, glancing beyond the top-hatted member of staff and through a pair of grand double doors into the interior of the building. Bloom was making his way across the lobby; then the doors closed, and Pope could see no more.

He looked at his watch: it was coming up to eight. It seemed likely that Bloom would be staying at the hotel overnight; perhaps this was where he always chose when he came to the capital.

Pope continued to the east, crossed Northumberland Avenue and walked beneath the bridge that carried the trains that made their way to Charing Cross station. There was a Costa Coffee on the corner opposite the entrance to Embankment underground station. Pope went inside, ordered a coffee and took it to a vacant stool at the window. He took out his phone and navigated to the Corinthia's website. He went to the booking section, entered today's date and said that he wanted a room for the night.

There was one available.

He took out his credit card and paid for it.

Chapter Eighty-Six

Pope bought an empty suitcase from Global Luggage on The Strand and a small toolkit from the nearby branch of Robert Dyas and then made his way back to the Corinthia. He climbed the steps into the palatial lobby area, his eyes drawn to the Baccarat chandelier with its crystals sparkling in the lounge where aperitifs were being served. He wheeled his case up to the check-in desk where a smartly dressed member of staff was tapping away on a keyboard.

'Hello, sir,' she said. 'Welcome to the Corinthia.'

'Thank you,' Pope said. 'I have a reservation.'

'Very good. Could I have your name, please, sir?'

'It's Euler – Frank Euler. I booked online.'

The woman typed on the keyboard and waited for the results to display. 'Here we are. Frank Euler. We have you down for one night. Is that correct?'

'Yes,' Pope said. 'Just the one.'

'Very good, sir.'

The woman took a blank keycard from a tray next to her computer, pushed it into an encoding machine and tapped a command on her keyboard. The machine chattered as the details were imprinted on the card's magnetic strip. The woman printed a second card, slipped both into a card wallet and wrote a number on the back. She handed the wallet to Pope.

'You're in Room 412,' she said. 'The fourth floor. The elevators are over there. Is there anything else I can help you with?'

'No,' Pope said. 'That's all, thanks.'

'Would you like a porter to take your case for you?'

'That's all right,' he said. 'I've got it.'

'Very good, sir.'

Pope wheeled his suitcase to the elevator lobby and pressed the button.

Vivian Bloom was in the hotel somewhere. He just had to find him.

⌣

The room was large, with a separate dressing area and a generously proportioned bathroom. It was decorated in gentle colours, with tall ceilings and wide windows that offered a view of Trafalgar Square and the illuminated needle of Nelson's Column. A small balcony opened onto an interior courtyard with a lit glass structure at its centre. The room had cost him three hundred pounds for the night; Bloom evidently had expensive taste – or, more likely, he was being accommodated with money from the public purse.

Pope waited for three hours, watching the television until his watch showed that it was eleven thirty.

It was time.

Pope carefully unplugged the television and carried it over to the bed, then laid it down on its face and examined its fixings. He took the toolkit from the suitcase, selected a screwdriver with a small head and then undid the retaining screws that fastened the inspection panel to the rear of the unit. He took a pair of pliers, found the cable that carried the current and snipped through it. He replaced the inspection panel, dropped the screws into their housings and tightened them, then carried the screen back to the bureau and stood the television in the same place as he had found it.

Pope went through to the bathroom to check that his disguise was still in place and, satisfied that it was, he left the room and went down to reception.

A different receptionist was on duty. There was a reduced need for staff during the night, as Pope had anticipated. He was pleased.

'I'm sorry,' Pope said. 'I tried to switch on the TV but it doesn't seem to be working. Do you think you could take a look?'

'Really?' the man said. 'I'm very sorry about that. Is it possible to wait until the morning?'

'I'd like to watch it now. Do you have anyone who can take a look?'

'Not really,' the man said, just a little flustered. He tapped a finger against the counter and gave a nod of his head. 'I'll go and have a look. I'm sure I'll be able to replace it if I can't fix it.'

'I just have to pop out,' Pope said. 'I'm going to grab a bite to eat. Room service is finished for the night?'

'Yes,' the man said. 'It finishes at eleven. Covent Garden is close, though. There are a number of late restaurants there. Some quite nice, I believe.'

'I'll do that,' Pope said. 'My key will open the front door, won't it?'

'Yes,' the man said. 'Just swipe it through the reader.'

'Thanks,' Pope said.

'And by the time you're back I'll have fixed your TV.'

As he walked away, Pope knelt down to tie a lace that didn't need tying. The reflection in an internal window offered a view back into reception, and Pope paused until the man had come out from behind the desk and disappeared into the elevator lobby. He waited until he heard the chime of the arriving elevator and the swish of the doors as they opened and closed.

He waited another beat and then went back to reception. He made his way around the desk. The man had left the computer unlocked, and

Pope took the mouse and clicked away from the home screen through to the booking system that the hotel used. It was Opera, the most commonly used reservations software, found in hotels around Europe; Pope had been given a course in how to use it years before, in order to equip himself for situations precisely like this. He clicked through the various menus until he found the details. He clicked the tab for 'Current' and was taken to a grid of names that contained shortcuts to all of the hotel's guests. Vivian Bloom was staying under his own name, and Pope opened the folio that contained all the relevant information about his booking. He was staying in room 324.

There was a magstripe encoder on the desk next to the computer, and Pope switched it on. He clicked on the 'Check-in' tab on the computer, typed *324*, set the expiration on the card for three days and double-clicked the button to create a new key. Pope took a blank keycard and pushed it into the slot of the encoder, waited for the necessary details to be written onto the stripe and then collected the card as the machine ejected it. He clicked back to the home screen and ensured that the desk was as he had found it.

He went into the elevator lobby. The indicator above the nearest elevator was ticking down to the first floor; perhaps the receptionist had already admitted defeat and was returning. Pope hurried to the end of the lobby, found the door to the stairs and pushed it open just as the chime sounded and the elevator doors opened. He pulled the door shut behind him and looked around: the stairs lacked the panache that was evident in the rest of the hotel, not much more than bare concrete with a metal handrail.

Pope put the keycard in his pocket and started to climb to the third floor.

Chapter Eighty-Seven

Pope emerged from the staircase on the third floor, next to the elevators. He paused there for a moment, listening to the whir of the motors above as one of the elevator cars descended down to the lobby.

It was quiet. He started along the corridor, the same as his own on the floor above. He heard the sound of a television in one of the rooms, and running water from a shower in another. He followed a sign on the wall that indicated the direction for rooms 320–329, and stopped outside number 324. He reached into his pocket for the keycard, holding that in his left hand as he reached for the holstered Glock with his right. He checked the corridor again and, happy that it was still empty, he drew the weapon. He lined up the keycard with the reader, pushed it into the slot and, as the light flashed green, heard the sound of the lock disengaging.

He pressed down on the handle and pushed the door, quickly slipping inside.

It was dark. Pope stood just inside the door for a moment and listened. He couldn't hear anything to begin with, but then he was able to pick out the noise of very light snoring. He closed the door, careful to ensure that it was as quiet as he could make it, and waited another moment for his eyes to adjust to the gloom. The room was the same as his own: a door to the bathroom on the left and the bedroom straight ahead. There was a little light passing into the room between a gap in the curtains; there were street lamps outside, and the yellow sodium glow was enough for Pope to make out the bureau, an armchair that looked as if it had been piled with clothes, and a suitcase on the floor.

Pope slid the keycard into his back pocket and crept inside. He passed the bathroom door until he was able to see around the wall into the rest of the bedroom. There was the same large king-size bed as in his room, with the shape of a single person sprawled out across it.

Pope closed in on the bed.

It was Bloom. The old man looked withered and thin in the unguarded attitude of sleep. His arms poked out of the sheets, gnarled and willowy. He was facing Pope, his head on the pillow, and his mouth was open just enough to let his breath whistle in and out.

Pope sat on the edge of the bed. He holstered the pistol and reached down, pressing the palm of his right hand over the old man's mouth.

Bloom awoke with a start. He tried to sit, but Pope was stronger and was leaning down; he was able to hold him against the mattress.

'No noise,' he said.

Bloom looked up at him. His face crumpled into confusion; Pope had almost forgotten that he was still wearing his disguise.

'Hello, Vivian,' Pope said.

The confusion was washed away and replaced with comprehension, and then, immediately thereafter, by fear.

'Are you going to be quiet if I take my hand away?'

Bloom nodded.

Pope uncovered Bloom's mouth. He pointed to the holstered Glock and then put his finger to his lips. 'Shh,' he said.

'I'm sorry,' Bloom said.

'You're sorry about what?'

'I—'

'Hush, Vivian. It's too late for apologies.'

Chapter Eighty-Eight

P ope told Bloom to stay in bed. He collected a chair from the other side of the room, placed it on the floor so that it was in front of the old man and then sat on it.

'I've got some questions, Vivian. You're going to help me understand what's been happening, and then you're going to help me fix everything.'

'You should probably think about your family, captain. They—'

Pope had known that Bloom would threaten his family, but his anticipation of it did not prevent the sudden flood of anger. He stood, pressed Bloom down onto the bed and then covered his face with a pillow. He smothered the old man until he had counted to twenty, and then he pulled the pillow away. Bloom gasped for breath.

'You're not in a position to make threats, Vivian. Do you know why that is?'

Bloom swallowed down a throatful of bile.

Pope stared at him. 'Because you have no leverage.'

'Of course I do,' he spluttered. 'I—'

'You don't,' Pope interrupted. 'You'd only have leverage if I had something to lose. I don't have anything to lose. I've lost it all already.'

'Captain,' Bloom said, holding up his hands as if he might be able to ward him off. 'We can sort this out. Let's talk.'

'We're *going* to talk, Vivian. You're going to answer my questions. And then I'm going to kill you.'

'You don't need to do—'

Pope held up a hand to forestall him. 'I know. You'll tell me what I need to know and then I can just leave. No one need ever know that I was here. You won't tell a soul. Right?'

'I'm not saying that. I—'

'You know my history. The people I've gone after – people who find themselves in positions like the one you've found yourself in – they *always* say that. Every time. And it's never made the slightest bit of difference. You know I can't trust you.'

'But think of your family—'

Pope felt a second flash of anger, but he tamped it down, fighting back the urge to smother the old fool for a second time. 'I do think of them,' he said with forced calmness. 'I think of them every day. And then I think of what you've done and how much you've cost me. Everything you said to me was a lie. You tried to kill me. You tried to kill Isabella. And then you took my family away.'

Bloom tried to stand, but Pope reached over with his left hand and pressed down on his shoulder. Bloom was old and weak and no match for him; he slumped back down on the bed again.

'I'm going to be reasonable,' Pope said. 'I'm going to give you a say in how you die. If you cooperate, if you answer the questions honestly – it'll be painless. Otherwise . . .' He let the sentence trail away. 'Well,' he continued, 'otherwise, it'll be something else, but you'll answer truthfully either way in the end.'

'What do you want?'

'You took Isabella. I recognised the men you sent. Why?'

Bloom looked back at him. 'You don't know?'

'Know what?'

303

Bloom watched Pope's reaction. He gave a gentle shake of his head. 'You don't know that Isabella is one of them – like Maia.'

'Don't be ridiculous.'

'No. I don't suppose you would know. Get my briefcase,' Bloom said, gesturing to the other side of the bed. 'I'll show you.'

Pope got up and moved around it until he saw the briefcase on the floor. He picked it up and dropped it on the bed in front of Bloom. The old man opened the clasps and took out a sheaf of papers. He flipped through the sheaf until he found the page that he wanted. Pope took it: it showed a graph, with two overlapping sets of data represented by coloured rows. There were twenty-four rows.

'What is this?'

'It's a DNA comparison – the red bars belong to Maia. The blue bars belong to Isabella.'

'They're similar.'

'No, captain. They're almost identical. They both have forty-eight chromosomes. You and I – well, everyone else, really – we only have forty-six.'

Pope felt the beginning of a headache. 'That doesn't—'

'Make sense?' Bloom finished when Pope faltered. 'Actually, it does. Sixteen years ago, your predecessor as Control sent Beatrix Rose to Venezuela to locate a scientist who had gone on the run from Daedalus Genetics. His name was Igor Koralev. The Americans wanted him back, but they didn't have the operation on the ground there like we did, and so we agreed to help. We didn't know what we were dealing with, of course. We didn't know what Koralev was working on, but we sent Beatrix and John Milton to get him back. They found him. It turned out that Koralev had stolen the fruits of his research when he went on the run. Daedalus had made progress with their work – Maia and the others were stable – but the genetic mutation meant they had to take a cocktail of drugs in order to stop them from losing control. Koralev had fixed that problem. The Americans were able to confirm that a baby girl was with him in Caracas, but after Rose and Milton found him, there was no sign of her. The baby was Isabella, Pope. Beatrix took her. We didn't know.'

'That's crazy.'

'Maia and Isabella have been together for a year. We think that Maia must have realised. They kidnapped Ivanosky. Our mutual friend told you what happened.'

'Our friend?'

'The man with the cap. Your contact. He says you call him Atari, too.'

'You have Ivanosky?'

'We do. The professor managed to get away from Maia and Isabella, but Atari found him before he could return to the Americans. We picked him up – he's working for us now. He told us what happened. Maia and Isabella took him to a laboratory that they had put together outside Juárez. Maia wanted him to run genetic tests on Isabella. He did, and he says that there's no question that she's the same as Maia and the others. But she's different, too. Better. She doesn't need to dose herself to prevent psychosis. There are none of the other side effects that they've seen, either. She doesn't have cancer like the others do.'

'They have cancer?'

'You didn't know that?'

Pope thought of Maia, and how she had looked ill.

Bloom continued. 'Isabella is the apogee of the research. Much as I find what they have been doing repulsive, I can't deny the obvious. She is the future, Pope. She is a billion-dollar asset. We had to have her, and now we do.'

'Atari,' Pope said. 'Who is he?'

'I'm afraid I don't know very much about him at all. I don't know his name, his history or whether he works alone or with others. He's a private operator. He finds things. Information. People. He sells it to whoever pays him the most.'

'And you're paying him?'

'For the past two years. We had no choice. I've seen what those monsters can do. You've seen. This is a new arms race, captain – the first country to make a breakthrough will be able to secure an advantage, like Oppenheimer did when he gave the bomb to Truman. The Americans are working on it, the Russians, the Chinese. Everyone. The Americans are years ahead, and they won't share. They didn't give us a choice, Pope. We had to take it for ourselves. They have defective research. Their assets are dead or dying. And now we have Isabella.'

Bloom paused, letting that sink in.

'Atari found you in Mumbai,' he continued. 'We needed someone to handle the exchange in Shanghai. You were perfect – you were well qualified, and we knew that the offer of helping you get your family back from the CIA would be all the motivation you needed. And then, when the exchange went wrong, you were still best-placed to go after Litivenko.'

'And then Isabella?'

'Yes, of course, although we didn't know what we know about her now. She was the link to Maia. I told Atari to use you to get her out after she was arrested. He'd already found you in Vietnam – months before. Your relationship with the girl – well, we thought you might be able to get her on your side. We didn't know if Maia was still alive, but we knew that if she was then Isabella would be the best chance to get to her. But the Americans got to Isabella before we did. And then . . . well, as you see, it took a turn no one could have expected.'

'Where is Isabella?'

Bloom looked up at him, but didn't answer.

Pope stepped closer to the old man and shoved him down, pressing him flat against the mattress and holding him there with his left hand. He took out the gun and held it against the old man's forehead with his right, the muzzle pressed between Bloom's eyes.

'I'm not going to ask again.'

'If you kill me, you'll never know.'

Pope pressed down harder; Bloom winced from the pain of the muzzle against his skull. 'But you'll still be dead.'

The old man looked up at him, his rheumy eyes blinking. He seemed as if he was going to call his bluff, but he must have seen something in Pope's expression that told him that that would be foolish. He swallowed, his Adam's apple bobbing against skin that was as thin and fragile as old parchment.

'Trafalgar Park,' he said. 'The Creche.'

There came the hammering of fists against the door. 'Sir?'

Pope flinched.

'Sir,' the voice said, more loudly. 'Wake up.'

There was more that Pope would have liked to ask, but he was out of time.

He took the pillow and held it over the old man's face.

'Sir!' the voice called. 'Please – wake up. Captain Pope entered the country this morning.'

Pope pressed down on the pillow, anchoring it in place as Bloom struggled. The old man arched his back and tried to work his fingers underneath it, but it was fruitless. Pope was heavier than he was, and he was pushing down. Bloom struggled for thirty seconds and then stopped; his legs spasmed once, and then twice, and then he lay still.

The banging on the door resumed. 'Sir – wake up! We need to leave.'

Pope went to the door. He looked through the peephole and saw one of the two men from before – Firth – standing in the corridor. He reached for the handle, pulled it down and yanked the door back. The man had a cell phone pressed to his ear; he was unarmed, and there was little that he could do as Pope aimed the Glock at him and beckoned him inside. Firth's eyes bulged wide, but he did as he was told, moving deeper into the room as Pope took corresponding backward steps.

'Shut the door,' Pope said.

Firth closed it.

They reached the point where the corridor opened into the bedroom, and Firth's eyes widened as he saw the motionless body on the bed.

The door closed behind them with a click.

Firth looked from the bed to Pope.

'Turn around,' Pope said.

'Please,' Firth said. 'I have a wife. I just got married.'

'Turn around now. On your knees.'

The man turned and knelt.

'The old man said that the girl you took is at Trafalgar Park. Is that right?'

'Yes,' he said.

'Have you been there?'

'I drove him today. Please. I—'

'How many men are there?'

'A dozen.'

'Who are they?'

'Soldiers. Nothing special. They're waiting for a proper detail to go in.'

'Where are they keeping her?'

'Top floor. With the other one.'

'Maia?'

'She's older. I don't know her name.'

'What did Bloom say about them?'

Pope wasn't interested in the answer; he just wanted Firth to keep talking so he wouldn't notice the knife that Pope had pulled from the scabbard on his ankle, nor that he had stepped close enough to reach around the man's head so that the blade was against his neck. He pressed down and sliced, opening Firth's throat, then clasped his free hand around his mouth in the event that he tried to scream. The noise was drowned by the bubbling rush of blood, but Pope held tight until the man's strength faded away. He dropped him to the ground, the plush carpet sodden with blood, and went into the bathroom to rinse it from his hand and the sleeve of his jacket.

He looked at his watch. It was nearly midnight. He didn't know how long he had. There was a second man who had been with Bloom that afternoon; would he come looking if the old man didn't show up to be evacuated, or was Firth responsible for him on his own tonight? There was no way of knowing. Pope dried his arm with the towel, leaving the faint stains of diluted blood across it, and went back into the suite. He took the 'Do Not Disturb' sign, opened the door and hooked it on the handle. He stepped outside, checked that he was alone, and, happy that he was, made his way down to the exit.

Chapter Eighty-Nine

P ope stole a Mercedes from a quiet side street a short walk
from the hotel and proceeded carefully, aware that to attract
unwanted attention now would be dangerous. He passed the
Houses of Parliament and turned right, the streets lit up and with
barely a soul abroad. He went by Westminster Abbey and out towards
Belgravia. There was a police car parked at the side of the street next to
the Victoria Palace Theatre. He saw the silhouette of the driver in the
police car, but nothing happened as he went by: the lights remained off
and the car was stationary as he crossed Buckingham Palace Road and
put it out of sight behind him.

His hands had been shaking as he had got into the car, and he
gripped the wheel tight in an attempt to stop them. He needed a drink,
but he knew that he didn't have the luxury of time. The bodies would
be discovered soon enough, and then they would start to work out
what had happened and who was responsible. It wouldn't take them
long to put two and two together; he had to find Isabella before that
could happen.

It would be difficult enough to get to her as it was; it would be
impossible if they were forewarned.

He thought about what Bloom had told him.

Could it be possible?

He reached back for anything that might lend credibility to the claim that Bloom had made and the documents that he had seen. Isabella had always been extraordinarily resourceful, but he had attributed that to her mother's training and her unusual childhood.

But . . .

Like Maia?

He didn't know where to begin with that.

He tried to think about something else. It didn't matter what Bloom had said; Pope didn't have to believe him. Isabella was at The Creche, being held against her will, and he was going to go and get her. That was the end of it.

He glanced across at the widescreen monitor set in the dashboard. The satnav predicted that it would take two and a half hours to get to Downton. The roads would be quiet, but there was a diversion in place on the A303 to allow overnight work to take place. It was one in the morning now. He would arrive in Wiltshire at a little after half past three.

He leaned back in the seat and tried to relax. It was difficult. He didn't have a plan. He didn't know what he would do when he got to his destination, save that he was going to find Isabella and get her out. He was badly equipped, too, with just the Glock, the ammunition in the magazine and his knife.

At least he was familiar with the place where Isabella was being held. The Creche was the old Group Fifteen facility where new recruits had been tested and trained. Pope had been there many times. The Group's instructors put him through an extensive training programme as he'd transitioned out of the Royal Green Jackets and started his new career. He could remember the building and its situation; that familiarity, and the possible element of surprise that he might hold, were his only advantages.

He merged onto the empty M4 and managed to relax a little, nudging the car up to seventy and settling in for the rest of the journey. He was tired, and he would have liked to be able to stop for a little sleep, but he knew that there was no time for that, either. They might know that he was coming. They would certainly know later today. He had to act tonight, right now, before Isabella could be moved out of reach.

There would be time for sleep later.

Chapter Ninety

Downton

P ope took off his disguise as he drove, tossing it out of the
window. He followed the A303, then took the A36 south to
Salisbury. It was half past two as he bypassed the city on the
ring road, the spire of the beautiful cathedral lit like a beacon and visible for miles around. He continued south towards Downton, following
Witherington Road as it passed the water meadows that surrounded
Charlton-All-Saints and eventually reaching the turning for Trafalgar
Park. It was a private road, guarded by a groom's cottage that had since
been rented to a local farmer. Pope remembered that there was another
road leading to the property farther along Witherington Road, and
he continued towards it. The driveway was grander, with a series of
wooden posts and a sign, painted a regal red, that stated that the property beyond was Trafalgar Park and that it was private. But it was too
open; the trees had been cleared, and he could see cameras mounted on
a tall metal pole a hundred yards along its length. He tried to remember
the terrain and zoomed the satnav so he could refresh his memory. The
road continued to the west and then turned to the north. There was a

farm between the road and the start of the estate. Pope decided that he would have a better chance of making a successful infiltration there.

He drove on, ditched his car on a patch of ground away from the road that was being used to store wrapped bales of silage and continued on foot. The road was narrow, little more than a single track, and it was enclosed on both sides by recently trimmed trees and hawthorn hedges and, beyond, by the rolling acres of arable land that made up so much of this part of Wiltshire. He reached the entrance to the farm and paused, checking again that there was no one else around. It was four in the morning now, and he was in the middle of the country; all he could hear was the hooting of an owl and, a long way distant, the grunting bark of a deer. The sky was clear, and there was enough moonlight for him to see the way ahead.

A sign said that the property beyond was Standlynch Farm. Pope took out his pistol and followed the track, hurrying between the trees for three hundred feet until he was at the first of the vast barns that were used to dry the grain from the harvest. There was a yard with parked tractors, disengaged machinery and old four-by-fours, then two more large barns, and then the farmhouse and workers' accommodation.

Trafalgar Park was to the immediate northwest, perhaps a quarter of a mile away. A rutted track led away from the farm, evidently used by the farmer to move his machinery into the fields to the west of the estate. Pope followed the track, settling into an easy jog.

There was no sight of guards, although Pope knew that the place would be defended. Bloom's man had told him so: a dozen men were here. There had been no need when he had been here before, but he doubted they would take any chances given the value that would have been ascribed to the captives now accommodated within. Pope realised that he was gambling on what Bloom had told him being the truth. He recalled the look on the old man's face and decided that it was unlikely he had found the wherewithal and inspiration to lie so convincingly. The Creche was an excellent place to take Isabella and the other asset;

it was discreet, it could be defended and its use as an MI6 facility had never, to Pope's knowledge, passed beyond a limited cadre of intelligence service personnel. And, now that Group Fifteen had been closed down and its agents were either dead or scattered to the wind, it could easily be put to another use.

He reached a junction. The farmer's track continued on into the fields, but there was a broad lawned promenade between neatly planted trees to the north. The avenue began beyond a neat wooden fence with a gate in the centre of it. Pope stopped next to the gate and watched. He could see the shape of the outdoor swimming pool that he remembered from his last visit, and, beyond that, the south wing of the mansion house. He stared at the hulking shape of the building, most of it hidden in the dark. He remembered it from his stay: the house was built of dressed stone under a tiled roof, and comprised a series of large rooms. He remembered a first floor that contained a baroque hall, drawing rooms, formal dining rooms and a library. A mahogany staircase offered access to the bedrooms on the second and third floors where the recruits and their instructors had stayed.

Pope clutched the pistol, thankful for its solidity and weight, but regretting that he was so limited when it came to ammunition. He took a deep breath, and then another. His nerves were alight and he felt an unaccustomed twitch of anxiety. He had no idea what he was getting himself into, and his year on the run had eroded his confidence. He was out of shape and out of practice, and going into any situation as blindly as this was folly. He closed his eyes and tried, one last time, to think of another way. There was none. If he didn't move now, if he didn't take even this smallest sliver of a chance, then he would have no hope later. Bloom's death would be discovered tomorrow, his role in the old man's murder eventually made plain and Isabella would be taken away somewhere he would never find her.

He knew, as he pondered options that he did not have, that he was doing this for Isabella, but also for himself. She was his salvation. She was his chance to right a procession of wrongs that had led, however indirectly, to the deaths of hundreds of thousands of innocents – and, eventually, to the implosion of his family and a sense of worthlessness that he had thought he would never be able to fix. Isabella was his chance to do that. She was the first reparation.

His misadventure had taken him all around the world: from the gilded riches of Zurich to the slaughtered cities of Syria, from his apartment in Montepulciano to the slums of Mumbai, through sleek Shanghai and dowdy Vladivostok, to Washington and then, finally, to the ignominy and personal tragedy of his exile in Vietnam. It seemed apt that it should end here, at a place that he recalled, in a village that was the epitome of England.

Pope knew he couldn't wait.

He knew there was no other way.

He had to push on.

He took a final, deep breath, slid the Glock into the back of his jeans and listened.

There was no one there.

He put his hands on the fence and vaulted over.

Chapter Ninety-One

Pope stayed in the cover of the trees on the left-hand side of the avenue. The promenade ended, the trees giving way to a wide lawn that enveloped the immaculate pool. The south wing of the house loomed ahead. Pope remembered how the mansion had been built: an original 'villa' had been added to, with large north and south wings; each wing was reached from the main building via a long gallery. The effect was that, from above, the collection of buildings looked like an elongated letter *H*. There was a large gravelled area to the front of the property. Two SUVs were parked there, moonlight limning the polished black bodywork and sparking off the opaque glass.

The pool was serviced by a neat pool house that held the pumping equipment. He hurried across to it and tried the door: it was open. He slipped inside, pausing for a moment to allow his eyes to adjust to the gloom. He remembered from his previous visits that the pool house also accommodated the backup generator for the main house. Pope went over to it. It was a single phase standby unit, reasonably large, running on diesel with a venting pipe that led directly to an aperture in the wall. Pope took out his phone, switched on the flashlight and laid it on the floor so the light played up onto the generator. He used the tip of his knife to turn the screws and remove the inspection plate. He found where the fuel suction line connected to the injection pump and sliced through it. A little fuel spilled out and then stopped.

He paused at the door of the pool house until he was sure that there were no guards who might see him, and after waiting an extra beat he left cover and made his way around the building towards the formal gardens, with the lily ponds and grandiflora.

He looked to the west and saw the gardens that he remembered. Beyond that, a helicopter had landed on a second lawn, its blades drooping down over the bulbous cockpit. He wondered how Isabella and the others had been brought here. They would have landed somewhere military – Brize Norton, perhaps – and then been transferred .

Pope froze as he heard a voice coming from the other side of the south wing. He lowered himself behind a box hedge, gripped the pistol tight and held his breath. He heard another footstep, and then another; he risked a glance, knowing that his silhouette would stand out against the otherwise even line of the hedge, but aware that he needed intelligence almost as much as he needed to maintain his secrecy. He saw the shape of a man, dressed all in black, wandering casually down the promenade away from the manor house in the direction of the swimming pool. The man was holding a submachine gun; he was too far away for Pope to make out what type of weapon it was, but he was sorely tempted to retrace his footsteps so he could try to relieve the man of it. He pondered for a moment, but decided against it. It would be difficult to do without making a noise, and he had no interest in alerting the additional security that he knew would be close at hand. He would wait, and manage until he was able to equip himself without taking a significant risk.

Pope waited until the guard was out of sight behind the trees and hurried towards the building. There were motion sensors on the walls that would, at the very least, trigger floodlights. Pope avoided them, aiming for a spot where their coverage would be interrupted by an outcropping on the wall.

He was facing the western side of the villa. The main entrance was on the other side of the building, beneath a grand Doric portico. That led into the hall which, in turn, offered access to the various rooms beyond. Pope knew that it would be impossible to get in that way; there would be more sensors, floodlights and security cameras. There would be guards, too; the man that he had just seen would notice him if he was on the return leg of his patrol. There was another entrance, near to where Pope was standing: steps led up to a door that opened into a saloon. Pope moved along the wall until he reached it, and then dismissed it; the door was more substantial than he remembered, and it would be impossible to open it quietly without specialist tools.

There was one more route in. Pope made his way around the building, passing the locked doors of the north wing gallery until he got to the north wing itself. The indoor pool was here, as well as the room with the equipment that heated and cleaned the water. There was a hatch there that must have been used to deliver coal at some point in the house's history. Pope remembered it from before, and that it had always struck him as a vulnerability. It had been little more than a wooden trapdoor in those days, and as he approached it he saw, to his surprise, that it had not been improved. The door was secured with a bolt that was, in turn, fastened by a padlock. It was a Master Lock that, at least, seemed as if it was new.

Pope looked around for something heavy and found a fist-sized rock in the border of the garden. He went back to the lock and looped the index finger of his left hand through the U-shaped bar. He pulled back, applying tension to the mechanism, and started to tap the rock against the claw side of the lock. It made a noise, but there was no way he could avoid that. He knocked harder and faster until the claw shook loose and released. He unthreaded it, slid the bolt back and then replaced the lock so that it was hanging loose. He opened the hatch, waited for a moment – convinced that he had heard the sound of footsteps – and then hurried inside. He was certain he could hear the crunch of boots on gravel as he gingerly lowered the trapdoor down above him. If the guard looked at the door with more than just cursory attention, he wouldn't be able to miss the fact that the lock was not securing the bolt; Pope gripped the pistol and waited, aiming up at the hatch. He would try to drag the guard inside if the hatch was opened, then get him out of sight and eliminate him as quickly as he could.

The footsteps drew closer, the crunch growing louder, and then they passed on. The guard hadn't stopped. Pope wasn't ready to relax, knowing that it could be that the man had seen the lock and was going to get reinforcements, but it was possible he had been fortunate. He wasn't going to wait to find out, however. He moved carefully through the pitch darkness of the plant room, avoiding the pump and the filters that served the pool, and crossed to the glow of light that seeped in through the crack between the door and the floor.

It didn't take long to find what he was looking for. The mains electricity for the property entered via a large fuse box. He unclipped the cover and let it swing down on its hinges. It was a modern unit, with a main switch, a residual-current device and a row of circuit breakers. All very straightforward.

He took a deep breath, gripped the butt of the Glock a little tighter and pulled the main switch.

The glow beneath the door was extinguished.

The lights went out.

Pope was sure that the backup generator would have switched on to cover the sudden loss of power, but instead of sucking fuel, it would only have found air.

The light stayed off.

And Pope moved.

Chapter Ninety-Two

.

I sabella stirred.

She had been sleeping soundly, but something had disturbed her. She kept her eyes closed and listened, trying to work out what it was.

She realised: it wasn't a noise.

It was the absence of noise.

She tried to identify what had changed. The regular bleeping of the medical equipment behind her had fallen silent. It had stopped.

She opened her eyes and attempted to raise herself up so she could turn and look. The restraints bit into her wrists. She had forgotten that they were there. The rough straps chafed against her skin and she became aware of the ache across her shoulders and in her arms and legs from being forced to sleep on her back. She tasted her mouth; the artificial sensation – almost metallic – that she remembered from earlier was gone, replaced now by the gumminess of a long and deep sleep.

Isabella looked down her body at her right hand. She clenched her fist and tried to curl her bicep. She was able to raise her hand an inch or two above the surface of the mattress before the restraint drew tight.

She raised her head as far as she could, craning her neck to the right so she could see down her body. The wristband was padded, soft enough that her skin wouldn't be abraded too badly if she struggled against it.

The cuff had been wrapped around her wrist so it was snug, and then fastened in place by a metal pin that was, in turn, threaded through two overlapping eyelets. The cuff was then attached to a retaining belt that looked as if it had been looped all the way around the mattress.

She heard something.

She held her breath, closed her eyes and listened.

There it was again.

A gunshot.

Muffled, not close, yet unmistakeable.

She tried to flex her bicep again. She managed to move her hand a little higher, the padded cuff tight against her skin. She closed her eyes and clenched her jaw and strained the muscles from her shoulder all the way down to her wrist. She felt her biceps go taut, the fibres burning, and she pulled harder. She raised her hand an inch from the mattress, and then another inch. Her teeth ground against one another and she pulled harder yet.

Chapter Ninety-Three

Pope came out of the plant room. The indoor pool had been remodelled in the years since he had been to the house, and in place of the tired room that he remembered was a plush and luxurious space.

He tried to remember the layout of the building. The basement of this wing had contained the pool, a shooting range and a gymnasium that had been laid with padded mats where they practised their close-quarters combat. The ground floor of the main building had comprised the baroque hall, the saloon, the library and the old dining rooms that were used for study: language classes, espionage theory and the tradecraft that would extend the working career of the men and women who would go on to become Group Fifteen headhunters. The main hall was connected to the north and south wings by galleries; he was in the north wing, and had decided that he would find the nearest stairs to take him up a floor, where he would then be able to use the north gallery to get to the main building. Firth had said that Isabella was being kept on the top floor. Pope remembered that storey had been reserved for sleeping accommodation. He would find her and get her out.

He stepped onto the marble floor and was nearing the door to the stairs when he heard the sound of footsteps. He whirled around, raising the pistol and aiming at the shadowy figure who was moving towards him.

A guard.

Pope pulled the trigger, the gun sounding loudly in the enclosed space and the recoil jerking his hand back up towards his face.

The bullet found its mark. The guard's onward path was interrupted, the man's foot missing the edge of the pool so that he toppled over and tumbled into the water.

Pope heard another sound, behind him, and turned to face it.

A second guard, coming out of a door he hadn't noticed.

The guard raised his arm.

Pope tried to dive clear.

Too late.

Chapter Ninety-Four

Ivanosky was still working. The laboratory on the second floor of the building was, he had been forced to admit, state of the art. Bloom had provided him with top-of-the-line equipment, including Illumina genome sequencing machines. The one that Ivanosky was using tonight was a HiSeq 4000, a fast system that amplified genetic signals clearly – even the faintest ones.

He had begun his work on Isabella by drawing blood. He had spent two hours creating what he called a 'library': a glass plate with depressions – called 'wells' – that separated the genetic material from different cells. Ivanosky converted the cells' RNA into DNA, divided the DNA into smaller pieces, and then appended each cell's DNA fragments with markers so he could trace each fragment back to the well from which it had been drawn. Finally, once the fragments were tagged, he collated them into a test tube and sequenced them.

He had instigated a broad swathe of tests, but the one that he was most interested in receiving the results of was the one that would sniff out even the smallest markers of tumour DNA in Isabella's blood. He couldn't dismiss the nagging fear that Isabella, like so much of the rest of his research, would be undermined by an insidious flaw that he could not counteract. He dared not raise his hopes too high until he was satisfied that she was not – at least for now – to be taken from him like the others.

He reached a finger up to his glasses and pressed them higher up his nose. The timer on the sequencer revealed that the processing was due to be completed in twenty-seven minutes. Ivanosky knew that it would be impossible for him to sleep until the analysis was ready, and so he would stay up and continue to work.

He looked around. The lab was good, but he was going to need staff. Bloom had promised that a team would be assembled, a collection of military scientists and civilian geneticists who would all be drawn to the project by the glory of what they might be able to achieve – their silence won with that promise, significant compensation and the Official Secrets Act. Isabella's capture promised discoveries that he had considered beyond him now that the M cohort were fatally compromised by their cancers. He knew that he was going to be busy, but he had resolved to oversee the recruitment process to ensure that the right calibre of scientists would be added to the team.

He looked back at the sequencer.

Twenty-five minutes.

He needed coffee. He got up from his desk and made for the kitchen. He wasn't even out of the door when the lights suddenly went out.

He paused, waiting for them to come back on again.

They did not.

Ivanosky swore.

He reached for his phone, but before he could take it out of his pocket he heard the unmistakeable sound of a gunshot.

He stopped.

Gunshots.

He froze, unsure of what to do, and then staggered through the darkness to the alarm that had been fixed to the wall. He slammed his palm against the button, but instead of the triggering of a siren, there was nothing. Silence.

Jesus.

'Sir?' Ivanosky spun. It was one of the guards. The man was holding a pistol and was a little out of breath. 'We need to leave. We've been breached.'

'I can't leave,' Ivanosky said incredulously. 'They've come for the girl. We have to get her away from here.'

'It's not safe—'

'You have to help me get her out,' Ivanosky spat over his objections. 'She's worth more than you could possibly imagine. Nothing else matters – do you understand?'

The guard paused, his brow furrowed. Ivanosky clenched his fists, becoming impatient as the man weighed up his order to keep Ivanosky safe in his custody against this new, competing request.

Ivanosky turned away from him and started to walk to the stairs. He would do it without help if he had to; the guard would have to manhandle him out of the building, and Ivanosky didn't think that he would do that.

He was right.

'Stay behind me, sir,' the man said. 'We get her and then we get out.'

Ivanosky let the guard go first, and then, relying on the feeble light of the crescent moon, he crossed the landing and reached the stairs that led up to the infirmaries.

Chapter Ninety-Five

The man had stepped out of a blackened doorway, a grey shadow in the muddy light, a gun in his hand. Pope recognised him: it was Parker, the other Group Fifteen recruit he had seen in Sioux City. Parker aimed and fired; Pope jerked to the side, but he was too slow to evade the bullet. It punched into his gut, somewhere above his left hip. The impact knocked him back a step, but the swirl of adrenaline in his blood meant that he was able to smother the pain; he allowed himself to drop to the side, falling away just as a second round tore into the space where he had just been, and brought his gun up to fire before he hit the floor. He pulled the trigger twice. The first shot was badly aimed and missed, but Parker, in an attempt to dive clear, put himself directly into the path of the second round.

Parker hit the marble and lay still; Pope couldn't see, but he guessed he had made a lucky shot.

Now the pain exploded out of his side, a sudden wave that was like glass shards dragged across his nerve endings. He gritted his teeth to stop himself from crying out, and reached down with his fingers. It was too dark to see anything against his black clothes, but he could feel the warm viscosity of his blood. Gut shot. Off to the side, better than it could have been, but he would have to get it treated or he would bleed out.

No time for that.

The first man was in the pool, his head down beneath the surface and his arms outstretched, his body gently twisting in the wan moonlight as his blood discoloured the water. Parker was unmoving.

Pope gasped with pain as he dropped onto his hands and knees, and then gritted his teeth again as he crawled across to Parker's body. He could see more the closer he got: there was a pool of blood on the pale marble, with a black flow running from an entry wound that had been neatly drilled in the top of his head. Pope frisked him; Parker had a Sig P224 and a spare magazine in the pouch on his belt. He discarded his own half-empty Glock, rearmed himself with the Sig and then gently levered himself back onto his feet.

The pain flared and he almost lost his balance. He put out an arm to brace himself against the wall. If he left now, perhaps he could get away. He could get clear from the house, follow the track back to the farm and take the road back to his car. He could, perhaps, get to it before he was found, and then drive to the nearest hospital.

But he couldn't do that. He had come here for Isabella. He had sworn that he would not leave her again, and he meant to keep that oath. He would repair the damage that he had done, and he was beyond caring if he died doing it.

He checked that the Sig was ready to fire and started slowly for the door.

Chapter Ninety-Six

I vanosky indicated the infirmary where Isabella was being kept and followed the guard inside.

The man came to a standstill.

'She's not here.'

Ivanosky stepped around the man and looked into the room. The bed was empty. The restraining strap was still fastened around the mattress, but the straps that had secured the girl's wrists to it were empty, dangling loosely over the side of the bed.

He heard movement from behind them and, as he turned, saw a flash of motion.

It was the girl.

She moved fast, avoiding him as she took three quick paces across the room. The guard had turned as well, but she was on him too quickly for him to bring his weapon to bear. She swept her right arm out, knocking the pistol from the guard's hand, and hopped in closer so she could drive her knee into his groin. He buckled at the waist, his head descending just as Isabella fired out a stiff right hook. Her knuckles connected with his chin and he stumbled to his right, putting his arm down to prevent himself from falling.

Ivanosky reached ahead and grabbed her, wrapping his arms around her torso and trying to lock his fingers together. The guard started to rise, but he was too close to her; Isabella pushed up, using Ivanosky as a pivot so she could add extra power to a right-legged kick that landed the flat of her foot against the soldier's chin. He straightened up and careened back against the wall, sliding down to rest on his backside.

Ivanosky tightened his grip, grunting with the effort as he hauled Isabella all the way off the ground and swung her away from the door. She butted him with the back of her head; pain flashed and he loosened his grip. He yelped, brought his face too close to her head and was defenceless against a second, stiffer blow. He heard the crack of the bones in his nose as they were crushed against one another. Isabella raised her arms away from her body, frightening Ivanosky with the exercise of sudden power, and easily broke his grip.

The guard pushed away from the wall. It was dark, but there was enough of a glow from an emergency light outside for Ivanosky to see that his face was a crimson mask, blood streaming from a cut in his brow. Isabella and the guard both saw the discarded pistol on the floor and sprang for it together.

Isabella got there first, grasping it in her left hand as Ivanosky dove for her ankle and tried to pull her back. He wasn't strong enough to stop her, but he was able to impede her long enough for the soldier to fall upon her, his arm sliding beneath her throat and closing tight, her larynx caught in the crook of his elbow as he pulled and started to choke her. He rolled onto his back and dragged Isabella with him. She stared up at the ceiling, unable to move, her airway blocked as he throttled her. She still had the pistol in her left hand; she tried to aim it, but Ivanosky wrapped the fingers of both hands around her wrist and pressed it down. She struggled against him; it was only the fact that he was above her and able to push down with all his weight that meant he could hold her arm in place. She was a young, slender girl, yet her strength was prodigious.

'Don't kill her,' he groaned through the effort.

The soldier didn't respond, and neither did he release the chokehold.

Isabella gasped for air. Her right hand was free. Ivanosky dared not release his double-handed lock on her gun hand, and watched impotently as her fingers traced up and down the side of the soldier's body, catching against his belt and then scrambling down until she found the pouch that he wore next to his empty holster. She felt behind the pouch for the cord that ran from the belt down into the man's pocket and pulled, dragging out a bunch of keys that he kept there. She clasped a key in her closed fist, reached up towards her head and then behind it, stabbing the metal tip into the soft tissue of the man's face. She stabbed again and again, stretching her arm all the way back so she could get to the side of the man's throat. The key was short, with only half an inch of the metal protruding from her fist, but there was enough to puncture the flesh and draw blood.

His grip loosened. Isabella bucked, shucking her shoulders and forcing his arms apart. She let go of the key, leaving it embedded in the side of the man's throat, and reached across her body with a punch that struck Ivanosky in the side of the head. Her prone position made it difficult to put any power into the blow, but he was old and it was more than strong enough to daze him. He lost his grip on her wrist.

Ivanosky was on the floor, his vision flickering with the throbbing from his broken nose. He was aware of a new person in the room, and as he blinked through the pain, he saw it was another guard. The man loomed over him, aiming down at Isabella with his own pistol.

'No!' Ivanosky yelled, kicking the man in the side of the leg enough to disturb his aim. He fired, but the bullet went wide, splintering a floorboard as it crashed home.

Isabella rolled off the soldier's body, clasped her gun in both hands and aimed up at the second soldier. He was unbalanced by Ivanosky's kick and unable to get out of the way; Isabella squeezed the trigger, and two shots from close range drilled him in the dead centre of his chest.

The man staggered back, his hands reaching up, blood already turning his shirt dark.

Isabella got to her feet. The first guard was trying to prise the key out of his neck and the second guard was on his back, his breath wheezing in and out of punctured lungs. Isabella raised the pistol; she aimed and fired, and then aimed and fired again.

Ivanosky looked up at her, blood running down his face. He held her gaze for a moment. 'Please,' he mouthed.

She raised the pistol, pressed it against his sternum and then pushed him until his back was against the wall.

'Please,' he begged. 'You're special. We could—'

She spoke over him, her voice like iron. 'Where's Maia?'

Ivanosky nodded with his head. 'Other . . . room.'

'Show me.'

Chapter Ninety-Seven

Pope found a flight of stairs in the basement of the north wing and dragged himself up to the first floor. They opened onto a generous lobby area that, in turn, offered access to a kitchen, dining room and what would once have been a family area but was now a makeshift armoury. The guards who defended the property had arranged their equipment here. He searched for a first aid kit, and to his relief he found one beneath the table. He opened the case and took out dressings, a roll of bandage, paramedic shears, antibacterial wipes and saline pods. He took off his jacket and pulled up his shirt, wincing with pain as he leaned over to the side to glance down at the entry wound. He couldn't see into it, but from the angle that the bullet had punched into his torso, he was confident that it had missed his guts. The wound was bleeding steadily; his first tasks were to clean it and seal it. He used the wipes to disinfect the wound, gritting his teeth against the waves of pain that were triggered every time he touched his flesh. He unpeeled a dressing, used the adhesive edges to fix it against his skin, and then wrapped his torso with the bandage to hold it in place. It was an amateurish fix, but he didn't have the time to do it properly, and he was constrained by the fact that he was forced to do it alone. It was possible that the interior damage was worse than he thought. But there was no way of telling whether he had internal bleeding; the first symptoms would be lethargy and nausea, and by the time they had manifested, it would already be too late.

Didn't matter.

He pulled down his shirt, put on his jacket and turned to the equipment. Pope saw neatly arranged racks that held a selection of firearms: two C8 carbines, a Heckler & Koch HK33 and two MP5s, and several Sig P226s and Browning Hi-Powers. Pope scanned the rack and picked out an Ultra-Compact Individual Weapon; it was a very short version of the Armalite AR-15. The UCIW employed a custom buffer tube and action spring design that allowed for the efficient cycling of ammunition while still presenting minimal overall length. He popped the magazine and checked that it was fully loaded with NATO rounds and slapped it home again.

Time to move. He had already been here too long.

He left the armoury and made his way to the gallery that joined the north wing to the main building. Every step was exquisitely painful. He leaned into the wound, his left arm pressing down against the dressing in an effort to keep it in place. He wore the UCIW on a strap over his shoulder, holding the pistol grip loosely. He continued along the gallery to the end, paused at the doorway and listened for activity. He heard nothing and, summoning up the remnants of his strength, continued into the staircase hall.

He heard footsteps from above before he saw the soldier responsible for them. The man was coming down the stairs, his legs visible as he stepped off the half-landing onto the final flight that would bring him to the first floor. Pope raised the UCIW, grabbed the folding foregrip with his left hand, aimed up the stairs and pulled the trigger. The selector was set to fully automatic and, as he held the trigger back, the gun quickly chewed through all thirty rounds in the magazine. Pope's aim was bad, and the bullets splintered the mahogany staircase in an ascending zigzag that cut the soldier down at the knees. He fell back, landing against the treads and sliding down to the ground. Pope let the UCIW hang on its strap, took the Sig from his holster and fired a mercy shot into the man's head from close range.

The noise of the fusillade had been deafening, and Pope knew that there was no way it would have gone unnoticed. He ejected the spent magazine, pressed in a fresh one and tried to climb the stairs.

He managed two treads before he was beset by an irresistible rush of nausea. The bile rose up his gullet and he bent to void it, the hot fluid mixing with the blood that was gathering on the stairs. Pope caught his breath and started to climb again, but instead he toppled forwards and landed on his stomach, the edges of the treads snapping into his pelvis and ribs. He tried to stand, but he didn't have the energy for it. The wound throbbed, and when he reached questing fingers to his side, he felt the damp warmth of more blood that must have pumped through the dressing.

He had no strength and the stairs looked like an impossible obstacle. He grunted with effort as he turned himself over. He would take a moment to catch his breath, and then he would try again. He clasped the automatic in both hands and marshalled his concentration; there would be other guards here, and it would do him no good at all to be distracted if they came across him.

He just needed a moment to gather himself, that was all. He felt his eyes begin to droop and slapped himself in the face, hard, then bit down on his lip until he drew blood. He tried to focus on the pain, using it to stay awake, but it started to fade away and his eyes grew heavy again.

Chapter Ninety-Eight

I sabella followed Ivanosky out of the room and across the landing. The lights were off here, too, and as she peered down the staircase, it appeared they were extinguished on the lower floors as well. The whole house was dark. The gunshots, the power; it was obvious the property was under attack, although she had no idea who might be responsible. She had to assume they were unfriendly, and act accordingly. She held the pistol tight in her hand, her senses stretching out as she probed for any sign that there was someone else on the floor with them.

The professor led the way into a second infirmary that appeared to be identical to her own. There was the same equipment – silent and blank, just as hers had been – and the same bed. Maia was lying there, restrained, just as Isabella had been. The window was uncovered, and a square of silver moonlight fell across her. She looked dreadful; Isabella tried to persuade herself that it was the poor light that painted her so pale and haggard, but she knew that it was more than that. Worse than that. Her illness had accelerated in the last few days at a pace that Isabella could barely credit. She had seen cancer's deliberate, inexorable progress in her mother, but at least Beatrix had had months. It seemed that Maia's cancer was different; it was ravenous, and it was eating her in chunks.

'Untie her,' she said to Ivanosky.

'She's not well,' the old man said redundantly. 'It's not a good idea. She'll be cared for here.'

The suggestion was so preposterous as to be insulting, and Isabella had to fight the urge to crack the butt of the gun against the professor's head. He must have seen the flash of her temper; he backed away, his hands raised, and then turned and crossed the room to the bed.

Isabella followed.

Maia opened her eyes. 'Isabella?'

'I'm here,' she said.

'What's happening?'

'This place – it's under attack. The power's been cut and—'

Isabella was about to say that she had heard shooting, but the clatter of automatic gunfire from somewhere below them made that unnecessary.

Ivanosky froze at the sound.

'Hurry!' Isabella urged him.

'You need to go,' Maia said weakly. 'Leave.'

'With you.'

'I'm sick,' Maia said.

Ivanosky pulled the retaining pin from the cuff around Maia's left wrist and made his way around the bed to work on her right. Isabella could see how frightened he was: his fingers were trembling, slowing him down as he fumbled with the bindings.

'You'll be faster without me,' Maia said.

'We'll get out together. Don't argue.'

Ivanosky worked the pin out of the second cuff and opened it. He tried to step back, tried to put space between himself and the bed, but he was too slow. Maia's hand flashed from the mattress to latch around his wrist, and she yanked against him to lend herself some leverage as she struggled up from the bed.

'Don't . . .' Ivanosky said, his protest cut short as Maia grabbed his shoulder with her free hand and spun him around, sliding her feet down to the floor as she slipped her right arm around the old man's body and drew him tight against her chest. He struggled, but despite her illness, she was still too strong for him. She grabbed his hair with her left hand and dragged his head back, exposing the leathery skin of his neck. She closed her right hand into a fist and, with Ivanosky's head still held back, drove the side of her fist into his throat. Ivanosky fell to his knees, choked once, and then toppled down flat on his face. His right leg spasmed, and then spasmed again, and then he lay still.

'For Aleksandra,' Maia said.

Isabella had seen too much death in her life to find the execution frightening, and she knew they had too little time to be able to dwell on it. Maia fell back against the bed, and Isabella went to her and helped her to stand. She ducked her head so Maia could rest her arm across her shoulders and secured her own arm around Maia's waist to help her keep her balance.

'You ready?' Isabella said.

'Yes.'

She helped Maia move away from the bed and, with Isabella bearing most of the older woman's weight, the two of them started out towards the door.

Chapter Ninety-Nine

They came down the stairs together, with Maia holding the banister on the right and Isabella pressed against the mahogany wainscoting to the left. Maia had collected a weapon from one of the dead guards, and by descending in this fashion, they were able to limit their profiles should a guard come up the stairs towards them, and also widen their joint field of fire. The stairs were wide and grand, with framed portraits of previous occupants of the house hanging on the wall.

The hall below was dark, save for the moonlight that crept in through an uncovered window. They reached a half-landing and turned onto the final flight of stairs down to the ground floor. Isabella stopped; she thought she saw something.

She squinted through the gloom until she was sure: there was a dead body on the floor and someone was sitting on the bottom stair.

Maia saw the figure, too. She raised her pistol and aimed.

'No!' Isabella said, reaching across and pushing the gun down.

Isabella stepped across the stair until her body was between Maia and the figure below, and then she continued to descend.

Maia stopped halfway down, covering the room below.

Isabella reached the man. She had recognised him: it was Pope. He was slumped against the wall. He had an automatic weapon on a strap that was slung around his neck, but the muzzle was pointing down between his spread legs. His head was forward, his chin resting against his sternum.

'Pope,' she said.

His head came up a little.

'Pope – it's me.'

He slowly turned to face her.

'Isabella?'

Maia descended the rest of the way. 'You can't trust him,' she said. 'He was working for them.'

Pope shuffled around so that he could look at Maia. 'No,' he said in a quiet voice. 'They tricked me.'

'I don't believe you.'

Pope looked to Isabella. 'They told me you were in trouble. Atari – he did. Been lying the whole time. Working for Bloom. That's why you're here.' He turned to Maia. 'That's why you're both here.'

'What about you?'

'I'm here to make amends.'

Pope braced himself against the wall and, with his arm held out rather than held against his side, Isabella could see that his jacket was sodden with blood.

'Pope—' she began, taking a step towards him.

'Been shot,' he groaned, although Isabella could see that without being told.

Maia gave him an appraising glance. 'Gut shot. He's bleeding out.'

'I'm sorry, Isabella,' Pope said. 'I've been a fool.' He looked down; she thought that it was a reaction to the pain, but then she realised he was fighting back tears. 'Came here to get you out. Bloom . . . he's dead. Killed him. I thought, if I could get you, I could take you somewhere you'd be safe. But I couldn't even do that . . .'

Isabella knew that they had to move. They had to get out of the house and far away. There were bound to be other guards here. They were vulnerable, and the longer they stayed, the greater the chance that they would be found. But Pope was injured and Maia was weak. Isabella didn't know if they would be able to make it out, and she doubted she would be able to help them both.

She was reaching out to steady Pope when she heard footsteps in the hall. Maia was on the third stair, and her gun arm flashed up, the pistol aimed just to the right of Isabella's head. The gun fired, deafeningly loud that close to her ear, and as Isabella spun around she saw a man knocked off his feet as the round drilled him in the chest. He landed on his back and slid to a stop.

Isabella's ears rang from the shot, and she could only just make out Maia's words. 'We have to leave.' Maia grabbed Pope by the arm. 'Where's your backup?'

He chuckled humourlessly, spread his arms and – wincing from the pain – said, 'This is it.'

'Weapons?'

He toted the short automatic and pointed down to the holstered Sig. 'These. Half a magazine in the automatic before it's dry.'

'Give it to me,' Maia said, holding out her hand.

Pope didn't demur. He ducked his head so that Maia could lift the strap over his head. She checked the weapon, popped the magazine and reloaded it with practised hands, and ducked her head through the strap.

'We need to go,' she said. 'Can you walk?'

'Think so.'

'Which way is out?'

There were four doors that opened onto the staircase hall. Pope pointed to one of them. 'There,' he said. 'Back of the house. I've got a car outside the grounds.'

Maia took a breath, and stood a little straighter. She put her left hand on the forestock of the automatic and held the pistol grip with her right.

'Let's go.'

Chapter One Hundred

They came out of the house and made their way around through the gardens. There was an enclosure comprising neatly clipped box hedges with other ornamental hedges within it, a fountain and two lily ponds. The southern side of the house loomed above them and they stayed within its curtilage as they followed Pope's directions and skirted around it.

They were at the corner of the southern wing when Isabella heard the roar of a powerful engine. She risked a look around the side of the wing and saw the running lights of a helicopter approaching from the southeast. It was coming in low and fast, barely above the tops of the trees, and there could be no doubt that it was headed for the house.

'Quickly,' Maia said.

Isabella looked around the house again and satisfied herself that there was no one who would see them. She went to Pope and waited as he draped his left arm across her shoulders. He held on to Maia with his right and, with him between them, they left cover and made their way towards the outdoor pool.

The helicopter clattered over the house and curled around in a tight turn that brought it back to them. It came over low enough for Pope to be able to identify it. 'It's a Merlin,' he said. 'Troop transport. It's reinforcements.'

They made it beyond the southern edge of the pool and started into the promenade of trees that Isabella could see ended with a gate.

The sound of the Merlin's engines changed. Isabella turned to see that it had descended, and watched as the wheels touched down on the open space next to the gravelled parking area at the front of the house. The helicopter was facing away from them. A rear loading ramp was lowered and soldiers hurried down it; Isabella guessed at ten, although it could have been more. She heard raised voices and then saw with fearful anticipation as the men started to run. They were armed, and their rifles were equipped with flashlights; they sent out powerful beams that jerked and swung as the soldiers headed towards Isabella and the others.

'They've seen us,' Pope said.

'Help him,' Maia said Isabella. 'Get to the car and then drive as far away as you can.'

'No,' Pope said. 'I'll stay. You said it yourself – I'm done for.' He pointed to the automatic. 'Give it to me.'

Maia shook her head. 'I have cancer. I'm already dead. You might have a chance – I don't.'

Isabella started, 'Maia—'

'I'll hold them up,' Maia said, interrupting her. 'Go. Get away from here.'

'No,' Isabella protested, cutting over her. 'We all go. We . . . we . . .'

The words failed her, fading away. She knew that Maia was right: they wouldn't all be able to make it. Maia and Pope were too slow. Someone had to stay behind to delay the pursuit. But knowing that, accepting that one of Maia and Pope would have to sacrifice themselves in order for the other two to stand a chance of escape, was no solace. Isabella had been here before. Her mother had sacrificed herself when she had known her time was up, immolating herself in an attempt to strike out the last name on her list; it seemed capricious and unfair that Isabella should have to face a similar situation now.

The men were at the edge of the house. Their flashlights painted the trees at the beginning of the promenade. They would be on them soon.

Maia reached out and took Isabella's hand. 'Promise me one thing,' she said, squeezing her tight. 'The professor is dead, but not Jamie King. He is as responsible for what happened to Aleksandra as Ivanosky was – or more responsible. And he is responsible for more than that. He—'

She was interrupted by a hacking cough, strong enough to bend her double.

Isabella reached her hand down to Maia's shoulder. 'I know,' she said. 'I promise.'

The fit subsided, and Maia raised herself up again. The men were closing in.

She lifted her hand and rested the palm against Isabella's cheek. 'Thank you,' she said. 'Go.'

Isabella eyes burned with unspent tears. Maia arranged the strap over her shoulder; gripping the short rifle in both hands, she made her way into the envelope of tended bushes and small trees at the edge of the promenade and disappeared into the gloom.

'Come on,' Isabella said. She grabbed Pope's hands and helped haul him to his feet. He was heavy, and he seemed to be weakening. She shrugged his arm across her shoulders and looped her own arm around his waist. 'We have to go.'

He was slow and cumbersome, and every step felt as if it might be the last that he would manage, but they set off.

Five steps.

Ten.

One after the other, they kept moving.

They reached the gate in the fence at the end of the promenade. It was padlocked, and there was no way that Pope would be able to scale the fence. Isabella was weighing up the options when she heard a clatter of automatic gunfire from behind them. She turned; she saw muzzle flash from within the dark border of trees, flashlights jerking and splitting as the soldiers scattered for cover, two flashlights sending shafts along the ground as the rifles to which they were attached were dropped.

Isabella aimed her pistol at the padlock and shot it off. She opened the gate and, after taking one final glance behind her, she turned back and helped Pope start along the track.

They disappeared into the night.

Epilogue

Laikipia County was in the Kenyan highlands and, even though it was on the equator, the early mornings were always cool and fresh. The sun was just broaching the jagged flanks of Mount Kenya, the proud peak that rose out of the rocky foothills at the edge of the savannah. Later, the sun would be strong enough to send woozy waves of heat up from the parched earth. For now, though, it painted pastel hues against the lightening horizon.

Jamie King gazed out through his binoculars. 'You see it?'

Teddy Carington had his own set of glasses. 'Magnificent,' he said.

King and Carington were in a private fifty-thousand-acre reserve. The landscape was formed by a series of valleys, lush grasslands that were studded with copses of wild olive trees and acacia bushes. King owned the reserve, and made it his habit to come two or three times a year to hunt, ignoring the fact that Kenya had banned big-game hunting years ago. The reserve was generously provisioned with plains game – zebra, giraffe, gazelle and hartebeest – together with several large prides of lion who hunted them. King never felt as alive as he did in these moments, roused before the dawn and then driven out to the bush to track down and kill his prey.

Carington had been his only guest this week. They had flown out together, leaving their families behind so they could spend the evenings discussing the progress of their project and the day's hunting.

King placed a bolt in the barrel of the crossbow, aligned the cock vane with the channel and nocked it securely into place. He could feel the adrenaline pumping around his veins; they had been hunting the lion for three hours and now they were close. The animal was a hundred yards away, dragging the carcass of the gazelle it had just killed into the shade of a large Moringa tree.

King glanced over at his tracker; the man looked back at him and gave a single nod.

He crept forward, leaving Carington a little way behind him, brushing through the chest-high red oat grass that obscured him from the animal. They were downwind of it, and he could smell the fresh blood as the lion lowered its head, bit into the shoulder of the gazelle and tore a leg away from the body. King watched it through the scope, placing the animal dead centre in the cross-hairs. His guides had explained that the lion was ten years old, and the leader of the local pride that had claimed this part of the savannah for themselves. The females were with the cubs, half a mile away. This lion wanted to eat alone, at least for the moment.

King slid between two acacia bushes and came to the dead parasol tree that marked the end of the scrub. The terrain ascended gently all the way to the Moringa tree. King's bow was custom-made from carbon fibre and it had cost him twenty thousand dollars. He considered that a bargain for the accuracy it delivered, and, anyway, he made that much between one breath and the next. The money was an irrelevance, especially when balanced against the beauty and efficiency of the weapon that he held in his hands. The bolt rail was perfectly polished, with absolutely no friction when the bolt was released to accelerate towards its target. It provided unmatched power to go with its accuracy; King had taken a young lioness this morning and he had heard the loud *thump* as the bolt punched into the animal's ribs, despite his shooting position being a good way away from the target.

The crossbow had been equipped with a monopod that was attached to his waist, rendering the weapon motionless when he shot it from a standing position. He pressed the stock into the notch between his shoulder and chin, sighted the lion once more, emptied his lungs and waited until he could almost feel the slowing down of his pulse. He squeezed the trigger, heard the pop of the trigger release as the bow fired and watched as the bolt streaked across the savannah. The lion yelped in pain as the bolt punched into its ribcage, the tawny fur quickly darkening as blood poured out of the wound.

'Good shot!' Carington exclaimed.

King loaded another bolt and nocked it back. The trackers were both armed with rifles; he waited for them to start ahead, their weapons aimed at the stricken lion. King took a breath, feeling alive beyond measure – and, the bow aimed ahead, he stepped out of cover and started to cross the distance to his prey.

The trackers drove them back to base for breakfast. The reservation had originally been a cattle ranch, home to hundreds of nomadic Masai who herded their cows and goats through the savannah. The big house at the centre of the ranch had been flattened and rebuilt in the months after King purchased it. Money had not been an object, and the property that had been constructed was truly stunning. The first architect had suggested they should build something discreet and sensitive, perhaps with a turf roof to help it blend into its surroundings, but King had angrily rejected the plan and replaced the architect with one more attuned to what he wanted.

His aim was to produce something majestic, a stunning building that would dominate the landscape. That goal had certainly been achieved.

The house was built out of locally quarried stone and was three storeys tall, standing over the grasslands like a sentinel. It had a weighty triple-height front door crafted from a single slab of oak that had been studded with metal rivets. The entrance hall beyond the door was grand, a tall space without windows that was lit by candles and reminded King of a tunnel leading into a centuries-old castle. A courtyard was full of the blazing morning sunlight, and that same light flooded into the living rooms and bedrooms that were arranged around it. There was a roof terrace with a bar, and each bedroom was served by a cobbled veranda.

The trackers parked the Land Rovers, and King took Carington around the back of the house to the pool terrace. They descended the wide marble stairs to the pool; it was a sheet of blue, ending with a sheer edge that offered a jaw-dropping view of the savannah beyond. The staff had set up a single table next to the pool, and King led Carington over to it.

'Thank you, Jamie,' the older man said as they sat down.

King waved his thanks away. The waiting staff were European, hired by his aide de camp after King had been dissatisfied with the quality of the locals. One of the waitresses – a pretty blonde-haired Swede – came over and took their order. King was hungry, and chose eggs and bacon. Carington ordered the same.

'Did you see the intercepts from last night?' King said as another waitress arrived with a pot of coffee.

'I did,' Carington said.

'Libya looks promising.'

King nodded. President Morrow had shut down the Syrian front, just as he had promised that he would. They had considered making another attempt on his life, but after the failure of the Sioux City operation and the death or disappearance of all the assets, they had decided to change course. The Islamists had been driven out of Syria and Iraq, and the resulting mess had been fought over by the Russians and the Americans. There was the chaos that King had expected, and he had been able to double the value of Manage Risk's contract with the government, in exchange for providing security for the construction companies that were descending on the lucrative reconstruction contracts like vultures feeding on carrion. Manage Risk's stock price had doubled, and that, in turn, had doubled King's own personal fortune.

The spoils of war were generous, and there was more than enough for all of them. The Qataris had their natural gas and the Saudis had their oil; both Sunni powerhouses had wanted to pipe their products across secular Syria for years, and now the regime had been removed that was possible. Carington was involved with a major pipeline company, and King knew that he had increased his shareholding in anticipation of the new work that would soon be coming its way.

'Life is good,' Carington said. 'We have a lot to look forward to.'

King looked over the older man's shoulder. There was a herd of elephants who often wandered through the ranch, and they had stopped at the watercourse that cut through the grasslands. They were only fifty feet away as they lowered their trunks to the water, the big female raising hers back up and spraying out a geyser that played over the dusty, wrinkled skin of her children.

He heard the rattle of the trolley as their breakfast was delivered. The waitress wheeled the trolley up to the table. There was a fresh jug of coffee and two immaculately polished stainless-steel cloches that sparkled in the morning light.

'I'm starving,' Carington said.

King hadn't seen the waitress before. She was dressed in the same uniform as the others, but she was much younger than either of the two women who usually served him. She had long dark hair and pale skin; as she realised that he was staring at her, she angled her head away.

'What's your name?' he said.

'I'm sorry, sir?' she said.

'Your name – what's your name?'

King turned away from the waitress, looking back up the terrace to where his guards usually placed themselves. He couldn't see them.

'What is it?' Carington said.

The waitress removed one of the cloches from the trolley, and as her hand came into view again, King saw that she was holding a pistol. The weapon was an arm's length away from him, and he recognised it as a Springfield Armory 1911. The sun glittered against the aluminium frame, and its shadow was cast on the perfect white tablecloth as the waitress aimed across the table at Carington and pulled the trigger.

It was a point-blank headshot. Carington's chair toppled over and he fell out of it, his legs thrown up as he bounced off the terrace floor.

King tried to back away, but he tripped over his chair and fell onto his backside.

The waitress swivelled and aimed down at him.

He put up his hands, as if that would do him any good. 'Please,' he begged.

The sun fell on her face and he realised who it was. The dark hair was a wig. He recognised the slender features, the clear skin, the eyes that shone with hate.

'Isabella,' he said. 'Please. This isn't necessary.'

She straightened her arm. 'This is for Maia,' she said. 'And my mother.'

The gun boomed again; by the waterhole below, the elephants looked up. Their curiosity sated, they started to slowly move away.

⁓

Isabella Rose walked briskly down the stairs. She had collected both shell casings and felt them, still hot, in the palm of her left hand. She held the gun in her right, another six rounds in the seven-round magazine.

She had been tracking King for a month. She had intended to end him at his home, but the news that he was to take a trip to Kenya had provided her with a better opportunity. His home was a multimillion-dollar Texas ranch, purchased from a bankrupt oilman and enhanced with military-grade surveillance and defensive counter-measures. Isabella had planned a way to get in and out of the property, but she had known that it would be difficult, even for her. This, on the other hand, was something else. He had guards, but he was vulnerable. It had been a simple operation to plan and execute.

She made her past the body of the Manage Risk guard she had killed on her way inside, sticky blood starting to clot around the wound in his throat she had opened from behind with the edge of the knife she wore on an ankle scabbard. She continued to the parking circle where the Land Rovers were parked and stepped around the body of a second guard, his throat sliced open in just the same way.

The engine of one of the Land Rovers was running and, as she approached, it pulled out to meet her.

She opened the passenger door and hauled herself up and inside.

Michael Pope looked over at her across the cabin.

'Well?' he asked her.

'It's done.'

Pope gave a single nod of his head; there was nothing more to say.

She had been here for twelve hours. The sunrise had been spectacular, a soaring palette of reds and purples and oranges that was heartbreakingly glorious, until the colours faded into the blue. It reminded her of the displays that she had enjoyed with her mother, the way the North African sun had exploded across the horizon until it finally rose all the way above the jagged peaks of the Atlas range.

She found that Beatrix was in her thoughts. Her mother had had a list of the men and women who had betrayed her. And, over time, she had struck each name off the list until her illness meant she was unable to continue.

Isabella had taken over for her. She had killed the last name on her mother's list. She had killed more since then, and she found that she was not ready to stop.

She had her own list now.

King had been on it, but now she could cross him off. There was one more name left.

Pope reached the end of the drive and the potholed track that led away towards Kimanjo.

He glanced over at her. 'Still want to try and find him?'

'A job's not worth doing unless it's worth doing well,' she said.

'Agreed.'

'And he's the only one left.'

'Won't be as easy to find.'

'No,' she said. 'But he can't hide forever.'

Dust billowed out from the rear wheels as Pope changed to third gear and picked up speed. The Land Rover bounced over the track and, in the distance, a young lioness glanced over at them from across the grasslands. Isabella looked farther to the left and saw that the lion was stalking a clutch of Grevy's zebra. The zebra, spooked by the sound of the engine, trotted skittishly away. When Isabella looked back, the lioness had disappeared into the bush.

About the Author

Photo © 2014 Tom Nicholson

Mark Dawson's books have sold more than a million copies and have been published in multiple languages. The John Milton series features a disgruntled assassin who aims to help people make amends for the things that he has done. The Beatrix Rose series features the headlong fight for justice of a wronged mother – who happens to be an assassin – against the six names on her Kill List, while the Isabella Rose series tells the story of Beatrix's daughter. Soho Noir is set in the West End of London between 1940 and 1970. Mark lives in Wiltshire with his family.